P9-EEG-507

The Stigmata of Dr. Constantine

Other books by Tom Dulack

Pork
The Vantage Ground

The Stigmata of

HARPER'S MAGAZINE PRESS
Published in Association with Harper & Row,
New York

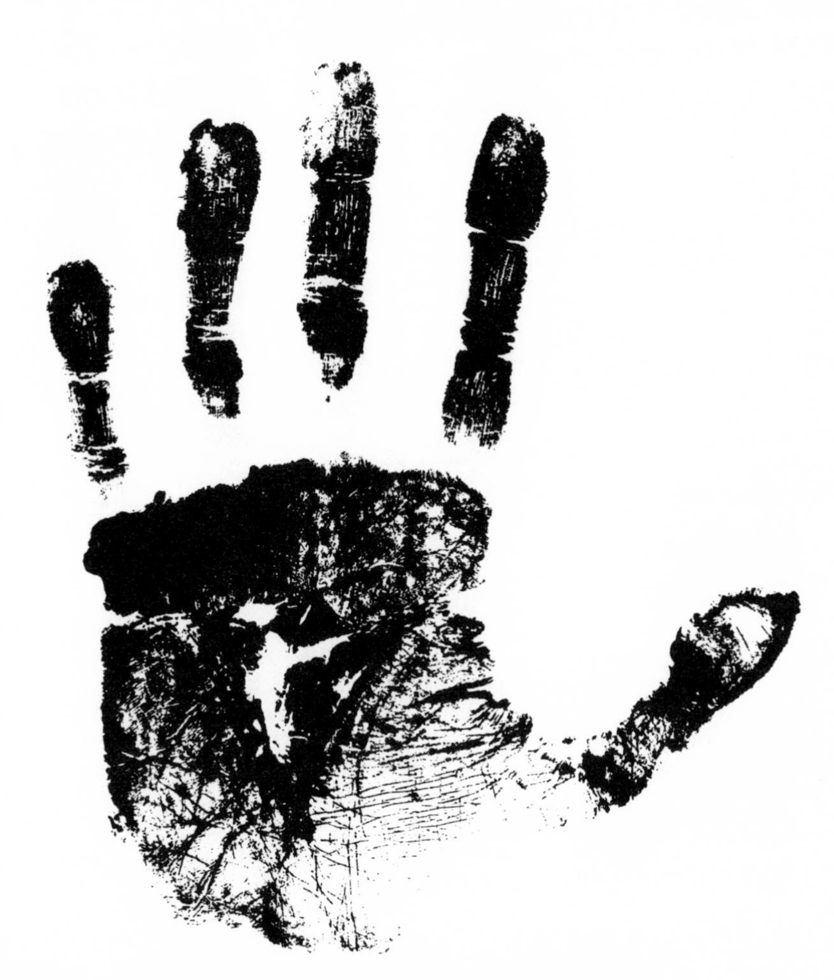

Dr. Constantine

A NOVEL BY

TOM DULACK

 For information address Harper & Row, Publishers, Inc., 10 East 53rd Street, New York, N.Y. 10022. Published simultaneously in Canada by Fitzhenry & Whiteside Limited, Toronto.

FIRST EDITION

Designed by Gloria Adelson

Library of Congress Cataloging in Publication Data

Dulack, Thomas J., date
The stigmata of Dr. Constantine.

I. Title.
PZ 4. D8874St [PS3554.U4] 813'.5'4 73-18662
ISBN 0-06-122100-7

FOR ALEX HORNKOHL

Oh, ages are yet to come of the confusion of free thought, of their science and cannibalism. For having begun to build their tower of Babel without us, they will end, of course, with cannibalism. But then the beast will crawl to us and lick our feet and spatter them with tears of blood. And we shall sit upon the beast and raise the cup, and on it will be written, "Mystery."

—"The Legend of the Grand Inquisitor,"
Dostoyevsky

CHAPTER 1

THERE WAS NO WARNING. The night before, Constantine stayed late at Margaret's. He was edgy during dinner, tense and expectant without knowing why, and drank too much. But he was a heavy drinker in any event. She served shrimp cocktails, which as a rule he avoided. However, because she'd made such an effort to please him, he ate the shrimp.

After, she served a mushroom quiche and then a rib roast. With the quiche Constantine drank almost the whole of a bottle of Liebfraumilch, and with the beef a bottle of Pommard. It was a fine dinner, Margaret was proud and happy, and Constantine was bored.

He wondered if he loved her after all. She was so young; half his age. When he'd met her ten months before, he'd been infatuated by her youth, her good looks, her virginity. The difference in their ages seemed negligible. Now he wasn't sure. Where previously he'd found her cute, fresh, clever, now she often seemed merely fatuous.

He drank whiskey and brooded. She cleaned the dishes. He tried to think of ways to tell her they were through. When she was finished with the dishes they watched the evening news, and he drank more whiskey. They went to bed.

While they made love he was far away. He thought of other women, imagined they were she; he thought of his ex-wife, and fleetingly of his daughter, Betsy, who was twelve. He wasn't with Margaret for a moment, but then, he thought, perhaps she was thinking of someone else too.

Around one he suddenly decided to drive back to his own apartment. Only then did she realize how drunk he was. She tried to prevent him from leaving. "You'll kill yourself," she argued. He gave her a push and slapped at her clumsily. She wept. In a rush of affection, he apologized emotionally and they embraced. He drove home with exaggerated caution, arriving without incident. And that was all. The evening had been entirely unremarkable.

He had one last drink in his apartment, sitting in the dark listening to the squalls next door of the Fernandez baby, who was colicky. He went to bed at 2:09. Later he remembered the time with puzzling clarity. He fell asleep at once. In the morning he awoke at the precise moment his watch stopped—7:02. He knew this because as he got out of bed he automatically switched on the radio and heard the announcer give the time. It was another ten minutes before he realized his watch was not running.

He felt terrible. His head ached and his mouth was dry. His stomach was boiling. *Those damned shrimp again,* he thought. When he was seven years old he'd developed a strange eczemalike infection; rashes and scabs covered his body. A dermatologist in Chicago prescribed ultraviolet treatments and advised his mother to remove anything containing iodine from his diet. Constantine remembered the visit to the dermatologist vividly; a terrifying misunderstanding had arisen. The doctor inquired whether he took in a lot of iodine. His mother replied, "We eat a lot of shrimp, and we use iodized salt." "Well," the doctor replied, *"I guess we'll have to cut it out."* Constantine took him to mean cutting the iodine out of his flesh grain by grain with a scalpel, and he became hysterical. After that, shrimp did not appear on their table for a long time. Eventually Constantine seemed to outgrow the allergy; in college he ate all sorts of shellfish and iodized salt as well without suffering any ill effects, until two years before at Christmas. Constantine ate a small portion of boiled shrimp at a party thrown by Prescott, his boss, and within twenty-four hours his body was blistered with hives and he'd lost his voice. Bill Morrison, his physician, treated the reaction (which he diagnosed as allergic) with antibiotics and the condition cleared up at once. Since then, until the dinner at Margaret's, Constantine had not eaten shellfish of any kind.

A strange mechanism, the body, he thought, sitting on the edge of the bed in his underwear, wondering if he was going to vomit. *Far more we don't understand about it than we do. Like the solar system.* With respect to the mysteries of the body, science was at the stage of finally arriving on the moon. Mankind had really progressed no further.

His blood was caustic in his veins. Each stroke of his heart raised painful tremors in his brain. The air in the bedroom was cloying, but he did not open the window. He lay back perspiring in the damp sheets, intending to rest a few moments more before dressing to go to the lab. Instead he fell asleep again and did not wake until ten.

He did not feel improved. The room seemed filled with an oppressive vapor that made breathing difficult. The bedclothes stank. He retained the hazy outlines of a revolting dream but was unable to recapture any particulars.

As he was shaving, he began to think about Gounod's *Faust.* He was puzzled why it should come into his mind; he was not familiar with the opera, did not like opera in general. Just the title came to him: *Faust.* Thinking about it for a while, he concluded that it was somehow connected with the dream. He was a logical man. Perhaps he had been dreaming of Margaret, and that was the subconscious link? Gretchen was named Margaret in Goethe's *Faust,* which he recalled vaguely from college. An old man seeking rejuvenation through plundering a young virgin's flesh. Flesch. He had studied under a famous hematologist named Flesch years ago. Constantine made a wry face at himself in the mirror; he often found the turns and catches of his memory objectionable. He finished shaving quickly, dressed, drank a glass of orange juice and left.

It was hot, breathless outside. The heat closed down on him and his starched collar rubbed welts into his neck. Even on the bridge, driving across the Thames River, there was no relief. To his right the July sun, already high in a cloudless sky the color of lettuce, turned the estuary into a painful mercury glare. On his left he could see the black shadow of a submarine gliding like a shark down the river from the naval base, toward the bridge, out to sea. A sailboat bellied along in the sub's wake. But the view on both sides was obscured by the high mesh fence the municipality had erected to discourage suicides.

All it discourages is a view of the harbor, Constantine thought moodily. If a man were intent on leaping from the bridge, no six-foot-high baffle was likely to deter him.

He took the first exit to the right and descended in a semicircle to the shorefront village of Groton. He turned left onto the street paralleling the river, the vast black arc of the bridge now high above him to the right. He looked straight ahead as he drove; the traffic on the water, the barges and tugs and outboard pleasure craft, did not interest him. Later he recalled noticing a brown-and-cream Chevy station wagon parked illegally outside the lobster pound halfway up the street; on the rear bumper was an orange Day-Glo sticker that said JESUS SAVES. Nothing else pricked his attention the rest of the way to the lab. He'd driven the same route every day for eleven years. He'd long since ceased to see much of the world he was passing through.

When he got to his office he was greeted by a bewildering construction of ladders and scaffolding. Two men in white uniforms were painting his office. Drop cloths shrouded his desk and the filing cabinet. The painters were loud and profane.

"What the hell's going on?" Constantine demanded.

They were indifferent, contemptuous. "You've been dispossessed, doc. It's your turn. You're on the schedule."

"What schedule? There is no schedule. Who let you in here? I've got work to do. Get out. Take that damned mess out of here!"

The painters showed him their authorization, signed, indisputably, in Prescott's hand.

"God damn it," Constantine burst out. "Who ordered that color?"

"It's part of the master plan," one of them said, puffing on a cigar. "It's called burnt orange."

"It looks like a whorehouse!"

The painter smiled, shrugged. "Talk to the management, doc." His partner, on a ladder, sweeping a roller across the ceiling in dramatic wet licks, was singing in Italian. Constantine turned away. The singing was blatant and off key, like the color they were painting his office.

Seething, he rode the elevator down to the cafeteria. He ordered toast and coffee and orange juice; he drank off the juice thirstily, but did not touch the rest. Except for the woman behind the cash register—whose name, to his further annoyance, he'd forgotten when she greeted him although he'd known her for five years—the cafeteria was empty. Now and then someone came in to buy a soda from the machine or a pack of cigarettes. No one spoke to him. He sat there for an hour, smoking, his wrists on the table, dropping ashes onto the buttered toast, staring at the fountain splashing in the green little court beyond the picture windows. He wished he could plunge his head into the fountain and keep it there until his headache vanished or he drowned.

At length, noticing that the girls in pink dresses were beginning to set up for lunch, realizing it was almost noon, feeling guilty, he rose and left. In the carpeted foyer, as he was waiting for the elevator, his boss, Jim Prescott, came around a corner and clapped him on the back.

"Been looking for you, Paul," he said. "I'm really awfully sorry about those bellies. There's just not a dime for the project." He hooked his arm around Constantine's shoulders, as he always did when he delivered bad news. "If you ever get the experiment off the ground—and to be frank with you, Paul, I think you're trying to pull one out of left field—but if you ever do get it off the ground, then it goes without saying, Paul, you'll get all the money you want."

Constantine leaned out of the embrace. "If we ever get the damned thing off the ground, we won't need money. We need money now."

Prescott came back after him and massaged his jacket collar. "Oh, come on, Paul," he chuckled as the elevator opened. "If there's a way to do it on a shoestring, you'll find the way. You always have, you always will. Just keep after it, Paul. I have every confidence." He laughed, and bunched the shoulders of Constantine's jacket, and half pushed him and half stumbled along with him into the elevator in an excess of jovial banality, just managing to recover his balance and duck back through the doors before they closed on his ribs.

On the ride up to his lab, Constantine reflected on the strange compulsions that drove a man like Prescott to call him Paul five times a minute. Did Prescott suffer from an identity crisis? Always touching you, pawing at you, breathing in your face. Constantine hated to be touched. Remarkable, he thought, that someone as shallow and incompetent could have risen so far in the company. He was only forty-five, six years Constantine's senior, his inferior in every way.

Afterward Constantine did not dismiss even this encounter as he searched for an explanation, thinking that perhaps some conjunction of interreacting chemical variants shared by him and his boss might have triggered the thing.

The painters were gone, but his office was not restored.

"They went to lunch," Geraldine told him.

"That little one who sings has a dirty mind," said Cathy.

"Oh, you're such a virgin," Geraldine said, and Cathy, the new girl in the lab, blushed.

"How do you like the color?" Geraldine asked Constantine.

"It makes me sick to my stomach."

"I think it's fantastic," she said. "I really get off on it."

He could not interest himself in their work. Everything irritated him. He was amazed that he'd ever thought Geraldine attractive. Thick-waisted, square-shouldered, built like a packing crate. And Cathy. He wished now he hadn't hired her. Straight out of college, she was timorous, uncertain, dependent, always running to him for reassurance. A month ago, when she applied for the job, he'd been faced with a choice between her and an older woman with better credentials. But the older woman was a thirtyish spinster, a bit of a rooster, and Constantine had opted for the pretty face. Now he regretted it.

She had lost another column, her sixth in two weeks.

"Maybe I'd better put you to work on something else," he said.

"I know I can pack a column," she insisted, hanging her head, compressing her lips with anger. "At school I packed beautiful columns. I don't understand what's wrong. Damn it, I know I can pack a column. An idiot can pack a column. Don't you dare take me off this project! Don't you dare!" She stormed into the cold room and slammed the heavy meat-locker door.

Geraldine laughed.

And I can't even fire her, Constantine thought, staring at the stainless steel slab she had banged in his face. He knew she had taken a big loan from the credit union to buy a new car. *So how can I fire her?*

"She's a virgin," Geraldine was explaining. "That's her whole trouble. She has sexual tensions."

Geraldine's experiment was going badly—it was the project Prescott had spoken to him about—and Constantine was annoyed with her for not seeming to take it seriously. As she prattled on, bursting into laughter when something new went wrong, he realized that if he stayed in the room with her for another five minutes she would provoke him into hitting her. So he left.

The hallway was crowded with wire cages filled with rats and mice and guinea pigs. Although the labs were air-conditioned, the corridors were not, and the stench made him hold his breath. The painters had reoccupied his office. He had nowhere to go.

"Damn it," he said, standing in the middle of the hall, his fists clenched. "God damn it!"

There were many things he could do, that he ought to do. The budget for the fourth quarter. The new literature on prostaglandins he'd been meaning to read for a month. But he was sick; his headache was diabolic. He decided to go home.

Although he'd been careful to park his car in the shade, it was an oven. Even with the windows down, moving, sweat poured off him. His sunglasses slipped up and down on the bridge of his nose. His shirt was wrinkled and stained. He squirmed on the hot leather seat and thought about Cathy.

Curious. In a few years, when she filled out, she would probably be a beauty. Long black hair down to her shoulders, parted in the middle, large mouth and nose, Italian, dark from the summer sun yet with a lemony quality to her color, or like a ripe pear; stunning, that black hair and suntanned skin against her white lab coat, and her teeth, white, startling, so that when she smiled you doubted they were real. Cathy. Whom nevertheless for some reason he did not find sexually interesting.

Why? Geraldine was, to put it bluntly, a tree trunk, a fire plug. And yet erotic, exciting. Maybe simply because she was so aggressive about sex. Was that all there was to it? Aggression? Readiness? True, during his lifetime he had encountered few women who were not attractive by virtue of their readiness (or determination) to go to bed with him. Perhaps it was vulgarity in a woman that was exciting; Geraldine was vulgar, Cathy was prim. And yet Geraldine was a WASP, in bed usually the worst kind. And Cathy was a Mediterranean, a devout Catholic to boot. Something about the libidinous consequences of the sensual saturation Catholic kids were subject to. Constantine knew about that at first hand; it accounted, he believed, for his own intense sexuality. His father was Greek Orthodox, lapsed. His mother was Catholic, Hungarian, and Constantine had received instructions in her Roman faith, had attended a parochial grammar school and spent one year in a parochial high school before he rebelled. Jews and Catholics—they were the best. Geraldine was a Protestant of some ill-defined stripe; her family lived in Pennsylvania, in Amish country (though they were not Amish). Still, Geraldine was erotic, whereas in spite of her theoretical advantages of blood and culture (never mind the fact of her gorgeous face), Cathy was not.

"Christ!" he said aloud, coming out of it. "I'd think about sex on my deathbed." He'd been in Mexico once on a vacation and spent a night in a small filthy village overrun by what seemed to him rabid dogs. Great packs of them, twenty and thirty strong, roamed the streets terrorizing people. Constantine recalled one sick old dog lying in a ditch, the victim of God only knew how many bouts of distemper, half paralyzed, his ribs sticking out, covered with flies, watching as a horde of yapping raving lathering mongrels yowled down the dirt street, tumbling over one another, keening, biting, their blood up, trying to get at a bitch in heat. The sick old dog glanced, twitched, sniffed, staggered to his feet and hobbled off in pursuit. *To the very last,* Constantine thought with a hard smile. *To the very fucking last gasp.*

In New London, stopped for a traffic light, he was approached by a ragged young man in denim pants and a T-shirt. He had a beard and wore a rope around his waist for a belt. In his arm was a stack of circulars. He thrust one through the opened window on the passenger's side.

"Trip out on the Lord, man," he said cheerfully. "The Lord wants you, baby. Don't say no."

"What?" The sun was in Constantine's eyes; he could not see the suspended traffic light to tell if it was green. "Get out of here!" The fumes of the traffic made him dizzy. "Get the hell out of my car!"

The young man was into the car up to his shoulders. He was grinning, hairy monkey face twisted into a leer. "Get your head together with Jesus, man. Jesus wants to rap with you. It's never too late. The Kingdom and the Power, man. That's where it's at!"

A horn sounded. The engine stalled. Constantine ground the starter, pumped the gas pedal.

"What do you want? Money? What? What are you mumbling?" There was a stripping sound as the engine caught and roared. Horns blared. Constantine squinched his eyes, trying to see the light. "I'll call a cop."

"Jesus is a heavy scene, He's coming right off the wall, no way he's gonna lighten up until—"

A chorus of angry horns prevented Constantine from hearing. Wadding the circular in his fist, he threw it at the face and stepped on the gas. The young man yelped, squirmed to extricate himself as he ran alongside, jerked free of the window just as Constantine's car squealed into the middle of the intersection. The light had changed back; he almost struck another car entering from the right. The driver screamed at Constantine and shook his fist. Constantine cursed back at him, gunned the car on through the clogged intersection heedless of the traffic, leaning on his horn, and sped off.

"Goddamned bum," he said, trembling. "Filthy goddamned lunatic! A public nuisance! They ought to sweep them off the streets, lock them up!"

To calm down, he stopped a few blocks farther on at a Friendly's, where he ordered an ice cream sundae that was served to him by a pretty teenager. It was the lunch hour, but the girl—Angela, according to the plastic badge on her breast—lingered at his booth and made small talk with him. The sundae was sixty cents. He tipped her a quarter. She dimpled a personal, almost intimate smile at him as he went out the door. He felt better, and by the time he reached home he'd forgotten all about the ugly incident with the Jesus freak.

He drew the blinds, stripped off his sweaty clothing, swallowed three aspirins with a glass of tepid water, turned on the air conditioner and lay down naked on the bed. He lay there silently in the cooling gloom, the hum of the machine masking him. His headache began to subside. He tried not to think. Images of a television commercial depicting by means of animated cartoons the progress through the bloodstream of the analgesic properties of a certain brand of aspirin played sporadically on his mind. He felt the tension in his arms and legs dissolving. Just before he fell asleep, he felt an odd tickling sensation in the palm of his left hand. Drowsily he scratched it. The last thing he thought was: *It means good luck. I'm coming into a fortune.*

He awoke at five feeling almost normal. A dull pain persisted in his temples, but he knew that all he needed now was food. He'd eaten nothing all day, he realized, except the sundae at Friendly's. *Angela,* he thought with a smile as he went into the bathroom. *Wonder how old she was. Sixteen? Old enough, old enough, however old.* He resolved to go back to Friendly's and chat with Angela again.

As he showered he considered where to go for dinner. Chuck's Steak House, maybe. On the water. Margaret liked Chuck's; they'd gone there together to celebrate his divorce. Should he call Margaret? Had he in fact told her he would call? Had they made a date for tonight? He couldn't remember, but he hoped not. Though he regretted slapping her, he regretted even more having apologized, having kissed her. "No, it's over," he said. "Must have been finished weeks ago." On the other hand, it would be impossible having an affair with a kid like Angela. She was barely older than Betsy. Old enough for sex, perhaps, but not for a relationship. "Well, maybe life would be simpler without relationships. Just screwing. Geraldine, Cathy, Angela. Just screw them when I want to and rule out binding ties from the start. Rule them out—make them put it in writing!"

He toweled off lightly, leaving his body damp so the evaporation would cool his skin, and prepared to shave for the second time that day. He had a coarse, fast-growing beard which was a penance to him. Taking down the shaving cream and the razor from the medicine cabinet, he ran the water into the bowl, wet his beard, lathered it and began to shave. He whistled snatches of a tune that had been flirting in and out of his head all day. He thought about Margaret again. Perhaps after all he should marry her. Living alone was really not satisfactory. He did not eat properly, he wasted time and money and energy taking women on dates. By combining their salaries they could afford to move into the country, maybe rent a house in Mystic, buy a boat. His alimony payments were crippling. Marriage might be the answer; if not to Margaret then to someone else. He needed order, regulation, routine to his life. He was becoming dissolute.

However, he had not been a notably successful husband the first time around. There was reason to believe that he was not temperamentally suited for the institution of marriage. What if he got married a second time, and it failed a second time?

No, no, no, he thought. *You don't need that. The Angelas of the world will do just fine for the time being. Just stay loose and unattached.*

The bathroom was humid. The mirror kept clouding up. Sweat formed on his forehead. In the light of the lamp above the mirror his damp torso gleamed as though he had been anointed. He drew the razor up along his throat, against the grain of his beard, over and over. His hand trembled slightly, he was so hungry. He would go to the Lighthouse Inn and have roast beef and potatoes, hot bread with melted butter, fresh berries in cream for dessert. And easy on the booze tonight. One martini, half a bottle of wine, no more.

Then he cut himself. It was just a nick, about an inch above his chin, at the corner of his mouth. He wiped his hand across the foggy mirror to get a better look at it. One bright red little seed, insignificant, but interesting. He stared at it, watching it grow, waiting for it to burst and trickle down into the white lather on his chin. The hot water gushed into the sink, sending vapors into his face, warm, fragrant. His reflection wavered. The drop of blood was shaped like a tear now, and now like a berry, the color of a garnet. It seemed to give off light, swelling slowly, expanding, beautiful, rich red and deep. He could see his reflection in its lacquered surface, sensed depths of mystery going down inside, as in a layered gem, textures, gorgeous, enlarging until his reflection vanished, dilating, filling up the entire area of the cloudy glass. Constantine held his breath, experienced a moment of vertigo, closed his eyes. And then suddenly, from behind him—for a long time he ascribed measureless importance to the clear impression that it came to him from above and behind—he felt something like a tremendous blow, as though a huge spike were driven through the crown of his skull into the core of his brain by a single immense stroke of a sledge hammer.

He uttered a weak cry and fell to the floor senseless, striking his forehead along the line of his right eyebrow on the edge of the sink, and the base of his skull against the toilet bowl. In the living room the telephone began to ring.

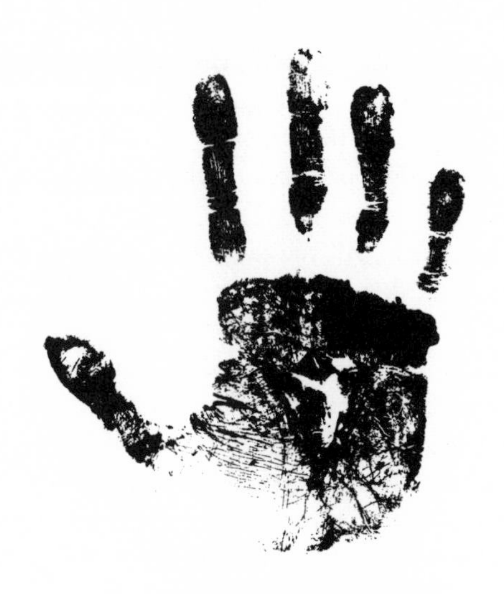

CHAPTER 2

"HIT HIM HARDER! You have to hit him harder!"

"I can't. I'm afraid I'll get blood all over me."

"You won't get blood all over you if you break his neck cleanly."

"It makes me sick."

"All you need is practice."

"You do it."

"No, you have to learn. Go ahead. Just bash his head against the counter."

"What if his tail comes off?"

"His tail won't come off!" Geraldine laughed at her. "Honest to God! Go ahead, smash him!"

Squeamishly, Cathy grasped the rat by the tail, holding him at arm's length. The animal struggled, trying to double back on his own spine and bite her. She took a breath, set her teeth, gave an awkward, half-hearted swing of her arm and banged the rat against the edge of the counter, instinctively closing her eyes. At the impact she squealed involuntarily with horror, dropped the rat and stepped back quickly, her hand to her mouth, as she saw what she'd done.

Geraldine shook her head. "All you did was break his spine."

"How awful. Now what do we do?"

"Have to kill him."

The rat was writhing on the counter. Geraldine, a cigarette in her mouth, calmly picked up an iron bar, flipped the rat on his stomach, arranging him so that his throat extended over the edge of the counter, then laid the bar across his neck and without emotion pressed down on it. There was a soft crunch as bone snapped. Cathy turned away for a drink of water.

"Nothing to it," Geraldine said. "But it's easier on the rat if you break his neck the first time. More humane."

"There must be a better way," Cathy said as Geraldine slit the rat's abdomen with a scalpel. "Why can't you just give him an injection or something?"

"His system has to be free of drugs." Geraldine removed the small stomach and, working swiftly and efficiently, began to hook it up to the three-foot-high contraption she and Constantine had devised. Cathy deposited the corpse in the garbage pail beneath the sink and then joined Geraldine to watch. The experiment was fascinating; it was only the killing she couldn't take.

Pandora's Box was Geraldine's name for the jerry-rigged device in which she was attempting to create an environment that would deceive the rat's stomach into believing it was alive. It was a box equipped with a homemade humidifier; a motor-driven peristaltic pump that sent glucose nutrient solutions into the stomach; glass tubes for collecting the acid secretions; a thermostat and heating coils taped to the walls; and a small desk fan with rubber blades which regulated the circulation of the air and was supposed to maintain a constant temperature. Because the company refused to fund the experiment, Geraldine had constructed the box from whatever scraps of garbage and leftovers she could beg or wheedle from other labs. Consequently something was always breaking down at critical moments. The thermostat would fail; the humidifier would malfunction; the fan would lose a blade; the pump would short out. There were too many moving parts, too much mechanical interdependence. Geraldine had killed forty rats in vain so far and now Constantine was dropping hints that he was losing interest. She thought he might abandon the project. She hoped he wouldn't. Though it had never worked successfully, she was proud of Pandora's Box, and defensive about it. It was like a fascinating toy; she enjoyed playing with it.

"The guinea pigs are easier," she explained as she attached the small red belly to some Teflon filaments. "You just press the thumb of your left hand against the base of the neck, and then with your right hand you get the heel of your palm under his chin and push his head back till it snaps. No muss, no fuss."

"Don't they bite?"

"Huh-uh. Trusting little buggers. Okay—it's ready. Let's give it the juice."

Locking the door, Geraldine turned on the humidifier and started the pump and the fan. The tiny organ suspended in the center of the box began to twitch. Geraldine smiled. "Looks all right. So far so good. You know, if this thing ever works it's going to be the cheapest experiment the company ever ran. Total expenditures until now are six dollars and seventy-five cents. Not counting the rats. But they're not worth anything." She adjusted a small valve on the roof of the box which was releasing drop by drop the drug they were testing.

As the solution moved a cubic centimeter at a time down the eye dropper tube into the rat's stomach, a violent reaction took place. The girls pressed their faces close to the glass. The organ shook and quivered spasmodically in an absurd and pathetic dance.

"It looks like it's suffering," Cathy said, feeling a surge of sympathy for the orphaned stomach. "Poor thing."

Geraldine, her eyes bright and intense, said nothing. She had killed a rat, disemboweled him, created an environment in which his stomach continued to live, and was nourishing the organ and subjecting it to a controlled, ingenious, potentially historic experiment. She had spent seven years in college at a cost to her parents of more than fifteen thousand dollars. Much of that time she had been lonely, tired and unhappy. But at moments like this all the sacrifice seemed worthwhile. She was repaid. It was wonderful.

"The temperature's going up," Cathy warned suddenly.

"Oh, no!"

"What's wrong?"

"Is it the fan?"

"The fan's okay."

"It's that goddamned thermostat again!"

"No," said Cathy. "Look—it *is* the fan, the motor. Do something!"

"There's nothing to do! I can't do anything. If I open the box I screw the experiment. God damn it!"

The belly was palpitating more rapidly. It jumped and squirmed like a minnow on a hook. Then, as the temperature climbed the critical few degrees that destroyed the delicate balances of the environment, the belly suddenly stopped.

Geraldine stared at the thing for a few moments, her face dark with disappointment, then swore under her breath and unplugged the contraption. "There's got to be a better way." She sighed. "Have to simplify the whole business somehow. It's too damned complicated. Shit!" She regarded her Pandora's Box crossly for a few moments more, then laughed harshly. "Fuck it. Let's have some coffee. I wonder where Constantine is. It's almost noon. He was late yesterday too."

The lab was an untidy but airy and pleasant room. From the large windows in the east wall the girls could look down on the small park below, adjacent to the cafeteria. There was an artificial waterfall, flowering shrubs and plastic benches along a gravel path beneath shady trees where in fine weather some of the employees ate their lunches. From these windows they could also see a stretch of the river, the sailfish and schooners spanking along in the breeze, the Orient Point ferry tubbing its way up the channel, spewing diesel fumes in her wake, the company barge moving out to dump tons of chemical waste into Long Island Sound.

Beneath the windows were two large machines. One, a centrifuge, resembled a stainless steel washing machine with a door in the top. The other was a liquid scintillation counter, with an instrumentation panel in different colors that reminded nonscientific visitors of a jukebox. A sign on it stated in red, white and black characters, CAUTION RADIOACTIVE MATERIALS. Near that was a refrigerator, and the counters the girls used for desks. In one wall, beneath a block of steel cabinets there was a large ovenlike steel structure with a sliding glass hood, ventilated in such a manner, like a chimney, that they could work with highly noxious or highly volatile chemicals, shielded from lethal fumes. In the middle of the room, running its length, was an island counter crowded with Corex tubes, beakers, pipettes, phials, homogenizers, fragile columns and tubes bubbled and blown into fantastic shapes like liqueur glasses—all the laboratory vessels, which had changed so little in their configurations since medieval times. The girls' lab coats hung from a rack near the door. Cathy's blue quilted ski suit, which she wore when she was working in the cold room, lay this morning on a stack of boxes of ammonium sulfate in a corner. Coffee mugs were pegged above the sink; next to the sink was a hot plate and a tray with jars of freeze-dried coffee, powdered cream, tea bags and sugar.

Cathy and Geraldine drank coffee and gossiped about Constantine. From time to time a black porter would pass down the hall wheeling a large cart filled with cages of rats, or mice, or rabbits, or dogs to be sacrificed in other labs for scientific purposes.

"I don't think he likes me very much," Cathy said. "He thinks I'm an idiot."

"You're too sensitive. He's okay. It's just that he's very ambitious, and he's selfish. I've known him for two years. The main thing about him is that he sees the people who work for him as extensions of himself. If you're useful to him, he treats you okay. When he decides you're no longer useful, he shits on you."

"Well, he's very good-looking."

"Don't get any ideas," Geraldine said, biting into a gingersnap. "I don't know this for a fact because I never went to bed with him, but there's a rumor that in his love life he's a practitioner of the three F's. Feel 'em, fuck 'em, et cetera."

"Well, all the same, I think he's very sexy. How old is he?"

"I'm not sure. Thirty-six, thirty-seven. In there. Maybe older."

"What's his wife like?"

"His ex-wife. A surprise. You'd expect him to be married to a knockout. But she's kind of dumpy, kind of dull. His daughter's good-looking, though. She looks a little bit like you, only blond."

After their break, Cathy donned her ski suit and went into the cold room to finish packing her new column. As she worked, interrupting herself every few minutes to blow on her fingers and rub her hands together, she thought about Constantine. She was thrilled to learn that she resembled his daughter. He was divorced, living alone; she wondered where. She wondered if he had a girl friend, a mistress; what she was like. A beauty, she guessed. He drove a Porsche. That was just right for a man like him. He must have a beautiful woman to sit beside him and speed through the Connecticut countryside.

She forced herself to stop thinking about him. She was determined to pack the column correctly; last night, lying in bed, she'd examined her conscience and decided that the reason her columns had been failing was that subconsciously she was trying to attract Constantine's attention. He was the kind of man, she had sensed, who took success for granted. She did not want him taking her for granted. On the other hand, if she continued to botch up her work he'd fire her, and she wouldn't see him at all anymore. So she applied herself with special care and concentration to the column, pouring small quantities of the resin and liquid buffer into a yard-long glass cylinder, waiting until the buffer drained off at the bottom, leaving the resin packed, adding more of the mixture, building up the base of resin through which eventually would pass the supernatant containing the enzyme fractions she was trying to collect. It was tedious work, but she was dogged. *I'll make him proud of me. I'll pack a column that will knock his eyes out.* There was almost no margin for error at this stage; if the column was improperly packed she could lose the entire sample through adsorption and adhesion to the resin; or the sample might flow through without any adhesion or separation whatever, so that the solution which emerged at the bottom was the same as what she poured in at the top.

Every ten or fifteen minutes she came out of the cold room and warmed up in the lab, where she began to prepare the sample of swine lung from which she hoped to isolate the prostaglandin enzymes. They were doing research into the effect of prostaglandins on muscle activity. Certain prostaglandins—enigmatic fatty acid derivatives—had been discovered to possess dramatic contracting properties in various types of muscles. Their ability to contract the walls of the uterus, for example, had already been utilized to produce a morning-after birth control pill. But it was a relatively new field, still largely unexplored.

Geraldine went down for lunch at twelve-thirty. Cathy ate hers alone at her desk from a paper bag: two carrots, a stalk of celery, some raisins and an apple. Whenever someone passed down the corridor she looked up eagerly, expecting to see Constantine. But he didn't come. The painters had completed his office and she thought it looked very nice. She wanted him to like it. She wanted him to be happy.

Geraldine returned at one o'clock and instructed Cathy in the technique for killing frogs.

"You take the legs like this, and then you bang his head on the counter, same as the rat. Then you have to pith him or he'll never stop jerking."

"I know how to do that," Cathy said. "Here, let me." Frogs were different from rats. It was hard to conceive of a frog feeling pain. She banged the frog's head, forced open his mouth and with a pair of large scissors cut an incision in the corner of the mouth and snipped across, back around the head, the frog leaping and jumping in her grasp, sliced the brain stem, which killed him, and then inserted a long needle all the way down the frog's spine, which extinguished the nervous system.

"Beautiful," Geraldine said with approval. "That's how."

"Frogs are easy." Cathy smiled.

"Constantine call in?"

"No. Unless he called when I was in the cold room."

"Funny." Geraldine frowned. "I tried to call him and there was no answer."

"You think he's sick? He looked so strange yesterday."

"He was just hung over. He drinks a lot. Turns into a mean, nasty bastard when he drinks. It's funny he hasn't called in, though. Oh, well." She shrugged. "Give me those scissors." She splattered another frog against the counter and began to cut him open.

In the cold room, Cathy took the sample of swine lung in buffer and placed it in the homogenizer. Then she finished packing the column. It looked fine. *I'll show him,* she thought. There was still a chance he'd come in before they quit. When the lung was homogenized, she poured it into a beaker. It looked like a strawberry milk shake. Filling up six plastic tubes, balancing them in pairs, she arranged them in the centrifuge and set the dials for a thirty-minute spin at fifteen thousand revolutions per minute. Breaking down the swine lung into the enzyme fraction was time-consuming. She had to draw off the supernatant, spin that down again and dissolve the second precipitate in more buffer for another separation. After which she saturated the last supernatant with ammonium sulfate. Then she returned the solution to the centrifuge one more time before collecting the supernatant, which—following dialysis—would go into the column.

Geraldine left at three to take her car to the garage, and Cathy worked on by herself cheerfully, happy to be alone. It would be nice if Constantine would stop in now and see her working overtime; he would have to be impressed by her dedication. She often did not sign out when she stayed late, so that he would not suspect her of simply grubbing for more money. If he came in now, they would chat, she would show him her superb column, maybe he would invite her for a twilight spin in his Porsche, a cocktail somewhere.

She set up the experiment in the cold room, applying the supernatant fraction to the top of the column and establishing the flow rate. She set the fraction collector beneath it. It was four o'clock. She would return at midnight to check it out. Tomorrow morning she was positive she would have a rich, beautiful, lively sample to present to Constantine.

She was thirsty and decided to go down to the cafeteria for a Coke. In the corridor, the floors were polished, the fisheye mirrors mounted on the ceiling at every corner gleamed. The walls were salmon-colored, the ceilings cream. The color scheme was the result of a study undertaken by the company to ensure the psychological well-being of the employees; it was supposed to reduce tension and eye fatigue. But to Cathy the overall effect was harsh. It was the lighting, she concluded—the impersonal quality of the antiseptic strip lights in the ceilings, always the same, day and night. *The trouble with this place,* she thought, *is that there aren't any shadows.*

She stopped in one of the neighboring labs to visit the rabbits Tom McGregor was working with. McGregor was testing a drug that was supposed to reduce cholesterol levels in the bloodstream. He had apparently left for the day; the lab was unoccupied except for the two white rabbits strapped to a metal surgical table. They were immense, the size of bed pillows. Attached to their skulls were pairs of electrodes hooked up to a large console with gauges and dials Cathy did not understand. Patches of blood stained their skulls, and Mac's lab coat tossed over a stool was also spotted with blood.

The rabbits were awake, and they looked at Cathy with their pink eyes, their nostrils flaring, their ears twitching. They were supposed to be anesthetized—Mac contended that they never felt a thing—but they were nevertheless awake now, clearly, and she could not imagine that they were comfortable.

She talked to them for a few minutes, wanting to stroke them, feeling sorry for them, warning herself not to sentimentalize their condition but responding to confusing emotions, confused by her knowledge that this pair of rabbits would be dead by tomorrow, to be replaced by two more exactly like them, and the day after by two more still, Mac having already killed over fifty rabbits in the experiment, which so far had not been a success. But it was necessary, she told herself. You had to believe that the rabbits were perishing in a good and even noble cause. Cholesterol, heart disease were killers. Still, she felt sorry for the rabbits lying there, strapped down, looking at her, the blood on their white fur. They summoned up disturbing memories of the pet rabbits she had owned as a child, smaller than these but also white; and all her other animals: three or four dogs, a dozen cats, turtles, goldfish, a canary called Max. One of her college professors had quoted some author as saying that in his experience people who were inordinately fond of animals were invariably cruel to other people. That struck Cathy as a great and malicious falsehood, although in her own case it was true that she had never been as affectionate toward another human being as she had been toward all her pets.

Anyway, she thought as she turned off the lights and went out, Mac said they didn't feel anything. She had to learn not to give in to emotionalism. Otherwise she would never survive here.

Her footsteps were soundless, absorbed by the shiny rubberized tiles. She walked past the cold-storage room where the carcasses of the dogs and cats and rabbits were tossed after the scientists were done with them, and down a flight of stairs and past the incinerator where twice a day the corpses were consumed.

She opened a door and entered another corridor, filled with the startling howls of anguished dogs. A sign on the wall cautioned: ACUTE DOGS—AUTHORIZED PERSONNEL ONLY!

The dogs were in a large room like a concrete bunker. Cathy looked in at them through a window. There were approximately a hundred cages in the room, in four rows, like stacks in a library, piled one on top of the other, three high, tall enough to let a dog stand on his hind legs and deep enough to permit him to lie down.

Most of the dogs were mongrels. The company bought them from the local shelters and dog pounds. The animals were employed as subjects in order to test the lethal levels of certain drugs and compounds. Some died in a matter of hours; it took others days to die.

It pained the girl to look at them. They were all barking, leaping madly straight into the air, flinging themselves against the doors of their cages, dancing on their hind legs and clawing at the wire mesh, their teeth bared, their eyes rolling white and crazy in their skulls. Some were bleeding from their paws where they had torn them; one was chewing in a frenzy at his tail; the uproar was sickening, but Cathy struggled to suppress the sympathy that was her instinctive response. She didn't know why exactly the dogs had to suffer this way, but she was confident there was a good and necessary reason for it as there was for everything that went on in Medical Research.

She walked quickly down the long corridor and let herself out through a door at the end. As she closed the door behind her, the tumultuous howls ceased abruptly. A visitor from the outside would never have been able to guess what was behind the door, which was painted a cheerful yellow, like daffodils.

She was in the reception foyer. It was carpeted from wall to wall, and there were deep chocolate velvet sofas, glass and chrome coffee tables, huge plants in ceramic tubs, sprays of plastic blossoms.

She lingered for a moment at a display case that took up an entire wall. Behind glass doors, on tinted glass shelves, were samples of the company's cosmetic line. Green aerosol cans of hair spray. Phallic silver tubes of deodorant. Plastic boxes shaped like miniature palettes, containing lipstick, mascara, eyeliner, rouge. Round jeweled pillboxes of blusher and powder base. False eyelashes. Cut-glass decanters of after-shave lotion and cologne. Lollipop vases of bubble bath and jars of bath oil in red, blue and translucent purple jelly beans.

It was very pretty. Cathy used nothing but the Kaizer line, which she purchased at a substantial discount in the company store.

She got her Coke in the cafeteria and returned to her lab. She took the elevator up so she wouldn't have to see the acute dogs again.

Back in her lab she opened one of the many articles on psoriasis heaped on her desk with the intention of getting a head start on a project Constantine was in the process of designing. It dealt with simulating psoriasis in rats in order to try to develop an effective medication for the disease.

> During the period of essential fatty acid deficiency (EFA), Burr and Burr in their now classic work discovered that a cessation of growth in young rats was a characteristic of the fat-free diet. In addition, during the deficiency period scaliness of the skin developed. The tip of the tail became heavily scaled and rigid. Hemorrhagic spots were often observed on the skin throughout the entire length of the tail. In female rats ovulation checked by vaginal smears was irregular and even ceased entirely in many EFA-deficient rats. In male rats prolapse of the penis was frequently noted.

Cathy yawned. It was terribly boring material. She hoped Constantine would change his mind about the experiment. It would mean four or five months of filthy, disgusting work. She turned the page, glanced, skipped a page, underlined another passage in red ink.

> Burr and Burr have developed temporary skin signs in adult rats by *ad libitum* feeding of a low-fat EFA-free diet alone or supplemented with cholic acid or cholesterol or both. The development of the dermal symptoms occurred very slowly, followed by a spontaneous cure.

Cathy closed the article, yawned again and stretched. It had been a very productive day. She was pleased with herself. It was six-thirty. Everyone else was gone. She liked the lab at this hour. It seemed to belong to her. She washed the coffee cups, cleaned up her desk, checked the sample and the column once more. She did not, she suddenly realized, want to leave. She sat at her desk, doodling on a pad, daydreaming. A porter came in to remove the garbage can containing the corpses that were the by-products of the day's scientific inquiries. She talked with him for a few minutes, warning him to be careful, those were radioactive wastes in the bottles in the sink. She doubted he knew what radioactivity was. But he was a nice, gentle, fuzzy-haired old Negro, and she liked him.

Finally, she got up to go. The sun was still high. Perhaps she would drive over to Ocean Beach for a swim. The summer was half gone and she'd been swimming only once. The trouble was that at Ocean Beach when she went alone men were always ogling her, pestering, trying to pick her up. She was afraid of them. Better to go home and catch up on her housework.

She was in the corridor when she heard the phone ringing back in the lab. She hesitated, then returned and answered it. It was Constantine.

"Geraldine?"

"No, this is Cathy." Her stomach muscles tightened.

"Cathy. What . . . what time is it anyway?"

"Six-thirty," she said. He sounded very queer. "In the *evening,*" she tried to joke. "Where have you been all day?"

"What day is it?"

"What do you mean?" She tugged nervously at the wire, wound it around her wrist. "Don't you know—"

"God damn it, tell me what day it is!" His voice came across very hollowly, as though he were speaking in the middle of a large empty chamber.

"It's Thursday, Dr. Constantine. July twenty-ninth."

"My God!" he mumbled.

"Are you . . . is anything wrong?"

There was a long pause, then he said slowly, "I—uh—I've had . . . it seems I've had a little accident." His tongue was thick, his words mushy; he sounded like people she had talked to just as they were coming out of anesthesia.

"It seems?" she asked, gripping the phone tightly, beginning to be afraid. "But . . . how can it *seem* . . . like you've had an accident? I mean, I don't understand how . . ."

"I've had an accident. Yes." *Was this Constantine?* she asked herself, all at once doubting it. *They've kidnapped him, drugged him, and they're watching him and he's trying to tell me something.* She had seen the same thing on television a few nights before.

"Are you all right? Have you been to a doctor? Do you want me to come over?"

"No, I'm fine. Don't worry. I'm fine." He pronounced each word separately. "I . . . I burned myself. I burned my hands cooking. Nothing serious."

"Have you seen a doctor?"

"I won't be in for a few days. Tell Geraldine that . . . tell her that . . . well, just tell her I had an accident and I won't be coming in. She'll know what to do."

"How did you burn yourself? Where? Are you sure you're all right?"

There was a long silence. She could hear him breathing. Then the connection was broken.

She paced up and down. She was very upset. He had sounded so remote. He didn't know what day it was. Was that believable? She felt she ought to do something; he was in trouble. But what could she do? Call Geraldine? Tell her? Tell her what? Maybe he was drunk. He'd got drunk and burned himself. Cathy had little experience with drunks; she didn't drink herself, did not know many people who did. How much did you have to drink before you couldn't remember what day of the week it was? He said he wouldn't be in tomorrow. She wanted to call him back. But how could she justify that? Maybe his girl friend was there. He didn't need her, Cathy, he surely didn't want her. There was nothing to do. All the same, she was convinced he was lying about the accident. Still, it was none of her business. He was his own boss, Prescott's fair-haired boy, according to Geraldine. If he didn't feel like coming in, that was his prerogative. If he was in trouble, he had friends, no doubt, of whose existence she was unaware. Friends who could help him, to whom he would turn.

There was nothing to do but go home. She thought about tomorrow, the certainty that she would not see him. It took the edge off her satisfaction over the column. She'd done it all for him, and now he wouldn't even be here to see it. Wasn't that how it always went? Wasn't that always the way?

She drove home depressed. A wasted day, she kept thinking. All for nothing. She turned on the radio. An Italian tenor was singing an aria from Boito's *Mefistofele.* Cathy's parents were devotees of opera; she had grown up with it in the house. She sang along with the tenor until she got to the bridge. There had been an accident, a trailer truck overturned. Traffic was piled up. She stopped singing because she had to concentrate on maneuvering her car through the congestion.

That evening as she was taking a shower, she began to sing the aria again; and then she recalled that it was the same tune the lewd painter had been singing the day before in Constantine's office. Which, she thought, was an odd though not very important coincidence.

CHAPTER 3

Yes, the voices singing in my head, I knew they would, I have always known it, I've known it since I was a child, I've been waiting for them, expecting this, it's true, I have always expected it. It was the subject I am sure of all those nightmares of my infancy, a previsioning and premonition, but as though in a foreign tongue I was not schooled to understand. I understand now, I have been ordained, I have the gift of tongues, and now I understand the singing voices and trace them to my childhood. I knew. I always knew it would happen like this. I am parched for silence. This cacophony, this quacking and cackling, gibbering of bats, *Walpurgisnacht* roistering and revelry, I thirst for silence, I would luxuriate in pools of silence as in pools of shade along the margin of a hot dusty road, endless, July heat on a yellow clay wagon track strewn with sharp stones, the dust matting the hair in your nostrils, coating your tongue, corroding your eyeballs, making them burn and water with hot salt tears or a summer shower of silence sprinkling down on me, my face turned upward gratefully to catch the cooling draught of particles of silence on my eyelids which crackle when I blink like dry parchment, my desiccated eyes. I offer my tongue swollen and black, my tongue that chokes up the brittle channels of my throat, to catch the drizzle of silences, the vapor, the dew, the distillate of all this pandemonium. But there is no shade, no pool, no cooling well or green oasis. I am in a desert where the stones spawn lizards that mock me with fire-red tongues and eyes like ruby chips, and I reel and gasp and suffocate in the holocaust of voices voices voices night and day and ceaselessly, decibels, volume, decrepitation, as though the salt-deposit layers of my consciousness were exploding in the incandescence of these tracts and wastes. At moments children sing to me, in voices like strings of pearls. Then whole antiphonal choirs like a surf running high and fast piling up along a rocky coast, booming that thunderous and calcifying heat of sound until I am dizzy and more than half blind and believe that I shall burst my flesh like an overripe fruit, split my seams and gush out onto the floor in a spongy pulp when—as if by design—the booming stops and is replaced by a coy teasing whisper, a tintinnabulating whisper that tickles like a feather in my ear. Voices, voices, bassi profundi, tenors, contraltos—brown voices, sugary voices, voices of ambergris, icy voices, voices like knives. Growling, barking, hissing, crying. I am ruptured, I am unmanned. I am unseamed from my nave to my chaps by this concatenation of pealing rackets and raucous gibes, these madhouse jinglings, discourse and riot, this infernal loquacity, language, idioms, accents, dialects—all these words, words, *words* (which I do not understand).

The discharges cannot amount to more than a spoonful every six hours—a spoonful from each wound; there are of course five wounds (as I always knew there would be): in my hands, in my feet and in my side. I say six hours though I have no reliable sense of the passage of time, and do not know with certainty how long, for just how long I've been afflicted so, it may be only minutes since I began to shave myself, it may be weeks or months: though the body speaks its own time, even in fever and delirium, the bowels, the kidneys, one's organs of increase can also tell the time, and

I estimate (the word makes me giggle), yes I *estimate* that I lose one teaspoonful—mark, Dr. Constantine, how precise, how scientific I continue to be even in this extremity, a tribute to the thoroughness of my professors and my education—a teaspoonful I say of blood with the passage of every six hours. Which signifies that given the altogether remarkable regenerative capacities of the marrow to manufacture blood afresh, there is virtually no possibility of my bleeding to death.

I say blood, but I'm not sure it is blood. It seems to change from one period to the next: at times it is a deep dark viscous red as like blood as anything I've ever seen, and it is this which is smeared on the walls of the bathroom and the door of the refrigerator like the greasy palm prints of a careless mechanic in a garage, and trailed across the carpet in the living room where I dragged myself on hands and knees a while ago, a journey from the bathroom of some fifteen feet that I have the impression (unreliable no doubt) required some fifteen hours, if not fifteen years—say fifteen lifetimes—blood, whereas at other times it appears to be more a bloody discharge, fundamentally something else combined with a small amount of blood, on the order of a menstrual discharge, and still again it has seemed almost colorless, a thick colorless fluid like snail slime or perhaps like whey, or even serum. . . . How it changes aspects like this I don't know, I am not sure it does change, perhaps it is the quality of my perceptions that continues to change. Perhaps my system has sustained a shock that has restructured the molecular order of things in my brain so that I no longer see, receive visual impressions on my optic nerve the way I did before, and no longer interpret what I see as I did formerly, the telegraphs from the eyeball to the brain being intercepted somehow, blocked, detoured, rerouted, rechanneled.

In other respects my vision has certainly certifiably been altered. Unless it is only that somehow inexplicably (I use that word! As if any of this could be explained. But for some reason I am not concerned, do not concern myself with reasons how or why, I am not even amazed—the amazing thing is my equanimity—I seem to be able to regard myself as if from a distance and my philosophical composure is wholly admirable, I seem admirable to myself, and my indifference to the scientific explanations behind the thing that has occurred strikes me as commendable. I do not neglect the possibility that this indifference may in fact be attributable to a comprehensive disability which renders me incapable of making the physical and mental effort necessary to speculate on the causes; I don't deny that I am overcome by a sort of spiritual torpor in its way sensual and gratifying, at moments almost sinfully luxurious, torpor, sloth, in spite of the pain and the caterwauling in my brain. More to the point, I realize that it is or will prove highly likely that there *is* no scientific explanation, which at the moment would not disappoint me in the least. But then, by definition, being feverish and hallucinatory, my conclusions are extremely unreliable—and when I am no longer feverish I can imagine that it might drive me to madness and death unless I discover the physiological and psychological patterns of cause and effect that have produced these lesions in my spirit no less than in my breast and my extremities) my *imagination* has been activated or stimulated fantastically so that I only seem to be receiving on my corneas the impressions of the corporeal world in a fashion dramatically (phenomenally) different from anything I have experienced before. But why do I make these distinctions? What is vision, what do we mean when we speak of a man's "vision" as distinct from his organs of sight? We mean his imagination. At least it's one of the meanings we give to the word. Vision. The idea presents itself to me with a curtsy: For the first time in my life I have a Vision!

I am not, and have never been hitherto, what you could call an imaginative person. My ex-wife likes to paint, that's me, her work, the portrait above the sofa, an image of me in oils, smirking at myself; at the present time it seems to be dissolving, the colors running together—it looks like a pizza pie and I find it much less offensive that way, much less than when it resembles me, hateful and hideous, a hateful commonplace person, badly painted; my wife is more commonplace than I am, and just because she paints is no certification of her imaginative powers. The truth is she is as devoid of imagination as my simpering and unattractive daughter, and I would gladly strangle the both of them.

My daughter. Betsy. She writes poems, poems which I am always hard pressed to admire as she seems to expect me to, because they are gibberish to me. Outlandish and incomprehensible. As she herself is. I don't understand poetry; not only hers, anybody's. *What woolsy matter drives the dervish,* she writes. What does that mean? I asked her, but she refused to answer, got indignant, lost her temper, mysterious and maddening. I don't understand her mother's paintings either, though it does not require a degree in Fine Arts to understand her portrait of me—comprising as it does an incomparable statement in its way of the sum of the malice and resentment which charged her third-rate soul. I think that's why I keep it hanging prominently: it is such a fine example of hatred and therefore a treasure in this homogenized world where nobody feels anything. Beyond that, however, it's true as that malicious lady was constantly reminding me: I do lack imagination. But I'm not ashamed of it. Imagination has never seemed to me particularly useful or desirable. In fact, it has seemed positively undesirable in my work. It consists basically of daydreaming, and in a lab like mine dreamers can get in trouble.

And yet now I begin to perceive that imagination and vision are perhaps synonymous. Woolsy matter is what my fey daughter sees where perhaps I see an enzyme. My ex-wife sees the world in terms of melting wax, and who can say that it isn't melting wax, who knows that I am not really as villainous as her revolting portrait makes me out to be? You may argue that the world is only what people agree to call it, a majority opinion, a consensus, which tells us less about the nature of the world than about the nature of prejudice and the power of political persuasion. There is an opinion current in psychiatric circles that a schizophrenic is merely a man who sees reality differently from the majority. I wonder if these wounds are really here, this pink snot oozing from my palms, or do I only see it and maybe if I go to sleep and sleep off this fever when I wake up my sight will be altered again and the wounds will be gone. In which case would I ever know for sure that I had them in the first place? It suggests the advisability of independent corroboration. Yes. Sooner or later I must show them to someone else, if only to reassure myself that I am not deranged.

In any event, I can see right through the furniture. I see the cells of the wood, and the molecular activity within the cells. I see the wood as a living thing, a honeycomb colony of interwoven molecules as active as a colony of fleas. And the crazy little bird crouched inside his Swiss chalet, I see him too there in his darkness, beady eyes glowing with vengeance, the gears revolving, the springs and levers, tick-tocking, flashes of silvery metal and dark lubricants, the bird straining on his coil, watching in the darkness, coiled to spring out and shriek at me. And the vase of flowers on the end table, I see the water percolating up through the stalk, I see the roots, I see the minerals in the water (they look like kidney beans). I see the chair and the flowers *as* chair and flowers but at the same time I see through them as well, and through—or at least into—the wall, which seems somehow liquefied, jellied, penetrable, as though I could walk through it or digest it like a pudding. But maybe I am imagining all this, and maybe I am dreaming. In my present frame of mind there does not seem to be anything to choose between these states or qualities or conditions. They seem very arbitrary terms, arbitrary distinctions for what is essentially one and the same condition.

My temperature is one hundred and eight degiees. Obviously impossible. I would be dead. But the thermometer recorded one hundred and eight just now in the bathroom. My eyes playing tricks, the mercury playing tricks? I do not urinate or defecate. But I can walk now; it's easy. I balance on the outside edges of my feet, and rather shuffle to avoid bending the instep, and it works as a method tolerably well, though I suspect I would be subject to cramps in my legs if I had to walk more than a few yards at a time. I am very weak. I am lying naked on the living room rug, which is befouled and encrusted with my suppurations. I think it is night though there is light from behind the drapes; it may be the mercury vapor lamps in the parking lot. I *feel* that it's night; I have no interest in making the effort to establish the point one way or another. The feeling is good enough for me.

The apartment resembles a charnel house. I keep thinking about the Manson family and Sharon Tate. My apartment looks like that. As though it had been ransacked, my portrait slashed with hunting knives, brutal, a sexual, almost ritual defiling of my image; the canvas hangs in triangular shreds, a solitary mutilated eyeball and a bloody inch or two of brow fixes me balefully, a crimson light beaming from the pupil lending a strange rosy cast to the room. The television screen is smashed. The Swiss chalet plundered, the bird dangling from the ruined doorway upside down, the wire noose around its throat. Lamps are shattered, drawers turned out on the floor. And everywhere brown blood smeared on the walls, the ceilings, like dried fecal matter, the stink, handprints on the white porcelain sink, footprints, writing on the wall, some cryptic, gnostic legend. I pretend I'm dead lest they return, in case they're watching me—I believe they are watching me, I feel their eyes on me, searching me out, as I lie here motionless, mutilated, naked on the floor, determined to thwart them, to frustrate their designs. I think I hear them in the kitchen, I hear their breathing, the knocking of their hearts, whispers, a footstep soft, muffled, the rustle of a garment. I hold my breath, lying here in the rosy darkness, I hold my breath and wait, determined to confound them—

(It is easier to crawl. I circumnavigate the boundaries of my rooms with more facility on my knees. I crawl to the phone. My ears are ringing, the voices clamoring in my skull. They do not let me think, they exhaust me, but I must take the chance, telephone, reestablish my reality, my presence even in my absence in the outside world. I dial, holding the phone gingerly on my fingertips, straining to hear through the roaring the voice on the other end) *Geraldine—Cathy—What time is it? What day is it?* (Can't hear a thing, I shout) *Tell me what day it is!* (Is there anyone on the other end?) *I've had an accident—*

Suddenly freezing, weak and trembling, I creep back to the bedroom, arriving at my bed in a state of shock and collapse. I doubt if I have the strength to pull myself up onto the mattress. But I manage. I manage, and lie there finally, panting, my body covered with greasy sweat, huddled beneath the blankets.

And think about Cathy Bianca. A sexual frenzy has overcome me concurrent with my attack, visitation, mutilation—I hardly know what to call it and I avoid calling it the one thing I know it should be called; for the moment (teeth chattering) I will settle for mutilation—an irrepressible sexual stimulation that is unbearable, a torment indistinguishable from the ravages of the fever and the bloody lesions that disfigure me, making me wonder if I would have the wounds without the erotic concomitant, wondering if the wounds are not some bizarre external manifestation of sexual desire, repressed libido—pleasure and pain mixed up and perhaps inseparable—nor is the pain the result solely of my ferocious sexual urge and fantastic imaginings finding no outlet or avenue of release, no discharge, because obviously a crucial portion of sexual pleasure derives from the pain of denying the desire, or from the perverse and fruitless entertaining of unrequited desire, which produces an ecstasy akin to the religious ecstasy of a hermit—and I am becoming prepared to believe that the quality of religious exaltation which is supposed to characterize the spiritual life of saints, hermits, reclusives of either sex is almost entirely sexual in nature so that the individual lives in an emotional environment of really inhuman erotic excitation *which never achieves a climax*, which it goes without saying is one (vulgar) definition of paradise. I have noticed before, throughout my life, that there is a predictable coincidence between disease and sexual desire. Both involve a disruption of the natural working of the physical and psychic mechanisms. With my wife, some of the most intense sex we shared came when one or the other of us was ill. There's an identity, or at least a parallelism, between the physical as well as psychological disordering that comprises both sexual excitement and feverish infirmity. Are they truly identical? Is sex a pestilence that attacks us like a microbe or a noxious germ—are we subject to contagions of sexuality, do we infect the objects of our desire, our spouses—is sexual intercourse then a brief, recurrent, incredibly violent disease? And then the pleasure—the painful pleasure—what does that indicate? That some part of us delights in self-destruction? In flagellation? In hair shirts and whips and beds of nails?

I would like to take my erection in both hands and tear it from my groin by main force. I would like to stuff it in my mouth and grind it between my teeth. I would like to impale virgin Cathy on it. And there is nothing to choose among them in preference of a sensation.

But why Cathy? This obsession with her. Especially at this moment of completest deformity (dead I would not be so deformed). I lie here shaken, trembling, gnawing on my lip, my eyeballs rolled back up into my skull, my penis rigid, huge, swollen, on fire. And I hallucinate Cathy, *bianca* and naked, a child, a baby, yet indisputably herself, transformed, kissing me with toothless gums, licking me, and I writhe like paper in a flame, I curl up inside myself, my muscles flutter and I cry out—my skull expands until it feels that it must explode, it's overheated, this fever, and while the child's cool slippery body snakeskin cool and glistening traverses mine and I taste the labial juices between her legs, as I excoriate her virgin orifices in my mind, an image foams up out of memory of graveyards in India, of crematoria, heaps of smoldering cadavers and ghastly shamans walking among the roasting flesh and plunging long pointy spears into the heated skulls, bursting them like grapeskins with small explosions.

This concentration on my phallus, this single-minded focus of my entire sensory apparatus on my genitals—it is a migrating, a convergence of all the components of my spirit to that region, as it were an osmotic flow and then a collecting in a pool of I was going to say erotic confluence but it goes further than the erotic, it is an eroticism that transcends considerations of mere copulation and orgasm, and develops or I wonder if it doesn't tap some cultural or racial levels of my unconsciousness impacted over centuries or better like lakes of petroleum gathered deep in the rock strata of our collective unconscious, probing, boring into that subterranean lake of myth and symbolism, releasing it in supercharged streams, bringing it to the surface, an eroticism of such force, as I touch my erect phallus and regard it, a royal purple scepter in truth and not merely in poetry, scepter and rule and the whole concept of masculine strength and power since the beginning of time, the rod—Moses' rod and Aaron's, and handing the scepter down from father to son, the scepter and not the crown that has signified rule and paternity, so that killing the king has always been equivalent to killing your father and the father raising the son in order precisely to be slain by him in that awful cycle repeated since the dawn of history, enacted no doubt in the frog-pond slimes of prehistory's consciousness, an idea immanent in creation before creation was aware of itself, like Prometheus refined into that legend of stolen fire from Olympus, all the potent myths and fairy tales concerning the children of Abraham seeking to grip the rod of majesty—it was all, my God, it is all so . . . *Freudian!*

Is that the extent of it, then? Nothing more?

"And now, students, let us consider the peculiar case of Paul Constantine. Paul hated his father and consequently masturbated to excess. Marrying a woman who reminded him of his mother, he subsequently had a love affair with a girl who reminded him of his daughter. The consequent confusion of identity reawakened Paul's adolescent fantasies and desires, which in the past had initiated, accompanied and been relieved by masturbation. His cultural conditioning and his place in society militating against his masturbating at the age of thirty-nine, however, he instead brought the stigmata of Christ down upon himself in a psychosomatic convulsion subconsciously designed to punish himself for having wanted to slay his father and sleep with his mother and to punish his mother for having failed to accord him her sexual favors. . . ."

My God, is that all? It would be worse than the recrudescence of the pain which, like the fever, comes and goes, abating, then flaring, sporadic and unpredictable. Just when I think I have learned to live with it, to accommodate myself to it, when I begin to grow philosophical, assuring myself that in the absence of the absence of pain, pain becomes the absolute and therefore no measure can exist by which I can establish what it would be like to be free of pain, my mind traveling like some sequestered theologian's, sequestered in a monastic cell in the Dark Ages, awash in sterile speculations concerning the nature of freedom, of relativity, the comparative strengths and even pleasures of subservience to absolute authority—that is, when somehow I manage to begin to contrive to deal with the pain, and even begin to believe I am on the verge of conquering myself and controlling if not the actual pain at least my reaction to it, it suddenly boils up with such redoubled fury that I want to shriek, except the pain is an immensity crushing the breath from my lungs, paralyzing my vocal cords, so I can only scream silently as it were, in pantomime, all my muscles screaming, and my organs and my nerves, though I make no sound. Nor can I control myself. That's it. It's as though I am being systematically denied the possibility of controlling myself. As though I am being compelled by a force that is quintessentially barbaric into a psychic environment where philosophical and moral conclusions do not exist. It is a definition of barbarism: the inflicting of pain, the enduring of pain (no, more: barbarism *is* pain)—a condition of suffering from which it is impossible to extrapolate a moral—suffering from which we cannot profit in any way—suffering which does not teach a lesson—suffering which *does not count!*

I tend, therefore, to pass my time in the arid analysis of the nature of the pain. When I was seventeen I tore the cartilage in my right knee in a bicycle mishap. Since then I have tried to explain to friends what it felt like; evidently it is like the pain of parturition: if you haven't experienced it, you can't imagine it. This is, of course, true to a degree of all pain—

not only is it literally unimaginable; since you cannot remember it it is indescribable. Nevertheless. Combine the pain of childbirth with the pain of cartilage tearing in the knee, with the pain of a raw nerve in a tooth (the moment when the dentist's drill begins to heat up the nerve ending; but take it further—lay the drill *on* the nerve and then leave it there), or consider your body from head to toe a throbbing abscess, consider pain of such dimensions that it converts itself to *sound,* of such dimensions that when you finally open your eyes, which have been pressed tightly shut in a muscular reflex like the rest of you, when you finally look you are profoundly startled and even disappointed that you cannot see the pain, that it has not assumed a corporeal form. Imagine that and you may have an idea of how these stigmata feel when they are at their most sensitive. Which is how they felt in the first hours almost constantly.

To tell the truth, those extremes are infrequent now, and when the pain does sweep across me, more often than not it is subject to some measure of containment which I impose on it by sheer force of mind; concentrating rigorously, I can localize it into my palms and feet and side, at which moments I readily admit, yes (how could it be otherwise?), that I feel a sensation as if spikes were being driven through my flesh; or as though my wounds were female couplings into which large bolts were being twisted, too large, stripping the threads, which must be what it's like to be raped, that sense of something immense and essentially unfeeling occupying you, tearing the tissues of the vagina, a *screwing,* or sodomy, anal rape, closer, yes, and that's the remarkable thing that again it's all so sexual, these torments, it reverts to that again and again as I seek for terms to describe what I feel. Sexual. The gashes in my hands and feet are, at moments, that is, they resemble vaginal openings, small bleeding mouths. But more important, as a result of the opening of these five new orifices in my flesh I feel vulnerable in a peculiarly feminine way, vulnerable, that's the word, the way a virgin must feel lying naked in front of her molester, on her back, her legs spread—as though the wounds of my visitation had developed curious new erogenous zones susceptible all of them to great pain but great pleasure also; there is something anticipatory in the sensation around the wounds in the vicinity of my bleeding, a tension and fear, a young girl, a virgin bride, I am like a virgin bride dreading her deflowering, suffering the first twinges of pain in anticipation of the actual physical penetration, and yet tense with excitement as well, wanting the despoliation, understanding in the depths of my blood that the pain itself will constitute a unique kind of pleasure lofty and perverse, wanting the fierce knife-strike for its own sake and all the mystery of the thing and its Jungian links to the primal aspic of creation . . . a young virgin girl but without losing my awareness of my virility either, my erect penis, excruciating to the touch, my testicles swollen to the size of grapefruits, the scrotum smooth and shiny, dark blue, the trapped polluted blood in there: in a word, bisexual. No, rather a kind of hermaphrodism with capacities for experiencing both male and female sexual transmissions. Transsexual. Which is to say, sexually nullified.

No. I am coming around. I don't know. I know enough, I am strong enough to face the fact that this thing has happened, that it is a medical fact, and neither a dream nor a hallucination. I also know, even when gripped by fever, that since it is a medical fact the condition is subject to a cure. Eventually I will be cured, I will be restored to what I was. It is a temporary condition, and I must endure it until I am sound enough in body and mind to make clear-headed analyses for treating it. Trying to formulate descriptions of the pain is useful, therapeutic—a vagrant sign of returning health, the reasserting of the habit of my mind to measure and classify things.

Until the pain returns, and once again I am cooked by microwaves, plugged into a magnetron, a vacuum tube, to a console broadcasting in programmed sequences billions of razor beams of electromagnetic waves of energy, making a grid of my flesh and jelly of my bones. It's as though I am being subjected to shock therapy, the lesions in my flesh sockets through which invisible terminals saturate my body with floods of electricity, without benefit of anesthesia, a dull chisel tapping out pineapple sections of my cranium, an eagle with his beak in my guts, needles probing my eyes. It is pain of such comprehensiveness that in spite of myself I break down and babble incoherent prayers. Only to take hold of myself in fury, with an effort I did not know I was capable of, grinding my teeth, biting my tongue, screwing up the muscles in my face, my whole body, contracting here on the floor into a protective, rigid, defiant, self-protective ball, crying, raving, over and over in the manner of a litany, a demented and blasphemous telling of beads: *Lord, Lord, what am I doing? I am half crazy to pray for relief, to pray to whom, madman! Why am I praying? I refuse to pray. Why am I praying? I refuse to pray.* I will not concede one atom to that filthy theological argument, to grant so much as tangentially that the supernatural plays any role here. No, no, and again no! I refuse to pray, I will not, and if my prayers were answered I would pray to have the wounds again and the pain again to refute my prayers. The concept of prayer is so loathsome, so unpalatable. I am not a child, nor a superstitious peasant woman. I am a man, a scientist, in the throes of extravagant suffering; I am being overwhelmed by it and therefore am not fully accountable for all that I say any more than a prisoner under duress—his fingernails being ripped off with pliers, his testicles being crushed in a vise—is accountable for the confessions he babbles hysterically. Any momentary lapses from my resolution then are not significant; they only signify that for the nonce terror and anguish have gained the upper hand; but I say this: if God himself came down and appeared at my bedside refulgent in a glory, even then, even then, yes, even then I would deny him. I would categorically refuse to believe—

I enjoy periods of lucidity now. It is like the angling of the globe, the revolving of the seasons, the move toward the equinox as periods of light and warmth gradually extend themselves against the sway of darkness and winter. I don't know how many days and nights have passed since I was stricken. My eyes have been phenomenally sensitive to light; I have kept the curtains drawn and the blinds closed tight, so I can never tell if the faint glow behind them is from the day or from the lamps in the parking lot. Once, I don't recall exactly when, I turned on the television with a view to establishing the date, the time of day, the weather in the external world. But the illumination from the screen proved too much. Moreover, the audio, no matter how I adjusted the volume control, was an indecipherable roaring and numbing pressure on my eardrums. It is the same with the radio.

So I lie here in the bedroom, or sit sometimes in the living room in a perpetual gloom of cool twilight, waking, sleeping, thinking, dreaming, the fever fitful and not particularly damaging anymore, possessing more the character of a narcotic that projects me into astral states of psychic buoyancy, psychic elasticity in which the walls of my apartment expand and contract, synchronized with my breathing. It is not an unpleasant sensation.

I hear the voices less now too. Obviously my illness has crested. I am getting well. The silly little bird pops in and out of his red-roofed chalet every fifteen minutes and delivers his pronouncement; it is purely mechanical, a bit of painted plastic and balsa wood on a spring, and I am no longer terrified. My portrait is once again nothing more than an uninspired and certainly uninspiring reproduction of my own anonymous features. The bloodstains on the carpets are negligible; they look as though a child had trailed a dripping ice cream cone through the place. Around the apartment there are almost no signs. I am alone, fairly comfortable, weak from lack of nourishment yet not critically so, the pain in my wounds mostly nettlesome now, a persistent itching as if the skin were in the process of healing itself as skin inevitably must. I am capable of rational thought and self-analysis for hours on end. All the terror has departed from my rooms.

But it shouldn't have departed. I realize that. For me to declare calmly that the terror has departed is more bizarre than what has actually occurred here. Clearly, I ought to be terrified. Somehow or other five monstrous wounds have been visited upon my body. I have no idea how long it's been since whatever this thing is happened to me. I am accountable to the people in the lab, to my ex-wife, to my daughter, to Margaret. I require medical care. I must explain, investigate, arrange, make right, correct the disruption of my life. Simply, *I have to do something!* My circumstances are terrifying. How is it then that I'm not terrified? Why, in spite of the terrific pathological abnormality of my circumstances, can I sit here in the semidarkness and congratulate myself on my tranquility?

There must be something else—an element that has nothing to do with physiology, with bodily chemistries. Perhaps that's why. Physiologically I'm returning to normal. The life-support systems of the physical structure are functioning efficiently again. And yet I do not act—I do not move to resume or try to resume the patterns of my former life because perhaps I am aware that there is a metaphysical element to contend with here, an element whose force and direction are not yet apparent, for which I must wait, which I must identify before I can do anything.

I note that I employ terms like "my former life." Does this imply a recognition that my seizure is a watershed in my life—a realization that I'll never be able to resume those patterns of my former life, that I recognize that I am unalterably changed?

I am waiting. I am waiting for something, some explanation to manifest itself. Or a resolution. The second act. This can't be all there is to it.

I will sit here in the dark and recuperate, gather my energies in preparation for whatever test or contest lies ahead. The conviction grows in me from moment to moment that much more is to come.

Nevertheless, I'm not afraid. I'm fatalistic about my immediate future.

Curious.

Ready for anything.

CHAPTER 4

> I saw how Jesus united with His bride in closest embrace. He laid His head over the head of His bride, His eyes upon her eyes, His mouth upon her mouth, His feet upon her feet, all His members upon hers so that His bride became one with Him and wanted all her Bridegroom wanted, saw all that her Bridegroom saw, and savoured all that her Bridegroom savoured. . . .

Cathy Bianca closed her eyes. One hand clutched the book of mystical writings in her lap, the other fondled the ears of a stuffed carnival rabbit lying on the pillow beside her. Brides of Christ, she thought. Saint Teresa of Avila. Saint Maria Maddalena of Pazzi. Saint Mechtild of Magdeburg. Virgins all. Brides of Christ. Virgins even after the consummation of their marriages, and yet the consummation transcendent, ecstatic. Lovers of Christ, beloved of the Lord, *lovers* . . .

It was a hot August night. There was a rip in the screen of her bedroom window that let tiny moths in and mosquitoes. Sweating, she twitched her rayon nightgown up over her thighs, moved her legs back and forth. A mosquito alighted on her thigh; she did not feel the bite.

Honey in the mouth, she was thinking. Jesus was honey in the mouth and music in the ear and a shout of gladness in the heart. "My Jesus is nothing but love, yes, mad with love," exclaimed Saint Maria Maddalena. Or was it Saint Teresa? Or Maria Maddalena writing about Saint Teresa? One of them, it didn't matter which, one of them tearing at the garments on a statue of Christ, crying rapturously, "For me You shall be naked, O my Jesus, for I cannot endure Your boundless virtues and perfections. I want Your naked naked humanhood!"

Cathy had been reading for two hours; she was in a state of curious nervous excitement that slightly nauseated her. Her mind was turbulent with confused images and contradictory yearnings.

The soul's amorous complaint. In grammar school the nuns had advised them to offer their sufferings as sacrifices to Christ. Ever since, she had equated pain with grace and virtue. Non-Catholics could never understand the utterance of a Saint Teresa, who spoke of the soul's amorous complaint to its Bridegroom, Christ, Whom the soul could never enjoy, the knowledge of which caused a pain that was paradoxically keen and sweet and delicious, a pain that seemed to pierce the very heart but which was glorious. Cathy understood.

His feet upon her feet, His members upon hers, she thought, squirming, feeling oddly voluptuous in the tangle of her nightgown and the sticky sheets. She understood the feeling Saint Teresa described, the feeling that her soul was fainting away in a kind of trance, conscious of having received a "wound of love."

When she was a child, she too had been capable of—or was it susceptible to?—a channeling of all her spiritual energies toward a union with Jesus. She had been devout, perfervid; at times she would pray herself literally sick.

Now, however, a great effort was exacted from her to maintain the purity of the associations that were awakened in her by phrases like "wounds of love." She loved God, she was still a devout Catholic, but she was in love too, and it was a profane love that impinged upon her reflections about

Saint Teresa of Avila and contaminated them. Thoughts of Dr. Constantine kept stealing across the surface of her devotional musings; almost without realizing it, she would pass from contemplating Jesus united with His bride to Constantine united with her, Cathy, sexually and profanely, Constantine naked, naked, his naked manhood inside her, which produced a charge through her imagination, a condition of excited painful longing that seemed to correspond point by point to the descriptions of psychic elevation she had been reading about. And then, when she at length did realize that she was thinking about Constantine and not Christ as she read the words "Oh my Lord and my God, how stupendous is Thy Grandeur!" she felt herself burning with sudden shame, as if she had committed some blasphemy, only in the next moment—rationalizing unconsciously—to repeat the words of Saint Teresa, as if they were a prayer and an explanation: "The soul sometimes leaps forth out of itself, like a fire that is burning and is become a flame. . . ."

She sensed it was not healthy, this exaggerated new interest in the ecstasies of Saint Teresa and her mystical counterparts. There was something morbid and escapist about it. She was vaguely aware that her infatuation with Dr. Constantine was responsible for it, that she was searching in this literature of mystical experience for an antidote to her passion for him, which—when she examined it objectively—she knew was hopeless. Moreover, the activities of these great saints, paralleling as they did in many respects things that she had thought and felt, served merely to reinforce her passion for Constantine and—by confusing it with her passion for her religion—lent it a dimension it would not otherwise have developed.

Which left her, she thought dispiritedly, in the unenviable position of being able to fulfill neither her spiritual nor her sexual requirements—assuming that one could draw meaningful distinctions between the two.

Although she did not drink, or smoke, or take drugs, she guessed she knew what it must feel like to be dissipated, as she wearily swung her legs over the side of the bed and placed her bare feet on the floor. Her eyes burned, her neck was stiff, her stomach kept turning over. She felt unclean, bloated, lifeless.

"You really have to do something about yourself," she said. She had been wallowing—there was no other word for it—in this state of intellectual and spiritual torpor for a week—for exactly the period of time Constantine had been absent from work. "It's really got to stop," she said irritably.

She scratched at her leg, was surprised to see a small smash of bright red blood on her thigh, and a mosquito bite raised white on her tanned flesh, the size of a nickel. She sighed as she looked around the room at the dirty wrinkled smelly sheets, the soiled underwear on the floor, the shoes and sandals, the wastebasket overflowing with Kleenex. It was a pigpen. Normally she was so fastidious. "Tomorrow I'm turning over a new leaf. Enough is enough."

Step one would be to forget about Constantine. Constantine was a dead end. He had a lover. How could he not have a lover? A tall, sophisticated knockout probably, rich, witty, talented. "So forget about him. He doesn't know you exist." Of course, it would be hard. But she would get over him. There were plenty of other good-looking eligible men around. Like that blond, bearded Jeff Milburne in Toxicology, who flirted harmlessly with her on occasion. True, he was married and therefore not exactly eligible. But he obviously liked her and had she ever encouraged him he would undoubtedly have begun an affair with her. And anyway, who could tell? Adultery was not the sin it used to be. Moral standards were changing all the time. The problem was her shyness. She had to stop being so shy, so frightened of men. Surely some accommodation was possible between her desire to lead a Christian life and her desire to experience a normal healthy sex life.

She would go to Ocean Beach tomorrow after work. And she would talk to the first man who approached her. She would talk to every man who approached her. That would be step two. She would put Constantine out of her mind once and for all. "And Saint Teresa too," she said with determination, snapping the book closed and returning the volume to the bookcase beside her bed.

Nevertheless, she dreamed that night, and her dreams were an exhausting amalgam of her desire for Dr. Constantine and the embodied images of the writings of Saint Teresa of Avila. She dreamed she was a child. She was in a church, kneeling before a life-size crucifix, only the figure on the cross was not Christ, it was Dr. Constantine, and he was naked. He was, however, very old and curiously diminished, as though he'd shrunk, and his hair was long, down to his shoulders, and he had a long gray beard. An angel appeared and spoke to her but she could not understand what the angel was saying. He was very beautiful, beautiful enough to be a woman. His face shone in a pink glory. He carried a long golden spear, the tip of which was on fire. Again and again he thrust the golden spear into her heart, and she felt it piercing her entrails. The pain was so great she groaned out loud, and yet whenever he withdrew the spear she cried out in protest because the pain was so sweet.

It was one of these cries that awakened her. It was dawn. She heard birds outside her window. Her body was covered with small bites. And the sheets, crushed between her legs, were wet and sticky.

"Have you heard from Dr. Constantine?" Cathy asked. "Is he coming in today?"

"Not a word," Geraldine said. "I called him last night to ask him something about the paper we're supposed to present at the Federations next month, but he didn't answer. You know what I'm beginning to think? I'm beginning to think there's nothing wrong with him at all."

"What do you mean?" Cathy asked in a rush of indignation.

"I've got a hunch he's looking for a new job and doesn't want anyone to know it. So he's faked an accident and now he's off interviewing someplace else."

"But why would he want another job?" It was a terrible, unthinkable idea. "What's wrong with this job?"

"Oh, the turnover in this business is terrific. Everybody is always trying to steal everybody else's top people. I wouldn't be surprised if Constantine never comes back."

Cathy felt faintly ill. "But Kaizer wouldn't let him go," she protested. "He's . . . he's too valuable."

"It's a cheap-ass penny-pinching outfit," Geraldine said, shrugging. "They don't give a shit. Witness Pandora's Box. They haven't spent a dime on that project."

"I don't believe it," Cathy said.

"Then why doesn't he answer his phone?"

"Maybe . . . maybe he was sleeping or something. Or in the bathroom."

"Maybe. And maybe he's in California too."

The possibility that Geraldine might be correct was profoundly upsetting. It was inconceivable that he had lied to her on the phone last week. He was obviously in distress when he called. On the other hand, he could have been so drunk he couldn't speak coherently. What if he was in California? What if he never did come back?

Distracted, unable to give her full attention to her work, she bungled three experiments in a row. Exasperated, Geraldine ordered her out of the lab.

"What the hell's wrong with you anyway?"

"Cramps," Cathy lied. "I'm having terrible cramps. They're killing me."

"You ought to get laid. Getting laid cures everything."

"I'll go lie down for a while in the lounge. Maybe I'll feel better."

In the hall, however, she saw Jeff Milburne, standing at the Xerox machine duplicating a manuscript. Impulsively she joined him, not knowing what she would think of to say.

"Hi," he greeted her, glancing up and smiling, then looking away as he fed the sheets one by one onto the glass plate and pressed the button.

"I . . . I didn't know they'd fixed this," she said. "I was just coming down to check it out. It was jammed yesterday."

"They fixed it this morning." He was wearing jeans and a tight short-sleeved knit shirt open at the neck. His arms were brown and muscular. He was really, she thought, feeling her heartbeat quicken, better-looking than Dr. Constantine. Really much better-looking. "I've been meaning to call you."

"You have?" She choked a little with sudden excitement. "Call me? Why?"

"Mears and a couple other guys, Heinrich and Bill, are looking for a crew for the sailing club. I thought you'd be perfect."

"But I don't know anything about sailing. I can't even swim."

"Doesn't matter. You're small. We need somebody small. It's a weight problem. You'd be perfect."

"But what if I fall overboard?"

"Then I can rescue you."

She looked at him. He raised his blue eyes to hers and she thought she saw something. He smiled. The machine wheezed and hummed and clacked, shuffling out sheets of copy, automatically separating and stacking them in a slotted bin at the side.

"That could prove to be interesting," she said, fluttering her eyelashes. But he didn't pick up her tone.

"It is interesting. And it's a lot of fun."

(And afterward, she was thinking, going warm inside, they would go out and have drinks. And after that—who could tell?)

"I'd love it," she said.

He smiled again and nodded. Evidently he had washed his hair—it looked clean and soft—and there were golden highlights in his beard.

"Good. I'll tell Mears. How's old Constantine treating you?"

"He's been out for a week. He's been sick."

"Really? I didn't know. What's wrong with him?"

"I'm not sure. I think he burned himself or something." She didn't want to talk about Constantine. "When do we start sailing?"

"Next week. Saturday." He turned the machine off and began stacking the copies. "I'll let you know the time."

"You live out somewhere near me, don't you? Out past Ledyard?"

"Yeah, that's right. I didn't know you lived in Ledyard."

"Well, actually in Gales Ferry."

"You have an apartment?"

"No, a little cottage. I live alone."

"Don't you get frightened?"

"Not really." She drew a breath. "You know, I was thinking . . . as long as we live near each other, it's kind of silly to drive two cars in on Saturday."

"Yeah, sure," he said easily. "I'll pick you up." He finished stacking the copies, cradled them in one arm and stepped away from the machine. "Well, she's all yours."

"Oh, I'm not using it. I was just . . . checking it out." She tried to think how to keep him there a while longer. "Have you been sailing a long time?"

"Since I was a kid. I grew up on the Sound."

"I've never been in a boat. I'll probably make a fool of myself."

He leaned his hip against the machine and crossed his ankles. He was obviously in no hurry to leave. Blushing, she made herself look him in the eyes. They did not speak for several seconds; there was something disturbed and wistful and exciting in his face. Her legs were weak; her toes inside her white Red Cross shoes were moist.

"You have freckles," he said finally in a soft, intimate tone. "I never noticed."

Clumsily she put her hand to her face and rubbed her nose as if she could wipe the freckles off. "They're a curse." She laughed self-consciously.

"No. I like them. Seriously."

"What else do you do besides sailing?" The words came blurting out of her incongruously.

"Tennis. Swimming. What do you do?"

She raised her small shoulders and let them fall. "I'm not very good at anything. I like to read. I read a lot. I'm reading *Anna Karenina* right now."

"That's pretty heavy."

"I like it. Do you like it?"

"Never read it. I'm not much for literature." There was a pause, something formal coming between them, which she tried to penetrate.

"I do like to go to the beach. I'm going this afternoon."

"It's a good day for it. You going alone?"

She swallowed, her mouth dry. "Yes." And then, as though stepping into an icy shower, coiled and tense inside: "Would you be interested in coming along?" She couldn't believe she'd actually asked him. She felt a little dizzy with it, but bold and happy too.

But he was regarding her with a queer expression, a little frown forming above his eyes, which were vaguely incredulous, his head tilted to one side. The expression confused her. Had she been too aggressive? Too pushy?

Then he was saying—ironically was it, mockingly?—"I'd like to very much, but I'm afraid I'll have to take a rain check. I'm going to the hospital after work to see my wife."

"The hospital?" she echoed, more confused. "Is your wife sick?"

He smiled, smugly, she thought. "No. She had a baby yesterday. A boy. Seven pounds."

"Oh," she said. "I didn't know. Congratulations."

She could not remember later what she said after that or how they separated. At first all she could think of was that she'd humiliated herself, and she wanted to go off somewhere and hide. Then she was angry with herself. She could not have felt more embarrassed if his wife had surprised them together in a motel room. It was mortifying, crushing.

In time, however, as she remembered his smugness, his supercilious smile, anger and contempt for him replaced all the other emotions the scene had aroused in her. What kind of a man was he anyway, hiding behind his wife and his baby like that? Didn't he have any pride, any self-respect? The worst rebuke she could administer to herself was that she had failed to recognize how weak and spineless he really was. What she liked was boldness, audacity in a man; she liked men who did not back off from the possibility, the challenge of emotional adventure. Could she imagine Dr. Constantine behaving like that? *He* would never deign to shrink behind a wife and child. She would bet on that. Dr. Constantine would never avoid the challenge of romantic adventures.

Then she remembered that she had promised to turn over a new leaf. *A fine way to begin,* she thought ruefully. But it was exceedingly difficult to keep from thinking about him. She tried telling herself she didn't care if he ever returned to work. Whether or not he took a job elsewhere would have absolutely no bearing on her own life. None. Why torture herself? It was all futile. Futile. He didn't know she existed. She had made a fool of herself with Milburne—wasn't that enough? Did she have to go out looking for humiliation? "I don't care if Geraldine is right. I don't care!" Who needed such anguish?

She would submerge herself in work. She would so fill up her brain with work that there would be no room in it for anything else. The nuns, after all, had known what they were talking about when, in grammar school, they had warned that an idle mind was the devil's own pasture.

It was a long, slow day. But she succeeded in mastering herself and did not make any more terrible mistakes in the lab.

At five o'clock, when she emerged from the Research and Development Building into the muggy afternoon sunshine, wearing her bathing suit now under her starched white lab coat, carrying her plastic beach bag, her purse slung over her shoulder, she paused beside her car to contemplate the bronze statue of Hermes—naked and gleaming in a posture of flight, his right index finger pointing at the blue sky—suspended over the pool on the lawn across from the parking lot.

It was the first time she had really looked at the statue. She could not have said what it was about it that made her stop now.

She did not know that the statue represented Hermes. If she had known, she could not have explained who Hermes was. Nor did she know that the wand he carried in the crook of his elbow was called a caduceus. She had heard of Aesculapius, but she thought he was a Greek physician, a contemporary of Hippocrates. She furthermore did not know that the snakes twisted around the caduceus were considered attributes of Aesculapius, and were symbols of rejuvenescence.

Mercury? she wondered. *It must be Mercury. But what's that thing called in his hand?* she asked herself, referring to the caduceus. She thought she was supposed to know its name, guessed she probably had known it once, in high school, and then forgot it along with all the other useless information she had toiled to learn as a child. *I'll have to ask someone,* she thought, turning away and opening the door of her car.

Half an hour later, as she lay on the sand at Ocean Beach watching a muscular young man in a very brief bathing suit throwing rocks into the water, she was reminded of the naked statue on the lawn, and by a process of association her mind went back to the dream of the previous night and it struck her that a substantial hypothesis could be constructed to the effect that her timidity in sexual matters was a consequence of her unusual religious proclivities.

Viewed one way, she had to admit, her religion, like her virginity, was an inconvenience. She wondered if perhaps she was only using her religion to shelter herself from involvement with other people, from the possibility of forging a serious relationship with a man. There was certainly nothing sinful about physical love. But an argument could be made that it was very sinful indeed to employ your religion as a device to protect yourself from the possibility of falling in love. An argument could even be made that a person who behaved like that showed symptoms of serious mental illness.

That was the problem. In this day and age, to be serious about religion was almost synonymous with being insane. Unless you were motivated to spend your life in a cloistered monastery (which she was not), it was virtually impossible to reconcile deep religious faith with the demands of the modern world. The Church itself seemed to recognize this; what was the ecumenical movement—the endless and vitriolic debates over birth control, abortion, married clergy, fish on Friday, the use of the vernacular—if not an admission of the fiendish uncertainties inherent in trying to define the nature of the relationship between the spiritual life and temporal life in the twentieth century?

And yet continence, virginity, the sacramentality of connubial love—these things were surely not negotiable. There had to be something you could with confidence call sin and something you could call virtue. Everything wasn't morally relative, was it?

Or was it? The unhappy truth was—a truth she could not the night before bring herself to admit—she felt sinful as she read Saint Teresa. There had been something lewd in her reaction. Cathy wondered if it might not be the case that there was also something specifically lewd in the experiences being described. "I am much embarrassed, my sisters," Saint Teresa wrote, "as to how to make you understand this operation of love." What was there to be embarrassed about? How could you be embarrassed to describe your relationship with God Almighty? Unless you recognized that spiritual love and physical love were only different sides of the same coin—or that spiritual love could be achieved only by the sublimating of one's sexual nature, which would mean that it contained an essence of that sexual nature.

But that was madness too. They would probably lock up women like Saint Teresa, put them in strait jackets and padded cells, if they were alive today. *All the same,* she insisted stubbornly, *both things* do *exist. Marriage is a sacrament. You can love God and love man at the same time. They should complement each other not contradict each other.* Maybe the clue was moderation. Maybe the error was *immoderate* love. Maybe the ideal balance in these matters depended on strict moderation. Or if not moderation, at least balance. *Maybe that's my problem—there's no balance to my life.* Which brought her back to where she began—she needed a man. She needed to fall in love.

Yet you could hardly fall in love if you could not force yourself to even say hello to a man. Which, evidently, she could not do, for—in spite of her resolution to talk to every man on the beach who approached her—when, at that moment, the young man who reminded her of Hermes came by and smiled at her, she rolled over onto her stomach abruptly and, trembling, feeling the blood burning in her cheeks—a spasm shooting through her, tightening all her muscles with inexplicable fear and hostility—she buried her face in her arms and lay motionless like that for ten minutes before she dared to peek over her elbow and saw that he had vanished.

It was six-thirty. The beach was nearly deserted now and the sea gulls were coming in to forage on the sand. The boardwalk was empty, though there were sounds of rifles popping and bells ringing from the shooting gallery, and on the rooftop terrace of the restaurant a few people were seated beneath the striped umbrellas, eating and drinking. She could hear the music of the merry-go-round on the other side of the immense parking lot. Three life guards in white pith helmets and orange nylon windbreakers, bandages on their blistered noses, were loafing around a lifeboat that lay belly up on the sand at the water's edge. A solitary swimmer was in the water, out deep by the diving raft. When he hauled himself onto the raft, Cathy saw that it was the man who had smiled at her.

It was still very warm. Although there were no clouds in the sky, it was hazy on the water. She could barely make out the Kaizer plant, and the huge green hangars of the shipyard and the cranes across on the other side of the mouth of the Thames. The Orient Point ferry, a rusting, peeling, dirty-white converted landing barge, chugged into the harbor on its last run of the day from Long Island. A few minutes later the Fishers Island ferry, a squat, clunky shoe box of a vessel, materialized out of the gray smoky haze, accompanied by a flock of screeling gulls flapping along above her wake, swooping and diving and skimming the waves.

Cathy tossed popcorn to the gulls on the beach, amused by the shrewish rush and flutter and squawk of the birds as they contended for the food. There were twenty of them, small brown birds, and then more arrived, larger white gulls who chased the small birds away, and then a golden retriever came running down the beach and plunged into the middle of the gulls, yapping frantically and scattering them.

Three high school girls in bikinis lying on a blanket several yards from Cathy, near the foot of the life guard tower, suddenly began to laugh and shout and Cathy looked at them. They were all as brown as pennies; their tans made her own seem anemic by comparison. They probably came here every day, lying on the beach from morning until sunset, with nothing to do except fortify the color of their skin and saturate themselves with Coppertone. Cathy guessed they were no more than sixteen, though their bodies were mature and they looked confident in their tiny swimsuits. Cathy's suit was one-piece, black and unrevealing.

Then she heard one of them utter the word "fucking." Cathy had never spoken that word; she did not think it. "Getting laid" was as close as she allowed herself to approach profanity. When under great stress, she might let slip a "damn" or a "bastard," but her most common expletive was "Sugar!" when something went wrong. She didn't seriously object to other people's swearing, any more than she objected to friends not sharing or sympathizing with her religious beliefs. But in the case of these girls there was something remarkable about those freighted syllables uttered in a childish voice so clearly and spontaneously into the soft, quiet evening air. She watched them surreptitiously, pretending to read her magazine, straining to hear what they were laughing about. They were smoking cigarettes, lying on their stomachs, their feet pointed at the water—which was beginning to hump and heave in long rolls of black cylindrical waves—leaning on their elbows, using the term over and over, and not, Cathy gradually realized, as a modifier but as a participle. They were talking about lovemaking. Their own.

"There we were, fucking our brains out in the back seat and—"

A breeze snatched away what followed, but Cathy could hear their laughter, and then she heard quite audibly: "So Susan said, 'Where do you two get off fucking while I only get to watch?' "

"No! She said that? What did Greg say?"

Cathy listened to them with a kind of contemptuous pity. They were so young and already so cynical. When, she wondered, did they begin having sex? Age ten? Twelve? And now, midway through their adolescence, what did it mean to them? One of life's greatest beauties, one of life's most precious mysteries, and already—judging by their comments and attitudes—these imbecilic children had squandered it in the back seats of cars, at drive-in movies, all beery and junked up and stinking of buttered popcorn.

It was comforting for Cathy to compare herself with them. All at once her virginity did not seem so odious to her. Rather it was possible to view her chastity as a mark of distinction. Not for her just any casual coupling devoid of high ennobling sentiments. No. The man who received her gift of virginity would have to be worthy of the prize. Promiscuity might be fashionable. According to the magazines, it was all but obligatory. But that was only to say it was common and vulgar.

Was she supposed to aspire to a life like theirs, like everybody else's? Wasn't she immeasurably superior to them, and to everyone like them? She would bet that not one of them had so much as heard of Saint Teresa of Avila, let alone Saint Mechtild of Magdeburg.

No, she thought, *no pimply Greg in the back seat of a car for me, thank you.* She began to feel very relieved. The three girls had helped her to understand the real nature of her problem. She was neither a sick neurotic nor a religious freak. She was a healthy, intelligent young woman who had yet to meet the man who measured up to her lofty and critical standards.

But that wasn't perfectly true either, she prompted herself. There was Dr. Constantine. She couldn't deny Dr. Constantine's worth. He satisfied all her stringent prerequisites. Urbane, handsome, mature, brilliant. With the added dividend that he was mysterious and inaccessible and somehow tragic. Tragic? Yes, tragic—she sensed in him an acquaintance with suffering, an intimacy with pain and disillusion, which paralleled her own. There was nothing complacent about Dr. Constantine, nothing fatuous or conventional or self-satisfied.

Face it, she said. *He's the most original and interesting man you've ever known.* Well, then. But she had been over all that repeatedly. She could not have him. He didn't like her. His indifference toward her was conclusive.

On the other hand, had she ever invited anything except his indifference? She could flirt with Jeff Milburne. But had she ever given Dr. Constantine the slightest encouragement to believe that she would welcome advances from him?

She tried to imagine herself as he saw her every day in the lab. It was not a flattering picture. Shapeless in her lab coat, rigid, tongue-tied, blushing, incompetent. He had no idea of the sort of mind she had. He had no basis on which to even guess that she read and understood books like *Anna Karenina* and *The Secret Sharer.*

It wasn't fair—to herself or to him—to assume that they could not enjoy a relationship that would be mutually fulfilling. *Who knows? Maybe we have a great deal in common.* He didn't know anything about her. Wasn't she obliged to at least make the attempt to convey to him that she was not the brainless awkward anonymity she seemed to be in the lab? *If he really got to know me, he'd like me, maybe,* she thought.

But how could she manage things so that he could get to know her?

Then it occurred to her that his illness offered her a rare and wonderful opportunity. He was home sick in bed. Perhaps alone. And if he was not alone? If his mistress was there? Well, so what? She would deal with his mistress. Maybe there was no mistress. It was better to know, one way or the other. If his mistress were there, if Cathy saw with her own eyes that he was in love with someone else, it would be instrumental in helping resolve her uncertainties, to accept the fact that she could never expect anything from him. Additionally, even if his mistress were there taking care of him, he would have to be impressed by Cathy's show of concern for him. No one else in the lab had visited him. He would have to be grateful. She would say she was worried about him, that she simply wanted to offer any assistance he might require. It was completely proper and decorous. It would be an irreproachable gesture even if she was not in love with him.

And if, by chance, there were no mistress after all—then anything could happen, couldn't it? Maybe she really could be helpful. Maybe he was alone and miserable and resentful at the indifference of his colleagues. Maybe she could actually make herself indispensable to him!

She would never have another opportunity like it; she would never know another excuse so suitable as this one to call on him uninvited at his home. It was audacious, but only she was aware how audacious it was.

She had to do it. It was intolerable living like this, not wanting to think about him, forbidding herself to love him, helpless to stop thinking about him. If for nothing else than reasons of preserving her sanity, she had to bring matters to a head.

I'm going to do it, she thought. *Come what may. I don't care. I'll go there tonight.*

CHAPTER 5

THERE WAS NO EVIDENCE of coagulation. The wounds in his hands were elliptical, about an inch long in the palm, and somewhat longer on the back of the hand; apparently the flesh had not been pierced all the way through from the back of the hand to the palm; rather it seemed as if there were two separate wounds, one on either surface of the hand, each fairly shallow, no more than a few millimeters deep. The openings in his feet were similar, but the wound in his side—to the left of and slightly below the heart—was at first little more than a contusion, a large bruise more on the order of a floor burn than an actual break in the dermal tissue. It was a week before it opened up and began to bleed. To the naked eye the tissue along the lines of the incisions was not damaged. Constantine knew that the sharpest scalpel in the world could not cut that cleanly. But more phenomenal was the fact that the blood did not coagulate.

For a time in those first days after he'd recovered from his fever and delirium, he speculated that perhaps the emissions from the wounds were not blood at all, but a rare species of pustulant discharge. Maybe, he thought, he had a kind of skin cancer as the result of working with radioactive materials. The wounds were not dissimilar to the cracks that opened up between the toes in cases of athlete's foot. Perhaps it was only an extremely virulent, extremely exotic fungus. Another theory that he entertained in the beginning was that his affliction had something to do with prostaglandins, which played a role in the coagulating process of various blood types. Suppose that his contact with them in the lab had somehow altered certain chemical balances in his blood, disrupting the equations of one of the clotting factors and thereby producing a quasi or pseudo hemophilia? It was a crazy idea, but no crazier than accepting the notion that there were supernatural explanations for the thing—a notion that from the start he refused to even consider.

Eventually, as he eliminated one bizarre and intellectually reprehensible alternative after the other, he had no choice but to conclude that his stigmata were the result of a psychosomatic convulsion for which there were no precedents. Not that this theory was any less bizarre than the others. But at least it was intellectually defensible. *There's no getting around it,* he thought. *I've done it to myself.*

It made his brain stop for a minute. It could not have been more stupefying (in fact, it would have been less) had he been provided with evidence that the stigmata were indeed a sign from God. It meant that without knowing it, without so much as suspecting it, he had been harboring within himself the ingredients requisite for producing a cataclysmic psychic convulsion of such intensity as to open five monstrous wounds on the surface of his body. For God only knew how long, he had been, in effect, a psychic time bomb.

Curiously, however, he was more embarrassed than alarmed. The injury to his vanity almost canceled out the injuries to his mind and his body. *What will they think of me?* was his first acute response. He was grotesque. He would be an object of loathing, contempt, ridicule in the lab if they ever found out. Prescott, for example. Prescott, who was so conventional that he was offended by long hair and beards and sandals. How repulsive Constantine would seem to him. As soon have gonorrhea, leprosy. He would have to submit to revolting examinations. They would delve into every shameful secret of his private life.

It would be intolerable. They would declare him either a mystic or a lunatic. He didn't know which was worse.

No one must ever know! he thought. *I have to get well, and keep it a secret, and no one can ever know what happened.*

Yet even as he said this to himself, he realized that he could not (or probably would not) be cured without resorting to medical assistance. Granted the stigmata were no doubt psychosomatic in origin. Granted also the disorder would have to be diagnosed and treated by a psychiatrist. The wounds themselves, however, were subject to nonpsychiatric therapy. In one sense they were like ulcers. What were ulcers except internal lesions brought about by psychic imbalances in the patient? But the psychic imbalances did not prevent a physician from treating them, even securing a complete remission irrespective of a remission of the patient's psychosomatic difficulties.

Logically, therefore, he ought to consult a physician at once. But he was immobilized by embarrassment. He could not divulge what had befallen him, what he had perpetrated on himself, even to an old and trusted friend like Bill Morrison. *I can just see myself,* he thought, wincing, *walking into Morrison's office with a big laugh.* Hiya, Bill. Hiya, Paul—what's up, kid? How's it going, Bill? Oh, not too bad, Paul, what's with you? Nothing much, Bill, except—well, it's the damnedest thing, but look here, I'll be damned if I haven't come down with the stigmata of Christ. Ha ha. Isn't that a killer? The stigmata of Christ, you say? Ha ha ha. Same old Constantine; always pulling my leg.

No. Never. He couldn't do it. And forget his friendship with Morrison. It would be the same with anyone—a stranger, an out-of-town physician. He would be overwhelmed with shame. Like an adolescent preferring to risk death from syphilis rather than confess to a doctor that he'd contracted it, rather than submit to the indignities of an examination, of treatment, of disclosure. Or like those occasions in his youth when in the confessional he could not bring himself to describe his sexual delinquencies to the priest, and so told lies and emerged from the sacrament more tainted than before.

But his lies in the confessional, the psychology of the syphilitic: they were owing to guilt. Guilt could paralyze a man. That was understandable. *But I'm not guilty of anything! What have I done? Why should I be so embarrassed?*

Well, embarrassment or not, he knew that to delay consulting a doctor would be a serious, perhaps even fatal, error. It was imperative for him to act emphatically, decisively. The longer he procrastinated, the harder it would be to cure the thing. It was only common sense. *You have five running sores,* he told himself, trying to arouse his imagination to an appropriate level of alarm. If he had just one rupture like that internally —a bleeding ulcer, for example—he would be over at Bill Morrison's office, or at the hospital, inside of five minutes. These were infinitely more serious because they were open to infection. Elementary considerations of self-protection demanded that he call Morrison.

"Now, right now! Get up and do it!"

But he didn't move. He couldn't. Maybe later, once he'd got used to the damned things. *We'll figure out something. Tomorrow. The next day. Maybe they'll just go away by themselves. No need to panic. That's right—give it a few more days. What we need is time—time to collect our thoughts —to review all the options and alternatives. Ascertain the direction of the disease, its drift, its movement, its ebb and flow. We'll just wait a while longer before we do anything, just wait and see. . . .*

Waiting, however, was not something he was temperamentally suited for. He had always been active, impatient, energetic. He liked to do things, to fill up his time. Now there was nothing to do and time became an obstruction standing between him and recovery, something to be dealt with consciously and manhandled out of the way. It existed in units for him, like bricks some days, like cinder blocks others. Often it was like huge granite slabs, which Constantine had to wrestle with as a stevedore contends with unmanageable pieces of cargo being loaded by crane and pulley, block and tackle, into the hold of a ship. He would labor, strenuously displacing unit after unit, moving the time by the hundredweight, by the ton, and then, exhausted, feeling that he'd accomplished a significant amount of work, he would take stock and in a Sisyphean nightmare discover that only an hour had passed and the volume of time to be handled, to be engineered from place to place, was essentially undiminished.

He regretted now never having cultivated a broader range of intellectual diversions. His teachers had always urged on him the required subjects in the liberal arts, insisting that an acquaintance with literature would help to make him well-rounded. But he'd disdained well-roundedness; was pleased to mature along angular, generally vertical lines. He was a chemist, a specialist; when he came home in the evening his brain was tired and it was not his idea of relaxation to employ it further. That was why he'd always resisted learning how to play chess or bridge. At the end of the day he wanted to curb the activity of his brain, not stimulate it. So he drank rather heavily, and was content to spend the evenings and weekends in either physical pursuits—boating on the Sound, swimming, tennis—or watching television, or listening to records. Now, however, he wished he'd acquired a taste for fiction along the way; it would have been a welcome and effortless diversion.

He couldn't even resort to records or television to relieve his monotony. One of the unfortunate lingering aftereffects of the shock of his attack was an abnormal sensitivity in his eyes and ears. Bright lights induced terrible headaches, so that often he had to wear dark glasses even at night. It was the same with his hearing; at first loud sounds of any kind were painful; he could tolerate his stereo only at volumes so reduced he couldn't enjoy the music.

It would have been helpful had he at least been able to go outside once in a while. Within ten days of his trauma, assisted by an ingenious arch support he fashioned by cutting up a pair of leather gloves, he'd taught himself to walk again with a minimum degree of discomfort. But he walked in a lurching shuffle which he could not correct or disguise and he knew that if he went outside he would call attention to himself, so he resisted the temptation. He might have driven his car, but he could not grip the steering wheel. So he was effectively incarcerated, placed under house arrest.

Nevertheless, he tried to maintain at least the externals of a routine related to the world he had inhabited prior to July 28. Without actually formulating his thinking in precise terms, he trusted that a rigorous adherence to the patterns of his previous existence constituted the best guarantee that he would eventually return to it. In this his psychology resembled that of the patient in a hospital determined to resist the dehumanizing process by which the hospital authorities try to strip him of his personality, cutting him off from all intercourse with the habits and patterns of his existence outside the hospital, in order to break him down and render him tractable —the patient who rejects johnny coats and insists on wearing his own monogrammed pajamas; who refuses to eat the hospital food and has special meals sent in from the outside; who attempts to personalize the vapid institutional anonymity of his surroundings with small tokens of his individuality: a pen-and-pencil desk set, a typewriter, a photograph of his family, his books.

Salvation lay in routine, he assured himself. It was vital to reestablish some order in his life: to clean the apartment, to prepare meals according to a schedule, to brush his teeth, to make his bed, to read the newspapers. *I mustn't let go of myself,* he thought. *I mustn't succumb. I have to keep struggling, keep myself fit.* It was very painful, but he persisted, and tried not to be discouraged when his efforts after two weeks were not rewarded by any evidence of improvement in the condition of the wounds.

His wife called to argue with him about some complicated business arrangement which he could not follow. He agreed with everything she demanded and hung up without telling her he was ill. Margaret called, and with a great effort of the will he impersonated a man who had fallen out of love. "It's all over, Margaret," he told her. "It's better if we just don't see each other anymore." He didn't know if she believed him; he didn't care. Maybe when he recovered he would explain. Maybe not. It wasn't important. The second week in August he made himself call Prescott.

"Paul! How are you, Paul? What the hell's going on? We're getting worried about you."

"The doctor says I've got viral bronchitis," Constantine said.

"Viral bronchitis? Your tech said you'd had an accident."

"No. That was nothing. Splashed some hot grease on my hands. Right after, though, I came down with this damned thing. It's knocked the hell out of me."

"Well, when do you think you'll be back on your feet, Paul?"

"Soon. I hope soon. But it's hard to say. It's a son of a bitch to treat."

"Well, I'm sorry to hear that, Paul. Everything's going to hell around here without you. You take good care of yourself, you hear me, Paul?"

"Yeah, okay."

"Anything I can do?"

"No, nothing, I'm fine."

"You sound God-awful."

"I am God-awful. But I'll be all right. I just need to rest."

Fortunately he had no friends in the apartment building. The place was inhabited primarily by military families and the turnover was rapid; nobody got to know anybody else, so except for the phone calls he was not disturbed.

But it was like being in solitary confinement. He wondered how long he could go on living this way before he went mad. Then he looked at his hands and with a dismal smile shook his head and murmured, "But of course, by certain conventional standards we have plenty of circumstantial evidence that you already are mad."

Cathy saw his Porsche the moment she drove into the parking lot, and knew that he was home. It was over two weeks since she'd made up her mind that evening at Ocean Beach to come to see him and then had her courage fail her—two weeks of remorse and self-pity and vacillation and furious self-denunciations. Now at last she was here, straight from work, in her white nylon smock and slacks and her Red Cross shoes.

But she still didn't know what she would say to him. The thing had grown so large in her imagination. She had to keep cautioning herself. "You're not about to commit a crime, for God's sake. There's no big deal." Prescott said he had viral bronchitis. There was no mystery after all, no need for apprehension. It was all quite ordinary. He was not taking a new position elsewhere, he had not been drugged or beaten. He was sick with a virus, and if she could be helpful to him, that would be wonderful, and if he was irritated with her for coming, well, what would she have lost? On balance, if he disliked her it would be preferable to his being indifferent to her.

She got out of the car and walked around to the front of the three-story red-brick building. It was without character, treeless, raw, baking in the sun.

She found his apartment number at the mailboxes in the foyer. Feeling shaky, she hesitated, was on the verge of changing her mind yet again. *You're crazy. What are you going to say to him? You'll make a fool of yourself.* And then, knowing that if she debated for another minute she would not do it—seeing with awful clarity herself at home later in Gales Ferry reviling herself—suddenly angry, as much with Constantine as with herself, she desperately pressed her finger against the buzzer and held it there for ten seconds.

Nothing happened. There was no reply. Perhaps he was sleeping? Perhaps he had gone out with the other one, in the other one's car; perhaps *she* had driven him to the doctor?

She rang again, and when again there was no response, her disappointment was tempered by relief. She'd tried. She had not backed down anyway. *I tried to see him, to help. It's not my fault if—*

Then there was a click and a rasp of static and he said, "Yes? Who is it?"

She went cold inside for an instant, felt panicky, wanted to flee, but when he repeated the question, impatiently now, she depressed the intercom button and said in a voice that was not her own, "It's me, Dr. Constantine—Cathy Bianca. Can I come up?" She waited; he did not speak. Half a minute passed. Her scalp was prickling with embarrassment and tears came into her eyes. She pressed her lips together to keep them from trembling.

Then: "*Who* is it?"

"Cathy!" she said, speaking without remembering to depress the button first. She fumbled with it, then said slowly, very distinctly and too loudly, "Cathy Bianca. Do you mind if I come up for a few minutes?"

The buzz of the door lock being released hit her like a small electrocution. She jumped, her heart pounding, and then stood staring at the door, and finally, leaping forward, only just managed to snatch it open before the buzzing stopped.

In the elevator she looked at herself in the fisheye mirror, which was a duplicate of the ones in the corridors at the lab. Even considering the distortion of her reflection in the curved mirror, she knew she looked terrible. Her hair was greasy and stringy; she hadn't washed it in eight days. Her nose looked like a mottled banana. She had neglected to do her eyes.

"You're out of your mind," she said, sick in her stomach with anxiety.

His door was ajar a few inches, but she knocked anyway. "Dr. Constantine?"

"I'm in here, in the bedroom. Come in and close the door."

She entered. She was in a narrow hallway, carpeted, gold. A small table with a pack of cigarettes on it and some keys. A bathroom opening off the hallway and the living room at the end. She saw a clock on the wall in the form of a Swiss chalet. She saw a corner of a painting of someone, a portrait, and a couch. The bedroom was between the bathroom and the living room.

"In here," he called.

"Yes, all right," she said, taking a breath and then entering his room.

It was very dark. The blinds were drawn and heavy green drapes were pulled together in front of the blinds; an inch or so of gray light came through the blinds where the drapes did not meet. He was lying in bed, covered to his chin, his arms beneath the spread. All that was visible of him in the gloom was his face.

"Sit down, over there by the door," he said. "Don't get near me. It's—what I've got—this is contagious."

She was there finally. In his bedroom. And he was alone. The folding doors of his closet were open; she saw his suits on hangers, his shirts, his shoes in rows. There were no blouses, no dresses, no indication anywhere that a woman shared the room. There was no mistress.

She sat timidly on the edge of her chair, her knees together, clutching her handbag in her lap. She could hardly meet his gaze.

"I'm sorry," she began falteringly, "if I'm disturbing . . ."

"I'm glad you came," he said. He lay quietly. With his arms at his sides beneath the bedclothes, he looked disturbingly unreal, as though he were an effigy on top of a sarcophagus, carved from stone. "I was going to call you. I wanted to see you."

"You were? You did?" She squeezed her handbag, rubbing the leather nervously with tense, damp fingers.

"I want you to do some things for me at the lab," he said, speaking slowly, his head motionless on the pillow.

"Yes. Anything. Of course," she replied eagerly. "That's why I came," she blurted, forgetting the elaborate lie she'd meant to use. She could see him now more clearly as her eyes adjusted to the twilight. He did not seem altered much, except that he was thinner; there were shadowy hollows in his cheeks and dark circles beneath his eyes. If anything, he seemed more handsome than before. "But . . . how are you feeling? Have you been seeing the doctor? I mean, are you—"

"Of course I've been seeing the doctor! Why shouldn't I be seeing the doctor? Are people suggesting that I'm not doing anything about getting over this?" He was agitated, and she hurried to reassure him.

"No. No one's saying anything like that. Why should they? I only meant—"

"That's all right." He stopped her, modifying his tone. He moved his head to one side and the sheet rearranged itself, coming down a little from his neck, revealing a portion of his collarbone and the outline of one shoulder. She couldn't see any pajamas, and she wondered with a sort of dreadful excitement if he was lying there beneath the thin covering naked. He sighed, frowned with an effort of concentration, as if it required an exhausting expenditure of energy merely to formulate a sentence. *He's so helpless,* she thought. *He's like a baby.* His hair, damp with sweat, was falling into his eyes. She longed to smooth it back, gently, with her fingertips, to soothe him and stroke his face. "How is everything going in the lab? Tell me—everything that's been happening."

Feeling more at ease, she reviewed for him the course of the prostaglandin research—"All my columns have been great since you left; I haven't lost a single one"—and told him about the apparent failure of a psoriasis experiment and what she thought might have gone wrong, and informed him that Geraldine was getting nervous about the paper they were scheduled to present at the Federations in September. "And Jeff Milburne's wife had a baby a couple of weeks ago, and Percy smashed up his brand-new LTD—some drunk hit him in Niantic but he's okay—"

Dr. Constantine lay with his eyes closed during her recitation, not responding in any way, so that she was beginning to wonder if he'd dozed off, when he suddenly interrupted her in the middle of a sentence, without opening his eyes, and asked, "Does anyone know you came here?"

"What?"

"Does anyone know—did you tell anyone that you were going to come here?" He was looking at her now and his eyes had a fierce light in them.

"No, no. It—it was a spur-of-the-moment thing. I was shopping in New London and—"

"Don't tell anyone."

"Well, of course, if you don't want—"

"Swear to me you won't tell anyone," he said vehemently.

"I swear, of course, I swear!" she exclaimed in confusion.

He stared hard at her as if trying to judge whether he could trust her; then his face softened and he seemed to relax by degrees and closed his eyes again, letting his head sink back into the pillow, the tension in his neck muscles draining. A minute went by without either of them speaking. She was rigid, sitting there on the straight chair, her back arched and aching, her knees pressed together, her hands and feet cold despite the closeness of the sealed room.

Everything she could think of to talk about seemed grossly inappropriate. The utter triviality and irrelevance of her life seemed to rise up in front of her reproachfully. *I'm a person with nothing to talk about. I don't do anything—I don't amount to anything.* It was crushing to understand her unworthiness, her presumption. *What do I have to offer him? What could I ever give a man like this?* She was proud, she was vain—she felt superior to everyone else, like those stupid girls on the beach that day, like Jeff Milburne. But where was the basis for her superiority? In what specifics was she superior?

She saw the sweat in the triangular depression below his throat, watched his Adam's apple move up and down as he swallowed, his head back, his neck bent slightly as if he were offering himself, exposing his neck to a knife thrust. He passed his tongue over his dry lips. His eyelids fluttered. She loved him and the thought was an agony to her because she was not worthy of him.

Then he spoke again. "I don't want to be bothered. The doctor says I need rest. That's why I'd prefer you didn't say anything in the lab about being here."

"I won't say a word."

"All right. Good. Now. I want you to do some things for me at the lab. Do you have a notebook? Write it down."

"Yes, I have. Here." She opened her bag and felt in it for the small red notebook she kept phone numbers and addresses in. A tissue floated to the floor, and when she bent over to pick it up she tipped over the handbag inadvertently and her compact and car keys spilled out. Flustered, she retrieved them, forcing a belittling laugh, glancing apologetically at him, arranging her handbag next to her chair with exaggerated care, crossing her legs, laying the notebook in her lap and raising her head expectantly like a secretary.

"I want to know," he began slowly, "what happens when you administer heavy doses of prostaglandin to a guinea pig."

"To a guinea pig? Why, he's going to get diarrhea."

He nodded. "I know that. What happens when you increase the dose beyond that?"

"Then he'll begin to go crazy."

"Beyond that. Take it all the way up, past his tolerance."

"Then he'll die."

"That's all right. I want to know what happens to his blood. Does anything happen to his blood?"

All at once his face contorted, as though he were suffering a spasm of some sort; he seemed to be in quick and intense pain. He caught his breath; she heard him grinding his teeth; his neck muscles protruded. The image came to her of him contending with something, battling, locked in some furious internal combat. And then it passed, whatever it was, in ten seconds it was over, and he expelled his breath in a whistle through his lips. His forehead was shiny; it was like a fever breaking. He stirred beneath the bedclothes. She watched him, open-mouthed, her pen suspended over the page. She was thinking that he hadn't coughed once yet. He had bronchitis and he hadn't coughed once.

"Where was I?" he murmured. "Sorry. What was I saying?"

"Do you feel well enough to continue?" she asked with concern. "I can come back later. . . ."

"No, it's all right. I get these attacks . . . attacks of headaches, terrible, terrible headaches, like migraines. Yes. Blood."

"The guinea pig's blood," she said, referring to her notebook.

"His blood chemistries. Analyze his blood chemistries at every stage.

Take it up to Harry Barton but don't tell him anything. No, I mean, it's okay, yes; just tell him I have a theory. Yes, I have a theory. Funny the ideas you get when you're sick. . . . Use the E derivative. But don't tell anyone you were here. This is an experiment I laid out before I got sick. Understand? If you tell anyone, if you breathe a word, I swear I'll— No, just understand, it's important that we're not premature." She wrote for a few minutes, scribbling, wondering if later she would be able to read her handwriting, and when she stopped he went on. "There's something else. About two months ago Geraldine finished up a project—she was synthesizing something, isolating radioactive derivatives from the adrenal gland. Get her notes and—no, never mind. That couldn't be it. No, God, that couldn't be it. Fungus. Yes, I forgot. Fungus."

"Fungus?"

"Bring me everything you can get your hands on in the library about fungus." She had to lean forward; he was mumbling now and she couldn't hear. "Fungus and iodine—see what we have in the library on iodine. Iodine's very important in this . . . equation. I'm sure of it. I want you to develop an experiment, another experiment—what effect does iodine have on the epidermal tissues of rats on fat-free diets. See if there's any literature on the subject. There must be something. Somebody must have done some work in that field. Design something; use your imagination."

"But design what? What kind of experiment?"

"Blood!" he said hoarsely. "The effect of iodine on blood cells. And don't tell anyone what you're doing. Not a word—"

He started to say something more, but once again, without warning, he was seemingly throttled by some terrible breath-taking pain. He rolled over on his side, exposing his back almost to the waist, the sheets twisting around him, and a groan came up muffled from the pillow. It registered once more on the girl that he was wrestling with something; it was as if he were being crushed in some gigantic embrace which he was resisting with all his might.

He rolled onto his back then, and she could see his face, which was scored and gouged with suffering. His mouth was open, his lips curled back, baring his teeth. His eyes were closed. His face was like a horrifying picture of—what was it?—suffering, but also almost ecstasy. *Yes!* she thought, astounded, rising now, standing over him. Ecstasy! *It's like orgasm,* she thought, her emotions all disordered, feeling as though she were on fire, knowing without knowing how she knew what orgasm was like. She began to tremble. She was preternaturally conscious of his nakedness, his body covered with sweat, his ashen face shiny, as she bent over him, smelling the odors of his body, so near, he writhing as if on fire too, as if his soul were leaping up, leaping out of himself, *"like a fire that is burning and is become a flame,"* she thought with awe and wonder while fragments of her dream weeks before, mingled with half-remembered phrases from Saint Teresa, churned and boiled through her brain. . . . The angel's golden spear: it was like that, as if a spear were piercing his very entrails, making him cry out, but the pain was sweet and delicious, *her* pain, for she identified with it so completely, with such a force of sympathy, that she felt it too, a great wound in her heart being probed and plumbed, stopping her heart, making her want to cry out with him and to absorb his pain, which was so sweet that she did not ever wish to be rid of it. . . .

And he was naked, yes, the naked spear tipped with an aureole of fire penetrating deep inside her, this naked lover bridegroom, rigid now as a statue, and she saw his manhood, awful, swollen, beneath the sheets that covered his lover's body, her beloved, and she wanted him to pierce her, she wanted to tear the garments from his body and inflict upon herself that wound of love, that precious grace, that hurt which she would pray would never heal. She could not stand. She wanted to fall on him, her head on his head, her eyes upon his eyes, her mouth on his mouth, and all their members touching in a union of perfect agony. She felt as if she were being pulled apart, torn this way and that first by desire, then by dread; then she could not distinguish between desire and dread—they came together and were the same thing, and the spear was deep deep inside her and she did not want to feel anything ever again except that soul-piercing ecstatic misery.

When all at once, even as she reached out her hand to take the sheet and snatch it from his body, he gasped and shuddered like someone resuscitated, like a person who had been drowned and was coming back to life, and he coughed and went slack all at once, and breathed deeply several times, and then she realized it was concluded. He went under into a deep sudden sleep, as if he'd been hypnotized. His breathing was steady. And she knew an immense desolate emptiness, as though all her spirit had been drawn out of her, and not knowing what she was doing, half blinded by tears, feeling faint and desperate and deranged, she uttered a little scream of terror and shame and disappointment, and fled stumbling from the room.

CHAPTER 6

The Bishop was pleased with himself.

"Yes, I think it went very well, Michael," he said to his assistant, a balding priest with a lean face and thick glasses who was arranging on the desk the day's documents, files, correspondence and reports requiring the Bishop's attention. "I think I can safely say I was front page."

"You were very impressive," Michael said. "As usual."

"Yes, I believe I was." The television cameras and the reporters had departed fifteen minutes before, but the Bishop was still excited. "Of course, to be honest, I came out of the thing looking more impressive than I really was. I mean, you know, my statement wasn't exactly extemporaneous. It didn't take a genius to realize the legislature would defeat the bill. I've been rehearsing what I'd say for a week. Well, it's all a bit of hucksterism these days, isn't it? You have to fight fire with fire. The important thing is, I was front page. We should also get major coverage on the evening news."

"It couldn't have worked out better," his assistant agreed. "Not even if the legislature had passed the bill."

"Oh, my God, that would have been a calamity. We don't *want* state aid for the schools. We have to get rid of the schools, and the sooner the better. They're reactionary and inefficient. Naturally I can't say that in public. So I blast away, and keep the pressure on the governor and the General Assembly, and when the tax exemption bill comes up they are all going to be extremely wary about coming out against God twice in the same session. That's the one I'm after. The tax exemption bill."

"Well, no doubt the governor will be calling as soon as the radio broadcasts your statement."

"I called him before the reporters arrived and told him what I was going to say. A political courtesy. Little things like that make a difference, Michael. He and I are having lunch tomorrow to discuss the situation."

"Amazing. I can't keep up with you," Michael said.

"That's because you're still awash in theological prejudice." The Bishop laughed. "Your head is still somewhere back in the nineteenth century. We're in the midst of the New Reformation. The second Protestantizing of the Church. Once you change your orientation to accommodate that fact, and not until, you'll continue to operate at less than one hundred percent efficiency."

Efficiency was an obsession with the Bishop. He'd built his career on it. He'd realized early on that the single most important and dramatic fact about the Church in the middle of the twentieth century was the ossification of its bureaucracy. In private conversations with intimate friends, he was given to drawing parallels between the clumsiness and inefficiency of the Church and the Romanov dynasty in 1917. "Call me an ecclesiastical Bolshevik," he liked to joke. "I want to sovietize the Church."

He had sense enough to keep his feelings to himself, having decided that advancement in the Church depended on deeds rather than theories. There was no dearth of abstract thinkers and sloganeers in the bureaucracy; there was, however, an acute shortage of hard-nosed businessmen highly schooled in the techniques of cost accounting and high-level business management.

He saw, even when he was a seminarian, that in spite of its fabled wealth the Church was drowning in red ink. It stood to reason that a man who could balance the books would not remain anonymous for very long. Accordingly, following his ordination, he took an M.B.A. from Indiana University's School of Business, and afterward, within a year of his first parish assignment, he had converted a twenty-thousand-dollar debt into a ten-thousand-dollar profit; and impelled by a crusader's zeal and a technocrat's capacity for economic reform, his rise through the hierarchy was swift. He was one of the youngest priests in the diocese. Shortly, he was the youngest pastor. He was a monsignor at twenty-seven, and at thirty-three the youngest bishop in North America. Now, a few months short of his fortieth birthday, he did not disguise his ambition to be named a cardinal. And whenever the subject arose among his friends of the inevitability of an American pope someday, the Bishop did not blush to think it might be himself.

"What works here on a diocesan level would work in Rome," he maintained. "Why shouldn't it? The problems are identical. All that's required is to disabuse yourself of the fiction that economics is something to be swept under the rug as somehow indelicate. Economics is everything. The Church is a fantastic business conglomerate—the greatest corporate conglomerate in history. But our business techniques are medieval. It's those damned Italians in the Vatican. All their spider webs of Byzantine illogic, their inquisitorial passions and hatreds and jealousies. They have to go. You just sweep them out of there, give them a pension and a gold watch and kiss them good-bye. You abolish half the commissions, and all the subcommittees—you streamline, cut costs, eliminate featherbedding—you apply Madison Avenue promotional techniques, you impose some order and common sense on your investment portfolios, you hire the best people to handle your accounting, you stop pouring floods of good money after bad. It can be done. It has to be done. Or else in the future the Church will never be anything else than a gilded mausoleum, a creaky, drafty old museum that has a kind of quaint, anachronistic, sentimental charm, inhabited exclusively by mumbling old Italian caretakers grubbing for the tourists' loose change and handing out towels in the urinals."

Although it was colorful, none of this was mere rhetoric. The Bishop had implemented his principles and his vision at every turn of his career. On his accession to the episcopacy, he immediately reduced his personal staff by sixty percent, laid off eighty percent of the lay teachers in the diocese —and forced the priests and nuns in some cases to double their work loads to compensate. He reduced the staff of the diocesan newspaper by half, raised the subscription price and solicited secular advertising, with the result that within six months the paper showed a profit for the first time in a decade. He overhauled the antiquated investment policies of the diocese as well. And he accomplished all this with a kind of amiable ruthlessness, naturally stepping on many toes and making numerous enemies along the way. But he was confident that his enemies could not argue with his statistics; he brought every argument down to the question of profit and loss, in which he was invulnerable. It was the sort of virtuoso performance that attracted attention to himself, and which like everything else he put to work.

"We're in a struggle for survival," he would expound to Michael as they dined in the episcopal mansion on a dish of *coq au vin* the Bishop had prepared with his own hands. "And in this day and age survival in the corporate jungle depends on economic innovation and political clout. The fat days of governmental benevolence vis-à-vis our feudal economic practices are a thing of the past. The state has the power—and what's more, a growing inclination—to tax us out of business. Which means that any churchman with a grain of instinct for self-survival had better realize, and damned quickly, that he's got to master political techniques or very shortly he's going to be out of a job."

His own job and his career never seemed more secure to him than they did that bright late summer morning as he discussed his news conference with Michael and prepared for the day's business. Politically he had been masterful. His combative instincts were high. He was willing to bet that the General Assembly would leave hands off the tax-exempt status of the Church. He had no intention of campaigning against that bill as he had in favor of the bill defeated the day before in the special session which would have provided financial aid to parochial schools; its potential for awakening resentment in the large non-Catholic population of Connecticut was too great. Instead he would continue to belabor the General

Assembly for the rest of the session on the school-aid issue, thereby maintaining an atmosphere that would discourage the average legislator from further mischief. He looked forward to the battle. He was confident he would win. The future looked as bright as the sunshine on the trees in the garden of the chancery.

Michael was reading the day's schedule out loud. The Bishop fiddled with a letter opener, suddenly impatient with the routine affairs ahead of him. All at once the diocese seemed too cramped, too provincial for his talents and energies. *I have to move out, move up, fast,* he thought. *A man could stagnate here.*

". . . At one-thirty you present a plaque to the editor of the *Visitor* for journalistic excellence in keeping with the high standards of a Catholic press in a free society."

"Wonderful," the Bishop said dryly. "Where?"

"Here."

The Bishop sighed. "Well, it won't take more than five minutes, I suppose. They'll probably want pictures too. All right. What else?"

"At two-fifteen a visit to Saint Margaret's Hospital."

"What for?"

"For a well-publicized blessing of the fireman who was felled the day before yesterday while fighting the blaze at the rectory of Saint Stanislaus in Uncasville."

"Is this your idea?"

"The man is a Negro. A Baptist."

"Hmm. Very shrewd. But you know, we don't want to spread ourselves too thin. There is a risk, after all, of overexposure. Too much of a good thing. We don't want to take over the whole newspaper, do we? Sin of pride and all that. Tell them I'm busy. We'll go to the hospital tomorrow. Remember, there's also that Vietnam veterans thing this afternoon. What time is that?"

"Three."

"Yes. Better to spread it around over a couple of days, don't you think? We'll do the black Baptist thing tomorrow. He'll still be there, won't he?"

"Oh yes. He's quite seriously disabled."

"Good."

"Your mother is coming for tea at four."

"Oh, my mother! Bless her. I trust we needn't worry about press coverage of that event. Strange, isn't it, how everyone can make political capital out of their mothers except the clergy. Why is that? It must be that there's some underlying sense—some innuendo of terrible failure—attached to the image of a priest's mother. We really are held in such horrible contempt by nearly everyone. In the old days we could counter contempt with fear, terrorize the populace—we wielded the power of life and death. Now look at us. A dentist has more clout. An undertaker. Just between the two of us, what this profession requires is some glamour. We should hire a public relations firm to make us look sexy. Oh, why not? It's all sham and fraud and titillation these days. If you can't beat them, join them."

"After your mother leaves," Michael continued in a monotone, as though he hadn't heard, "you are free until six, when you are the guest of honor at the Daughters of Isabella annual Renewal Banquet. Whatever that is. You have to present a scholarship to a Puerto Rican child named Milagros del Rosario, who is a thalidomide baby, born without arms."

"Oh, Lord!" said the Bishop, flapping his own arms against his sides. "You will write the speech for me, Michael, won't you. There are limits."

"Finally, at eight-thirty you give an address at the Jaycees in Noank."

The Bishop felt very depressed. After the euphoria of the press conference, the day in front of him promised to be a profound anticlimax.

In fact, however, it proved to be rather stimulating; he was agreeably surprised. He spent the morning writing letters, and read a chapter in Camus's *The Plague;* the fiery fanatical character of the priest with his apocalyptic visions interested him as a counterbalance to the compassionate intellectuality of the doctor, with whom the Bishop identified. But he felt sorry for the preacher. Then he and Michael had a superb lunch of crabmeat and a fine dry German wine, which improved his spirits considerably.

In the afternoon the meeting with the editor of the diocesan newspaper turned out to be lively and amusing. The editor was young, bright and attractive, and after the Bishop presented the plaque and the picture-taking was concluded, they retired to his office and talked for an hour about a variety of innovations the editor was planning. The Bishop endorsed all of them, and as the editor departed promised to stop by the paper's office for lunch in the near future.

"You have to stop making dates with insignificant people," Michael admonished him.

"There is no such thing as an insignificant person, Michael. Not in the eyes of God." The Bishop smiled.

On their way to the VFW ceremony, he stopped the car outside a grade school whose mother superior he loathed. "Let's run in for a minute and stick a flea in her habit," he suggested. "Nasty old bat. I'd like to pitch her down a flight of stairs." Unfortunately the nun was absent, away on a retreat, and the Bishop was disappointed. "School falling down around her students' ears, their minds filling up with rubbish, and she's off praying!" he grumbled.

At the VFW ceremony he gave a short speech, reading from notes Michael had prepared for him, in which he denounced the war and all its sponsors without seeming to impugn the valor of the effort and the patriotic sacrifice represented in the room by the members of the VFW and the released prisoners.

"How was I? How was I really?" he demanded afterward, seeming to forget that the words he'd spoken were Michael's.

"Front page. Absolutely front page."

"I thought so too. But then one is never sure. Stop here. I want to get the paper."

He was pleased with the coverage of his news conference, but felt the story did not convey the explosive impact he thought he had imparted through his performance in front of the cameras. "They left out some damned good stuff. Well, maybe they'll include it tonight on TV."

His mother, a handsome woman in her early sixties, wearing a tailored linen suit, her gray hair rinsed blue, was waiting for him when he returned.

"You're late, darling," she said, kissing him.

"I've had a very hectic day, Mother. Did you see me in the papers?"

"Yes, it was wonderful!"

"I've been better," the Bishop said, kicking off his shoes. "But I've been worse too. What are we reading today?"

"Book Five of *Paradise Lost.*"

"Great. Just what I need. Don't be too offended, though, if I happen to doze a bit while you're reading. I've been up since five, and I didn't get to sleep till after two last night."

"You should take better care of yourself."

"I am a man possessed, Mother. You know that. Here's the tea. . . ."

They took their tea, chatting and gossiping, the Bishop bored but affectionate. Afterward his mother read aloud to him while he napped, stretched out on the couch. When he woke at six, she was gone.

A good woman, he said to himself. *Deadly dull, but good.*

At the Daughters of Isabella that evening, the Puerto Rican child who had been born without arms made a very deep impression on him.

"That kid really tore me up," he said as they drove to Noank.

"Yes, heartbreaking," Michael agreed. "Lovely and intelligent."

"Her name is Milagros. That's Spanish for miracle, isn't it? Wouldn't it be nice if a miracle would happen to her?"

"A miracle did happen to her. The scholarship was a sort of miracle. It'll make a big difference."

"Oh, yeah. The scholarship. Of course. But I'm thinking about her arms. Milagros del Rosario. The miracle of the rosary. Fine kind of miracle."

"Miracles don't happen anymore."

"Thank God," the Bishop said fervently. "Yes, the sad fact is that if I could choose to suspend the laws of nature for one moment in order to miraculously provide the girl with a pair of arms, I would have to decline to do it. A single miracle would set us back a hundred years, wouldn't it? I wouldn't have any choice at all, would I? The Italians would have a field day."

"What would you do, in fact?" Michael asked him suddenly.

"If some saint came down with a pair of new arms for her?"

"Yes."

"God, I don't know. What a question. I suppose I'd quit the priesthood and take a job lobbying in Washington for Ralph Nader. Or run for Congress or something. Or slash my wrists. What would you do?"

"Run out and begin buying up stock in the company that made thalidomide," Michael replied cynically, and the Bishop laughed.

But for the rest of the evening, until he went to bed, the Bishop could not stop thinking about the Puerto Rican girl whose name was Miracle of the Rosary.

CHAPTER 7

For the following week and a half, Constantine called his lab technician every other day. There was nothing to report about the guinea pigs, no significant changes in their blood chemistries before they died from massive doses of the prostaglandin derivatives. The literature that Cathy mailed to him—he would not let her visit him again, he said, for fear of infecting her—concerning iodine studies and fungus research were likewise of no value in helping Constantine explain what had befallen him.

The answer has to lie in the blood itself, he thought. *Obviously. Instead of trying to simulate the condition in a rat or guinea pig, the sensible thing to do is analyze the blood.* His earlier conclusion that the stigmata were the result of a psychosomatic disorder had in the intervening weeks been seriously qualified in his mind by the stubborn refusal of his blood to coagulate. He had never been a bleeder, although as a child, during one period when he was nine or ten, he had many inexplicable nosebleeds. But there had never been a coagulation problem, and as far as he knew there was no history of hemophilia in his family. Nevertheless, the blood he leaked experimentally into a drinking glass was still liquefied after seven days. *It's a two-pronged problem,* he thought. *Physiological and psychological.* Was it possible that a psychosomatic calamity could be so severe as to alter the properties of his blood chemistry?

Blood was one of the most diabolically complicated subjects in the profession. Constantine didn't know very much about it. What he did know was that coagulation was the climax of an incredibly complex and delicate cause-and-effect drama featuring the interrelated actions and reactions of myriad blood components, only a fraction of which science understood. Tracing the course of the coagulation process was like watching people in a discotheque dancing under flashing strobe lights; you only saw tantalizing glimpses of the action and had to intuit the rest.

Nevertheless, he ought to have his blood analyzed. He would learn something. But whom could he trust to do it? How could it be managed without his revealing what had happened to him and thus risking exposure of the whole shameful situation?

Then he remembered Conrad Flesch. Flesch was an internationally renowned hematologist under whom Constantine had studied years ago at Harvard, when for a short while Constantine had been a medical student. Flesch had ended up at the Mayo Clinic. He was an old man by now, but if he weren't dead there was no reason to suppose he was not still at the Clinic. *I could send a sample of my blood to him. Make up a story. Ask him to send me his findings. It would be safe, and Flesch is a genius. Whatever he found would at least be a starting point. . . .*

The next time he talked to Cathy, he asked her to send him a dozen Vacutainers, the small glass vials they used in the lab for collecting blood.

"I'm starting to work again," he explained.

"Work with blood?" she asked. "Whose blood?"

"No, not blood. Something else. I can't tell you. It's . . . a secret."

"How are you feeling?"

"Much better. Yes, a lot better. I think I'll be back soon."

But when the bottles arrived, he did nothing. He had a new idea by then.

"Cathy, would you do me one more favor?"

"Anything!"

"I've ordered some books. I wonder if you could pick them up for me. The bookstore is in Hartford. It's right across the street from Constitution Plaza. Next door to G. Fox. They won't mail them without being paid and I'm in a hurry. Will you pay for them and bring them over? I think it's safe now."

"Tonight," she said. "I'll be there tonight."

"Good. Thanks."

"You sound much better."

"I am. Yes. I think I've almost got this thing licked."

That evening, painfully, laboriously, he straightened the apartment, and shaved, and forced himself to get dressed. He put on slacks and a shirt and tie and eased his feet into a pair of loafers. As an afterthought, he put on also a blue-and-white-striped seersucker jacket. He wrapped his hands in clean bandages he made by cutting up a bed sheet, and then sat down in the living room to wait for the girl.

The wounds ached this evening, the pain rising and falling in a pattern that would have translated on graph paper into a range of peaks and valleys. He wondered if the pain was somehow associated with the girl. The stigmata had not been especially troublesome for some time before she came to see him, and then it had all opened up again with full force, as bad as it had been the first few days. Since then, he'd experienced only moderate discomfort, but tonight it was very bad. It was almost as though some mechanism was at work inside him bent on precluding him from even talking to her. Or was it sexual desire being somehow converted into anguish expressing itself through his injuries, an inflaming of himself that produced a literal disorder corresponding to the psychic inflammation that resulted from erotic excitement?

She had seemed very beautiful, very desirable. He could not tell whether she had changed as he had, but where before he'd been indifferent to her, comparing her unfavorably with Geraldine, now her beauty assailed him. Perhaps, he mused, it was merely the fact that all of a sudden he could not have her that made her so desirable. A rudimentary notion in sexual matters: inaccessibility was a powerful erotic stimulant. And Cathy now all at once was as inaccessible to him as though he were in jail.

He thought about convicts, the high incidence of sodomy and homosexual rape in prison. Sexual deprivation had to be the cruelest aspect of prison life. He wondered if it was also an aspect of the lives of monks, hermits, religious reclusives. Was penal servitude really a literal servitude of the penis? It would be interesting to know if "penitential" derived from the same word as "penis." And what of castration? Did a castrated man experience the same excruciating frustration when he saw a desirable woman? Did all women become Helens of Troy by virtue of the impossibility of his ever again having any of them?

She was late. She said she would be there by seven-thirty, and it was half past eight now, getting dark outside. It was nearing the end of August and the days were measurably shorter. He looked out the window. It was raining lightly. The asphalt in the parking lot was slick; the cars gleamed in the floodlights.

He was very impatient for her to come, but he was also apprehensive, dreading another attack. Or was he really impatient for the attack? The other time he had slept afterward for ten hours and when he awoke felt, for a while, strangely cleansed, revitalized. There was a sense of spiritual well-being which he attributed to Cathy's obvious devotion to him. A simple thing: a pretty girl was infatuated with him. She was a stimulus to his all but moribund vanity. Thinking about it now, however, he questioned whether it was not the pain itself that had produced a temporary improvement in his frame of mind. Shock therapy was supposed to work that way. And from descriptions he'd read of the process, he guessed that what he experienced the evening Cathy had been with him was very similar. It was as though lightning bolts exploded inside him, as though blowtorches played over his body and his brain. And the next day he felt better.

He sighed. His mind was tired from thinking. He wished he could massage it like a cramped sore muscle, and loosen it up and relax it.

Cathy arrived half an hour later.

"I'm sorry," she said. "You wouldn't believe the traffic in Hartford." Her hair glistened with raindrops. She was wearing a short sleeveless white dress and sandals; her skin looked golden. He sat on the arm of the couch, his hands in his jacket pockets, and did not move from there while they talked.

"How are you feeling? You look good."

"Yes, I'm feeling a lot stronger," he said. "Just put the books down over there on the table." The package, he was relieved to see, was sealed, as he'd instructed the man in the store.

"It really surprised me," she said, "when I got there. I mean, that it was a Catholic bookstore."

"Why did that surprise you?"

"I never would have thought you were interested in religious subjects."

"I'm interested in them in a scientific way," he replied evasively. He had to devote careful attention to maintaining his balance, concentrating on what he said the way a man who has drunk too much concentrates on trying to walk a straight line. "Are you thirsty? There's some whiskey in the kitchen. Above the sink. Please help yourself."

She appeared surprised momentarily, then seemed to realize quickly that he was still convalescing and that his asking her to fix her own drink was not unusual. "I don't normally drink," she said. "But if you have a Coke or something . . ."

"I think there's some soda." He sat on the arm of the couch while she went into the kitchen, his muscles tense with the effort and the need to hold onto himself, to impress her with the idea that he was all right, to not fall apart again. He wanted her to report to Prescott; he needed more time.

"You aren't a Catholic by any chance, are you?" she called from the kitchen. He could hear her cracking open an ice cube tray. He wondered with sudden fear if there were any signs in the kitchen of blood, anything lying about to incriminate him.

"No. Well, I used to be. Not anymore."

She came back, holding the glass of soda in both hands, smiling at him. She seemed more confident, less like a doe transfixed in the glare of headlights, about to shy off and bolt at any second. She seemed very happy to be there, and her happiness and her radiant smile made him despondent.

"I never would have guessed," she said, walking around the room, glancing at the titles of books, pausing for a moment in front of the portrait, finally sitting down across from him and drinking her soda, raising it to her lips with both hands, looking at him over the rim of the glass. "Do you still have any feelings about being a Catholic—one way or another?"

"No. I'm an atheist. I don't believe in God. What about you?"

She hung her head briefly. "I believe in God. But I don't object to people who don't," she added quickly. "It's a very personal thing with me. It's my own problem."

"You're a Catholic?"

She nodded. "I suppose it's an anomaly, being a scientist and everything. But that's just the way it is."

"Do you go to church regularly? Do you receive the sacraments?" He felt twinges in his hands and feet and the wound in his side was very hot, but he didn't think he would be overwhelmed this time; it seemed to be under control.

"Pretty regularly; yes." She shook her head involuntarily, as if she were somewhat embarrassed by the admission. "Very regularly, I guess, actually."

"There've been a lot of changes in the Church lately. It's not the way it used to be when I was young. What does it all mean to you?"

"I don't know," she said after a moment, thinking, her face serious and composed. "What do you mean?"

"How do you believe? Do you believe in . . . in miracles and things?"

"Miracles?" She looked at the ice cubes melting in her glass. Then placed the glass on the coffee table. "That's a funny question. I haven't really thought about miracles in a long time. I don't know. I suppose I do. I mean, I suppose I believe that God could perform miracles if He wanted to. I guess He doesn't want to."

"I think a miracle happened to me once," he said slowly.

"To you?" She seemed skeptical but interested. "Really? When? How?"

"A long time ago." He started to remove one hand from his pocket to rub his eyes, which were burning, then remembered and stopped. "No. It's nothing. Just a lot of damned stupidity," he said bitterly.

"Oh, tell me. I'd love to hear," she said, prompting him with childish eagerness.

"It wasn't anything. A psychosomatic illness, that's all. Perfectly rational explanation. There's always a rational explanation for everything."

"Tell me anyway," she said.

"There's nothing to tell!" She looked instantly stricken and remorseful and he regretted hurting her, but it was progressively more difficult to maintain the conversation. It was as though he were becoming intoxicated; he thought that shortly he might begin to babble. He had to fight back a growing urge to strip off his bandages and show her.

"I was reading somewhere," she was saying, looking into her lap, "that all illness is psychosomatic."

He did not reply and for a minute or so they could hear the rain falling and then the baby next door crying. She was uncertain now, evidently wondering how she had offended him and wary of saying anything that would upset him further. For his part, he wanted to reassure the girl, wanted to convince her that there was nothing extraordinary about his illness, sensing as he did that she was—in ways he could not spell out—potentially a therapeutic agent for restoring his psychological health. However, he had to contend with an irrational antagonism toward her and an impulse to cruelty. He wanted to hurt her, to insult her, to make her suffer a measure of the denial imposed on himself by the stigmata that prevented him from embracing her, kissing her, carrying her off to his bed. And this unlikely combination of emotions, he realized, was very dangerous. She might help him; it would be a great, immeasurable relief to tell her everything, to show her. But he could not trust her—a conventional Catholic, in love with him probably. There was no way to predict what her response would be. Nor his, if she disappointed him. *I might kill her!* he thought.

"How are you coming," she asked at length, speaking tentatively, nervous now, tapping her foot, playing with her watchband, "with your work on the iodine and fungus project?"

"Fine. Yes, it's going . . . well."

"I'm dying to know what you're doing."

"You'll know everything when it's time for you to know."

They were silent again; she emptied her glass, and then with a set little smile regarded the ice cubes intently as if they contained the answer to a scientific problem. At length, when the silence had grown seriously uncomfortable, she raised her eyes and looked around for something to use to force the conversation.

"Who painted the picture?"

He cocked his head and seemed to scrutinize the portrait of himself with aversion.

"My wife," he said. She couldn't tell if the aversion was for the picture or his wife. "Hideous, isn't it?" he murmured.

"Oh, I wouldn't say it's hideous. It's not very much like you, but—"

"It's exactly like me," he said feelingly. "It's so much like me that at times I'd like to put a knife through it!" He gave a shake of his head, irritated with himself, with his weakness and loss of control. She made a polite remark he didn't hear; he was thinking he had to get rid of her, to send her away, before he said something really irreversible, before he lost all control.

"Yes, look—well, I'm sorry, Cathy. But I'm suddenly not feeling well. . . ."

"Yes, of course." She got to her feet quickly. "I'm sorry. I didn't mean to tire you out."

"Tell Prescott you saw me. Tell him I'm fine but it's a slow recuperation. Tell him I'll be back to work soon."

"All right. You'll . . . call me at work?" She looked as though she were about to cry. He tried to make his voice gentle, fighting a great rage in him.

"Yes. I'll call you. Thanks for the books."

"Don't get up," she said, managing a strained smile. "I can get out by myself."

She bent down to pick up her glass. He saw that the rug near her chair was speckled with brown blood spots. But she didn't notice them and a moment later she was gone.

Weary, his limbs aching, his mind numb, Constantine removed his jacket and his tie and kicked off his shoes. Then, too tired to undress further, shivering, he lay down on the couch and fell into a sleep filled with erotic dreams of Cathy.

The *Catholic Encyclopedia* listed in its bibliography under "Stigmatics" over a hundred books and articles including R. Biot's *L'Énigme des stigmatises;* J. Lhermitte's *Mystiques et faux mystiques;* J. Lindworsky's "Gedankenkraft: Versuch einer Theorie der Autosuggestion"; and D. Zimmer's

"Über Stigmatization und ihre Erklärung." There was a long article on the phenomenon and several articles on individual stigmatics. In addition to the encyclopedia, the bookstore in Hartford had had in stock two biographies of contemporary stigmatics—one of the Capuchin monk Padre Pio, and the other of the Bavarian peasant woman Theresa Neumann. For the next few days, Constantine occupied himself exclusively with avid research into the material. It did not seem paradoxical to him to be interested in the Church's position on the subject. Other people had borne the stigmata. As a scientist he was obliged to look at every side of the problem.

The word came from the Greek; it originally meant a brand made with a hot iron. Cattle and slaves were "stigmatized" and in some countries professional soldiers as well. It was a mark of shame, of servitude. They branded soldiers to keep them from deserting their posts.

There was no special religious significance to the term until Herodotus used it to describe tattooing practices in certain ancient religions. In modern medical usage the term was current to signify characteristics of various kinds of hysteria, as well as symptoms of syphilis and gonorrhea.

It came as a surprise to Constantine to learn that stigmatization was not one of the Church's enthusiasms. In general the Church seemed to view the phenomenon itself, as well as miraculous claims attaching to individual stigmatics, with a reserve that approached condemnation. He hadn't expected to discover that the Church was no longer hospitable to the idea of miracles. It was funny. He should have known. He remembered again the incident from his childhood—which he'd referred to when he spoke to Cathy—that convinced him he'd experienced a miraculous cure; in retrospect he could see it was a portent of the way things would go in the Church that his miracle had been subjected to ridicule.

He was in the fifth grade. Ten or eleven years old. At the apex of his religious susceptibilities. He remembered the tremendous assaults on his senses and emotions: the colors, the smells of wax and incense and sweet sticky wine; the feel of old cassocks and lace and linen surplices; the organ music and the bells and the singing of the choirs, so powerful that he wanted to weep sometimes with a confused and triumphant yearning that shook him bodily; the fantasies engendered over long periods of solitary vigil during the forty hours' devotions, at night in the ghostly shadows of the empty clanking church, praying himself into a trance as he stared into the sinister gloom around the high altar—it was all very heady and potent. At that age his defenses against the accumulated force of the sensual stimulants were few and weak and underdeveloped.

They went to mass and communion daily. He served mass three or four times a week. Catechism was the first and most important class of the morning. Every half hour a bell rang and they would interrupt whatever they were doing to pray out loud. They prayed together before leaving for lunch, and they prayed again when they returned. They prayed also at three o'clock before going home, and were encouraged to pray at meals and bedtime. They studied Bible history three times a week, and the priest quizzed them regularly on matters of faith and morals. When they weren't attending mass, they were attending novenas, stations of the cross, forty hours' devotions or Holy Week services. Or they were rehearsing for these events, or singing in the choir.

The nuns knew nothing. They were terrifying. The long rosaries looping from their waists dangling and clattering against their shroudlike skirts as they walked, the beads the size of acorns, weapons as often as not, wielded against students like bicycle chains, deadly things, the crucifix a spike, heavy enough to split your skull, the nuns whom you hated and feared. They were saturated with prejudice and superstition. Awash, wallowing, in fairy tales and lies. To hear them speak, if there were any natural order in the universe, God had put it there for the sole purpose of violating it spectacularly every five minutes or so. Those hard stupid embittered women with their fists clenched, their minds clenched like knuckled fists. In consequence of their tutelage, a student would logically graduate as a sort of quasi mystic with a perforated nervous system and a proclivity for hysterical swoons.

Constantine's "miracle" happened in that context. He suffered as a child from chronic tonsillitis. His fear of a tonsillectomy was such, however, that each winter when his tonsils became infected he would not tell his parents, preferring to suffer the attacks in painful silence. In the winter of his fifth-grade year his tonsillitis coincided with the feast of Saint Blaise. On that day each year the priest blessed the throats of the parishioners with two crossed candles tied with a ribbon into an X like a pair of scissors. Saint Blaise was the patron saint of sore throats and, the nuns held, was credited with innumerable cures of ailments connected with the pharynx.

It was a cold wet gloomy morning. Constantine lay in bed shivering from the pain of his swollen tonsils. When he swallowed he saw fire. Then he remembered what day it was, and Saint Blaise, and he felt hope and sudden conviction that Saint Blaise would cure him.

He couldn't sit still during mass. He squirmed with impatience and Sister Perpetua, kneeling behind him, kept thumping his spine. No element of challenge attached to his emotions; he was not testing Saint Blaise. He simply believed he would be cured. And he was. With the touch of the crossed candles on his exposed throat, the pain vanished. He was overjoyed but not surprised; his cure seemed perfectly in keeping with the limits and procedures of the natural order as it had been defined for him by the nuns.

But after mass, in the classroom, when he went up to the desk to confide the wonderful news to Sister Perpetua, thinking she would be pleased with his firsthand corroboration of everything she had taught them, the nun was furious, threatened to beat him if he clung to his blasphemous story, demanded to know "Who do you think you are?" that God should visit a miracle on his puny and insignificant tonsils. When he told his classmates they sneered at him. "Bullshit, Constantine," they said. He took the tale home to his parents, but they didn't believe him either; they only smiled indulgently and exchanged looks that made him blush. After that there were no more miracles. Until now.

They should see me now, Dr. Constantine thought with a humorless smile. *What would they say, how would they deal with me?* They'd always predicted he'd come to a bad end.

The official Church attitude was ambivalent concerning stigmatics. They locked up the stigmatic monk Padre Pio as though he were a criminal, forbade him to give interviews, to submit to medical examinations, to publicize his stigmata in any way. Of course their position was double-edged. They did not forbid the pilgrims to flock to the monastery in southern Italy to see Pio celebrate mass; they didn't prohibit his hearing confessions. And to give them their due, it was logical enough—if you looked at it from their vantage point—to refuse to permit a thorough and objective medical examination. If the stigmata were a miracle, submitting to clinical probing might be construed as impudence in the eyes of God.

A miracle to believers was self-evident. Nonbelievers were never likely to be persuaded by a library of medical proofs.

Nevertheless, Constantine thought, it would have been helpful if even one stigmatic had been objectively examined. Concerning Padre Pio there were numerous statements and affidavits from doctors who treated him for ailments independent of his stigmata. But in that all of the doctors were Italians and Catholics, their opinions and their judgments of what they saw were suspect. Theresa Neumann, it was true, did attempt from time to time to authenticate what the commentators called her charism, but the authentications were invariably subject to ground rules of her own devising and therefore not trustworthy. In her case, furthermore, her very desire to prove she was authentic served in Constantine's interpretation to indict her. It suggested pride in the stigmata, an insistence on her sanctity that was, in the context, sinful.

On something as fundamental as that—whether the stigmata were a mark of God's grace or displeasure—no agreement existed among the authorities. Commentators pointed out that the stigmata usually occurred in conjunction with a state of ecstasy. In the Church's reckoning, ecstasy was apparently a weakness, a fault in a person's psyche, which was unable to support powerful emotional pressures. Ecstasy was, clinically speaking, a breakdown of the personality not dissimilar to psychosis and therefore "bad"—negative—sinful. It was curious too that although many individuals completely undistinguished by their faith and morals had been granted the stigmata, many exemplary religious figures—indeed, the overwhelming majority of the saints—did not have them. For every Saint Francis of Assisi, who bore the marks, there were a thousand others who did not.

It was also instructive to note what seemed to be a historic incidence of the power of suggestion as it applied to the rate and frequency of stigmatization. The word appeared only once in Scripture. Saint Paul, in an ambiguous passage, wrote that he bore *the marks* of the Lord on his body. Most authorities accepted this to mean figurative rather than literal marks, though Constantine was confused by their logic. By medieval times, as the focus of Christian celebration shifted from contemplating Christ triumphant on the cross to a devotion organized around an increasing compassion for the sympathetic identification with the suffering of Christ crucified, great preachers like Saint Bernard of Clairvaux were propagating stigmatization as a superior avenue to the glories of mystical contemplation (the early fathers, in any event, did not appear to view ecstasy in an ambivalent light). However, from what Constantine could glean in his unsatisfactory researches, Saint Bernard was talking about the practice of self-inflicting the stigmata to induce ecstasy; the *Catholic Encyclopedia* listed the blessed Mary d'Oignies and Robert de Monferrant as representative examples of this sort of worship.

Until Saint Francis of Assisi as it were popularized the stigmata, however, the number of people possessing the charism, or alleged to possess it, was either very small or badly documented. After Francis died in 1226 and his stigmata were publicized by his ambitious followers, the incidence of stigmatization increased dramatically.

Because of the nature of the mystery—and the mystery-oriented nature of the Church—it stood to reason that no attempt was made to document the subject systematically. A vast catalogue was published at the turn of the century purporting to be the definitive study and containing 321 names and biographies of stigmatics, but in its methods it was woefully subjective and negligent, filled with irritating lacunae, obfuscations, pietisms and omissions. No reputable Church authority took the thing seriously.

The problem was, Dr. Constantine saw, that by the time the scientific world and the techniques of academic scholarship had made an impression on the Church sufficient to permit or encourage a thorough investigation of the phenomenon, the facts necessary to the success of such an endeavor had long since vanished. And, coincidentally, just when a temper in the Church was developing that allowed for the investigation of the mystery, the incidence of stigmatization showed a drastic decline. Since the catalogue by A. Imbert-Goubeyre was compiled in 1894, very few cases of stigmatization were recorded. In the past sixty years there were only a handful, and most of those were discredited after perfunctory inquiries.

Which went far to explain the welter of contradictions and confused theory and countertheory that characterized the available literature. For one thing, some stigmata were invisible. Saint Teresa of Avila and Saint Catherine of Sienna had invisible stigmata. What was especially notable about these two saintly ladies was the extravagant sexuality of their ecstatic visions, a facet which Constantine—himself prey to intense flights of erotic fantasy since his visitation—was quick to remark. To him, however, erotic ecstasy notwithstanding, invisible stigmata were no stigmata at all. "Sorry, my dear Teresa," he would say, "your stigmata weren't much more miraculous than a migraine headache or an upset stomach. Today you wouldn't even make a college textbook on psychosomatic illness."

Psychopathological considerations were closely associated with most of the cases he read about. It was well known, for instance, that subjects in cataleptic states induced by hypnosis, when asked to repeat movements performed in front of them, repeated these movements mirrorwise. It was the same in most instances of stigmatization. The wounds of Christ were reproduced by the stigmatic in the same pattern he saw in the image of the crucified Christ he was praying to or which appeared to him in his ecstatic vision. Consequently the wound in the side in many patients appeared on the left and in others on the right side of the body. Constantine was interested to learn that although recent archaeological findings in Israel had shown that criminals were crucified through their wrists and ankles, not through their palms and feet, no known stigmatic ever displayed wounds anywhere except in the palms and feet. Which, thought Constantine spitefully, ought to lay to rest once and for all the supernatural side of the thing. If Christ were conferring the stigmata, He'd reproduce the wounds the way they were on His own body. It would be instructive to see whether, in view of these archaeological discoveries, future stigmatics would develop the wounds in their wrists and ankles.

It was all, he concluded, as supernatural as an ingrown toenail. Furthermore—and most telling, this, so far as the supernaturalists were concerned—the stigmata were not limited to the Christian world. Moslem ascetics were known to have developed stigmata as the result of immersing themselves in profound contemplation of the life of Mohammed, their wounds corresponding to the wounds Mohammed allegedly received during his religious wars. And atheists received them too, like himself, Dr. Constantine.

He would derive an almost childish comfort from coming across some similarity between an aspect of his condition and one of, say, Saint Gemma Galgani's (a curiosity in that although the Church flatly refused to pass judgment on her stigmata, the stigmata did not stand in the way of her canonization). "Yes, that's how it is with me!" he'd exclaim on reading that Agnes Steiner went for weeks on end without sleeping. He wondered at this pleasure, at the satisfaction and solace gained by knowledge of a shared experience no matter how bizarre. He was avid to discover further connections between himself and the others.

Padre Pio, he read, had received the stigmata in circumstances that vaguely paralleled his own. In the choir of the church one morning during mass, the young priest had without warning let out a terrible shriek and fallen to the floor as though he'd been shot. The wounds appeared instantaneously, and he possessed them constantly forever after that (as opposed to some stigmatics, whose wounds appeared and disappeared according to the rhythms of emotionally suggestive seasons on the Church calendar). Even in the biography of this internationally revered man, however, there were contradictions. Some accounts argued that Pio had experienced invisible stigmata for weeks before the lesions appeared that morning; other accounts denied this. Constantine had felt only a curious itching in the palm of his hand a few hours before he was stricken. And, though he was delirious for days and could not be certain of the sequence of the development, he was fairly confident that the stigmata had appeared instantaneously. As opposed to this, Theresa Neumann evidenced sensitivity and discomfort for many weeks in the areas where the wounds ultimately formed. Then the wound on the back of her right hand took shape fully eight days after the wound on the back of her left hand appeared. The wounds in her palms did not open up until the following year. In this, Constantine felt confirmed in his original hypothesis that the injuries did not extend all the way through the flesh—they were essentially superficial, four separate coordinated wounds instead of two with entrance and exit paths.

Saint Gemma Galgani, in common with Theresa Neumann, was a victim of recurring childhood illnesses. Theresa Neumann was subject to frequent attacks of vertigo; a fire on a neighbor's farm apparently traumatized her when she was twenty; she experienced numbness in her arms and legs and pains in her back. Like many other stigmatics, she sustained a severe blow to her head when she was young. Temporary blindness, paralytic seizures in her left arm, attacks of deafness in her left ear, appendicitis, pneumonia were all part of her medical record. A long list of infirmities, longer than usual, but not uncommon to the majority of stigmatics. In Gemma Galgani's case, however, variations in the stigmata, differing from the experiences of other stigmatics with similar histories of childhood illness, were related. In addition to the "conventional" stigmata (the weirdness, thought Constantine—how turned around one could get, how quickly an environment took hold of a person, refashioning his notions of what was natural and what was not—the weirdness of that modifier, "conventional," used like this), Saint Gemma was given to sweating blood as Christ was purported to have done in Gethsemane (as the purported Christ was alleged to have done? Strange how one was compelled to talk about Christ as though His existence were a fact, since qualifying every reference to Him was clumsy and onerous, so that for convenience, if you wanted to treat of the stigmata and stigmatics, perforce you took a short-cut form, exposing yourself to the risk of ending up *believing* when all you started out to do was practice verbal economy. "Snares! The situation is fraught with peril, Constantine. *Apage!* Devil, get thee behind me!" Strange too how much easier it was to credit the existence of the devil than of the Christus—*Christus:* a denatured word, that, perhaps the euphemism he sought, the suffix blunting the arrowhead of the final crossed *t,* deflecting its impact —yes, Christus it would be from now on); Saint Gemma, a mournful, pretty, sloe-eyed girl with hair parted in the middle and sensuous mouth puckered in her photo for a phantom kiss, also developed from time to time scourge marks on her back, the scourging at the pillar of *ecce homo,* the Christus, on her back and—where else?—her breasts, perhaps, but how would anyone know that, to whom would the virgin girl expose her breasts? And finally, for Saint Gemma, marks of the crown of thorns appeared along her hairline, which taken all together amounted to a sizable piece of mystical pyrotechnics, for sheer theatrics tending to relegate many other more highly regarded stigmatic saints to the shade. Though when it came to pyrotechnics the champion of them all was Saint Francis of Assisi, who could levitate. A sure cure, thought Constantine, for the problems of ambulation created by pierced feet. In a league by himself, old Saint Francis was, though Padre Pio was not exactly a piker either; Pio could bilocate, which at the least made him competitive with Saint Francis. For that matter, you'd find a lot of smart money willing to back bilocation over levitation in a showdown.

Constantine's medical history was not helpful as he tried to assess the weight of his own stigmata in the light of lore and tradition. True, he had injured himself several times playing sports when he was a child, but the injuries did not seem in retrospect very significant. He had never been given to violent spasms or mysterious paralyses. Measles, chicken pox, sprained ankles, wrenched knees, tonsillitis. A pedestrian record. With the exception of the dermatological problem. On the one hand, it was reassuring to know that his medical history had little in common with those of most other stigmatics. On the other hand, he was conscious of a definite regret too because it seemed to signify that he was truly nothing more than a medical freak, depriving him of even the distorted comfort that would have followed from a feeling of kinship or community with all that absurd legion of fellow sufferers, a sense of his place in a continuity or tradition. He remained outside that, alone—a scientist and an atheist—and neither his science nor his atheism offered him any support.

When he was finished with his research, he felt if anything farther removed from an answer than before. All he had really established with any certainty was that he was the only living stigmatic in North America. And that come what may, he was never likely to be canonized.

The domestic routines he had imposed on himself as a buffer between sanity and complete dissolution were now very irksome. Without realizing it, he began to cheat. His schedule of meals was difficult to adhere to because not only did he have very little appetite, all the dishes he used to like now revolted him. He had started by determinedly pouring his cereal, boiling the coffee, drinking his juice. At noon he'd poach a couple of eggs, which he ate on toast. For dinner he'd broil a small steak he had sent over from a neighborhood market that still delivered orders to its customers. A cocktail before dinner. A cigarette after, and a glass of Scotch. Most of the time, however, he only toyed with the food it cost him such effort to prepare; he was rarely able to empty his plate; invariably he felt gassy and torpid for hours after eating. Soon his breakfast was reduced to an orange and a cup of tea; lunch, to a few soda crackers and a saucer of bouillon;

dinner, to a bit of bread and butter with a tomato-and-mayonnaise salad. Finally his diet came to consist of tea for breakfast and an orange in the evening. Surprisingly, though of course his weight declined, he did not experience any serious impairment of his strength. It was a revelation to him how few calories were really necessary to maintain health and physical fitness.

He grew a beard. Shaving was too hard to justify, and he rationalized that he had always been curious to see how he would look. The beard came in rapidly, and was unexpectedly gray. He combed and trimmed it dutifully for a few days, then lost interest in matters of personal hygiene, and after a while ceased to bathe or clean his teeth.

He declined to admit to himself that he was losing his interest in such things. He devised excuses for everything. He was so physically inactive, he argued, that it was only natural for his appetite to be depressed; never going out, he was less in need of daily baths than would otherwise be the case. It made no sense to clean the apartment, change his clothes, make his bed. His only visitor in five weeks had been Cathy, and he'd made up his mind that he could not risk seeing her again. On the phone he tried to sound coldly professional to her. Once, after she brought the books, she had rung his bell, but he refused to answer and that rebuff had apparently cooled her ardor somewhat. So he let the apartment fill up with dirt and stench. *As long as I remain mentally alert, mentally involved,* he told himself, *I'll be okay. That's what's important. It doesn't matter a damn if I brush my teeth.*

To this end of mental alertness, he applied himself diligently every morning and evening to the local newspapers, and on Sunday to *The New York Times.* He read everything, from the first page to the last, including the obituaries and the classified ads. But his brain was sluggish; he had been away from the news of the world for weeks, had lost the continuity of the rhythms of world events, so that much of what he read of the developments in foreign capitals seemed incomprehensible. It was drudgery wading through such stuff twice a day, but he kept at it for a long time, in the spirit of the middle-aged executive trying to work off some of the unsightly fat around his middle by a program of regular exercises—sit-ups, push-ups, knee bends morning and night—red-faced, veins enlarged, puffing and gasping through the five minutes of torture, hoping each day that the muscles will be more supple, that as he becomes accustomed to it again exercise will grow progressively easier; impatient for tangible results. Try as he would to concentrate, however, Constantine's mind would wander. In an article on Cambodia, he would pause at the name Lon Nol, and think how absurd it was for anyone to be named something like that, and then he would try to imagine what Lon Nol would think of a name like Paul Constantine, his mind moving lazily through eddies of irrelevance and verbal associations, following a course of least resistance, like a leaf in an autumn storm flushed into a river, drifting, snagging now and then on twigs and undergrowth along the bank, becalmed for moments in stagnant pools, then sliding on, down, until, decomposing, it ended on the stream bed, a part of the soggy mulch. Lon Nol, Sta Lin, Ho Chi, Ni Xon. Becoming absorbed in the shape of a letter, seeing pictographs instead of words, a *t* a harpoon at times, a fish hook, a protozoan beneath a microscope at others. The *Y* of Yalu a dousing wand at one moment, a candelabrum the next. He would read the entire article containing the reference to the Yalu River, and when he was finished be unable to recall what he'd read, having been thinking about dousing wands, or men dangling from stocks, or arms raised in benediction, or slingshots, or crosses. His brain felt spongy; it offered no resistance to pressure. Constantine would jerk himself awake, swear, rattle the paper irritably, and toil through the next article like a man fighting sleepiness, opening his eyes wide, resisting the urge to blink, shaking himself. But the drowsiness would steal over him, seducing him away from the printed page.

The one topic in the papers he did not have to struggle to maintain an interest in was science. Articles dealing with medical curiosities always brought him to attention. The successful separation of Siamese twins in Newfoundland. The death of a heart transplant patient in Houston. The heartbreaking case of a child in Boston dying of leukemia. For weeks after he'd ceased to bathe or change his clothes, scientific articles continued to excite him.

In time, however, even that failed to affect his deepening lethargy. He skipped a day's reading, tried to make up for it the following day. Fell three days behind. Vowed to save all the neglected papers and read the whole lot on Sunday. Settled instead on "The News of the Week in Review," and then couldn't finish that. And, like the executive trying to exercise fat from his waist, each break in the routine making it doubly hard to resume, Constantine eventually gave up reading papers entirely and let them pile up in the hallway, one on top of the other, like cordwood.

The trouble was that the outside world was irrelevant to him with all its insipid concerns insofar as it did not have a bearing on some facet of his stigmatism. Whether or not the People's Republic of China reached an accommodation with Tibet over a border dispute seemed far less important than that both Tibet and China were filled with people who without exception did not have the stigmata.

He used to fantasize the existence of a colony of stigmatics—someplace like a leper colony, a tropical concentration camp or Alpine sanatorium for the confining and treatment of their ailment. He wondered how he'd like such a place. The relief of being able to discuss his symptoms, to share the experience, to unburden himself of the terrible monotony and isolation, would be balanced, no doubt, would be offset by the loss of—what?—a perverse pleasure was not the correct term, nor pride. Perhaps a perverse satisfaction, in spite of all the horrors, in the singularity of his position.

After all, he would catch himself thinking, *everything else aside, I am the only one.*

He stopped answering the phone. Then, because he couldn't stand its ringing, he had it disconnected. He didn't care what they thought at the lab. Let them gossip and speculate. The lab seemed extraordinarily distant. He could scarcely remember what it was he used to do there; it was as though he'd been away from it for six years instead of six weeks.

Then one night in the middle of September Prescott came. He rang the buzzer for long minutes. Constantine saw him in the parking lot afterward, standing by his car, looking up at the building, saw him circling the Porsche suspiciously. Fernandez, the next-door neighbor, pulled into the lot and Prescott talked to him for a while, pointing up at Constantine's darkened windows and shrugging. A few minutes later, there was a loud rapping at the door and he heard Prescott calling his name.

Constantine sat in the dark for an hour until he was sure Prescott was gone. Then he turned on the lights and looked around. He was shocked.

The apartment was filthy. The bedroom reeked of his unwashed body, the kitchen of rotting food, the two odors of decay not dissimilar and not particularly offensive to him. He was used to his own squalor by now. The gold carpet was speckled in every room with blood. Soiled bandages and lumps of gauze lay where he'd dropped them; he couldn't remember when he'd stopped changing his dressings, substituting a pair of cotton socks, which were vile and black and crusted. He hadn't bathed in weeks. His beard was long and scraggly. His teeth were discolored.

It was as if Prescott's pounding at the door pummeled something loose in Constantine's psyche, permitting him to see at last from a fresh perspective what he'd permitted to happen to himself.

They were after him. Prescott might have got the superintendent to unlock the door. They could have caught him. He was deeply alarmed.

I've got to do *something!* he thought. He had been waiting for weeks, stupidly, aimlessly waiting for something to happen, waiting for the stigmata to disappear. But they were not going to disappear. He had to act, to seek help.

He remembered his old teacher again, Conrad Flesch. He would send a sample of his blood at once. If anyone in the world could figure out what was going on, it was Flesch. And he would make an appointment tomorrow to see a psychiatrist. They were after him; he had to be cured. And psychiatrists were bound not to violate a patient's confidence. They couldn't even divulge a patient's address. They were like priests in the confessional.

And he had to move. Quickly. In the next few days. He had to find another place to live and cover his tracks so that neither Cathy nor Prescott nor his ex-wife nor *anyone* could find him until he was restored.

It's a blessing, he thought, *that Prescott came tonight. A goddamned blessing!*

CHAPTER 8

Dr. Conrad Flesch was two hours behind schedule. It was a twelve-hour drive from his home in a suburb of Rochester, Minnesota, where he lived in semiretirement, to the lodge in Quebec where he was to begin a four-week fishing vacation with his daughter and her husband. His eyesight had begun to fail in his old age, and he did not like to drive at night. So he had hoped to leave at six. But the previous evening he'd been unable to find the Shakespeare fiberglass fishing rod his grandson had given him for Christmas; his bad memory, always an inconvenience, had lately been a plague.

A fruitless two-hour ransacking of the cellar and the attic that early fall Friday morning preceded his discovering that he had absent-mindedly stowed the rod in the spare-tire well of the station wagon a week before

—to ensure, he guessed with a sigh, that he would not mislay it in the meantime.

It was eight-thirty by then. He knew he would not be able to make it to the lodge in an unbroken stretch of driving, that he would have to spend the night in a motel, so he dawdled over his breakfast and read the newspaper.

At half past nine, when he was finally ready to leave, as he was searching for his car keys a package arrived by special delivery, for which Flesch signed. It was a small box wrapped in brown paper and bound tightly in double thicknesses of twine. A letter was Scotch-taped to the back. The return address meant nothing to him; the name, though, Paul Constantine, he felt he ought to remember.

Seated at the desk in his study, Flesch opened the letter. It was typed, and the letterhead read: KAIZER MEDICAL LABORATORIES—DEPARTMENT OF PHARMACOLOGY.

> Dear Dr. Flesch: I don't imagine you remember me. I was a student of yours at Harvard in 1958. I'm the one who got drunk and smashed the coffee table at your party in the spring of '58. I'm working in Groton, Connecticut, now for the Kaizer Pharmaceutical Company, and I've recently come into possession of a blood sample that I find remarkable. I would very much appreciate your opinion of the enclosed specimen. I realize how busy you must be, and so I'm reluctant to tell you that I consider it a matter of the utmost urgency. I think you'll agree when you analyze it that your time and effort have not been misspent. Apologizing for this intrusion, hoping that you are enjoying good health, and anxiously waiting to hear from you, I remain yours truly.

Paul Constantine . . . Flesch sat with the letter and the package on the desk in front of him, and thought back to his year at Harvard in 1958. Paul Constantine. A party? Which party? He'd entertained students in his Cambridge apartment almost weekly. It had been a productive year. His book on diseases of the blood had been published the previous spring to enormous acclaim. *Time* magazine had run a lengthy story on him. At Harvard Flesch had been lionized. His students, though, were a dull and conventional lot, the weekly dinner parties on the stodgy side. But—yes, there was a boy, a nice-looking, sandy-haired medical student, a little surly, somewhat arrogant, with a prickly, sarcastic intelligence, always a step or two removed from the others, disputatious, often sullen, a heavy drinker. Yes. Flesch remembered. Paul Constantine. He remembered that dreadful party, young Constantine unusually disruptive, gulping down almost a quart of whiskey, stumbling drunkenly over his own feet and crashing headfirst into the coffee table. At first Flesch feared he'd suffered a concussion. He'd opened a deep scalp wound that bled for an hour. Flesch wanted to take him to the infirmary, but Constantine refused, insisted on driving home, and the next day, his head bandaged, he attended class. Although he never apologized for his behavior, he was apparently ashamed of himself because he never came back to another party for the rest of the term.

A strange young man, Flesch thought, able to picture him now in considerable detail. With occasional flashes of brilliance. Not by far his best student, but attractive, individualistic. At the time, however, it occurred to Flesch more than once that the boy seemed misplaced, as though he'd made a mistake in his choice of profession.

"But why the devil is he sending me this specimen? Surely someone at Yale or at Harvard or in his own lab can analyze it for him. He ought to be able to analyze it himself."

He looked at the package. "Utmost urgency . . ." Why the mystery, the taint of melodrama?

The sample, packed in Styrofoam pellets, had been sent in a sealed phial. He held it up to the light for a moment, thinking. It appeared to be whole blood, in EDTA, no doubt, since it hadn't clotted. Amazingly, there was no evidence of decomposition; no separation of plasma and serum. He had never seen anything quite like it.

Any other day he would have driven over to Mayo and run some tests on it himself. But he was late, he had to leave. So he lifted the phone and dialed his old friend and colleague at the Clinic, Hermann Seltzer, and asked him if he would send one of his techs out to pick up the specimen.

"Do a CBC on it, and while you're at it give me some general chemistries too and, let's see, yes, a prothrombin time. . . ."

"Sure, fine," Seltzer said. "Do you know what you're looking for?"

Flesch paused before answering, scratched at the old cigarette burn on his desk with the point of the letter opener, then said, "Matter of fact,

Hermann, no. I don't have a clue. If you find anything interesting give me a call, will you?" He gave Seltzer his address in Quebec and his phone number at the lodge.

Before he left he returned the blood sample to its wrappings and placed the package in the refrigerator. Then he explained about the technician to his housekeeper, and finally, at a little after eleven, he set out on his vacation.

The friend to whom Flesch entrusted the blood sample, Hermann Seltzer, was at fifty-two thirteen years his junior. Before Flesch retired, they had spent eight years of successful collaboration together at the Mayo Clinic. Seltzer would not concede a particle of intellectual superiority to the older man. But Flesch was forever famous while Seltzer was equally forever equally anonymous, and, though Seltzer chose to ascribe the disparity in their fortunes to fate and bad luck, the real reason was to be found elsewhere.

It went back to the autumn of 1943, when, as a young intern at Methodist Hospital in Indianapolis, Seltzer examined a twenty-three-year-old black woman suffering from a hemorrhagic disease. Because the patient was a female and there was no family history of previous hemorrhagic disorders, Seltzer automatically ruled out hemophilia as an answer. In routine fashion he then tested the woman's platelet count, her capillary resistance and her bleeding time; they were normal. Her fibrinogen and calcium levels were normal too. The prothrombin, or clotting, time of her blood, however, was abnormally prolonged; whereas healthy whole blood taken from a vein with a syringe clotted generally in five to ten minutes, the patient's blood required nearly ten hours to clot. Following administration of the other standard tests which at that time were thought to be definitive, evidence seemed to indicate that the patient was suffering from a congenital prothrombin deficiency—a deficiency of one of the four major factors in the chemical chain reaction which, in the aftermath of an injury, led to the manufacture of fibrin and the coagulation of blood.

But Seltzer was not satisfied with this diagnosis. Afterward he himself could not explain why. Conventional wisdom argued that the case was one of congenital prothrombin deficiency; Seltzer had always deferred to conventional wisdom. Nevertheless, that autumn of 1943 in Indianapolis, he experienced for one of the few times in his life a moment of pure inspiration that led him to disdain conventional wisdom.

His patient, he decided, was in fact deficient in a hitherto unknown clotting factor. He devoted the next six months to proving it.

Employing well-known techniques for removing prothrombin from normal plasma via the addition of barium sulfate, the young doctor proceeded to establish, in a series of what he believed were wholly original experiments, that although the addition of plasma devoid of prothrombin restored his patient's clotting time to normal, the addition of a prothrombin preparation derived from a normal plasma source had no effect at all on the clotting time. In 1943 there were only four recognized clotting factors: fibrinogen, prothrombin, platelets and calcium. Inasmuch as the levels of all four of these factors in his patient's blood had already been shown to be normal, Seltzer concluded with great excitement that he had singlehandedly discovered nothing less than a new clotting factor.

The Seltzer factor! he thought ecstatically. "They'll call it the Seltzer factor!" he told his wife, who—though she did not know a platelet from a corpuscle—was overjoyed to think that her husband would be famous.

Seltzer was a cautious man; in his profession caution was, of course, a virtue, but Seltzer took it to excess. Normally he had little confidence in his own abilities. Moreover, unlike those people who were governed by a fear of failure, for reasons never clear to him he was forced to labor under a fear of success.

It dated to his childhood, in the schoolyard, in games. He would go to the plate or the foul line telling himself, *I can't do it, I know I can't do it, I know I'll miss.* When in fact he would strike out or miss the free throw he would feel a greater sense of vindication in having foretold the outcome than disappointment over his failure. In time this character flaw evolved into a kind of pompous pseudophilosophy behind which he tried to mask the truth of his fear from himself and everyone else. "Don't expect anything," he would lecture his young bride, Marylou. "In this life if you don't expect anything you'll never be disappointed." And his bride believed him, neglecting to perceive—in her passion for the man, whom she considered a genius—that in spite of his never expecting anything he was nevertheless continually disappointed all the same.

It became a complex which found expression in a variety of self-defeating postures; none was more revealing than his negative rhetorical constructions. To girls in college he wanted to date, he would say, once he'd summoned the nerve to say anything, "I don't suppose you're not doing anything Saturday?" Or: "I don't suppose you'd care to go out with me some night?" When the girl would refuse he would tell himself bitterly, "Of course she's busy, I knew she wouldn't go out with me, I knew it." And he would keep telling himself that he knew it until his knowledge began to seem a triumph of foresight instead of the humiliating rebuff he could not bear to admit it really had been. Even when he proposed to Marylou he couched the proposal in defensive negatives: "I don't suppose you'd ever consider marrying me?" And was shocked when she said that she would.

However, in the winter of 1943–44, Seltzer dared for a change to be optimistic. He had discovered a new clotting factor; there was no doubt in his mind of that. And, though he realized his discovery was not in the same league with those of the Mendels and Einsteins of the world, he felt he could reasonably expect substantial rewards to proceed from his findings: international recognition in his field, lectures at prestigious congresses, job offers, federal grants, foundation awards. His future seemed assured.

But at this juncture his lifelong conservatism and habits of caution betrayed him.

He felt that his presentation had to be airtight. As he put it to his wife, "I have to sew up every loophole. I can't leave anything to chance. I have to anticipate every objection. They're like a pack of wolves; they always go straight for your jugular." So he set out to duplicate and reduplicate his procedures over and over again. "It has to be one thousand percent," he insisted. "They'll murder me otherwise." A second decision he made that had fateful repercussions was to tell no one of his discovery. "They're all pirates," he argued. "They can steal your socks without taking off your shoes."

What Seltzer did not know, however, was that other investigators in different parts of the world had concurrently made the same discovery. Owing to the war, communications in the international scientific community were practically nonexistent, and so the researchers in France, Norway, Australia and elsewhere worked on in ignorance of the research their colleagues were pursuing. In any event, Seltzer could not have guessed what was happening in Europe. But similar investigations in the area of identifying the new clotting factor were under way in the United States. Some of Seltzer's associates at Methodist Hospital knew about them. But since no one at the hospital knew what he was doing, no one told Seltzer that a major development in the coagulation field was imminent.

The result was that when at last Seltzer was satisfied that he had constructed an "airtight" case, in the very week he sat down to write up his discovery for publication, Owren's discovery of Factor V in the Rikshospitalet in Oslo was revealed to the world, to be followed soon after by corroborative papers from Dr. Quick, Drs. Fantl and Nance in Australia, and Dr. Seeger, who was the first man to purify the clotting factor which the young Indiana intern had hoped to name the Seltzer factor but which instead forever after would be known by Seeger's name for it, accelerator globulin.

Given a different temperament, Seltzer still might have published his findings profitably. He had become, however, the victim of a fixation that was his undoing. Factor V was—almost without his knowing it—a final crucial test of his self-defensive pessimism, which argued that losing was inevitable and only hurt more if you tried to win. He would never again in his life, he thought, have an opportunity like this. His discovery was legitimate. He was the first. To be "scooped" by others, to have to share his discovery with others, to have it qualified in any way, was intolerable. His confidence—weak at the best of times—in this crisis utterly collapsed. His paranoiac view of the scientific community as pirates and cutthroats waiting to rip open your jugular convinced him of the futility of publishing his findings. No one would ever believe that he had independently discovered Factor V, let alone that he'd been the first to discover it. He would be a laughingstock. He was devastated. He never published his work, never told anyone except his wife what happened. Afterward, not surprisingly, he was never the same.

His father had used to lecture him, "You only get one chance in this life, Hermann. When it comes, get hold of it, ride it all the way. Because you'll never get another chance." In the spring of 1944 Seltzer was persuaded that he'd had his one chance and had bungled it. The experience took something vital out of him; he began to hate to go to work. Methodist Hospital seemed a mockery of the career that might have been for him. Eventually he couldn't stand it any longer, could not bear dealing with his colleagues, came to detest Indianapolis. In 1946 he left.

Between 1946 and 1958 he accepted a residency in Saint Louis, set up in private practice in a suburb of Detroit, went into partnership in Dubuque. He and Marylou had two children, a boy and a girl, both very handsome, talented and energetic. He made, as all doctors did, a salary far in excess of what his abilities would have earned him in a comparable situation in another field. But he was dissatisfied the whole time, and it wasn't until he finally decided to retire from clinical practice and devote himself to research that the pain of the Factor V disaster began to fade.

His children were grown and married, he had two grandchildren, he had financial security. As he surveyed the boundaries of his life and his prospects, he saw much to be thankful for. If it was indeed true that a man got only one chance in life, it was equally true, he came to feel, that a man could also in a limited degree start fresh; it was not necessary to drag the encumbrances of youthful disillusions behind you to your grave. You could readjust the angles of your vision: expecting nothing did not ipso facto preclude a man's learning to enjoy the small but numerous pleasures and diversions available to anonymous middle age.

He joined the staff at the Billings Hospital in Chicago. His fascination with blood was as strong as ever, and research produced a kind of oblivion in him that was healing. There was something near to total abstraction in the study of platelets (which came to be his specialty); the spherical little structures with their cactuslike spines viewed through an electron microscope undergoing their endless metamorphoses, now crescent-shaped, now like miniature dumbbells, quadrangular one instant, hectagonal the next, disgorging dendritic spikes and penises and filaments, devouring their own appendages, dilating, deflating—the platelets with their phenomenal predilection for massing at the site of a disrupted vascular surface to seal off the bleeding—this chimerical life of theirs, so vital and so various, offered Seltzer a surrogate microscopic world that bore almost no relationship to the world which had robbed him of glory.

On the whole, for the first time since the calamity of 1944, Seltzer could describe himself as reasonably adjusted to the terms of his existence. He was at last content.

In his new circumstances, he even ventured to publish a couple of modest papers on purpuric lesions, which happened to attract the attention of Conrad Flesch. Flesch was impressed by the tenacity of Seltzer's meticulous presentations and the thoroughness of his methodology. On Flesch's initiative the two men met at a convention in Milwaukee, and despite their differences of style and personality, they were compatible. Shortly thereafter a position on Flesch's staff at the Mayo Clinic opened up; Flesch asked Seltzer to fill it and, flattered, Seltzer agreed.

The relationship that grew up between the two men in the ensuing eight years before Flesch's retirement was very singular in that they became friends without either of them really liking or approving of the other. In Seltzer's view Flesch was lazy, sloppy, eccentric and often irresponsible. Seltzer also resented the careless ease with which Flesch was given to assimilating the most obtuse and contradictory principles and synthesizing them into cogent theories while Seltzer had to scrape and scratch and grind for everything he got. In addition, Seltzer was put off by Flesch's total disinclination for the nuts and bolts of research; research bored him; basically Flesch was a theoretician who—once he developed a theory—gave it to Seltzer to prove and immediately lost interest in it.

For his part, Flesch was amazed by Seltzer's narrowness. Aside from chess—which he played the way he ran the lab, conservatively, unimaginatively—he seemed to have no outside interests, no interests at all other than human blood. Flesch liked football, trout fishing, classical music, movies. He liked to drink French wine and argue politics. But to Seltzer blood was everything, it was his life. "He is so humorless," Flesch would complain. "You wouldn't believe how boring he can be." He would joke about Seltzer's compulsiveness. "Some people see the world through rose-colored glasses. Hermann sees the world through bloodstained slides."

That Flesch made fun of him behind his back, however, did not cause any serious problems in either their professional or their social relationship. Each in his own way felt superior to the other, Flesch philosophically and

Seltzer scientifically, which produced a balance of advantages and disadvantages vis-à-vis their respective vanities. Their partnership accordingly was cordial and by and large a success.

Hermann Seltzer was fifty-two the morning he received Dr. Constantine's blood in his office. It was his birthday. He had begun to lose his hair in college; by now he was almost completely bald. He was a slightly built man, about five feet eight, and by careful dieting he kept his weight around 160 pounds. For his age he was very fit. That morning, however, while moving a sofa for his wife, he'd felt something pop in his back, and he was worried. He'd had some problems with his vertebrae a few years before, and now, as he sat at his desk vainly trying to find a comfortable position for his spine, he wondered if he might need an operation.

It was an aggravating day all around. One of his assistants was leaving to have a baby, and he had before him the unpleasant task of firing another assistant. He had to write letters of recommendation for three students who had been studying in the lab over the summer. Marylou was giving him a birthday party that evening, his children and grandchildren would be there, and he was expected to barbecue the ribs. And his back was killing him.

So he did not place particular importance on the blood sample Flesch had sent to him. He gave it to a technician in Hematology with instructions concerning the tests Flesch had requested, made a note of Constantine's name and address, which he took from the wrapping, and then put it out of his mind.

He didn't return to work for two weeks. The day after his birthday his back got worse. The following morning he couldn't get out of bed. To his wife's importunities that he see a doctor he replied bad-temperedly, "I know what they'll say. They'll want to operate. They have one-track minds. You think I'm going to let those clowns put a knife in *me?* Not on your life!" He lay in bed in great pain for a week. The rest was beneficial; the back responded. The second week he was able to move around, gingerly, through the house in robe and slippers. When a plateau of recuperation seemed to be reached, however, beyond which he did not advance, he at last resorted to the care of a chiropractor recommended by one of his wife's cousins, and after a single agonizing gymnastic session in the quack's office he was cured. Seltzer felt so ashamed that he never told anyone, and sternly swore his wife to absolute secrecy.

By the time he resumed his duties in the lab he had quite naturally completely forgotten about the blood Flesch had sent to him. A huge backlog of paper work had accumulated on his desk in his absence, which required the better part of his first morning back on the job to deal with. Just before he was going to break for lunch, he came upon the report of the experiments Flesch had requested. He read it first with disbelief and then with anger and when he was finished he jumped up and went off in search of the technician who had performed the work, a thirty-five-year-old chemist named Clairborne.

Seltzer was a perfectionist and was intolerant of sloppiness and errors on the part of his subordinates. And when he was angry he was tactless at best and often abusive. Coming into Clairborne's lab, he waved the report accusingly in the man's face and said without preliminaries, "I don't suppose that you'd care to explain what the hell this is all about?"

Clairborne, having performed dozens of experiments for different people during Seltzer's absence, did not know which report Seltzer was flapping at him. "What the hell is what all about, Hermann?" he asked innocently.

"This! The specimen that Conrad sent over before I left."

Clairborne looked at the report. "Oh, that. Strange, isn't it? But it's true."

"You aren't trying to tell me that there are *no* clotting factors in that blood?"

"We couldn't get the plasma to clot." Clairborne shrugged, leaning against the sink and sipping from a coffee mug. "What can I tell you? We did everything. Nothing happened. It just wouldn't clot."

"How," asked Seltzer with heavy sarcasm, "do you explain this phenomenon?"

"I don't." Clairborne sipped his coffee, screwed his mouth into an expression of distaste. "All I do is run the tests. That's what I'm paid for. *You* get paid for explaining the phenomenon." Then he modified his tone a little. "It's odd," he said, throwing the dregs into the sink and rinsing the cup. "But it's not the screwiest thing that ever happened around here."

"There's obviously some monumental error in your procedures," Seltzer said challengingly. He looked at the technician, angry and supercilious; Clairborne had been at Mayo two years longer than Seltzer, but he had only a B.S. and Seltzer's M.D. conferred on him the privilege of status, permitting him to look down on the younger man with relatively the same contempt with which the Ph.D.s regarded his degree, which they considered pedestrian. Clairborne, however, refused to be intimidated; what he did he did well—he knew it and was proud of it. He did not feel obliged to put up with Seltzer's pretensions.

"I don't make monumental errors, Hermann," he said stiffly. "I used the same old procedures—the same ones I've used a thousand times before."

"I don't suppose you'd be kind enough to show me your data," Seltzer said with hostile courtesy.

"I'd be only too happy," Clairborne replied in the same vein.

He took a notebook from the drawer in his desk, laid it on the counter in front of Seltzer without a word and, affecting indifference, returned to what he was doing before Seltzer had arrived. Seltzer sat down and applied himself to the notes, looking for the error logic told him had to be there.

Given the standard procedures, it was impossible to fail to restore the normal clotting time of plasma no matter what deficiencies the plasma might present. The whole theory behind coagulation research was predicated upon the inevitability of activating the coagulation process in laboratory conditions. It was by means of this foolproof procedure for inducing coagulation in the plasma of even hemophiliacs that it was possible to deduce—by simply eliminating alternatives—which among the twelve recognized factors were deficient in any sample. If all the clotting factors were shown to be present, at normal levels, and the whole blood refused to coagulate, then the investigator would feel justified in concluding that the blood was deficient in a new or unknown factor. This is what had happened with Seltzer in 1943. But everything depended on the fact that the clotting time of all plasma could one way or another be restored to normal. If plasma were deficient in prothrombin, for example, you found out by adding prothrombin to the sample. The same applied to the other factors. It was the nature of plasma to clot in response to certain time-tested procedures; it was a fact of its nature as immutable as the fact of the nature of water's insistence on evaporating when exposed to air. Water that did not evaporate was not water; plasma that could not be made to coagulate in a test tube was not blood. There was no room for debate. The results of Clairborne's tests were a contradiction in terms; the results were impossible. A procedural error was the only explanation.

Yet from the moment he opened the notebook Seltzer really did not expect to find an error. The tests were very simple. Any first-year chemistry major in college could perform them. Clairborne was a very competent man. It had to be something else. Impossible. But it had to be something else.

Seltzer closed the notebook, pinched his nose between his thumb and forefinger, looked over at Clairborne, writing up another report, cleared his throat and said quietly, "I'm sorry, Greg. I apologize. It has to be one of two things. Either the reagents you were using are somehow defective—"

"They're not," Clairborne said flatly without looking up.

"No—I didn't think so. That would be highly unlikely." He thought for a moment, tapping the counter with a pencil. "Then it has to be something in the blood that inhibits the activation of the clotting factors. But what the hell could it be?"

Clairborne straightened up and turned around. Although he did not like Seltzer—no one in the department really did—he respected him, and now the earlier friction was forgotten as his professionalism asserted itself. They sat there together pondering the problem.

"You know," he said after a time, "I realize this doesn't make any sense but this has the earmarks of some kind of elaborate practical joke."

"What do you mean? How could it be?"

"I know. It can't be. But I feel like somebody's pulling our leg. Did Conrad tell you anything about the donor? Is there a history of bleeding?"

"He was going on vacation. He was in a hurry. He didn't say much. I guess I'd better call him up."

"It's probably something ridiculously simple. Get me another sample and I guarantee I'll find out what. The data was okay, wasn't it?"

"Yeah. Fine."

"Maybe I did make a mistake. . . ."

"No, it's fine."

"Well, if you want to follow it up let me know. But I'll need more blood."

"Yeah, okay." Seltzer got up. "I'll let you know. And—uh—look: I'm sorry about before, Greg. My apologies."

"Forget it, Hermann. Glad to have you back."

Seltzer did not spend the rest of the day thinking about the problem. He had many other things to attend to. He interviewed several applicants for vacant positions, checked on a number of experiments in progress, did some work on the budget. But that evening, following dinner, he began to run over the puzzle in his mind. It bothered him. At length he telephoned Flesch, but no one answered.

The rest of the week was very busy for him. Against the background of the other important work under way in the department, the blood of Dr. Constantine began to seem a mere curiosity. It wasn't until Friday that Seltzer got around to calling Flesch again.

"Hermann! How are you?"

"Fine, Conrad, fine. How's the vacation going?"

"Terrible. Filthy weather. Cold and wet. But the fishing's good. Why are you calling?"

"You asked me to. Remember? About that blood sample you sent over the day you left."

"Oh, yes. Constantine's. Damn, I'd completely forgotten."

"What do you know about the donor?"

"Nothing. Constantine didn't say who the donor was. At least I don't remember his saying anything. I left his letter at home."

"What about Constantine?"

"He used to be a student of mine years ago. Works in a lab in Connecticut—Kaizer."

Jotting down this information, Seltzer asked, "Could it be his blood?"

"His? I wouldn't think so. Why do you ask? What have you found anyway?"

"Nothing much." The lie came out instinctively; Seltzer immediately wondered why. "Nothing terribly interesting. Some marginal prothrombin levels, a few other small things. Nothing significant."

"That's very strange," said Flesch.

"What's strange?"

"Well, why the devil did he send me the stuff? He said it was very urgent I should analyze it, said something about its being well worth my time."

"Clairborne suggested that it might be some kind of far-fetched practical joke."

"Could be. He was a bit of an eccentric, as I recall."

"Eccentric?"

"Well, maybe that's the wrong word. He was erratic. Drank a lot. Rather a violent sort. He smashed up a coffee table or something at a party when I was at Harvard. I don't really remember a great deal about him. So you didn't find anything. Funny. He made it sound so damned important. Well, you never know about people, do you? Thanks anyway, Hermann. I'm much obliged."

"Any time," Seltzer said. "See you when you come back. We'll play some chess. Hope the weather improves."

So, he thought. There was something. Urgent. Flesch said Constantine made it sound urgent. So there was something fishy enough about the blood that even Constantine was aware of it. But of how much was he aware? Why, in fact, hadn't he run the same clinical procedures on the blood himself in Connecticut? Why send it all the way out here? Why the mystery? Constantine obviously knew something; equally obviously he didn't know what Seltzer now knew. He made it sound urgent. That changed everything. *This could be something. This could be something very big!* He wanted to know more. He would have to get in touch with this Constantine, find out exactly what was going on. Kaizer. Conrad said he worked for a lab called Kaizer. Connecticut. He would have to check on that. At the same time he decided it would be prudent to detour whatever curiosity Clairborne was still feeling. If it was really big, Seltzer wanted it for himself.

The following Monday morning he arrived in the parking lot just as Clairborne was getting out of his car. He was with Miss Evans, a blond M.A. working on her doctorate, with whom—the gossip had it—Clairborne was having an affair. The three of them walked to their offices together, chatting about the weather, and Clairborne's engine, which was knocking, and the high cost of living. Miss Evans was still sleepy and said little.

"Oh, by the way," Seltzer said, trying to sound offhanded. "You remember that blood we got from Flesch? I talked to him. There was indeed a history. Hemophilia. Unfortunately the donor died."

Clairborne lifted his eyebrows. "Is that right? Too bad. A funny business, that was. Too bad. I would have liked another crack at some of that plasma. It bothers me."

"Bothers me too," said Seltzer. "But not much we can do about it now."

"Too damn bad," said Clairborne, frowning. "Well, see you later, Hermann."

"Right."

"Bye, Dr. Seltzer," Miss Evans said. Seltzer watched them move off, staring at her legs. She had beautiful legs and wore short skirts.

Lucky bastard, he thought.

He worried for the next few days over the most effective way to approach this Dr. Constantine, Paul Constantine, who worked, he had confirmed, at Kaizer Pharmaceutical in Groton, Connecticut. It had been a mistake not to press Flesch for further details about him; on the other hand, his instincts had warned him against arousing Flesch's interest; for the same reason, he could not now apply again to Flesch with questions about his former student. He was probably a chemist, maybe a Ph.D. He didn't figure to know a lot about human blood. But then where had he obtained the sample? He knew something. But how much? And how to approach him without alerting him to the full extent of the potential significance of whatever it was he'd stumbled upon? *I have to get answers without his asking too many questions.* He also had to face the possiblity that Constantine was perfectly aware that he was onto something extraordinary. In which case Seltzer would be out of luck. For the time being, however, it seemed to him best to proceed on the assumption that Constantine knew very little.

At last he sat down to try to compose a letter to him. His rhetorical abilities, however, were modest, and the necessary subtleties were nearly too much for him. He wrote and rewrote, crossed out entire sentences, agonized over phrases and parts of speech. "Remarkably interesting" gave way to "extremely interesting" and then, after much self-doubt, in the final version Seltzer struck out the "extremely" and let "interesting" stand alone, thinking it more disingenuous. In the same vein, "very eager to talk to you" underwent similar transmutations until it emerged in polished form as "it might not prove mutually disadvantageous if we discussed this matter at greater length." "Hoping to hear from you soon," which seemed innocuous when he wrote the words, seemed in retrospect, after he'd sealed the envelope, quite alarming, and he tore the envelope open with a curse and copied the letter one more time, altering the offensive phrase to read more circumspectly, "Very truly yours." This was the final draft of the letter he mailed:

> Dear Dr. Constantine: Owing to the fact that Dr. Conrad Flesch was going on vacation the day he received the sample of human blood you sent him, he asked me to perform the experiments you requested, Dr. Flesch and I having been friends and colleagues here at the Mayo Clinic for the last ten years. I am sorry to be so remiss in reporting our findings to you, but illness has kept me home in bed for a couple of weeks. Unfortunately, we are unable to provide you with a comprehensive analysis of the blood at this time owing to the limited quantity we had to work with. However, our preliminary findings have proven interesting, and I consequently feel that it might not prove mutually disadvantageous if we discussed this matter at greater length at a time and place determined by your convenience. Very truly yours, Hermann Seltzer, M.D.

A week passed, two weeks, three; there was no reply. Seltzer was disappointed but resigned: Constantine obviously knew what he had—or had come to learn it in the meantime—and was working on it now, and was not about to share his discovery with a stranger at the Mayo Clinic. *That's that,* he thought. There was nothing else to do. *I never really expected anything to come of it,* he told himself. *It was one in a thousand.* He tried to forget about it.

The weather began to get cold; the leaves fell from the trees. Seltzer painted the storm windows and hung them. The heating man came out to clean the filter on the oil burner. Seltzer returned to his platelet studies. And then he really did forget the whole matter.

Almost a month after he'd sent it, his letter came back from Connecticut unopened. It had been forwarded from the pharmaceutical company in Groton to an address in Waterford. It was stamped in purple ink: "Addressee unknown."

Seltzer was immediately plunged into resentful despondency. An abrupt, an evasive or even a discourteous reply from Dr. Constantine he could have accepted. But to have his letter—the letter he had labored over, torturing the recalcitrant language into a semblance of cogency at what a cost: *three hours!*—to have it returned unopened, unread, struck Seltzer as a mortal insult.

Who the hell is this guy? Who does he think he is? Doesn't he know anything about professional ethics, basic fundamental human courtesy? What kind of an operation are they running out there, staffed with irresponsible drunks and lunatics. All this Alfred Hitchcock stuff. You do somebody a favor, you upset your whole schedule for a week, and then what happens? They don't have the simple courtesy to— No address. He moves around, no forwarding address; they don't know at that company where he is? What kind of an operation is that?

He couldn't eat his lunch, he was so upset. At length he could not contain his anger. He picked up the phone and called Connecticut. *Give them a piece of my mind,* he vowed. *This is the Mayo Clinic, after all! Give them a goddamned earful, that's what!*

He asked for Dr. Constantine's lab. After a minute or so the switchboard operator informed him that there was no Dr. Constantine listed in her directory. On a hunch, Seltzer asked to be put through to the Department of Pharmacology. He spoke to a female technician and told her he was trying to locate a Dr. Paul Constantine. She said that he didn't work there anymore.

"This is Dr. Hermann Seltzer at the Mayo Clinic," he said. "I am calling on behalf of Dr. Conrad Flesch, whose name should be familiar to anyone in your department who is not completely illiterate. I wish to speak with someone who can tell me where Dr. Constantine is."

"I'll connect you with Dr. Prescott," the girl said. "Just a minute, please."

A moment later another voice came on, Prescott, he said, the head of the department. Seltzer identified himself and explained why he was calling. There was a pause and then Prescott said, "I'm afraid I can't help you. The fact is that I don't know where Constantine is. He doesn't work here anymore."

"But surely you have some idea where he is working!"

"Matter of fact, Dr. Seltzer, I don't," Prescott said. "He terminated his employment with us somewhat—" He hesitated. "Under somewhat *peculiar* circumstances. No one here has seen him or heard from him since the end of July. Are you a friend of his, Dr. Seltzer?"

"Yes, we—we went to school together." Seltzer lied impulsively, his anger dying away in response to the tone of the other man's voice, the troubled uncertainty, the phrase "peculiar circumstances"—again the mystery, everything associated with this man Constantine off center somehow, enigmatic. "It's terribly important that I get in touch with him."

"You heard about his accident?"

"Accident? No; what accident?"

"Something happened to him last summer. He apparently had an accident of some sort. He called in one day. Talked to one of our techs. Said he'd burned himself, burned his hands. It was very strange."

"What was strange? What's strange about burning your hands?"

"Oh, not the accident. His behavior subsequently. After his accident he came down with bronchitis. I tried to call him several times to see how he was getting along. You know, the first month or so—I expected him back from day to day—but he never answered the phone. And then he had the phone removed. I wrote to him but he didn't acknowledge my letters. I finally drove out to see him one day, knocked on the door of his apartment. But he didn't answer. The neighbors told me he was home, they were sure he was home, but he wouldn't open the door. Finally I had no choice. I wrote to him and told him that unless he made some kind of declaration of his intentions, I had no choice but to let him go. He never answered that letter either. Then he moved, and I don't know where he is now. I'd like to know too. I have a check for him, and his stuff in the office—"

"You mean he never came back to clean out his office?"

"Some expensive things here too. His typewriter, an oil painting, an Oriental rug. I don't know what more to tell you, Dr. Seltzer. The whole thing is—well, I'm just mystified. That's the only word for it. Mystified."

"How well did you know him?"

"We worked together for ten, eleven years or so. I knew him very well. He used to come to my house socially. We were friends."

"Was he dependable?"

"Very dependable. A fine scientist. Nothing—nothing!—absolutely nothing in the past, nothing he ever did, prepared me for anything like this. It's been just—a bolt out of the blue, you might say. I just can't explain it."

"But in this day and age a man can't simply vanish into thin air," Seltzer said. "Somebody has to know where he is."

"This is a pharmaceutical company, Dr. Seltzer. Not the Bureau of Missing Persons. I daresay somebody does know where Paul is. I'm only saying we don't."

"But don't you care? I mean, how is it possible that—"

"It's none of my business, Dr. Seltzer. Paul knows he has money here, the typewriter, his belongings. If he wants it he can come and get it. As far as I know he hasn't committed any crimes. If he has, the police would be looking around for him. He has a right to do what he wants. I've never considered it my place to track him down. The fact is I'm damned annoyed with him. He left me in the lurch, you know. Projects hanging in the air, that sort of thing. I'm not sure I want to see him, to tell you the truth."

"But if he were in trouble—"

"You think he's in trouble?"

"I don't know."

"There *is* something funny going on, isn't there?"

"I really don't know. Look, I'll be back to you in a few days. It's important, I think, that we locate him. If you want to, you can call back here to satisfy yourself as to who I am. I've done a lot of work with Conrad Flesch."

"*The* Conrad Flesch?"

Seltzer made a face. "Yes, *the* Conrad Flesch."

"Oh, sure. Flesch and Seltzer. I didn't make the connection. Well, it's an honor talking to you, sir. Blood, isn't it? You're the blood people."

"That's right, we're the blood people. Incidentally, what exactly was Constantine working on when he had his accident?"

"Oh, let's see. I can't remember right off. I'd have to check. Prostaglandins mostly, I think. And some skin studies. Psoriasis, as I recall."

"Human blood?"

"Human blood? No. No, nothing like that."

"You're sure?"

"Yes, of course I'm sure. I can check my records, but I'm sure he wasn't working with blood. It's not his field. Why do you ask?"

"Nothing, really. Just an idea. If you hear anything will you please get in touch with me immediately?"

"Of course."

"I'd be very much obliged."

"And vice versa."

"Right. Anyway, I'll be talking to you again, I think."

"Fine."

"One other thing. His title. Is he a Ph.D. or a medical doctor?"

"He's a Ph.D."

"Right. I remember. Well, thanks very much."

"Pleasure talking to you," Prescott said.

Brother, this is something, Seltzer thought in high excitement. *Boy, you're really onto something!* The man had an accident. Burned his hands. A month or so before he sent the blood to Flesch. Won't answer the phone. Takes off, leaving money behind, and Oriental rugs. Constantine had to be found. But how did a man in Seltzer's position go about it? Prescott was right; unless he'd committed a crime the police would not be interested. He could be in South America for all anyone knew. Or dead. Of course there were places to begin. Seltzer would like to see the data he was working on when he had his accident. Interview his friends and associates. No question you could track the man down. But it would take time and money, and Seltzer didn't have enough of either.

At work he was nervous, excitable, indecisive. He talked out loud to himself. His colleagues gossiped about his absent-mindedness. Then one morning when he arrived at his office there was a message stuck into the dial of his telephone. "Dr. Prescott called. Connecticut. Please call him back."

"Prescott," he said when the connection had been made. "This is Seltzer. What's up?"

"Hello, Dr. Seltzer. Sorry to bother you. But you know, I haven't been able to stop thinking about Paul. So finally last night I drove out to where he used to live. Talked to his landlord. Get this. He said that Paul left the apartment in terrible shape."

"Constantine was in terrible shape, or the apartment?"

"The apartment. He said there were . . . *stains* everywhere."

"Stains?"

"Bloodstains."

"Bloodstains!"

"On the carpets, on the bathroom wall, everywhere. He said it cost him two hundred bucks to clean the place up. He said Paul still owed him fifty. He took the rest out of the deposit. He was mad as hell. What do you make of it?"

"Did the landlord call the police or anything?"

"No. He thought Constantine was molesting little girls or something. What do you make of it all?"

"Dr. Prescott, please. Don't say anything to anybody. I can't explain right now. Just sit tight on this, please. I'm coming to Connecticut. I'll be out there as soon as I can. Then we'll talk. I'll give you a full explanation. It's very important. I can't tell you how important over the phone. I'll see you very soon."

"When you asked me about blood the other day—" Prescott started to say. But apologizing hastily, Seltzer cut him off and hung up. He sat at his desk sweating, his eyes glittering, his hands damp, feeling acid pouring into his stomach. But he was smiling. His excitement nearly suffocated him. Ambitions, dreams, aspirations that he hadn't felt in almost thirty years stirred in him.

Maybe, he thought fervently, *maybe Dad was wrong.* Maybe after all, he thought, once in a great while, life did in fact offer a man a second chance.

CHAPTER 9

"... THERE WAS BLOOD everywhere. I think now that I was aware of the blood before I was conscious of the pain. But I was very feverish and hallucinating too so I guess it's possible that I really experienced the pain first and added, so to speak, the detail of the blood later to my memory picture because after I'd stopped hallucinating and calmed down it seemed more logical. I mean, the natural cause-and-effect sequence has the wound produce the pain, not the other way around, as you know. But now I can't be certain. I was feverish for four or five days. Once I took my temperature and it read one hundred and eight, which of course is impossible. I only tell you that so you'll appreciate the intensity of my delirium. When I woke up on the bathroom floor, well, I forgot to tell you, I had a pretty bad cut, over the eyebrow, right here; you can still see the scar. So maybe that was the blood I was first aware of when I woke up. Which doesn't resolve the question of the other—of the—well, stigmata."

"You're reluctant to use that word, Mr. Brown?"

"I don't know why. It just seems so odious. I'm not a religious person. I'm absolutely not. But it's convenient, isn't it? Stigmata. Funny. I'm almost convinced now that the pain did come first. It was like hornet bites in the beginning, exactly as though I'd fallen into a hornet's nest. The pain was highly generalized. It was at least a week before it localized itself in the particular areas of the stigmata. Since then the quality of the pain has undergone a significant modification. I mean, it seems significant to me. It's like a toothache, a really bad toothache, an abscessed molar. I wonder if I use that image because so often the wounds conjure up oral ideas in my imagination. As you can imagine, I spend a great deal of time looking at them because I don't have very much else to do. Anyway, that's what it's like. A toothache, an exposed nerve, throbbing. It never lets up. But I've adapted to it. Strange what a man can get used to as long as it's predictable, as long as you can depend on the situation or environment or whatever to be more or less stable from day to day. In the beginning it was the not knowing that almost drove me crazy. The uncertainty. One moment agony, the next relief. Now—well, I almost can't remember what it was like not to have this pain. But that's bad, isn't it? It implies a subconscious acceptance of the thing."

"Tell me more about your sensory impressions of those four or five days of fever and delirium."

"Yes, I'm sorry; I realize I've been digressing. It's hard not to. It's all so mixed up in my mind. I felt battered at first, violated, my whole body ached. I was lying on the floor, face down, and I think I was afraid I'd broken my neck. I was afraid to move, to try and move. Though the feeling was also a little like when I was a child—you remember when you were a kid and you'd wake up in the middle of the night turned around in bed, completely disoriented? Remember how that felt, the terror? That's what it was like when I regained consciousness. That annihilating fear. I felt all turned around.

"The bathroom was filled with this pinkish mist. Have you ever seen a homogenized lung? It was that color. Perfectly rational explanation, I hasten to add, nothing at all phenomenal about it. When I had my, the seizure I guess we can call it, the manifestation, I was, as I told you, shaving. The hot water was on full. I remember it was clouding up the mirror, condensation; I had to keep wiping it off to see. When I fell, the water of course continued to run. We have a big boiler in the basement of my apartment building, never had any trouble—as you do in a lot of these new apartment complexes—with inadequate supplies of hot water, though I never appreciated how much hot water we had until— Sorry. I keep wandering, don't I? Is that a bad sign? Well, anyway, as near as I can estimate, it was approximately twenty-four hours. The water was running all the time so the bathroom was filled with steam. I'd cut my brow, blood had dripped into my eye. Which accounts for the pinkish mist—"

"You said that you felt violated; that's the term you used."

"Yes. My whole body ached."

"Was there anything sexual about the character of that sense of violation?"

"Yes! Exactly! Sexual! I felt as though I'd been somehow, I don't know, raped. Spiritually sodomized. I felt very embarrassed. Understand, I say I felt embarrassed. As I look back on what happened, I can't avoid giving a sequential structure to the components of the event which distorts the true picture of my frame of mind. There was no sequence, literally speaking, to my impressions. I was shocked, frightened, feverish. It was precisely as though I awoke to an environment, a dimension, in which time sequences, the very concepts of time as an entity, had been pulverized. For a while I was timeless. The sexual thing was simply there, all around me, for four days, like that pinkish mist."

"Have you ever had any homosexual experiences?"

"No. Never. I know what you're thinking. But I don't think we should get sidetracked by the sexual business. Maybe I shouldn't have mentioned it. I don't feel that it's a critical factor. And it's such a cliché, isn't it? Mother fixations, nipple rejection, all those Freudian banalities. Well, just to keep the record straight, to get it down on your tape recorder, yes, there was another element to the sexual thing, I might as well tell you. Women have always been very important to me. I never had any trouble getting whoever I wanted. I've had lots of love affairs. I'm not bragging. It's just a fact. Women have always found me attractive. I've taken advantage of that. So I was shattered when I realized that suddenly I'd been rendered repulsive to the opposite sex. I asked myself what woman would ever let me touch her with these hands? Who would ever trust herself to go to sleep with a man who had things inside him that could lead him to disfigure himself like this? That weighed on me very heavily. The loss of my sexual self-esteem. Also those first few days I had an extraordinary incidence of erotic dreams. Oddly enough, Margaret didn't figure in any of them. Margaret was my girl."

"Your daughter?"

"No, my daughter's name is Betsy. My girl friend. It may be significant, because I was with her the night before. We had dinner. By and large Margaret and I had a very satisfactory love life, so it seems odd to me that she didn't figure in any of my dreams. Stranger still, Cathy, the new girl in the lab, did. And I never had any sexual inclinations toward her. Though she's pretty enough. But mousy."

"What did you do after you woke up in the bathroom?"

"I'm not sure. Somehow I got to my bed. I don't know if I walked or crawled. There were blood spots all over, not bad really, though when I was delirious the place seemed like a slaughterhouse from the blood, but anyway there's blood on the carpet from room to room and it's hard to see a pattern to my movements based on the blood, the spoor. If my life depended on my venturing an opinion, I think I would say that the wounds in my hands either opened up while I was unconscious in the bathroom, or almost immediately after I woke up, and that they developed more gradually in my feet over, say, the next forty-eight hours. The injury in my side at first was nothing more than a bruise, seemed like nothing more than a bruise, a long cuneiform welt; the skin wasn't even broken, I don't think. Later it began to bleed too, and it hasn't stopped, of course, since then. I lose about a cup of blood every day, sometimes a little more, sometimes less. The bleeding in my hands and feet, although it's persistent, is much less copious than in my breast. I was thirsty all the time, this desperate burning thirst, and I would get out of bed two or three times an hour, it seemed, to get drinks. I drank a lot of water, and almost a case of soda and quarts of orange juice. I was on fire. It's interesting that I don't recall urinating, though of course I must have.

"I would say that I dozed off and on—but the sensation was different from dozing, more like a trance. Imagine a trance on a scale of one to ten with ten being consciousness. Most of the time I was swimming down around three or four. Occasionally I would drift up as high as eight or nine, which is when I was more or less aware of where I was and what had happened to me. I heard music a lot and a voice talking, a male voice, deep, a basso, but spaced out, like when you operate a record at half speed, you know what I mean, that terrific distortion. It must have been the radio or the TV next door, the Fernandez family, my neighbors—they had a colicky baby that cried a lot, which was rough in a place like mine where the walls are paper thin. The phone rang a lot, Margaret, I suppose, and once in a fairly lucid interval I managed to call the lab and talked to Cathy. It's funny. I knew I should call for help, the police, Bill Morrison, my doctor, something incredible had happened, I'd been attacked, mutilated by a maniac who for all I knew was still in the neighborhood, or maybe even in the building. That Manson thing came to mind recurrently, you know, the murders in California. I kept seeing Manson's face and then it would shade off into the face of some terrible dirty hippie type who tried to bum a ride from me that day, the beard and those crazy eyes, and Manson with that mark on his forehead, self-inflicted, branded, like the Wandering Jew.

"So I knew I should call for help. But even then somehow I was embarrassed, I think, afraid to tell anyone. Maybe even then I knew I hadn't been attacked—that the whole thing was psychosomatic—and I was simply reluctant to admit it consciously because it seemed shameful."

"When did you first realize that there had been no intruders in the apartment?"

"Well, early on I checked the door, at some point I checked the door, the safety latch, and it was locked, you know, a sliding bolt and chain. But I didn't register the significance of that. It was reassuring, I was safe, the door was locked. It was much later, I think, when it first struck me that the blood wasn't clotting, that the detail of the lock became meaningful. Even when I was delirious, you must understand, there was a layer, a stratum of rationality, or a current of rational thinking asserting itself, some facts getting through to me, and I thought it was extremely odd that the blood refused to coagulate. The cut over my eye had developed a firm scab.

And this in spite of the fact that the wounds in my hands were superficial compared to the gash on my forehead. They are superficial even now—it seems as though they would have to clear up entirely within a week to ten days. Anyway, it was at that point, when the anomalies concerning the clotting factors in the various wounds began to get through to me, that I realized no one else had been in the apartment. I'd been staring into the mirror, after all, shaving. I was struck from behind. It would not have been humanly possible for anyone to sneak up on me. But since there was no other rational explanation, I guess I'd ignored the obvious discrepancies. That's how I interpret my response to the whole thing at this one moment in time. I ignored the discrepancies because the only other alternative to my having been molested was so utterly repulsive."

"What alternative?"

"That it was a—a miracle. A mystical experience. That I had the stigmata of Christ. The psychosomatic alternative didn't occur to me until later."

"You seem very belligerent on the subject of religion."

"I guess I am. Yes, belligerent isn't a bad word. I'm a scientist. An investigator. The same as you. I've trained myself all these years to try and think rationally. I believe that there are principles of natural law behind every so-called phenomenon. Religious people disgust me. Priests disgust me with their medieval quackery. The whole anti-intellectual bias of the thing, the appeal to inexplicable, supernatural forces. Yes, at times I get very violent on the subject. The pope, birth control, all that. I could beat up people over issues like that."

"Were you raised in a religious background?"

"Roman Catholic; yes."

"When did you give it all up?"

"When I was fourteen or so. My wife, my ex-wife, was Catholic too. We had some pretty good fights about religious things in our early years."

"Good?"

"Well, you know—bad, I mean. Especially when we had Betsy. My wife wanted to have her baptized, and I refused. She finally saw the light. Or maybe she baptized her in the bathtub behind my back. I don't know. Anyway, I realize how important the fact of my religious training is, that there's an obvious cause-and-effect relationship between my religious education and these stigmata. Some childhood trauma that's at the heart of the problem, that we have to identify."

"You seem to have considerable faith, Mr. Brown, that therapy will cure you."

"Absolute faith. You take my Catholic childhood, my history of dermatological problems, the pressures I've been under since the divorce. I mean, what else could it be? Obviously I've done this to myself somehow. God knows how, but there's no question in my mind that the wounds are self-inflicted and psychosomatic. I grant you the physiological symptoms are bizarre, but not unique after all. Stigmatization is a recognized medical fact—I've been doing research into the thing the past few weeks—and the syndrome is a textbook case, is it not?"

"That depends on which textbooks you read. I'm afraid our time is up, Mr. Brown."

"Does the case interest you?"

"It would interest anyone."

"Then—you're willing to treat me?"

"That's another question."

"What do you mean?"

"Well, I'm not perfectly convinced at this point that you want to be cured."

"What? What the hell are you talking about? Why else do you think I've come here?"

"There could be a hundred reasons why you've come here. None of them having anything to do with a genuine desire to be cured. As I understand it, you haven't submitted your condition to a medical examination. Why is that?"

"I was . . . embarrassed. It's a long story. To put it briefly, I don't relish the prospect of becoming a scientific guinea pig, some kind of medical freak. And I don't know a single clinician who could resist the temptation to turn this into a circus. As a matter of fact, I have done something. I sent a sample of my blood to the Mayo Clinic, to a hematologist I studied under at Harvard. Conrad Flesch. I asked him to do an analysis. So far I haven't heard from him. For that matter, I'm not sure he's even still there, or even still alive. Anyway, damn it, of *course* I want to be cured! Do you think it's fun being like this?"

"I don't know. I've had patients in similar straits who felt a certain distinction by virtue of what they felt were unique disabilities. I'm sorry; let me make a further point. By your own admission these wounds may be the result of your work with prostaglandins. You've had a history of dermatological problems connected with iodine, and you ate shrimp the night before it happened. You were working with radioactive materials. There is at least as much very real possibility that your wounds have absolutely nothing to do with psychopathological aberrations as that they do. Yet you've made virtually no attempt to verify or disprove that, aside from a few half-hearted and badly designed experiments your technician performed."

"I told you—"

"Yes, I know. That you were embarrassed. But you have to understand, Mr. Brown, it's going to be a serious waste of our time and your money to initiate a long course of therapy only to discover that your wounds are the result of, for example, radioactive blood poisoning."

"But they're not!"

"You don't know that. And you haven't tried to find out. You say you came down with an extraordinary case of hives after eating shrimp at a Christmas party, which your doctor diagnosed as an allergy and treated successfully with antibiotics. The logical place to begin, it would seem to me, is to try first to determine whether your wounds are the result of an allergic response to something, As a precondition to accepting you as a patient, I have to insist that you do at least that much in your own behalf, to demonstrate at least that much genuine desire to be cured."

"But that's impossible! Do you realize what allergy tests amount to? How extensive they are? I could never keep it a secret. You don't understand that—"

"I apologize for interrupting again, but we really have gone beyond our time. I have other patients. Let me put it to you a different way. Do you see this?"

"It's an aspirin."

"What if it were not an aspirin? What if I could guarantee you that by swallowing this pill you would be instantly and permanently free of your stigmata? Think about it. It's a very important question. Would you take the pill? Don't be hasty. Think about it. Would you really? Are you sure? You see, Mr. Brown, until you can say yes, and mean it, I don't think you're ready to be helped. When you're ready, call me and we'll talk again."

When the patient had gone, the psychiatrist jotted down some notes on the session.

> Acute dermatosis. Lesions in hands, feet and breast. Prelim diag: hysteric self-induced and self-perpetuated. The skin subject/sensitive to disturbances in autonomic nervous system and endocrine activity. Possibility compulsive contact, self-inflicted damage stemming from unconscious conflict. With mother? Wife? Religious authority? Generally excoriation of skin more fundamental than pruritus usually complained of (c.f. Noyes *Mod Clin Psych*). But here, no significant pruritus; massive excoriation. Element of masochism. Hostile dependent maternal relationship? History of dermatosis, interpreted by patient as allergy to seafood.
>
> Prognosis complicated by Brown's scientific education. Wanted to be clinician. Quit studies after two years med school. Why? Religion. RC background. Marked aversion to term stigmata. Wounds of Christ. Check stigmatization. What saints? Francis of Assisi? Paul. St. Paul? Did St. Paul have stigmata? History of dermatosis in family? Genetic? No mention of father. Compulsive insistence on natural causes. No outward symptoms characteristic hysteria.
>
> Possibility maintains excoriations in aggravated state during sleep periods. Discount claim blood does not decompose. Work on that. Blood pressure, pulse, normal. Otherwise, average health and physical fitness for man his age. Weight loss minimal in spite of alleged prolonged fast.
>
> Interesting. The wounds of Christ. Paul Brown. Why does he call himself Brown? Would bet it's not his name. Hope he returns.

The psychiatrist's name was Levy Auerbach. His office was on Park Avenue in New York between Sixty-ninth and Seventieth. He was young, thoughtful and diffident, which set him apart from most of his colleagues in the profession. And he was modest about the capacities of psychiatry to effect cures, which also marked him as unusual. Given his temperament and intellectual bent, Auerbach often thought that had he been born a Roman Catholic he might well have become a priest; and he would have discharged his clerical functions with the same skepticism about the sacramental mysteries of the Church that he brought to the institutional mysteries of his branch of medicine. He wanted to be useful, to help people. For all its limitations, the practice of psychiatry had, early on in his education, seemed to offer the most promising of many inadequate options for accomplishing this.

He spent fifteen minutes or so writing his comments on the session with Mr. "Brown." These he appended to the several pages of shorthand transcriptions he'd made during the session, which later he would augment with material taken from the tape recorder, concluding just as his receptionist ushered in the next patient, Mrs. Rosenquist from Queens.

Mrs. Rosenquist was a thin gray woman in her middle fifties; she reminded Auerbach of a cheap garment that had been laundered too many times. She was suffering from what he had finally diagnosed as mucous colitis deriving from psychosomatic origins. For a long time she had been convinced that her gall bladder was inflamed (a diagnosis which her family doctor had inexcusably confirmed). Her life was a misery. A rootless, vicious husband, a feckless son, a pair of daughters cut from the same cloth as Goneril and Regan, the mysteries of menopause—all had combined in a conspiracy to crush her. Fragile as a pigeon's egg, she would have been destroyed too except for the intervention of an unlikely *deus ex machina*, a neighbor by the name of Mildred Schwartz, a tough old friend with a congenital distrust of the medical profession. Mildred Schwartz had prevailed on Abbie Rosenquist to consult a psychiatrist before submitting to surgery. ("What's a dollar, Abbie?" Mildred had said. "A dollar's for today, your gall bladder is forever!") Now, after nine sessions, Mrs. Rosenquist was making encouraging progress; more important, she had retained all her vital organs.

They would have sliced her up sooner or later, Auerbach thought, as Mrs. Rosenquist removed her coat and sat down across from him and began to talk. If it hurts pump them full of drugs, chop them up, rip it out. No matter that in three weeks the symptoms could all return. Remove the colon next. The appendix. The pancreas. That was their mentality. It was puzzling, the esteem in which most people held surgeons. Auerbach would as soon deliver himself to the ministrations of a hog butcher as to entrust his body to a surgeon.

Mrs. Rosenquist would never know how fortunate she was; the absurd, self-serving and grotesquely misnamed Code of Ethics prevented Auerbach from denouncing her family physician. She probably wouldn't have believed him anyway. Her conditioning being what it was, she would probably defend him up to the point where he murdered her, and then plead his case in the hereafter. For that, as for so much else, there seemed to be no remedy.

Mrs. Rosenquist talked. Her husband was beginning to complain about the cost of the therapy. Her daughters were confused by it and somewhat jealous. The family had all been made to feel obscurely guilty; Abbie Rosenquist was experiencing for once in her life the satisfactions of the exercise of power. Auerbach was glad for her. From time to time he would murmur something, nod, smile, encouraging her. It didn't matter at this point what she was saying; he didn't have to listen very carefully anymore. It was helpful for her to talk because she thought it was making her well, and apparently she wanted to be well. Not all of them did; that was the toughest part of the job—deciding which patients required their pain and suffering.

Auerbach had been convinced for a long time that to a substantial proportion of people—perhaps even to a majority—sickness was more often than not a luxury. In his own case, almost the only opportunity he had to read Shakespeare or to listen to a violin concerto or to meditate was when he was home sick in bed. His wife waited on him, his children behaved themselves and were respectful. At the least, illness was a luxury. It could also be a defense, as indeed psychosis was demonstrably a defense. But beyond that, pain, illness, real suffering in many people often became a defensive weapon, an instrument they wielded against their antagonists with remarkable effect. A doctor had to try to figure out what he was dealing with in a woman like Mrs. Rosenquist: did she *need* her pain—was the inflammation of her large intestine her only possible form of retaliation against the boor she was married to? And if so, how did he, Auerbach, best serve her best interests? Could he in conscience disarm a woman like that and return her to her tormentors defenseless?

Ultimately, he believed, people had a right to suffer. Plato would have punished sick people, expelled them from his utopia on the grounds that the culprit, by permitting himself to become infected, committed an antisocial, criminal act. But surely, Auerbach thought, a man had as much right to make his body feel miserable as to make it feel well. Surely a man ought to have exclusive and final authority over the disposition of his own flesh and blood.

His practice had made a relativist, even an existentialist, of him. He was fascinated by the moral ambiguities of disease. Whereas for most of his colleagues disease was an absolute—pain constituting an "evil" and the absence of pain constituting "good"—to Auerbach the nature of disease was far more complex and profound in its implications. "That's a clear case of conjunctivitis," a doctor might say. "Yes," would be Auerbach's reply, "I agree that it's conjunctivitis. *But what does it mean?*" The majority of his colleagues were unable to comprehend the question, let alone answer it. But to Auerbach the question was the only interesting and certainly the most important aspect of the case. Any moderately intelligent technician could diagnose conjunctivitis and even prescribe treatment for it. Determining the philosophical coordinates of a particular case of conjunctivitis, however, was a challenge immeasurably more intellectual, with potential benefits far in excess of simply relieving the soreness in a patient's eyelid. It was the only challenge, furthermore, in Auerbach's opinion, that should appeal to an intelligent man.

The trouble was few of his colleagues were very intelligent. Most of them were highly trained, skilled technicians, and nothing more. And the surgeons were the worst of them. Absolutists all. Identify the source of the discomfort and then chop it out. That was their creed. To Auerbach, absolutism in anything was synonymous with barbarity. As soon ask a receptionist in a dentist's office about the moral ambiguities of disease as ask any surgeon of his acquaintance.

Not that he couldn't appreciate why so few of his colleagues (surgeons aside) were sensitive to the existential implications of their work. Believing what he believed, seeing the way he saw, made life uncomfortable for Auerbach; one preferred certainties, of course. Relativism was a kind of endless philosophical anxiety. You never knew exactly where you were, exactly what you were prescribing, whether it was right or wrong to prescribe anything, whether it was right or wrong to try to "cure" someone (assuming you could define the term "cure" with any exactness, which usually you could not). But in Auerbach's view, not knowing where you were was insufficient reason for arbitrarily insisting that you were someplace else. Philosophical anxiety was distressing; however, self-delusion did not seem a dignified alternative for a rational person.

This "Brown," for instance. Ninety-nine out of a hundred doctors in New York City would doubtless agree that his stigmata were "bad" and that he needed to be "cured" of them, and that a "Brown" without the stigmata was demonstrably "better" than a "Brown" with them. Auerbach preferred to reserve judgment. Consider, he thought: "Brown" comes asking for something he calls "help." But asking for it doesn't necessarily mean that he really wants it, or even that he knows what he means by it. If the stigmata are truly psychosomatic, then a part of "Brown" has demanded them. Another part of him rejects the stigmata and wants to be cured. To which part ought the psychiatrist give priority? It was altogether possible that the self-punishing tendency which produced the stigmata was more valid than the tendency to self-protection which brought the man to my office. Who knows—maybe "Brown" *deserves* the stigmata, maybe he requires them as a long-term purgative essential to correct a way of life that's grown intolerable. And maybe it's the weak, despicable, degraded side of him that brought him here in an attempt to ensure the perpetuation of his vicious or self-destructive life patterns. Maybe something good and clean and decent in "Brown" has rebelled against some moral degeneracy in his character, producing excoriations that are figurative as well as literal denunciations of moral decay.

Which, thought Auerbach, was a nice theory except that it brought the case very near to conventional Roman Catholic thinking: namely, that the stigmata were a blessing.

Well, why not? So consider the possibility that they are a blessing. If "Brown" is in fact ill, mentally dysfunctional, then it doesn't make much sense for me to operate out of his identical assumptions. He refuses to consider the stigmata in a religious context. Conventional wisdom suggests that I therefore might profitably do just that.

If he returned—and Auerbach had serious doubts that he would—it would be very interesting. There probably wasn't much to be done for him, however. One out of how many—twenty, thirty—did he ever feel confident he had helped? And never had he seen a case as spectacularly complicated as this one. Given his track record then, it occurred to Auerbach to ask himself from time to time why he continued in his profession. Wouldn't it be more logical in view of his skepticism to do something else, where the moral concerns were less ambiguous, where he could perform useful work more efficiently and be sure that he was in fact performing useful work?

He had often considered trying something else. But he always came back to the argument that he could not imagine a profession more interesting than his present one. It was that simple. His work stimulated him. Furthermore, he was convinced that at the very least he was keeping a handful of people like Abbie Rosenquist out of the clutches of other practitioners, who were less intelligent, conscientious and scrupulous than he. That wasn't much to rationalize a vocation, Auerbach realized. But it was enough.

Mrs. Rosenquist departed at four-thirty. His receptionist informed him that Mrs. Auerbach had called to say she would meet him for cocktails at the Pierre at five. And Mr. Wellek had telephoned to break his appointment, which had been the last one on Auerbach's calendar for the day, so that he was now free to leave.

As he put on his coat and scribbled a few last-minute memos to himself, he reflected that he had heard almost nothing Mrs. Rosenquist had told him. But she was smiling when she went out of the office, and a little bit aggressive. She would, he guessed, get a few licks in tonight when she confronted the other Rosenquists. That was something. Unfortunately for "Brown" at this stage, there would be no such even so minor consolations. "Brown," he sensed, had a long way further to fall before—if ever—he began to rise again.

Poor bastard, he thought as he closed the door and went out. *Of all the people in the world I wouldn't want to be tonight, old "Brown" is just about number one.*

CHAPTER 10

EVERYTHING WAS CHANGED. Geraldine had left at the beginning of October, and Cathy couldn't stand her replacement, a boring self-satisfied dunce named Donald Jurgens. He was slow and incompetent and so—instead of firing him—the inverted Kaizer logic was to bring in another technician, Gloria Snively, a fat housewife with horrible acne, to help him. Although it did not seem possible for anyone to be less capable than Jurgens, Gloria Snively set new standards. As a result of her colleagues' combined sloth and negligence, not only did Cathy have to do her own work, she had to supervise theirs as well, especially inasmuch as her new boss, Dr. Albright, tended to blame her for their mistakes.

Albright arrived at the end of October, preceded by a reputation for genius. He was brilliant, Dr. Prescott explained to Cathy—a hard-driving, dedicated scientist, tough but fair. "He'll make things hum around here,

Cathy, I promise you that. And he's a much better administrator than Paul ever was. Let's face it, Cathy, Paul could be pretty sloppy at times, pretty disorganized; now admit it."

In fact, Albright turned out to be a pompous, petty, small-minded hypocrite. He was also a lecher; he made it clear in the first few days that he thought of himself as sexually irresistible, and that he intended to take Cathy to bed eventually—behaving as though it were a foregone conclusion that they would one day be lovers—the only impediment being his crowded schedule and lack of time. He was a comical-looking man in his early forties, short, potbellied, with an absurd little mustache and a gap between his front teeth. But he was immensely impressed with himself and assumed everyone else was too.

He would stroll into the lab puffing his pipe and looking preoccupied with mighty ventures, poke around in Cathy's notebooks, find an excuse to lean up against her, to brush against her breasts with an elbow, to pat her bottom, and then after a few bad jokes laden with sexual innuendo—which Jurgens would yodel at sycophantically—he would wander away with a leer and a wink and Jurgens would say something like "Goddamn brilliant, isn't he? What a mind!"

She did not know how much more of that she could take. All the challenge and excitement had been siphoned from her life. She hated getting out of bed in the morning. She was headachy and bad-tempered. Thinking that she needed to expand her social circumference, she joined a bridge class, in the hope of meeting interesting people and forming new friendships. But the class consisted of seven middle-aged women and a deaf man in his seventies who walked with two canes, and Cathy dropped out after the first session. She then made plans to join a karate class, but at the last minute lost her nerve.

She wondered if going on a retreat would improve her spirits. There was a cloistered convent in Bethlehem, not far from Waterbury, that she knew of from a high school classmate who'd spent a week there one summer. Regina Coeli it was called. She could go there. But her vacation wasn't until June, and she had her car payments to make, and she had no money in the bank. So a retreat was out of the question.

She started to eat compulsively and quickly gained ten pounds. Then she embarked on a starvation diet which made her cross and gloomy and weepy. She performed her tasks in the lab without interest or enthusiasm.

Had anyone told her that her dissatisfaction and lethargy had anything to do with Dr. Constantine's terminating his employment at Kaizer and thereby vanishing from her life, she would have disputed it. She believed he was no longer a factor in her psychology.

When Prescott had informed them that Constantine was not returning, she had felt hurt and betrayed. Geraldine had been right all along. No doubt from the beginning he'd planned on leaving the company. What was especially hard to accept was that he had not even called her to say good-bye. She felt jilted and foolish and resentful.

But almost immediately a series of self-defensive mechanisms in her went into operation. *There was never really anything between us anyway,* she rationalized. You couldn't very well talk about a man jilting you when there had been no mutual affection in the first place. She had never meant anything to him. And in time she persuaded herself that he had meant much less to her than had been the case.

She could not forget, of course, that night in his bedroom—the terrifying seizure, her strange identification with his pain that was like the descriptions of orgasm she had read in novels. But after a while even that incident lost its significance, faded, seemed less inexplicable. She had been nervous, overwrought. His suffering had frightened her. She'd gotten a little hysterical. She could scarcely remember what she'd felt. It was too embarrassing to think about.

She made herself concentrate on his many imperfections, and it seemed to work. By Halloween she could tell herself—and believe it was the truth—that she didn't care about him anymore. *He's a closed chapter in my life,* she thought. *Good riddance.* But subconsciously her interest in him remained alive and vital, and the phone never rang in her living room but what a part of her did not hope (and half expect) it was Constantine.

Contributing to her sense of psychological aimlessness and malaise during this period was a concurrent crisis in her religious life. The practice of her faith was gradually losing its meaning. The sacraments no longer seemed to furnish her with spiritual sustenance. When she went to mass now she said her prayers the way she worked in the lab—mechanically, by rote, without enthusiasm or satisfaction. She tried to interest herself again in Saint Teresa's autobiography, but the book seemed dry and schoolish. Where once Saint Teresa could excite her to the point of physical illness, now reading her was drudgery.

In a search for inspiration, she attended a jazz mass in New London, celebrated under the auspices of a Catholic study group at Connecticut College. But the experience failed to revive her flagging commitment. She was repelled by the alien music; the whole thing seemed ludicrous, even blasphemous. It mystified her that the Church would sanction such a sacrilegious travesty.

A few days afterward, the so-called underground movement in the Church was brought to her attention by an article in *The New York Times*. All over America small groups of alienated Catholics were bearing a new kind of witness in an effort to renew themselves and their Church. They were making communal confessions, celebrating "home masses" in which the faithful administered the sacrament to each other. The article discussed worker priests and liberated nuns, and their roles in the movement, which *Time* magazine said was "based on a reversion to fundamentalist Christian principles, often a barely coherent but deeply felt neo-Primitivism that is shaking the Roman Church to its foundations."

The idea appealed powerfully to Cathy. She wanted to learn more. The movement seemed to contain a promise of an alternative to the expanding emptiness and vaguely alarming disquietude of her spiritual life. But she didn't know where to go, what else to read, what to do, how to place herself in contact with any of these groups. They were, after all, underground, and viewed with dark suspicion by the more orthodox elements of the Church.

Then a young man she'd met at the jazz mass ran into her in a supermarket one Friday afternoon in Groton. He was sallow and ungainly, with overly long thin arms, thick glasses and bad teeth, and because he was not attractive Cathy felt no animosity toward him. She inquired whether he had attended any other jazz masses. He replied that he had not. "Who needs that Mickey Mouse?" he asked rhetorically. "Those people up there," he went on, referring to the study group at Connecticut College, "aren't doing anything except playing with themselves." He was nice, and he seemed intelligent, and he made her laugh. They strolled the aisles, pushing their carts, talking and laughing, and when they had paid they stood, their packages in their arms, on the sidewalk in front of the store, both hesitating to part.

"Well," he said finally, with a rather glum smile, "be seeing you around, I guess."

"Yes. Take care," she said vaguely, starting to walk off.

"Hey," he called. "You wouldn't be—I mean, how about a cup of coffee or something?"

"I'd love to," she said, stopping. "But I'm in a terrible hurry, as a matter of fact." It was a lie; another lonely boring weekend lay ahead of her. "But —well, maybe just for a few minutes."

There was a Friendly's nearby. They sat in a booth; he ordered coffee and she sipped hot chocolate.

"What's your name anyway?"

"Cathy."

"I'm Fred."

He worked in a hospital as an orderly. "You know, lugging the guts down to the lab, delivering dead babies to the morgue. It's a job."

She had worked summers during high school as a medical technician. "I used to collect blood," she said.

They talked about hospitals and drank cup after cup of coffee and chocolate. Eventually Cathy brought up the subject of the jazz mass again and the study group. "Boring," he said emphatically. "Kid stuff. They think they're so strung out on Jesus. They don't know anything."

"Yes," she agreed. "I found it all very hollow, meaningless."

He nodded. "Bad religion and bad music. Bad vibes generally. A bummer."

When he was fourteen he believed he had a vocation. He actually spent four months in a seminary " . . . until I got fed up and split. I was an atheist until I was twenty. Religion just wasn't relevant to life as it's really lived, as far as I was concerned. I guess I'd have stayed an atheist if I hadn't met this chick in the hospital. Her name's Marcia. She was recuperating from an appendectomy. She'd been crashing in a commune up around Boston. They were into drugs and mystical phenomena and gigs like that. She took me up with her one weekend. Knocked me for a loop! They're into everything up there. Speaking in tongues, extrasensory stuff, dope. Oh, yeah, they're into drugs, but it's strictly controlled. They have a sacramental perception about drugs. It gives you a new insight into the concept of sacramentality." The commune, he claimed, was like a laboratory of religious experience. "Everybody's bound together by love," said Fred, his eyes behind his thick glasses growing larger. "Family love. The atmosphere isn't like anything else. It's indescribable. You can just feel it"—he clenched his fist to illustrate—"when you walk in the door. Love! Twenty, twenty-five kids feeling as one! Talk about communion!" The whole arrangement was organized around a single-minded determination to "break through—to *achieve* Christ, the way you're supposed to achieve Him in communion but never do. Twenty kids all devoting themselves to Jesus, to the aim of *realizing* Him. Can you imagine the psychic power of twenty people all channeling their spiritual energy in the same collective effort? You could knock down buildings with the psychic force of twenty people. I tell you, I got back my faith in about five minutes."

He had to leave then to go to work at the hospital. She gave him her phone number, fully expecting him to call her the next day. When he did not, she was somewhat surprised, and felt perhaps a little lonelier over the weekend than she would have if she hadn't expected him to call, but it was not a serious disappointment.

Thinking that it might improve her disposition if she found a different place to live, she applied at a number of realtors and every day after work she drove around the area inspecting apartments. But they were all too expensive, so as an alternative she made plans to redecorate her cottage. She bought paint and brushes and sandpaper. She moved all the furniture out of the living room and stacked it in the cramped dining area and her bedroom. Her aesthetic model was a picture in one of her magazines: a New York apartment with white floors that looked very smart. So she painted her floor white too, and when she was finished it was sensational and she was extremely proud and happy. But the floor would not dry. A week later it was still like glue. She tried using her hair dryer on it, set the thermostat at 85. But, inexperienced and impatient, she'd applied the paint too thickly and the layers beneath would not dry. Finally, not caring anymore, she put her rugs down, knowing they would stick to the floor, and dragged her furniture back in, gouging and tearing and scoring the soft paint, which peeled and stripped like human flesh and was quite horrible to look at, and afterward she stayed out of the living room.

The weather turned bad. A ponderous low pressure area moved in over Connecticut and would not go away. It was cold and rainy day after day. The house was dark and smelled like a cellar. Her clothes felt limp when she put them on in the morning. At work she quarreled with Gloria Snively and was sarcastic and insulting with Jurgens. Dr. Albright warned her sternly that he held her responsible for the spirit of dissension in the lab.

Then one night as she was watching a mindless television program, Fred called.

"You remember me telling you about those people in Boston? Well, I'm going up tomorrow. I was wondering if you'd be interested in coming with me—just to see what it's like."

Gratefully, even joyfully, she accepted. It might be just the thing to dispel her apathy and bad temper. If nothing else happened, she might at least make some new friends. She looked forward to it very much.

"We're all trying to get back to fundamentals. That's all it is—fundamentalist Catholicism. We're very Christ-oriented, but it's like a form of what you might call catacomb Christianity. You know, in the beginning the mass was very simple. 'Do this in commemoration of me,' Christ said at the Last Supper. And that's all the mass consisted of for centuries. Sharing the bread and wine, a couple of prayers, maybe a song. It was spontaneous. Communion meant community. It was a family thing—communistic. What we're trying to do is to recreate that concept of a Christian family."

Cathy and Fred were sitting in a Howard Johnson's, eating breakfast while a mechanic was fixing Cathy's windshield wipers, which had failed during a cloudburst.

"How do the drugs fit in?" she asked.

"Well, the theory about the drugs is a little abstruse, but basically we use drugs as a shortcut to Vision. The idea is to try to become one with Christ. But given the way we've been educated, we have to get rid of a lot of intellectual preconceptions first. The point is, there's more than one kind of reality—there are alternative realities in the universe that we have to learn to explore."

"I don't know what you mean."

"Well, in our society we get locked into a rigid, undeviating view of things at an early age. It can't be helped. Like when I was a kid in New York I was in a special school for bright children. I was in first grade, I think it was, and I remember painting a picture—it was a black sun in a green sky. The teacher got mad. The sky is blue, she said. And the sun was yellow. Any fool could see that. She made me change the picture. But the fact is, *I* saw a black sun and a green sky. Do you understand what I'm driving at?"

"Not really," she confessed.

"The point is that if I had to be told the sun was yellow, then as far as I'm concerned I must have been perceiving things differently from my teacher. Which means that you could argue that the sun is more than one color. That there's an alternative reality to the sun, to the color of the sun. You get it?"

Cathy apologized; she was afraid she did not get it.

"Look," Fred said patiently, speaking slowly. "When we're young, we see the universe as it really is. Then we go to school and we're brainwashed into accepting an imposed reality that's a lot different from what's actually there. Look how imaginative kids are before they go to school. Well, what we call imagination in a kid is another word and a distorted concept for a true Vision. The kids see things the way they really are. The straight world can't deal with that; it's incomprehensible and inconvenient. So they say the kid has a lot of imagination. And when you have a kid who really sees, they say he has an overactive imagination and send him to a psychiatrist to cure him!"

When they were back on the highway, Fred pursued the subject further. "There are at least two sides to the natural world. Probably more. Or maybe there are no sides; maybe the natural world is a curve, or something like a Möbius strip. Anyway, at the moment my own perception is limited to the idea of sides, two sides. Now you take yourself. What you see when you look out the window registers on your mind as a picture, a flat surface. You can't help it. That's how you've been indoctrinated to see. But with the help of drugs—if you use them carefully and treat them as sacraments—

it's possible to break through that surface and experience the *other* side, the alternative reality."

"But isn't there a danger of becoming addicted?"

"Not if you're careful. Not if you do it in the right spirit. People who get hooked are sick to begin with, they're trying to escape from something, they approach drugs in a negative spirit. We have a positive orientation about them. We're trying to achieve Christ. He isn't going to let us get hooked. You always trip with a guide, someone to take care of you. It's like Dante. You know the *Divine Comedy?* That's the prototype for everything —the journey, the descent into a conical world of mystery. You'd be surprised how important the cone is in occult methodology. I've tripped on LSD a lot, and it's always a conical journey. You go down and around, spiraling, exactly like in Dante, until you get to the bottom, the last circle, with everything frozen, and then you go a little farther, *through* the bottom, and then—" He smiled happily at her, his eyes shining as he remembered; she thought there was something quite beautiful in his homely face at that moment, something sweet and clean and radiant. "And then you're out on the other side, and climbing in the sunlight!"

"But I still don't understand what all this has to do with becoming one with Christ."

"There isn't any one single anthropomorphic God. Christ is limitless. Limitless! He's everywhere. He's everything. He's the energy that drives the universe. So before you can be at one with Him, you have to break through this façade, this learned artificial perception of false reality. You have to break through to the other side. Drugs can be helpful for some people. Other people don't need them. But if you use them, you only use them until you get there. Then you don't need them anymore. In fact, then they'd be counterproductive. It's like peeling a psychic onion. You get there progressively, getting rid of layers and layers of the preconceptions that are keeping you from the true vision of reality, step by step, stage by stage."

It was all very murky to the girl, but it was exciting too, and if she was skeptical about a lot of what Fred told her, and anxious about some of the implications of the narcotic aspect of life in the commune, she was also eager to experience it all firsthand.

They lived on the second floor of a large two-story frame house in a run-down neighborhood of abandoned storefronts and crumbling warehouses that was earmarked for redevelopment. "Someday," Fred said scornfully. "They've been talking about urban renewal here for ten years. They'll never do anything. It's a big civic rip-off. Lots of artists have studios around here. Some very weird types. But nobody hassles us."

Walls and partitions had been removed from two apartments to create a loftlike room almost fifty feet in length and half as wide, with a high ceiling. In one corner was a stove and a sink and an old refrigerator. Mattresses were scattered on the floor and orange crates served as tables, complementing a few sticks of junk-store furniture. The windows were boarded up, but the room was adequately lighted with candles and lamps. Though it was messy, with bundles of newspapers stacked along the walls and pieces of clothing strewn everywhere, and you had to walk around wine bottles with candles in them and plates and cups and shoes, it was clean enough and warm, and Cathy thought it was somehow romantic. She liked it, and she liked the people who lived there.

They were all, four girls and six young men, approximately her own age. The number of residents was a fluid thing. "Kids just come and go," she was told, "as the spirit moves them. We never say no to someone who wants to crash whether they're into Jesus or not. If they're not when they arrive, they usually are before they leave." A core of six of them, including Fred's friend Marcia—a plump barefoot girl in a granny dress and pigtails who was especially friendly to Cathy—lived in the house permanently and maintained it. They had odd jobs, in filling stations, in supermarkets, selling tickets in movie theaters and molding scented candles in head shops. "Everybody contributes something," Marcia said. "It doesn't take much to live when you've got your head together. You'd be surprised." Some weekends as many as thirty people stayed in the house.

"Where does everybody sleep?"

"Here." Marcia smiled. "We share. We share everything."

Cathy hoped they did not expect her to share a bed with any of them. When Fred had talked about love she did not understand him to mean sex. It worried her a little, but Marcia was so relaxed and apparently good-natured, and took it upon herself to put Cathy so at ease, that after a while she did not believe there would be any trouble. If worse came to worse, she thought, she could sleep with Marcia.

The common denominator of the group was their alienation from the orthodoxy of the Church. Like Cathy, they had all been devout and conventional Catholics who came gradually to sense an irrelevance and aimlessness in their lives, which they ascribed to the dead forms of their religion. They spoke feelingly of spiritual emptiness and crisis. The ecumenical movement was evidence not of the Church's renewal but of her attenuation.

"Ecumenism was just a ploy—innovation for the sake of innovation," a huge man with a thick black beard informed her gravely. He wore a tubular silver cross around his neck which converted into a hashish pipe. His name was Alan and he worked in a Boston library, part time. "The ecumenical movement," he went on, seated cross-legged on the floor, drinking wine from a paper cup, "is essentially a patch-up job—like trying to plug the leaks in a sinking ship. It was forced on the Church by the defections of the faithful. It was an attempt to be all things to all people. It was the first time in history that the Church was forced to react to a situation instead of taking the initiative. Changing the liturgy, desanctifying saints, redefining mortal sin—all that is a sign of panic. I think Pope John was a lovely human being, but history will show that he presided over the dissolution of the Church as we've always known it. What you have today in Rome is the equivalent of a rump parliament. In effect, there are a dozen Catholic Churches in America today. The real drive for renewal is going on in places like this. It's very much of an existential thing—a search for spiritual alternatives in the face of the collapse of the old theology."

Cathy thought he was brilliant. He spoke eloquently of Teilhard de Chardin and Kahlil Gibran in the same breath. He had a sonorous voice, rich and luxurious as his black beard. In spite of his considerable girth, he was very handsome.

As the afternoon passed quickly, she realized how superficial her own thinking about religion had been. She did not know what existentialism was. While of course she had read portions of *The Prophet,* she had never heard of this formidable theologian de Chardin, nor of another writer they invoked frequently, Thomas Merton.

They made her feel timid and ignorant, on the one hand; on the other, she was delighted to be there. It was exactly what she wanted and needed —a group of serious friends, as serious as she was, who were deeper, more thoughtful and better informed than she, who engaged in stimulating abstract discussions, for whom religion was a vital living thing. She thought the commune was fabulous. It was the perfect antidote for her apathy and spiritual numbness. She could feel herself, almost by the hour, being renewed.

Even when they smoked marijuana—Alan unscrewing the cross and stoking it and handing the pipe around—Cathy, though she declined the invitation to join them, accepted what was after all the first technically criminal act to which she had ever been an accessory with an equanimity she would not have possessed in any other circumstances. Smoking grass might be technically illegal, but it would take a truly perverted mind to condemn these gentle and considerate and serious new friends for smoking it.

Moreover, the grass seemed to heighten their perceptions. The conversations became even more interesting, more intellectual. They talked about the relationship between sexual ecstasy and religious mysticism. The terms were practically interchangeable. The antisexual bias of the Church was Paulist; it had nothing to do with the truth of the nature of the revealed Christ. Even today nuns took their final vows in a marriage ceremony; they became brides of Christ. It was impossible to separate the sexual from the mystical. A slight dark Greek boy with curly hair, Phillip something, had spent a year in the Trappist monastery in Gethsemane, Kentucky. He'd lived in the same room that Thomas Merton once occupied. He claimed that self-flagellation was still a part of a Trappist's discipline, and that novices were closely watched at first for incriminating signs that they derived masochistic gratification from whipping themselves. But you couldn't really draw distinctions between sexual pain and religious fervor. They were interwoven. "Yes," Cathy ventured. "It's like Saint Francis, the story of his hair shirt. They say that when Saint Francis died they couldn't remove the hair shirt he'd worn all his life because his body hairs had grown through it and become part of the shirt." They were overjoyed with her analogy.

She drank cup after cup of sour red wine, and felt warm and protected and loving and loved. Fred was right. You could knock down buildings with the collective emotions generated from within this group of gentle conscientious intelligent Christian friends.

After supper Marcia quoted from Scripture and they discussed the ambivalent text. From time to time one or the other of them would compose a spontaneous litany. *It is a church,* Cathy thought joyfully. *This is what the Church must have been like in earliest times.*

At one point in the evening, the room illuminated exclusively by candles now, the smell of marijuana sticky-sweet in Cathy's nostrils, the wine, to which she was unaccustomed, having made her soft and dreamy, a thin pretty girl with long blond hair called Jennifer began to chant something in a language Cathy had never heard. Her head back, her arms upraised, her eyes opened but apparently sightless, she sang out a repetitive phrase in a soft melodic voice that sent a shiver through Cathy.

"What's wrong—what's happening?" she asked.

"She's speaking in tongues," Marcia replied, taking Cathy's hand comfortingly.

"It's . . . it's beautiful," said Cathy, "but it's a little scary too."

"She's very close to the Lord," Marcia said, looking into Cathy's eyes and squeezing her hand.

The phenomenon lasted for about five minutes before the girl came slowly out of it, and looked around with a vague dazed smile. Marcia got up and went to her and placed an arm around her, and Jennifer laid her head against Marcia's plump bosom while Marcia kissed the top of her head and stroked her hair. Then they lay down together, embracing each other and kissing. It all seemed so natural to Cathy, like a kiss of Peace, so easy and free of self-consciousness. It was beautiful to watch them, lying there in each other's arms, like children, kissing innocently. It seemed to her a manifestation of Christian love, the love that abided in the energy of the universe which was God and could not therefore be displeasing or offensive.

She felt Alan's eyes on her. He was lying nearby on one of the mattresses, still fully dressed in jeans and a dark blue tank top shirt, his huge hairy chest and round belly, thick as a keg, rising and falling with his steady breathing, powerful and good, a good thoughtful brilliant man, and Cathy experienced a flow of uncontaminated love for him, for all of them, and she reached out and took his large hand in her tiny one, and it was like extending herself to all of them, reaching out to touch them all, establishing a pure and intimate contact with them through him, achieving a strange and wonderful sense of sodality with these new brothers and sisters. She lay down beside him and closed her eyes, calm and happy as a child, secure, unafraid, and waited, feeling complete and euphoric, for whatever would happen, waiting for him to touch her. However, he didn't move, and soon he was asleep, snoring; and, smiling, holding his hand, soon she was also asleep and did not hear the moans and sighs of Marcia and Jennifer, who were not asleep in each other's arms across the room from her.

CHAPTER 11

CONSTANTINE STOOD in the window of his second-floor apartment watching the blue syncopated sparks flashing from the roof of the police cruiser. A crowd of some twenty blacks was standing in the street mute and hostile as the police hustled two teen-agers into the rear seat of the car. One of them was bleeding from a scalp wound inflicted by a bicycle chain. A second police car pulled up, prompting Constantine to move away from the window, letting the plastic shower curtain fall back into place.

The police frightened him. They came on the average of twice a day; he was always certain they were coming for him.

He sat at the wooden table next to his bed, his head bowed, his long beard reaching to the third button of his overcoat, his gloved hands clasped lightly between his knees, waiting for the police to go away.

Six weeks had passed since he had talked to the psychiatrist. In that time he had lost, he estimated, fifty pounds. His clothes hung on him. His skin was yellow and waxy, and the outline of his skull was painfully defined. His neighbors thought he was sixty; he welcomed the error: he could not have hoped for a better disguise.

Suddenly he heard screams in the street, glass shattering, an explosion that might have been gunfire but which could as well have been a cherry bomb. The door banged open below, he heard scuffling sounds, and a woman swearing on the landing, and a baby crying. Then the door closed, and somewhere another door closed, and the building was quiet. Soon things were quiet in the street again too.

Constantine was used to it by now. In the month he'd lived in the neighborhood he'd witnessed half a dozen street fights, a couple of muggings, and a stickup in broad daylight. Two apartments in his building had been burglarized, a girl had been raped. But Constantine was not alarmed. He knew he should have been. He was virtually the only Caucasian on the block. Nevertheless, he enjoyed a strange immunity. No one ever bothered him. Even the teen-agers who loitered menacingly outside the soul food restaurant on the corner looking for trouble merely fell silent whenever he appeared. "Here comes old man Brown," they would say, and they would stare at him wordlessly as he shuffled past, his shoulders rounded, his hands in the pockets of his voluminous overcoat. When, as often happened, he opened the door to the hallway of his building and came upon a couple of drug addicts shooting up, they would turn their backs on him, press against the wall and let him go by.

After the police departed, he switched on the lamp in the tiny kitchen and heated some water on an old hot plate. There was a gas range with three burners, but he couldn't make it work. His only nourishment these days was a cup of tepid bouillon which he drank in the morning and at night. Pouring the water into a translucent soup bowl, he added the bouillon cubes, sat down next to the cold radiator in the other room, placed the bowl on the radiator and carefully began to remove the crusted woolen glove from his left hand. The glove peeled off like a scab. Constantine looked, sighed. It was the same. Fresh, pink, pulsing, vulvular, discharging an opaque ocher fluid.

In the beginning he'd examined himself every time he awoke in hopes that during his sleep his wounds had vanished. For a while during the autumn his hopes were fortified by the conviction that one morning they *would* be gone, that they would disappear as phenomenally as they'd arrived. Lately, however, he not only did not expect them to vanish, he was beginning to fear what would happen if they did.

He owed thousands of dollars. In the past six weeks he'd lived in three different places, left unpaid rent behind, broken leases, deposits. He had no money, no credit. He'd sold his car, sold his securities to pay the alimony and keep his wife at a distance, pawned his clothes, his luggage, his furniture. He owed the phone company, Master Charge, the credit union. Even if the wounds disappeared, he wondered how he could possibly go back, how he could plausibly explain his long delinquency.

And yet he wanted to be whole and healthy again. He kept insisting on that. He thought about the psychiatrist, who was never far from his thoughts. He had been mistaken, that man. Constantine had been ready to swallow the pill. Maybe not that very day, that particular instant. He had hesitated then because he was trying to be honest, to be responsible, and, no, he truly wasn't ready at that moment. Especially considering the terms which Auerbach had put to him. An instantaneous cure. An instantaneous cure for anything, which was to say a miracle, would be nearly as traumatic as instantaneous mutilation. Everything was organic, there were organic rhythms, seasons, cycles. A person had to get accustomed to the idea of being well. The body had to readjust to health by slow degrees; so did one's psychology.

But it was wrong to assume—as no doubt the smug psychiatrist in his fancy Park Avenue tower was assuming superciliously—that he didn't want to be cured. He had returned to Connecticut with a strong intention of calling Auerbach during the week and telling him he was ready. He even believed that he would meet Auerbach's precondition and submit himself to an allergist.

However, things happened. Things, he maintained, over which he had no control. He was victimized by circumstances. Convinced that he was the object of a manhunt—and forgetting that the specialist at the Mayo Clinic would not be able to contact him—he abandoned his new apartment and took a room at a different address under the name he'd assumed at Auerbach's, Paul Brown. That cost him a month's rent plus a month's security deposit. But the racket from his neighbors was intolerable, and the landlady was too inquisitive, so after a week he moved again, to the squalid apartment in New London. The moving, the scraping for money, negotiating with used-furniture dealers—it all combined to deplete his energy and left him with a feeling of deep lassitude. His intention to see an allergist lost its definition. What was the point? He knew the stigmata were not an allergy. Auerbach knew it too. Auerbach was merely trying to break his will. *I'm not a child,* he thought resentfully. *I won't let him treat me like a feeble-minded child.*

Nevertheless, paradoxically, he intended every day, every tomorrow, to telephone Auerbach and say, "I'm ready." And it would be the truth. He thought he would swallow the pill. But he continued also to procrastinate. He tried to analyze why. That kind of procrastination was a pattern of his life. Even before. Like his problems with paying bills. He knew the debts would not vanish of their own accord; furthermore, he would have money to pay them in his checking account. But often, with certain debts, he simply could not bring himself to sit down at the desk and write a check. Nor did threatening letters budge him; if anything, they made him more intransigent, gave him a genuine excuse for not paying. Only when the debt was finally turned over to a collection agency was he moved to concede, though grudgingly, feeling resentful and injured, usually including with the payment a scathing and self-righteous letter of his own. Which seemed to justify the course he had adopted: running up bills, drawing on credit, as an excuse to hate and abuse his creditors.

The psychology had parallels with the way he put off going to the dentist when he'd lost a filling. It wasn't a matter of fearing the pain of the dentist's instruments; the filling might be small, easily replaced with a minimum of discomfort. But Constantine would nevertheless delay making an appointment to have the tooth repaired, and the cavity would flake and chip and rot, becoming larger, more serious; he would realize that with each passing day of indecision he was guaranteeing that the operation would be difficult and very painful, he might lose the tooth entirely, and still he would not make the appointment which ultimately, he knew perfectly clearly, was unavoidable. Which in turn raised the question of whether he truly desired the pain, and if so, why? How could a man want pain? No, that was Auerbach's position. It wasn't that. It was something else. He was missing a connection. He concluded that he wanted something else, and wanting it interfered with his arriving at a decision, so that the final inconvenience was a by-product of the something else.

He tried to be rational. During that time the whole pressure on him was to retain his habits of rational thought. He couldn't call Auerbach until he had figured out what it was preventing him from calling Auerbach. And the constant grinding application of his rational faculties to the question was putting him in jeopardy of becoming irrational. *Which is another way of saying,* he thought in despair, *that I don't* want *to call him after all—and that's simply not true!* He *had* wanted to; something prevented him that first week or so after he'd gone to New York. Now he could not call because of the financial mess which had evolved in the interim. So did it make any sense to keep aggravating himself over a problem that no longer existed? Even if he finally came to understand why six weeks ago he had delayed making the decision, it would avail him nothing now when entirely different and external factors precluded his doing it. And yet it was still to be done, because the external factors, like the chipped tooth, would only grow bigger if he didn't. Aside from which, it was becoming increasingly difficult to imagine himself without the stigmata. They were now as much a part of him as the hands and feet that contained them.

His mind ached; he was fatigued. He lay down on the lumpy mattress and closed his eyes, trying not to think. The bowl of bouillon chilled on the radiator and formed a yellow spiderweb of scum. He forgot about it. He lay there shivering, listening to the creaks and bumps and groans transmitted from the other apartments through the useless heating pipes. It began to rain; he could tell by the sounds the cars made passing through the street, their tires sounding like tearing silk. As the rain increased he could hear it in the gutter pipes. Later the rain turned to sleet, millions of needles spraying against the windowpanes, which shuddered and rattled in the rotten casement. Once he heard footsteps pounding along the sidewalk as though someone were being pursued. Again, a horn beeping. He dozed off. When he awoke the sleet had stopped and everything was silent, so silent there might not have been a world outside the confines of his walls, so silent that he was not sure for a few moments that he was not still asleep.

He rose and turned on the light in the kitchen. The cup of bouillon looked like a bowl of urine on the radiator. The silver paint was blistered and scabby; he wondered when there had ever been heat enough in those pipes to blister the paint. He knew he ought to eat, but he wasn't hungry. He took some moldy cheese from the refrigerator and, crumbling it, scattered the fragments on the floor and then sat down at the table to wait for the rats to come.

It was strange. For all the rats he'd sacrificed in laboratories over the years, killing them and dissecting them, removing their livers, their hearts, their brains—hundreds of them, perhaps thousands—it wasn't until he'd come here to live that he really began to understand what marvelous animals rats truly were. They were quick, tough, handsome and intelligent. He couldn't understand why everyone feared and detested them. They were harmless and often very companionable. Given a few more weeks, he was confident he could domesticate them. Already he was close to persuading them to eat out of his hand. He preferred them to cats; they were more candid, more amusing.

There was a hole in the ceiling where the plaster had fallen out. He could see slats and tufts of dirty insulation. He wondered why the rats never arrived through that hole. He guessed they came up through the rotten floor beneath the sink, or from behind the stove. But he never actually saw them enter. They simply materialized. One moment he was alone and the next there were the rats, invariably two of them (though whether the same two he could not be sure), glossy and beautiful, running back and forth silently, eating the cheese he had spread for them.

"Forgot to feed you last night, didn't I? My apologies. I trust you dined elsewhere and weren't terribly inconvenienced."

"Affectation, affectation," said one of the rats.

"What do you mean, affectation?" Constantine demanded.

"Charlatan," said the second rat, gnawing cheese.

"Fake, fraud," added the first.

"I suppose this is your idea of gratitude for all I've given you?" Constantine said with irritation.

"You were levitating again last night."

"I was not!"

"Floating around the ceiling," said the first rat. "Upside down."

"You said you were going to try to stop that."

"It's a cheap trick."

"Go to hell!" said Constantine indignantly.

"No will power."

"A cheap trick. You ought to be ashamed. Parlor stunts. Done with mirrors, no doubt."

"Very bad form, levitation. Plaster saint," they jeered.

"I don't know what you're talking about. Go to hell!"

"Levitation, bilocation," they chorused. "Vanity, vanity. Filthy disgusting cowardly liar."

Furious, Constantine looked for something to throw at them. The only object close at hand was the bowl of bouillon. He flung it across the room with a curse. The soup splashed yellow against the wall, a sunburst, the bowl shattered, and Constantine sat straight up in bed and looked around. The light was out. He didn't remember turning it out. He didn't remember lying down.

A pathetic trickle of heat was spluttering and fizzing in the radiator. Constantine got out of bed and sat on the floor, wrapped in the blanket, huddling against the radiator coils, shivering, imagining the vagrant warmth as much as actually feeling it.

Freezing to death, he thought, was supposed to be the easiest way to die. Though jumping off a high bridge was supposed to have advantages too: the exhilaration of the long fall, like flying. And the pain would have to be negligible. One did not hesitate to end one's life; what finally stopped you was the fear of pain. But the suicides who dove off the Golden Gate Bridge did not die from drowning; they died on impact. And the impact didn't hurt. There was nothing you could really call pain in a great blow like that. Pain always followed a blow in the face, for example, by several seconds. Constantine had driven his face into the steering wheel once in a collision, and he remembered a strange sensation of euphoria that lasted for a considerable interval before he felt any actual discomfort.

The Golden Gate, he mused. Was it any wonder they went off the

Golden Gate in such numbers? A name like that. Why not call it the Pearly Gate?

The pain after such an impact, from such a height, would have to be an extremely delayed reaction. By the time the reaction could take hold there was nothing left to take hold of. You'd be dead by then. Which made it almost perfect. The only hitch being the godlike exhilaration of that brief spectacular plunge. Surely somewhere near the end of it you would experience an immense regret that you could not duplicate the feat. Your last seconds would be filled with, or at least qualified by, frustration, which would spoil the purity of the act.

No problem like that with freezing to death. They say you began to feel warm, finally, snug and cozy, and then gently drifted off. But there was the discomfort of the cold first.

Gas would be better. He might be tempted to do it with gas, except that the oven didn't work. And then besides, there was the wholly undignified posture, on your hands and knees like a brute quadruped, your head in the oven, half man, half turkey, and the farting smell of the gas, your last moments filled with demeaning images and associations. No, it would have to be glorious, exalting, the final concentrated expression of your quintessential reality.

It was the early hours of the morning. The window, in the light from the lamps outside, looked like a rectangle of bacon grease. It was freezing cold. He got to his feet, letting the blanket slide to the floor, and hobbled into the bathroom to urinate. Then he went to the window, drew back the plastic curtain and looked out. The street was deserted. He estimated that it was around two. He walked up and down the apartment for a while thinking about nothing in particular. Then he went out.

As he limped and shuffled down the street in the direction of the city pier a few blocks away, he noticed a wreath nailed to the door of a small wooden bungalow; he assumed that someone in the house had died. But a few doors farther on, he saw in the window of a market a cardboard crèche, and he thought with surprise, *Christmas? Can it be Christmas already?* He couldn't remember Thanksgiving. Was it December already?

Where had November gone? It was impossible. "Christmas," he said. "Christmas!"

The river was black and glossy, unruffled by the gusts of wind that flapped his coattails against his calves. A night watchman making his rounds along the pier approached Constantine, a flashlight in his hand, his boots striking sharply on the wood; Constantine drew back into the shadows of some packing crates until he passed.

Across the river, the lights of the shipyards and the oil refinery and the labs where he'd worked were reflected in the water. A tanker tied up at the oil company dock was outlined in white lights. Off Avery Point, beyond the University Branch, a beacon flashed. There was no traffic on the river, only an occasional pair of headlights on the high bridge to his left.

He walked upriver to where the submarine tender was moored. On her bridge a Christmas tree swayed in the wind, the red and blue bulbs quivering. Berthed alongside her, like a baby sea cow, was a submarine. As Constantine watched, a sailor came up out of a hatch and called something to a man on the ship, who leaned over the railing and replied. Constantine could hear their voices but not their words. Then the sailor vanished.

Retracing his steps, Constantine walked along the railroad tracks, following the river, until he came to a ferry slip behind the dark and silent train station. The pier and the adjacent parking lots were floodlighted, but no one was around. Constantine heard the church bell on the top of the hill in New London tolling three. He walked out to the end of the pier and stood looking down. The water made sucking sounds against the pilings.

I would go numb in a couple of minutes, he thought. *In this coat I couldn't swim if I tried. It would drag me down, right straight down to the bottom. It would be over in no time at all. It would be all over—*

A siren in one of the factories on the other side caused him to raise his head. He saw a tugboat with orange running lights poke out from behind the tanker and move up the river past the shipyards toward the bridge.

Up the river, Constantine thought, *always up the river, back to the source.* He had traced this same Thames back to its source one summer afternoon three years before with his wife and Betsy (who were both bored). He had always wanted to go to England and see the source of the other Thames, which he'd read was up somewhere in the Cotswolds in Gloucestershire.

He used to read with great interest accounts of international expeditions undertaken at enormous expense to determine the source of the Amazon.

The Amazon. Men always looking to the Amazon for an explanation of their puny masculinity. It was no accident that men persisted in battling back up jungle streams, fighting their way back to sources which when they found them were only leaky little holes in the rocks of mountain grottoes. No mystery either that the most satisfying death was to launch oneself off a high bridge and die in a river like the Thames, so tempting to so many mariners who had traveled through this water above and below the surface that the authorities had had to erect tall mesh baffles on the bridge to keep them from going over the side in droves.

"Five minutes!" he said, trembling, staring into the water with such intensity that after a time it no longer seemed like fluid, until it seemed like polished mahogany, as though he could walk on it. "All I have to do is step out there, and it will be over, it will be all over." The water rose along the pilings, silent, inviting him. He felt weak, and faint, and insubstantial. He would dissolve like a puff of smoke. The wind could blow him over the edge like a dry leaf. In minutes he would die. He inched his toes closer to the edge. Little bits of rotten wood crumbled beneath his feet and drizzled down into the water, which continued to ascend toward him as though high tide were coming in all at once, in a single concentrated swell. It was almost level with the pier now; it must be swamping Groton on the other side, pouring into the plants, short-circuiting the great generators, sweeping men and machinery before the flood; in another moment it would take him too, curl around his ankles and drag him down and it would be oblivion, black and wet and warm. The wind howled, tugged at his coat, staggered him with blows, there was a howling in his brain, building to a great climax of storm threatening to bring the bridge down too, buckling its foundations like wet cardboard and sending the ships up onto the highways in a tidal flood and cosmic mockery and terror and chaos.

And then it all ceased. The wind died, the water declined, the roaring in his skull was shut off. He heard the church bells tolling four. He heard a dog barking and a tugboat hooting. He stumbled back from the edge of the pier with tears burning his eyes like sweat, crushed and mortified by his fear and cowardice.

"Dr. Auerbach? This is Paul Brown. Do you remember me?"

"Yes, of course, Mr. Brown." Constantine waited but the psychiatrist was silent.

"I tried to commit suicide last night."

There was another silence before Auerbach spoke. "But you changed your mind."

Constantine was irritated by the vapid reply. "I know, I know all about all the aphorisms and truisms; you don't have to tell me. I know what you're thinking. The callers don't jump, the jumpers don't call. That's what you're thinking. But this is different. I was close." He was in a phone booth in the concrete yard of a Shell station. "I was very close. You'd better believe that." It was a gray afternoon; the air was sprinkled with white flecks of either ash or snow, he couldn't tell which. "The next time I'll do it."

"I hope you won't," said Auerbach, sounding guarded.

Constantine shifted his weight, leaned on the door, which creaked against his spine. His shoes crunched a bit of broken glass. The soles of his feet ached. "I would like to talk to you. I'd like to see you."

"You don't want to kill yourself." It was not a question.

"But I will! Unless I can talk to you right away."

"All right," said the psychiatrist a moment later. "When can you come in?"

"I can't. That's the point. I can't come in. I'm . . . too weak, too sick to travel. I was wondering . . . I mean, I was hoping that . . . well, can you possibly come here?"

"I don't know where you live," Auerbach said evenly.

Constantine told him the address. "It's only a couple of hours on the turnpike from New York," he added. "I know, I realize how expensive . . . but somehow, well, I'll get the money somehow, don't worry about the money. Will you come? It's . . . I'm afraid that . . ."

"You're afraid?"

"I'm afraid I'll lose my mind. That I'll go crazy and kill myself. I'll go to an allergist if you insist. I haven't gone yet because . . . I've been prevented. But I *will* go—if you agree to come up and talk to me first. Will you?"

Almost thirty seconds passed. Cars pulled up to the pumps, ringing the bells. It was unmistakably a dry snow now swirling around. Constantine waited. At last Auerbach said (as Constantine had known all along he would say), "Mr. Brown, you have to come here. It has nothing to do with time or money. My coming to you would only serve to defeat the purpose."

"I told you I *can't* come! I can't travel!" His voice rose. "You don't realize what it costs me just to come outside in the daylight like this, to make this call—the risks I take, the physical effort."

"If you're serious about wanting help, you'll find a way to get here," Auerbach replied. "Try to understand. If I come to you, not only will I not be able to help you, I'll actually make your problem worse. Believe me—if you're as convinced as you seem to be that I can help you, you have to give me credit for knowing what I'm talking about. The first, perhaps most important step for you has to be a decision on your part to get yourself to New York. Strictly speaking, I can't help you. I can't, strictly speaking, help anybody. All I can do is try to help someone help himself. The power to cure you coexists with the powers that injured you. Sorry to sound pedantic. But it's the only way I know how to explain it. And those powers coexist inside yourself. If and when you want to be cured, you'll find a way to come to New York."

"Why do you insist on that 'if and when'?" Constantine demanded.

"Sorry. That's my perception of the case. I'm not convinced."

"What do you need to be convinced? You want me to kill myself to prove it?"

"That would only convince me that I was right."

"How will you feel," Constantine asked vindictively, "if you learn that as a result of your refusing to come to New London I in fact did kill myself?"

"Very saddened," Auerbach answered seriously, convincingly. His tone disarmed Constantine. "Very depressed. Very humble. Very helpless."

Constantine was silent for a long time. Then he said despondently, "Is it all right if I call you again, maybe? Even if I don't come in?"

"Yes. Call me whenever you want to."

Constantine was silent again. Then he asked sheepishly, "Would you do me a favor?"

"If I can."

"Will you accept the charges for this call? I'm in a phone booth and I only have twenty-five cents."

With the coin lying on the counter, Constantine leaned heavily against the phone and shut his eyes. He was sealed off. There was no more latitude to his life than there was to the phone booth. He couldn't kill himself, he couldn't live with himself. He had nowhere to turn, no one to turn to.

Except . . . Cathy! Cathy Bianca. He hadn't thought of her in weeks. Not that she could help. Or would even want to. She might no longer be living in the area, in Connecticut. She might be married. In any event, he would seem a horror to her: old, debilitated, mad. Or was it possible she'd take pity on him? *What if I just told her? What if I showed her and explained the whole thing?* It would be a relief, a freeing of himself from at least a portion of his mental anguish. And it would place the burden of responsibility on her—the responsibility to act, to react, to make a decision. Perhaps she still loved him. He could trust her anyway; she was perhaps the only person in the world he could trust. *And I have to talk to* someone. *If I don't, I'll explode. I'll go berserk. And that's all I need. To go berserk, and start breaking up the place, and the police coming with the ambulance and the strait jacket. Oh, yes, that's all I'd need. . . .*

Before he could change his mind, he picked up the quarter, pushed it into the slot and dialed Information.

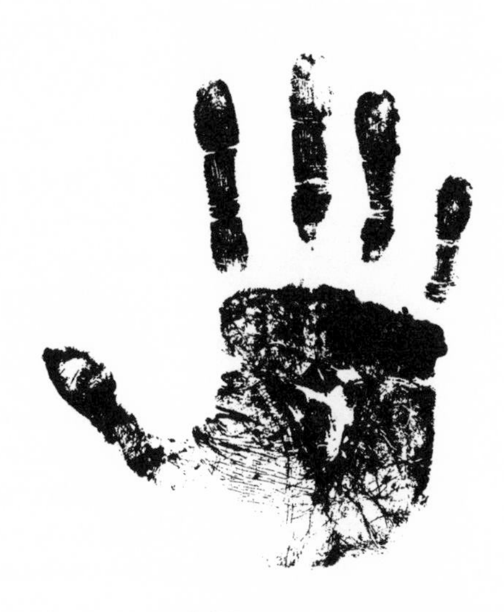

CHAPTER 12

THE MINUTE SHE HAD WALKED into the apartment, she told her friends, she could feel a "holiness" suffusing her. A kind of mystical energy had been coming out of him; she compared it to radioactivity. "I remember thinking that something tremendous had occurred, but spiritually more than physiologically. I mean, he'd been reduced almost to a skeleton physically, but he seemed gigantic spiritually, and beautiful! He was transformed. He glowed. I never had such a feeling."

And the fragrance in the air—like a blending of the scents of spring flowers, violets and lilies of the valley. But somehow more than merely a fragrance; it had been a sensation of mingled taste and smell. She recalled also the taste of honey that had immediately filled her mouth.

Constantine lay on a mattress, covered with a thin blanket, pretending to be asleep.

"Saints smell like that," a man's voice said.

"Saint Francis smelled like violets too," said someone else.

"And Saint Francis had the stigmata."

"I know. God Almighty!"

"It's just tremendous!"

"And do you remember about the honey, what Jennifer said when she came out of it last week?"

"That's right. Jennifer said she had the taste of honey on her tongue."

"What else? What else happened, Cathy?"

She was wearing jeans and a soiled sweat shirt with PROPERTY OF HOLY CROSS ATHLETIC DEPARTMENT printed on the chest. On her left wrist was a small bandage. As she talked, pulling nervously on a joint, her friends pressed around her in a circle, she was still tense and excited and confused. She struggled to put into words all she had thought and felt. But her powers of language could not command the myriad images and associations which had churned through her mind, nor could she understand the extent to which they had been influenced by her experiences week after week in the commune. Furthermore, propriety would not allow her to speak of some of the things that had transpired.

"I don't know," she said, casting down her eyes. "It was very awkward at first. I was amazed by how he looked, of course. I was really staggered. I mean, do all of you understand? He's only thirty-nine! He doesn't eat anything! He doesn't require food!"

"I can't believe it," Marcia said.

"I tell you I worked with him. I know him!"

"Why not?" asked Alan. "It's only hard to believe because we're all still so limited. The man has had the breakthrough. He's light-years ahead of us. The thing happens in front of our eyes and we can't see it, we can't accept it. If Christ walked in we'd doubt our senses."

Constantine opened his eyes cautiously and tried to identify the speaker with the deep authoritative voice. He saw a large bearded man with a powerful chest and an enormous belly; he was wearing some kind of silver ornament around his neck. He looked intelligent and sympathetic. It would be all right; he sensed he could trust them. He did not feel threatened; in fact, he felt quite the opposite. He had resisted coming with her, but now he was glad. He was safe at last. They would take care of him. Cathy would take care of him and sleep in his arms. His ordeal—the shame and the torment and the diabolic loneliness—was over.

Cathy poured wine into a paper cup. "At first we just talked. I talked. I don't remember everything because I was so high, I felt all strung out, and these waves of energy coming out of him, washing over me . . . I felt all scrambled up. I guess what got us on the subject was me talking about the scene here. It was crazy—I mean, with me politely pretending I didn't notice anything unusual, like I'd just stopped by for a drink or something. He didn't say anything for the longest time, didn't offer any explanations. He just sat there looking at me with these eyes—God, I've never looked into eyes like that. You could see right down into his soul through them. . . ."

She had been terrified; now, surrounded by her friends, after the event, she did not recall the terror, only the subsequent exaltation. She had worn a short skirt and a black turtleneck sweater beneath which her breasts were unconfined. He had said nothing at first, and looked at her the way he did because with her arrival the pain had returned with renewed savagery. He could feel the wound in his side opening and closing like the gills of a fish, pulsing wetly, sore and fiery. The pain seemed to enamel his eyeballs, and for a time he did not see her at all.

Feigning sleep, Constantine listened to her recitation—she sounded like a schoolgirl delivering an incompletely prepared lesson—as he remembered rising from his chair and standing in front of the greasy window, looking out sightlessly, his hand moving without volition to his side, feeling under the coat, his fingertips brushing the area of the wound beneath his heart, the pain like teeth in his flesh, like a beak, and seeing vague forms in the street through a mist of pain.

"I think I got into a very involved description of Fred's theory about the Möbius strip, which I probably got all wrong, and . . ."

(The cone, and Dante, spiraling down to the bottom as in the Inferno, and then breaking through the bottom and emerging, on the other side, climbing in sunlight.)

His perception of her beauty, which he took in like a plant absorbing oxygen, his sensitivity to every nuance of the girl, the smell of her cologne, like a garden after rain, the movement of her breasts beneath the sweater, the shine of the stretched nylon on her knees above the black zippered boots, the crucifix around her throat, as she talked confusedly about alternate realities and drug-induced phenomena and Christian love.

("I'm an atheist. I'm an atheist! I'm a scientist and an atheist! I don't believe in God!"

"Dr. Constantine, what's really happened to you?")

"I don't remember . . . I just can't remember!" She was crying now, and Marcia put her arms around her and hugged her. "He had these gloves on. It was cold in the apartment. He was wearing that overcoat and these gloves. I don't know. I think I guessed before he— One minute he had the gloves on, and the next . . . there he was. There they were, his hands. I . . . I don't know."

"Leave her alone. Take it easy, Cathy. Give her a drink."

She had been hysterical. She did not retain a memory of all that followed —of her brief swoon, of waking up in his arms, of kissing his hands and pressing them to her breasts, of her uncontrollable weeping, of her raving, her profanities, scurrilities, prayers, of begging Jesus to come to her, to kill her, to plunder her, of tearing at her clothes and biting her own wrist until it bled.

"What happened afterward, Cathy?"

"Afterward," she whispered, wiping her eyes, glancing at Constantine, "afterward it was . . . very loving. It was very spiritual. . . ."

It was as if his eyes were filmed with blood. He saw her indistinctly, through a red luminous haze like the mist that condensed in his bathroom that day when he awoke on the floor and felt crucified, afraid to move, thinking his neck was broken.

He thought, *It's like an erotic fantasy coming true.* Perhaps the whole thing, from the beginning, had been nothing else, and nothing less. From the start the experience of the stigmata had been overlaid by a subtle, perverse sexuality which was paradoxically related to his sudden and drastic loss of self-esteem. But there had been no focus to that sexuality; it was a sexual wash with no object of desire to fix on, with no real desire in any conventional sense of the word. It had been the pain and fear and tension of sex as a major permanent condition, and now unbelievably, with the girl in his arms, those months of vague aggravation and excitement, like the itching of one's skin beneath a months-old cast, voluptuous irritation that made one writhe with a frustration not very different from the intense pleasure of self-gratification, it all came together into a focus in this virginal child, so that he wondered if the intensity of his repressed emotions had not somehow actually conjured her up, whether she was not an essence of his own spirit condensed, a precipitate of himself. In which case to make love to her would be tantamount to making love to himself.

But wasn't that all it ever was anyway for him, or had been all his life —self-abuse, abusing himself on a woman's body, trying to immolate himself over and over, his promiscuity less a repetitious quest for impossible gratification than a search for equally impossible self-destruction?

He pressed his mouth to hers. Her lips were cold and dry and unresponsive. It angered him that she was unresponsive, and taking her by the arms, he shook her. Rivets drove through his palms, but he didn't care; he squeezed her harder and brought his mouth against hers once more, violently. His teeth broke her lips and made her whimper, and, inflamed, he screwed his mouth tightly against hers, feeling for her tongue with his teeth, wanting to bite her and taste her blood.

They were on the bed then, she was lying back shielding her eyes, her face turned to the wall, her breathing quick and irregular, and Constantine was on his knees between her legs, his hands beneath her skirt, stroking her legs, her thighs. She felt exposed, like a small girl showing herself to companions. Then he gripped the tiny zippers that ran down the length of her boots and opened them, stripping them off, the leather falling open, peeling away like bark, and she shuddered and sighed as his face came into contact with the insides of her thighs as if he had unzipped all of her and she was peeling open and something external and confining and protective were falling away. He moved his face along her thighs, which were tense and cold, kissing her, pushing the skirt up over her hips, and then lay there sprawled between her legs, breathing in the warm familiar forgotten always alien pungency, wanting to lie there forever without moving.

But she dislodged him with a spasmodic thrust of her hips, and he rose slightly to pull at the flimsy nylon, tearing her underthings, at which she gave a small strangled scream as if he had torn her flesh instead. But she arched her back and raised her hips to accommodate him, and he felt the hair of her thighs, flossy above her knees and scratchy where she shaved below, little black needle points, and probing for her with his tongue between her legs, the mucous pulpiness bitter to his taste, and then bitterly he was inside her, coming up on top of her, and she, struggling to remove her sweater, her arms above her head, pulled it free, and seeing the wounds in his hands again gave a rapturous exclamation and seized his hands and kissed them. It was excruciating for him. A groan escaped his lips, which excited her tremendously, naked except for her skirt, and she kissed him and murmured deliriously into his sticky flaring palms:

"I want to feel you, I want to hurt you, does it hurt when I do that? Are you in great pain? I want you to be in pain, I want your pain, I want you to hurt me so I can share your pain, I want to *be* your pain. . . ."

Her tongue was a nail exploring the core of his lacerations. She licked at his sores like a wounded animal, as if she were licking her own wounds, not his, while he, between her legs again, had the sensation that his face was covered with her blood, that her life was flowing out of her into his mouth menstrually in this protracted declension.

But there was no release in all of it, as after such a term of celibacy there should have been, no release even in his orgasm, which came retching up out of him painfully as though he were passing streams of slivered glass mixed with his semen, which she drank down, coughing, choking, her face wet, streaked with his semen and hot tears. Everything remained clotted inside him, he felt tumescent, suspended, and he strained to get hold of her again, straining inside her to let go, as, on top of him, sweat blistering the visible bone between her breasts, she gripped him with her thighs and screwed herself down on him, her eyes shut tightly, her face distorted in a silent scream, seeming for the moment (and at different fleeting moments as her expression underwent serial metamorphoses) to resemble one by one all the women he had ever made love to in his life.

They were almost all of them like her, slender with almost boyish figures, half-formed girls, he being repelled by large fleshy women with great carnal pendulous breasts, preferring girls like Rosemary, *Rosemary,* he thought as this stranger gouged at his shoulders with her fingernails, flaying him, the smell of their bodies like warm glue, and she raved obscenities—Rosemary, who was a lesbian, or at least had lesbian tendencies, herself as fascinated by large-breasted women as he was repelled by them, whom he got pregnant, who aborted over his protests, which made three germinal Constantines on different parts of the continent to have been flushed down toilets to whom (or which) he had never given a thought until this moment, the abortions in a sense the fruit of this child's womb, boiled up out of her and presented like phantoms to his imagination. Rosemary! A boy with a vagina. Which was all of a piece with that other woman, the other little Italian who Cathy now became for an instant, who liked to masquerade, with him as a woman dressed in her lingerie, and play with him, which had been more thrilling than he had ever dared to admit to her—those sexual reversals that said so much about all his inhibitions and strengths as well as flaws in his character, like the girl in Greenwich, Sheila, who had an anal fixation, who liked to have anal sex with him, performing on him, because she could not come otherwise, also lesbian, who confessed that she fantasized his anus was a vagina, excited to kiss him after he'd been eating her, tasting herself on his tongue and mouth, so that she could imagine what it was like to eat herself. The images of these women came back one after the other, like the images of the long-forgotten abortions, forming out of the hot textured vapors between this child's legs, intruding between him and her, between the precise and focused concentration that was the instrument of his potential release.

"You smell like honey," she said. "It's like streams of honey pouring out of you, like streams of fire, hot honey all up in flames, I see flames shooting out of you. . . ." She tried to drink from him. Her face was smeared and bloated. In a paroxysm she gnawed at his hands.

It was black and filthy, a black mass she was performing on his body, trying to wound herself on him, celebrating her own pain, trying to ingest him, in some other realm, another dimension, sex the alternative reality, what she was talking about earlier, what she must have meant, an environment, a substitute world full of magic marvels and metamorphoses, sex almost a culture if not a continent with its own geography and laws and natural order (or natural disorder), and he could lose himself in it too, he could go down with her, submerge himself, vanish; he wanted to follow her down into her cone-shaped sex like Dante even though the alternate reality was the Inferno, he would go with her, he was going with her now finally as their rhythms synchronized and she gasped and shuddered and, rising, twisting, her stomach muscles tight and hard, she began to scream.

It was a long chilling drawn-out piercing sound, to Constantine's ears like the screech of a dying rabbit, a rabbit being torn apart by hunting dogs, or dogs in a laboratory, acute hounds, dying slowly of poison, or women in labor. It was a sound that made him energetic suddenly with cruelty, sadistic as he drove himself against her, driving himself back to his childhood, the night they set the cat on fire in an orgy of what was commonly called sadism but was really masochism, the pleasure shaped less by torturing someone or something else than by damaging your own sensibilities—and it had been an orgy, a clear sexual thing, so that although he was too young for orgasm he wet his pants with excitement, and now he remembered that also, how it felt, the voluptuous letting go, and he felt it finally building like that again in him as the girl, on her back, her damp long hair tumbled out in sea tangles on the mattress, her spine bowed, covered with sweat and slime and blood, writhed as though currents of electricity were jetting through her arteries, the hollow soulless feline wail issuing unbroken from her purplish lips, lips to bite and rip and chew, thought Constantine, descending on her, his arms around her shoulders, touching her eggshell skull, wanting to kiss her wanting to crush her skull to seize her by the nape and swing her like a cat by the tail until her pussy spine snapped, feeling all over again the same hysteria and lascivious pleasure and the lewd exalting pain.

Then she was silent. Suddenly she was staring up at him in silent amazement, and he began to talk to her for the first time, moving in and out of her without knowing it, not knowing what he was saying, crooning at her like a mother crooning to a sick infant. She stared at him, like a sick infant who cries so hard she can't catch her breath and goes rigid in her limbs and turns blue, her mouth open, her eyes glazed, with Constantine holding her, finally at the point of tearing himself loose but trying perversely to hold it, to heighten the pleasure and the pain, holding back, delaying, stroking her head with a fierce total concentration of tenderness and hallucinated loathing, her face loathesome, purple, her lips swollen with trapped blood, engorged—and at length she gasped profoundly, her eyelids fluttered, and with tremors buckling through her she came, and as she came and came she was transfigured in his arms and he was holding Betsy, coaxing and gentling her in the middle of the night, imposing himself on his infant daughter, perfusing her with his own strength and health and psychic power, fury and affection in balance, willing her back into focus, his whiskery cheek nuzzling her damp feverish face, brushing off the nightmare panics from her brain as he stroked the hair on her eggshell skull and felt for the soft spot cautiously with his thumb, shushing her and murmuring nonsense until her sobs turned to hiccups and her tense little muscles softened, and her breath grew normal and she snuggled in his arms.

And at last Constantine let go and felt it all flowing out of him. The girl gave a cry. "Oh, I'd do anything for you!" And he dissolved. "I'd rob, I'd steal, I'd kill, I'd burn in bleeding hell for you!" And Constantine contracted and dissolved and re-formed and ran out of himself until nothing was left and he was conscious of nothing but a consuming thirst.

"Yes," Cathy affirmed quietly to her friends. "It was very loving. Very tender and beautiful."

There was a pause. Then Fred asked, "What are we going to do? You think maybe we should inform the priest at—"

"No," Cathy said firmly. "He's mine. He belongs to me."

"He belongs to all of us," Alan reminded her.

"Yes, that's true," Cathy conceded. "But not the Church. They'd take him away from us."

"She's right. The Church would crucify him."

"We're the Church," said Cathy. "We take care of him. Nobody else can even know about him. Not a word."

"If you ask my opinion," said Alan, "we are about to bear witness to extraordinary things devolving from that man. You mark my words. I can already feel a heightening of our consciousness."

The others solemnly agreed that their collective consciousness was at a much higher pitch since Constantine arrived. And they also agreed that great things were imminent. And for all that they felt, as Alan did, that Constantine belonged to all of them, no one objected when Cathy crawled into bed next to him. They understood.

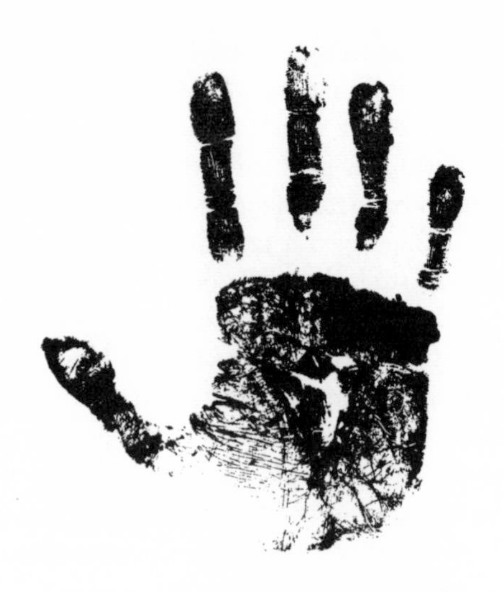

CHAPTER 13

The Bishop had just spoken on the phone with one of his contacts in the General Assembly in Hartford, and he was elated.

"What did I tell you, Michael? Did I or did I not predict that they would be afraid to come out against God twice in the same session?"

"What happened?" Michael asked.

"He says he can virtually guarantee that the tax bill will not get out of committee. It's dead!"

"Congratulations. You've done it again, haven't you?"

"I *told* you. Didn't I tell you? Well, admit it, didn't I?"

"Did I contradict you?"

"No, but I detected skepticism, I detected something less than one thousand percent faith in my reading of the low political mentality that prevails in Hartford. This calls for a celebration. Cancel all my appointments. I'm going to take you to lunch in a little place I know in Groton where they serve the most exquisite stuffed flounder."

"I don't like flounder," Michael objected.

"Nonsense. You'll love this flounder. I promise you. Let's take the Corvette. And I think we had better wear civilian clothes. I'm supposed to be having lunch with the mayor. It wouldn't do to break a date with the mayor and then be discovered eating somewhere else. Twelve o'clock sharp."

"I really don't like flounder," Michael insisted unhappily.

"It's first-rate. You'll see."

For the next hour the bishop composed replies to his mail into the Dictaphone machine, and studied the auditors' reports on a badly managed parish near Ledyard. At eleven forty-five he changed into a pair of pearl-gray double-knit slacks, a dark-blue turtleneck sweater and sunglasses. At twelve o'clock, punctually, the horn of his white Corvette (a birthday present from his mother) sounded in the driveway. The Bishop smiled. Michael was almost inhumanly efficient. *It's what we need,* he said to himself. *Lots more like Michael.*

Half an hour later they were in Groton, shoulder to shoulder at a crowded bar in a tavern called Hoagy's, filled with beer-drinking construction workers in hard hats from the shipyard across the street. Although Michael had long experience of the Bishop's unconventional tastes and habits, he was not prepared for Hoagy's.

"Don't you think we're rather out of place?" he muttered.

"Isn't it great?" the Bishop exclaimed. "Two martinis, please."

"These men are looking at us."

"Extra dry. Straight up. With Beefeaters gin."

"I'll just have a beer." Michael sighed.

"Don't be silly. They make excellent martinis here. I feel in a mood to celebrate and we can't celebrate with beer. You know, it's amazing to me how—how *clerical* you continue to look even in mufti. I fancy even in a bathing suit you would manage to look like a priest."

"I feel very ill at ease without my collar. And frankly I find all this disguising and slumming of yours undignified. Furthermore, it's childish and absurd."

"It's fun," the Bishop replied. "Don't spoil my fun."

"You look like a middle-aged Lothario," Michael observed sourly.

The Bishop laughed. "Lothario! What a word. Now here we are—don't they look lovely? Nothing like a clear cold glass of sparkling gin on a clear cold sparkling wintry morning when I have just won a smashing political victory! Cheers, Michael. Cheers!"

He took a large swallow, blinked, smiled and relaxed against the bar, nodding at the drink with benign approval.

"There's something adventurous about it, you know," he said a moment later, "about changing one's identity, penetrating alien spheres of activity. It's good for you. It's a kind of therapy. It's so easy to stagnate in a job like ours. So easy to lose touch with the outside world. For instance—when was the last time you were in a place like this?"

"I have never been in a place like this."

"There you are. My point exactly. How can you hope to administer to your constituents if you don't know who they are, how they live, what they think, what their concerns are? You have to get out and mingle with them. I love it. As an occasional change of pace. It smacks to me, being incognito like this, of the high old romance of, for example, *Henry Fifth,* that scene the night before the battle of Agincourt. You know that wonderful scene where the king is disguised, out talking to the troops, and they're all complaining about having to die for the crown, and he gives that marvelous line, 'Why, thou owest God a death.' "

"That's *Henry the Fourth.* Part One. Hal says it to Falstaff."

"Are you sure? Are you positive, Michael? I would swear it was *Henry the Fifth.* I would absolutely bet my life on it."

"Then you would lose your life. It's *Henry the Fourth.*"

"Oh, well." The Bishop shrugged. "It all amounts to the same thing. The bit of romance, the bit of intrigue."

"To me it sounds like charlatanism."

"Granted. But what with one thing and another, I imagine there's no avoiding a pinch of charlatanism now and then in our profession. There's an historical tradition that shapes us. The miracle—the magic—the witch doctor performing his voodoo. It's always been—well, you use the word charlatanism. I prefer to think of it as theatricalism. We were the first thespians. You know, the inextricable connection between art and religion. The festival of Dionysus. The temple qua theater. Et al. It's a source of power, strength. Theatrics wedded to economics—a prescription for the revival of the Church in the twenty-first century. Let's drink to that, Michael. To the New Reformation."

"I have serious doubts there'll be a twenty-first century," Michael said, sipping his martini.

"Nonsense. Look at those submarines across the street. The nuclear fleet. Mankind's last best hope of ensuring the integrity of the coming century. The most failproof guarantee ever devised by the mind of man against global self-destruction. It's true. People don't realize it yet, but mankind has once and for all ensured the survival of the species on this planet—and it's those incredible submarines that we can thank. It's thrilling. Why are you looking at me that way? I'm deadly serious. It's one reason I like to come here. I drink to Hyman Rickover. I have very little doubt that a hundred or two hundred years from now Rickover will figure in the pages of world history as one of the three or four preeminent men of the century. Along with Chairman Mao, Pope John, et al. God bless you, Hyman Rickover, wherever you are. And so once again the pattern will be shown to have prevailed wherein a genius of the Jewish persuasion has been instrumental in making the Gentile world safe for the untrammeled pursuit of anti-Semitism." He emptied his glass, looked at the disapproving expression on his assistant's face, laughed out loud and ordered two more cocktails.

"I haven't finished this one," Michael protested.

"Then hurry up. You can't waste it. Economy begins at home. These martinis are coming out of a diocesan emergency fund. We must hold ourselves accountable for every cent. Self-discipline, Michael. Rigid, undeviating self-discipline is the key to success."

"One might include in that category self-denial. Some vagrant notion that I hope hasn't passed completely out of your advanced consciousness."

"What are you talking about?"

"I'm talking about that corner of the Church's mentality that in its old-fashioned way insists on viewing self-indulgence as a sin."

"Oh, sin. I don't know anything about sin. Sin is quite outside my range of competence. There is only efficiency and inefficiency. That's all. And I must say I take exception to your implying that I'm self-indulgent. How many hours sleep have you averaged this week?"

"What's that got to do with anything?"

"Come on, come on. Tell me."

"Six, seven. I don't know. Seven, maybe eight."

"I have averaged four. You don't get to my place in life by being self-indulgent."

"No, I suppose you're right," Michael said with a private smile, adding, "It also doesn't hurt to have a rich, doting mother behind you working tirelessly for your advancement." The Bishop was extremely touchy about the money in his background; Michael knew it and liked to provoke the predictable overreactions to the subject whenever the Bishop began to get pompous.

"My mother," the Bishop snapped as Michael gave him an innocent look, blinking myopically behind his thick glasses, "was precious little help in getting me through the seminary in three years, and she was not there at Indiana stroking my fevered brow as I was compiling the best academic record in the history of the business school, and she was not there when I—" He broke off, recognizing the expression in Michael's eyes, realized he was being baited, was angry for a moment, glared at his assistant, and when Michael finally broke and laughed, turned his face away and growled, "Oh, go to hell. Go to bloody hell!"

He drank his second martini more slowly. The crowd at the bar thinned out. After a while the Bishop returned to the subject of submarines. Hoagy's stood in the middle of the shipbuilding neighborhood and everyone who patronized the place was involved in one way or another with underwater boats. So the tavern was filled with memorabilia of a generation of submarines. On the back bar, on the old wooden and glass cabinet doors, above the shelf of jars containing salted almonds, beer nuts and pickled pigs' hocks, were dozens of photographs of submarines—being launched, christened, submerging, emerging—submarines on which Hoagy's patrons had over the years worked or served. Another panel of the back bar was decorated with cigarette lighters, close to a hundred of them, mounted with ornamental crests, tiny figures of plastic heraldry, representing what appeared to be every ship in the underwater fleet. On the wall opposite the window that looked out on the shipyard were wooden plaques memorializing the SS *Bergall*, the *Norwhal*, the *Thresher*, the *Dace*.

"It's the most compelling sight in the world for me," the Bishop said, "watching one of them moving down the Thames, putting out to sea. Awesome. There's an anthropomorphic quality about a nuclear sub. It looks so much like a whale or a shark, but it's man-made. I was reading somewhere some science fiction writer who was seriously suggesting that our machines may be an evolutionary step. You know, he was saying that eventually machines will begin to think for themselves. That maybe they amount to a survival-of-the-fittest sort of adaptation against the pollution of the atmosphere and the oceans. That somehow man is in the process of preserving his brain in these indestructible machines. Don't you find that exciting?"

He was animated, his eyes seemed to flash, he spoke quickly with a frenetic quality. Michael knew it wasn't the gin. Not all of it. The Bishop had a capacity for unusual degrees of self-excitation; at times the play of his mind, his imagination, the scope of his interests and the novel angle of his views and conclusions seemed to intoxicate him. There was at such moments, at this moment, something narcissistic in the Bishop's fascination with the attractiveness of his own voice, his own ideas. He had, Michael figured, with just about total success channeled what must have once been an enormous sexual energy into other areas, achieving an uncommon integration of his emotional and intellectual potentialities. Yes, sexual was the word to describe his frantic yet single-minded pursuit of an idea, or a project, or a goal. Michael—sexless, save for an infrequent masturbatory fantasy—viewed himself as the ideal complement to the Bishop in terms of the coloring of his temperament, personality and intellect. Ten years younger, he nevertheless saw himself as indispensable in the checks and balances he imposed on the Bishop's flights of emotionalism and vanity—excesses, these, in each instance, and inherently dangerous and destructive—indispensable to his present success and future advancement. In addition to which (though he considered the two of them, in spite of the difference in their ages, exceptional friends, and his loyalty absolute), he thought himself the superior mind and talent of the two.

"It's a catalyst for philosophy," the Bishop was saying, referring to the neighborhood, the submarines, the necessity for the clergy to come out from their cloisters periodically to sample what he called the "real world." "You can't contemplate a submarine and its metaphysical implications in these terms without having your mind stretch. It's extremely healthy. You begin to see life from a different perspective. As a churchman, you begin to realize the absurdity of debates about contraceptives or the length of the hemline of a nun's skirt. The trouble with theology is that it bears so little relationship to philosophy. It's not concerned with how people live, how they should live, how they can live. It's only concerned with itself. I'm always referring to what in former times we called 'the flock' as 'my constituents.' It annoys people. But that's what they are. We can't presume to do anything for anybody distinct from what the Red Cross or the Blue Cross or the Salvation Army or the Welfare Department does for them *unless* we take off our cassocks and stoles and get out and mingle with them in places like this. It's incredibly valuable, instructional. That's the problem: Instruction.

"My God, do you realize what intellectual eunuchs the seminaries continue to produce even today, in this day and age? Closet queens, drag queens, intellectual and spiritual transvestites. The clergy is a zoo, Michael, let's face it. A freak show. That's why I'm in favor of a married clergy. Maybe if they had normal sexual relationships with women—more or less periodical ejaculations—they would be better equipped to confront the unsettling facts of life in the twentieth century. If the truth were to be known, I for one would like to call a moratorium for ten years on the teaching of theology in the seminaries. Just do away with it. Give ourselves a rest. Free the children's minds. Let them open their eyes. There's no question in my mind that the single most potentially self-destructive preoccupation of the Church is theology. We will have two orders of the stuffed flounder, please, served in the dining room. Thank you, we'll take our drinks in there."

"I don't like flounder," Michael objected once more. "I'll have the sirloin."

"Nonsense. You will have the flounder. And thank me later. It will be memorable."

The dining room contained eight or ten tables with mismatched tablecloths. It was decorated with fish nets and lobster traps hanging from the ceiling and an artificial fireplace in one wall with plastic logs and cellophane flames. There were photographs of Hoagy's son in a midshipman's uniform. A painting of John F. Kennedy, with his son at the funeral superimposed in the foreground, saluting. Through the steamy windows they could see one of the great hangarlike bays of the shipyard where the conical orange snout of a submarine was taking shape beneath the welders' torches.

"I've always been crazy about the sea," the Bishop said as they waited for their meal. "Oddly enough, I've never owned a boat. All my life it was a toss-up between wanting a boat and loving fast cars. The fast cars won out. Mother, bless her, put her foot down on my having both. One or the other, she said. I went for the cars. There's a certain sex appeal, don't you think, to dashing through the diocese in a Stingray. The kids identify with me. I seem like a swinger to them. It's a positive public relations image. But a boat! No, something still too decadent, too bloated about a churchman on a yacht. Too aristocratic.

"But I've always loved the sea. To the detriment of my career, in fact. Yes, it's true. I think I would have risen even faster had I accepted an assignment in the middle of the country somewhere. But I always had my eye on this diocese. I wanted to be the bishop here because it's close to the sea. You know, the one benediction I really enjoy giving each year—the one that comes from the heart, when I don't feel like a fool or a hypocrite—is when I bless the fishing fleet in July. Ah, here's our flounder at last."

A pretty girl in a sweat shirt and blue jeans served them; the Bishop joked and flirted with her easily, making her blush. When they were alone again, Michael said, regarding the fish on his plate without enthusiasm:

"You are quite the ladies' man."

"I could be," the Bishop agreed evenly. "I'm very sensitive to female sexuality, very responsive to it. I would have been a huge success in the Renaissance—in the court of Alexander Sixth, for instance. I'm a Borgia at heart—Roderigo Borgia sans murder, rape, violence and incest. I would have been very happy in that environment—aside from being surrounded by all those Italians, of course. This flounder is rather a disappointment," he said, laying down his knife and fork. "It's been overcooked. Damn it!"

"I think it's superb," Michael said vindictively. "You were right. It's memorable."

"Oh, what do you know about food? You couldn't tell a baked flounder from an overshoe. Damn it! I feel like sending it back."

"We're in Hoagy's in Groton. We're not at The Four Seasons. Don't make a scene. A fish is a fish."

The Bishop looked petulant; he sat back in his chair, pushed his plate away from him, drummed his fingers. "But it was so *good* last time."

"Derive a moral from it."

"Will you please stop chomping on the damned thing!"

"I'm hungry. It's good. I didn't know I liked flounder. I'm indebted to you."

"A cow eating hay has more discrimination." He signaled to the waitress and Michael braced himself. But the Bishop merely ordered another drink, and after a while his humor was restored. "I'll have lobster tonight. It will taste so much the better by contrast with this insipid piece of carp. That's what it is, you know. It isn't flounder at all. It's an evil-smelling slab of planked carp!"

"That's it," Michael said with his mouth full. "That's the way. Be philosophical."

Late that evening the Bishop sat at the small writing desk in his bedroom dressed in silk pajamas, composing a letter to the *Hartford Times* dealing with the furor which had developed in response to an editorial urging abortion reform in the state. There was a knock on the door, and Michael, still fully clothed, entered.

"I'm glad you haven't gone to bed," the Bishop said, not waiting to hear why his assistant had come. "I'm trying to formulate a position on this abortion issue that's in keeping with my progressive image without at the same time infuriating all the conservatives. It's tough to try and waffle on this one. How the hell does anyone get pregnant in this day and age unless she wants to? I wonder how the abortion statistics break down in terms of religion. I bet there's a majority of Catholics. Who don't use the pill. Damn it! Maybe I just shouldn't say anything at all. The President gets away with it. Why not me?"

"We have a stigmatic in the diocese," Michael said.

The Bishop laid down his pen and turned to look at his friend. "Is that a fact," he said after a moment in a quiet voice. Michael was looking at his shoes, as though it were his fault. There was a silence. Then the Bishop said, "A stigmatic. You said a stigmatic."

Michael cleared his throat. "I'm afraid so. And—he works miracles."

They were silent again for a few moments; Michael sat down on the edge of a straight chair near the bed, his hands flat on his thighs. The Bishop frowned.

"Go on," he said.

"It's very peculiar," Michael resumed. "I heard some garbled rumors a couple of weeks ago, but I discounted them. Obviously. An incredible thing like that. Who could believe it? But. The rumors persisted. Then, a little while ago, I got a call from Boston, from the Cardinal's office, wanting to know what we knew about reports of a stigmatic in the New London–Groton area. I told him we didn't know anything, that it was news to us. The Cardinal is very agitated. What happened was, a woman claims that her daughter—" He broke off and lowered his face in embarrassment, shook his head then spread his hands in a kind of appeal to the Bishop, whose expression was inscrutable. "A girl, nine years old, has leukemia. Or rather *had* leukemia."

"Had?"

"She's at Mass General. There's been a total remission of the disease. A total remission. Which the doctors say is—well—miraculous."

"How does the stigmatic figure in?"

"The child told her mother that in the middle of the night, a week before, a man described as such-and-so appeared in her room and told her she would recover within seven days. He had a beard, was dressed in old clothes, and he was bleeding from the hands. Naturally the hospital denies that it would have been possible for such a person to get inside. Anyway, a week later the disease—well, as I said—a total remission. Of leukemia! The doctors had given up hope."

The Bishop sat silently for two minutes, thinking. Then he said with sudden bitterness, "The family is no doubt Italian."

Michael nodded. "Their name is Morini. The girl's name is Antonietta."

"What else? Is there anything else?"

"There's the possibility of a cult forming. The stigmatic seems to be attracting some kind of underground attention—hippies, drug types, unsavory characters."

"I'm sick," the Bishop said. "I'm sick to my stomach, Michael."

"Yes, I am too. If it's true, it's appalling."

"What's his name? Who is he?"

"Don't know. The girl knows more, apparently. She says they talked for a long time. But evidently the people from the Cardinal's office who questioned her were less than diplomatic. They frightened her and now she won't say anything else."

The Bishop leaned his chin on his fist. His eyes were almost closed. The boyish cast was gone from his face. He looked old.

"Medievalism," he murmured finally, shaking his head in weariness and disgust. "God, is there no getting rid of it?"

"The Cardinal wants something done."

"Of course the cowardly silly ass wants something done!" the Bishop erupted. "Dumping a stigmatic in my lap! Doesn't have the guts to deal with it himself!"

"Well, he says it's in our diocese."

"We're going to get him out of our diocese. Posthaste. I promise you that. I will not have my diocese thrown into a reactionary uproar by some grotesque—" He was so angry he stammered. "Do you realize what this would mean? The boost it would give to every antediluvian theologian who . . . what an impediment it would be to everything progressive we've tried to do? A miracle worker yet! That's all I need! They'll have him on Dick Cavett! No, Michael. No, no, no!" He pounded the desk.

"It'll just be our luck that he's genuine too."

"Oh, I haven't the slightest doubt. It would be too easy if he were fraudulent. Michael, keep this quiet. I don't want anyone to know about it. Go to Boston, talk to the child. We have to locate this man and then deal with him."

"How? I mean, there's no law against being a stigmatic. What can we do to him?"

"Murder him if necessary. I mean it. I think I'd be prepared to murder him. God, doesn't it drive you mad? You work and work and work—and just when things appear to be taking shape, just when you begin to see daylight, some son of a bitch develops the stigmata and begins performing miracles on your doorstep! I don't know what we'll do with him. Put him in a monastery. Send him to Rome and let *them* deal with him."

"He may not even be a Catholic."

"Lord! What if he's a Jew? Michael, please. Get to work on this. Don't do anything else. Find him. First we have to find him. Then we'll figure out something. And for God's sake keep it quiet. What do you know about stigmatism?"

"Nothing."

"There must be books on the subject."

"There was that Capuchin in Italy, Padre Pio. And Theresa Neumann in Germany . . ."

"What a mess!"

"You're going to be watched very closely on this one."

"Don't I know it. Well, read up on the subject."

"Pio was supposed to be able to bilocate, or levitate, or something. And I think Francis of Assisi was a stigmatic."

"God, it's all so—so *sordid.* I feel as though a very dirty trick has been played on us."

"Maybe it's all an exaggeration," Michael suggested, but without much conviction. "It's nothing but rumor and conjecture so far."

"The remission of leukemia is no conjecture."

"True. Well, I'll drive up to Boston first thing in the morning."

"Be discreet," the Bishop warned. "Be very discreet. Once the media get hold of this, we're dead."

"In other words, for once we'd rather not be front page."

"God forbid!"

When Michael was gone, the Bishop tried to comfort himself with the reflection that he was blessed in having a man like Michael at his disposal to deploy against the enemy. Michael's cold analytical intelligence was the ideal antidote to the subterranean passions and superstitious hysteria no doubt bubbling at the source of this obnoxious phenomenon. If anyone could smother the thing before it got out of hand, Michael could.

Nevertheless, it was small comfort. The Bishop couldn't work—the abortion issue seemed inane now and irrelevant. He couldn't think clearly. After moving restlessly through the house for about an hour, drinking cognac, brooding, he went to bed. But he couldn't sleep. He lay in the dark listening to the wind that had risen, contemplating all the bizarre possibilities posed by the existence of a stigmatic residing within the boundaries of his ecclesiastical jurisdiction. Somewhere out there the stigmatic was lying in bed too—or traversing the Atlantic seaboard, bilocating, working miracles—maybe thinking about the Bishop.

"It's intolerable," he groaned into his pillow. "This awful, awful medievalism . . ."

When he finally did fall asleep, he slept badly, dreamed atrocious things. It was, on the whole—as he was to confess much later—the gravest challenge of his entire career.

CHAPTER 14

He wasn't certain how it happened. For that matter he wasn't certain what had happened. The girl, of course, had been cured. They had shown him the accounts and her picture in the papers.

But while he did not question the accounts, studying the picture he could not swear that it was the same child he had the vague impression he'd seen that night. There was nothing really distinctive in her features. A fat round little Italian face.

On the other hand, there were the stupefying details of her story: her description of him appearing in her hospital room with his bleeding palms exposed. But, impressive as that was, a rational explanation was possible. One of the members of the commune used to baby-sit for the Morini child, had visited her in the hospital, had told her about Constantine. So a form of autosuggestion might be at the root of it somehow—the child seeing what she wanted and expected to see.

Except that she had been cured. A total remission of leukemia. The medical authorities professed to be astounded. And that was almost the least of it. There were, after all, precedents for the remission of leukemia. It did sometimes occur. The papers talked about a case in Arizona in which a leukemic child contracted measles and shortly thereafter was cured of the blood condition. These things happened and nobody knew why. Fair enough. Constantine was prepared to accept as natural—even though inexplicable—the Morini child's cure except for one thing: on the night in question, at the exact moment the girl claimed to have seen him in her room, they were all trying, in a strange ritual peyote ceremony, specifically to cure her.

Alan was responsible for the idea, which was inspired by stories a Jewish anthropologist told about her recent investigations into peyote rites among the Navahos. The girl—Joyce Weintraub—had lived on a Navaho reservation in New Mexico for six months doing research for a master's thesis. She maintained that she personally witnessed a number of "miraculous" cures stemming from peyote sessions which involved mystical conditions similar to those various members of the commune had achieved via different agencies.

Alan wanted to try to cure the Morini girl. Joyce was enthusiastic. "Why not?" she said. "It works. I've seen it done. The Navahos cured a blind woman one night at a peyote meeting. They literally restored her sight. I saw her before and after." The Navahos believed that peyote was a medicine of great potency. It was more than a medicine; it was a divinity, or a kind of tabernacle in which divinity reposed much the way the consecrated Host of the Catholics embodied the living Christ. "What do you think you're reading about in the Bible when you read the story of the loaves and fishes, or the turning of water into wine? Those weren't miracles. They weren't violations of the laws of nature. They confirmed the laws of nature. The only reason things like that don't happen very much today is that science has altered our conception of the universe. Nature hasn't changed. It's only that scientists have redefined it and sold most of us on their definitions. That's what it's all about, why we're here—all this amounts to a process of reeducating ourselves. Which involves learning how to forget everything we've been taught in school."

It would all be of a piece, Alan added, with the general tenor of the group's activities and investigations up until that time. "And with the doctor here we have an element in the equation of really incalculable potential. A psychic catalyst that can set off a tremendous chain reaction."

Constantine was skeptical, but he did not object. Since arriving in their midst he'd tried to remain ambiguous concerning his spiritual proclivities. The respect they accorded him bordered on reverence. He was vulnerable to their attentions, flattered, and he was grateful for the haven they'd offered him. Reluctant to jeopardize his unexpected and gratifying security, he thought it advisable to let them believe whatever they wished to believe about him; the truth was that every other alternative to that course was mortally dangerous. So he agreed to participate in the peyote ritual, although guardedly and equivocally.

Nine of them were present that night. They lighted a charcoal fire in an outdoor grill which they placed in the center of the room, clearing a space among the mattresses and the junk-store furniture and the orange crates and heaps of old newspapers. Joyce collected flowerpots filled with earth and canning jars of water and arranged them around the grill in a circle. They had among them over a hundred peyote buttons. All of them had gotten off on the drug many times previously. "We'll utilize the energy in the earth and the fire and the water," Joyce instructed them. "The peyote will help direct the energies to Toni Morini."

She seemed exceptionally beautiful to Constantine. She was wearing a long green full-sleeved dress patterned with bright splashes of red and yellow flowers. With her hair clipped back behind her ears, a necklace of wooden Indian beads around her throat and copper bracelets on her wrists, she resembled a fantastic gypsy sorceress. He couldn't stop looking at her. She seemed not quite human.

She placed several candles in wine bottles. The wax and the candle smoke were charged with latent power too. She brought out a buckskin drumhead and a pair of Indian rattles like maracas she'd been given by friends on the reservation. "Music is important. Drumming and the rattles. Constantly. The rhythms will dictate themselves to you. Let the instruments do what they want. They'll tell you. We'll chew the peyote until we get off, and pray. Concentrate on Toni Morini. Pray for her, however you know how to pray or feel like praying. See her face. Try to feel what she's feeling. Identify with her. Try to become Toni Morini." Constantine was not to ingest the peyote. It would be counterproductive in that he was already at the stage of consciousness which the others could only approach assisted by the drug. "Pray hard. If you feel like singing, sing. Singing is very important. When you feel you *have* to sing—when you begin to sing songs you never knew you knew—it's a sign that we're getting somewhere. And believe!"

Seated in a circle around the charcoal fire, they chewed the peyote buttons solemnly. They took turns drumming and playing the rattles. At first they played clumsily and self-consciously. In a few minutes, however, they established a definite and—to Constantine's unpracticed ear—sophisticated rhythm. Although some of them were musicians, none was very accomplished. Yet they played like professionals. He saw looks of surprise on some of their faces.

Alert and expectant, Constantine waited for something to happen. But for a long time, aside from the eerie subtleties of the playing, nothing did; his wounds felt unusually sensitive, but that was all. He tried to concentrate on the Morini child; he was unable to pray for her, but he tried to concentrate on helping her get well. He thought that if he failed to concentrate he might be responsible for the miscarriage of the experiment. Nevertheless, he couldn't concentrate, could not imagine the child. He could not create a single image in his mind, either of children or of hospitals. His brain was a deposit of dead ash. He felt guilty.

Well, he consoled himself, *it doesn't matter.* What did it matter? The drumming and the rattles were pleasant and interesting. Soothing somehow. He was warm and comfortable. He could sit there on the floor with his legs crossed and admire Joyce's profile, Joyce seated next to him, their thighs touching lightly. He fancied he could feel the warmth from her body; it was her body distracting him, preventing him from concentrating on the child. She was radiant, in her flowered gypsy dress almost regal, her eyes closed, her jaws moving slowly as she masticated the peyote button, her profile in the candlelight like the face of an Egyptian princess. Her copper bracelets glowed with a peculiar incandescence, as though they were sources of light rather than reflectors.

The drumming was mesmerizing. He felt drowsy. Cathy, in her jeans and sweat shirt, seated to his left, was murmuring something he could not make out. He smelled the flowery scent she was wearing, and the tension of expectancy was drawn out of him as though by a magnetic force. He went slack. He seemed to be ensconced in a sexual warmth emanating from Cathy as the drumming went on and on, and the rattles hissed like wet logs in a fire.

He tried to define what he felt for the girl. It was not love. Yet it was not unlike the emotion he had felt for his mother when he was a child, an emotion composed of gratitude, dependence, the need to create an identity by means of her admiration and approval. It was something like that but it was also intensely erotic, an emotion you could not call love in any conventional sense but in the absence of which you could not talk about love in any sense whatever, and which was rendered still more complex by a coexistent quality of affection that could only be described as fatherly.

It did not seem possible for him to experience so many diverse, even self-contradictory sentiments at the same time. It would have been baffling enough had he felt them all serially, as he had the first time they'd made love, when from moment to moment Cathy seemed like all the women he had known in his life. Now, however, all those disparate emotions had come together in an illogical, impossible compound.

Impossible, yes. Impossible to figure out. He was floating. He didn't want to think, could not think. He was passive, receptive, a sponge, a blotter. . . .

Then he became aware that one of the girls, Paula, had been crying for several minutes without his noticing. Soon someone began to speak, random quotations from the Bible. It was a powerfully built young man who had arrived from Texas that afternoon, with a voice that sounded to Constantine like organ music. "For it is written," he declaimed, "I will destroy the wisdom of the wise—if I must needs glory, I will glory of the things that concern my infirmities." A thrill went through Constantine; he shivered with pleasure. Another of the girls was singing; she was sitting on the other side of the fire, swaying back and forth, clasping her knees, singing something incomprehensible in a pure, lovely soprano.

Cathy uttered a long sigh; it was the way she sighed at times when they were making love, as he entered her.

Constantine found himself sighing too and smiling foolishly, nodding his head in time to the melody the girl was singing, the melody producing in him a voluptuous languor tinged with melancholy. Briefly he recalled the child, the child who was the occasion of his sensuous torpor, who was lying in a hospital bed a few miles across town, dying. The image was not intrusive. After all, he thought abstractedly, dying could be sensuous too. Death could be voluptuous. Viewed in one admittedly rather perverse light, the death of a child could be construed as positively erotic.

Suddenly a bitter taste invaded his mouth. On the instant he was intensely thirsty. There was a jar of water near his foot. He tried to reach for it, only to discover that he could not raise his hand from his lap. The bitterness filled his mouth like an expanding volume of noxious gas. He was nauseated. His stomach muscles contracted in a series of spasms that flooded his abdomen with a pain that caused him to inhale and inhale again and prevented him from exhaling as the gas was compressed down into his lungs, scorching them, and he thought with amazement and certainty, *I'm having labor pains!* He closed his eyes and clenched his teeth, expecting momentarily to vomit. But the spasms subsided and he could breathe again, although the bitterness remained on his tongue, and opening his eyes, he looked around.

The room was luminous. It was like a photographic negative of the room in which everything lighted by the candles was black and all the darkness glowed with a refulgence the color of silver nitrate. He looked at the quivering flames of the candles and saw circles of darkness. The faces of the people behind the candles were black empty jagged holes, as though their features had been eaten away by acid.

The drumming and singing had ceased. He heard in its stead a sound like a great wind blowing through the room, a tremendous storm, howling, and though he could not feel the wind and the flames did not flutter, his extremities were freezing. The wind mounted in rhythmic waves which set up reverberations inside him. He vibrated like a drumskin. It was as though a great angry bird were locked within him, beating its wings.

His head was like a huge stone weighing hundreds of pounds, pressing down crushingly on his spine. He wanted to turn to look at Joyce, with a confused impulse to ask for help, thinking that somehow she could alleviate the horrible pressure on his vertebrae before his spinal column was pulverized, but his head was too heavy to turn except by fractions of an inch at a time; he had the impression that it took an hour to accomplish the maneuver, an hour of torturous unrelieved effort and concentration which left him exhausted. When, finally, he was facing her he saw that her ears had grown to points and were covered with black hair like a wolf's. She was still Joyce, beautiful, a gypsy queen, but her ears were enormous, rising on either side of her skull like horns. The red and yellow flowers were sprouting from her dress, which had turned to grass. He wanted to tell her, he felt that she was unaware of what was happening to her, but when he tried to speak he couldn't move his tongue. His mouth was petrified.

And then he was looking at Cathy behind him and to his left, looking at her without turning his head—he lacked the strength to make another revolution of his head—and he had the illusion that he was seeing the girl through the back of his own skull, and saw that she was taking on the aspect of a frog, or if not precisely a frog at least something definitely amphibian. Her mouth was elongated, her forehead flattened out and corrugated. Where her ears should have been two gills were pulsing. Her eyes waved about on antennalike stalks, the eyeballs like jellied marbles. She was bright blue. And near her was another amphibian, one of the girls, the soprano, Jennifer, iridescent, making anguished croaking noises.

Constantine felt impelled to speak, to admonish them. He cleared his throat and the sound inside his head was like a peal of thunder rolling up and down a desert canyon. It deafened him. He thought his eardrums would burst. Nevertheless, he tried again and again to shape words with his frozen mouth, and at length he thought he was speaking, he knew he was speaking because he could see the words issuing from between his lips in immiscible particles, floating up in front of his eyes, multicolored, like shreds of weightless vomit, floating around the room like nodules of oil in water, some soft and pulpy, others sharp-edged and glittering, some slimy, some mossy, some covered with greenish scales.

The floor began to decompose around him. It seemed to evaporate floorboard by floorboard until he was balancing over a black void on a single narrow plank which was very elastic and rode up and down with a motion like a raft on a choppy lake.

Then, to his immense relief, the floor materialized again, and he could turn his head freely. Joyce was Joyce again completely, and Cathy had black hair and human features, and Constantine sighed, thinking it was all back to normal. A moment later, however, he happened to direct his gaze across the room at a woman seated with her back against the wall, her face illuminated by the darkness shed by the candle in her hands, whom he knew he had never seen before in his life even as he told himself that she was disturbingly familiar. It was her dress, he decided, a blue dress with a starched white pilgrim collar. Suddenly he remembered where he had seen the dress: it was Betsy's dress, a birthday present from him on her tenth birthday, the exact dress, but the woman, his daughter, was older than he, very large-breasted, and now he could see, yes, it was indeed Betsy, only Betsy thirty years into the future. She was sobbing violently, convulsed with grief, and he thought that her tears explained the bitter taste in his mouth: he had been tasting his daughter's grief, the bitterness of her sorrow, just as the hammering in his breast he knew now was not a giant bird but the throbbing of his daughter's anguished heart. She was weeping for him. He was certain. His own anguish was insupportable. He attempted to call out to her, to call her name, but his tongue was forked now like a reptile's, and he could only hiss at her before she vanished into the pool of darkness created by the candle she was holding, flowing into it like a stream of water into a drain.

And then it came to him. He had a moment of transcendent percipience that seemed to scald his brain, and he understood that although he had not touched the peyote buttons he was experiencing the full collective impact of all the peyote the others had been chewing for several hours. And with this realization he slipped off.

He did not know what followed after that. There was a transition he could not account for, a period devoid of sensation. Simply cold space. Immediately after which he saw whatever he saw; according to the Morini girl he appeared in her room. Later, he recalled a feeling of euphoria so concentrated that he thought confusedly he'd been making love to Cathy. It was like going off a high bridge, striking the water after a protracted rapturous fall, what he'd always imagined that would be like, exploding against the iron water, the derangement of all his senses at the frozen instant between the explosion and the delayed surge of pain.

And there was a child in a bed. It could have been Betsy. He had seen Betsy earlier. It could have been she. He would not have been prepared to say that it wasn't.

But at that instant, the others felt it. Everything stopped. He had to depend on their reconstructions of the moment, and each of them felt something different, and some of the most graphic testimony came after the fact, days later, when the miracle had been authenticated, but they all agreed that they could feel it. The drumming stopped. Everyone at the same instant looked at Constantine. He seemed to be in a trance. His eyes were open but he saw nothing. One said he'd stopped breathing. Joyce said he was cold as ice and had no pulse. They all later claimed to remember that the temperature in the room dropped several degrees in a matter of seconds. He was rigid; his spine was arched. He made gurgling sounds in the back of his throat. Then his eyeballs rolled up into his skull, he gave a deep groan, shuddered, and collapsed in a swoon.

All this took place within ten minutes of the beginning of the ceremony. None of the others had time to get high on the peyote.

When a week later they learned that the Morini girl had been cured, Constantine was frightened and mystified. It had been all so indefinite and ambiguous. His instinct was to deny he'd played any part in the child's recovery. He felt threatened.

The others, however, were convinced. There was no question. It was a classic case of bilocation. They argued with him; they badgered him. They would not let him deny it. He had been in two places at one time. He had cured the girl. It was more sensational than anything Joyce had seen on the reservation. They had nothing to do with it; the peyote had nothing to do with it; he'd done it alone.

Eventually Constantine's resistance weakened. As time established a distance between him and the event, his memory began to accommodate itself to their version of what took place that night. He "remembered" details that were previously obscure. The color of the girl's pajamas. The arrangement of the furniture in her room. A vase of flowers on a nightstand. Phrases he had uttered.

Soon all uncertainty vanished, the ambiguities were resolved. Yes, they were right—he had been there. He'd performed the thing. He was exclusively responsible. It was he, not God, he insisted. It was irrelevant to speak of God in this connection. His atheism did not waver. He had done it himself. He was not interested how this had been accomplished. It was sufficient for him to know that he had accomplished it. Furthermore, in the weeks following, he duplicated the feat over and over again, spontaneously, without the stimulus of a peyote ceremony.

He tried to explain to them what it was like, but it was very difficult; the language was not designed to encompass mysteries of such magnitude. All the same, he tried. It seemed important to fix this fresh phenomenon with words.

It was, he said, almost more of an emotion than a sensation—an emotion of weightlessness, as though he existed in outer space, free of gravity, or at the bottom of a pressureless sea, moving in slow motion, spiraling along the curve of a Möbius strip of space-time in an environment resembling both air and water but distinct from either; a kind of optical illusion, only of all the senses—Constantine as though in a precognitive state of protoconsciousness, a sensory mechanism not knowing what sensory was, not knowing what knowing was, himself unformulated: a condition characterized by a dreamy, queerly pleasurable derangement of sense and elements, as though air were a fluid and water could be respired. It was not a dream, nor a coma, nor a trance, though it combined ingredients of all three. It was less than sleep, but less than wakefulness too. His body *ceased* for what seemed to be long periods of something similar to (though ultimately different from) Time; it was as if for a space of an interval of a medium which you might denominate Time if you could delete from the word every nuance of the concept of chronology, he existed as a distillate of himself, or as a gas. He was plasma and serum, fully aware of the disparate natures simultaneously expressing themselves in him, but never losing sight of his larger identity as blood, a different entity altogether.

When he was like that, he had what he called, for lack of a more precise term, visions—although they involved nothing optical, unless you were able to conceive of optics as a transliteration of taste and smell. They were like formalized intuitions during which (or as a result of which—it was so indefinite) intercourse transpired between essences of himself and people he knew he did not know but with whom he shared a strange and tangible intimacy, as though they were characters from books he had read as a child and forgotten; who appeared to him out of context, or at best in extremely attenuated contexts, posed for example against the background of a detail of weather, a stormy night on a palisade overlooking the Pacific, or some fragment of an interior like a glimpse of a billowing curtain, or a polished brass doorknob in a bedroom, or a floral pattern in a hotel somewhere. Pretty children (he had a "feeling" they were pretty and blond, or female and slight) and old men and women who "gave off a kind of odor, something antiseptic, like the ward of a clinic" ("I had the sense one old lady was in her seventies, I had the sense that she was suspended over a gorge or a waterfall, in the middle of the night, in a nightgown like a yellow fog, like reflected moonlight"), whom he did not so much converse with as seem to contemplate, again the way one contemplates a character in a novel or a play: a character who cannot converse with you, is not aware of your scrutiny, and yet between whom and you something passes back and forth, a sympathy is exchanged, in the process of which you become a vital part of the character at the same time he becomes an equally vital part of yourself—an exchange like a transposition of psychic energy, the perfusion of the character with some psychoelectric cadences of himself.

Although he was always very confused about the parameters of these psychic transports—he could not detail names, or dates, or seasons, or places: they invariably remained just beyond the farthest reaches of his overextended powers of concentration—he became convinced that during them he applied himself to sick children and made them well, to crippled old ladies, restoring the use of their limbs; he was convinced that through his intercession the blind could see and the mute could speak. "It's as if I *adsorb* the illness. They seem to pass through me somehow, exactly as if I were resin in a column chromatography experiment adsorbing their afflictions."

There was no regular pattern to his transports. One day it would happen around noon and last for five or six hours; another day he would "leave" in the evening and not "come back" until early in the morning. Some days nothing happened. Other days he would go off without his friends realizing he was gone. According to Cathy, he would be sitting erect in a chair, his eyes open, lucid, carrying on a conversation for the entire period during which—as well as he could testify—he was engaging in woolsy forms of extraspatial intercourse with phantom essences in another dimension.

He would "return" from these psychic excursions fatigued, heavy with the impression of great distances having been traversed, infinities of time and space having been circumnavigated.

Other incidents of spontaneous remission of serious disease were reported. They brought him the papers. He read the accounts with fascination and a cold mounting pride.

> For the fifth time in the past two weeks, the scientific community finds itself powerless to explain an apparently spontaneous remission of an "incurable" illness involving the intercession of a reported stigmatic. Authorities at City Hospital in East Providence disclosed yesterday that Catherine Petrocelli, aged 9, of 1419 Kenmore Ave., paralyzed from the waist down for 13 months as the result of an automobile accident, has regained full control of her motor resources—in other words, Cathy Petrocelli can walk again although doctors had determined that she would be crippled for life.
>
> Mr. and Mrs. Rocco Petrocelli, the child's parents, although beside themselves with joy and delight, were reluctant to discuss the matter with reporters on advice from their parish priest, Monsignor George Pocobello of Holy Name Church. Nevertheless, they did confirm the account of Mrs. Ruby Peluso, head nurse in the Pediatric section of City Hospital, where the child had been undergoing tests for a kidney infection, that little Catherine attributed her cure to a "vision" in which a bearded man displaying the stigmata of Christ—open bleeding wounds reminiscent of the nail wounds purportedly inflicted on Christ's body at the Crucifixion—"appeared" before her one night and told her to have faith, promising that within 48 hours she would walk again.
>
> It was the fifth time in recent weeks that the stigmatic has been cited in connection with a so-called spontaneous remission of a medical condition deemed incurable. In each case—one in Boston, two in Hartford and one in Framingham in addition to the Petrocelli girl—the patients have been children between the ages of seven and eleven, female, Roman Catholics, and of Italian descent.

Dr. Meyer H. Goldberg, chief of staff at City Hospital, discounted the idea of any miracle. "With all due respect to the religious sensibilities of the parties involved," he added. He went on to say that, "There are almost an infinite number of purely physiological variables operating in the functioning of the nervous system, any one of which might be the cause of Catherine Petrocelli's recovery. We may never know what happened."

Monsignor Pocobello released a statement cautioning against an "emotional overreaction" to the phenomenon. And a spokesman for the Office of Diocesan Affairs, speaking for the Bishop, declared that for the time being, "We are suspending judgment pending a full investigation. This is a very serious, very delicate matter, and an objective assessment of all the facts can only be jeopardized by a climate of emotionalism."

Nevertheless, for the moment emotionalism seems to be the order of the day in the predominantly Italian neighborhood. Throngs of motorists have been streaming down Kenmore Avenue for the past 36 hours, and the sidewalks and lawns in front of the Petrocellis' two-story red-brick bungalow have been packed from early morning to late at night with people hoping to catch a glimpse of the girl. All this is in spite of freezing temperatures, sleet and snow. Bark has been peeled from the leafless oak tree in the Petrocelli front yard, and a lilac bush has been all but uprooted by souvenir hunters.

And commerce has reared its head along the tree-lined street: a brisk business has been reported in scapulars and rosaries, and this morning a bookseller operating out of a blue Volkswagen bus sold 37 copies of a life of the stigmatic priest Padre Pio, an Italian, in less than an hour.

In an adjacent column was a related story about the other four children who had undergone unexplained cures. The Morini girl. A seven-year-old named Carmen Bozzuto in Framingham, who had been deaf since birth. An eight-year-old in Hartford, Anne Marie Carusello, with multiple sclerosis. And Lucille Damiani, age ten, also from Hartford, with rheumatic fever that vanished instantaneously one night, leaving no sign of aftereffects. All of them having been "visited" by the stigmatic.

There were discrepancies in the children's descriptions of their nocturnal visitor, but Constantine did not think they were significant. One had him "very old, like Grandpa, with a long gray beard." Another said, "He looked about as old as Daddy," who was thirty-four. The Morini child stressed his kindliness. But the Bozzuto girl had been vaguely alarmed by him, claiming to have seen "fiery sparks in his eyes." All the children were hospitalized at the time of the visitations. Each was under sedation. They all testified that his hands were bleeding.

Even though Constantine could not specifically recall these particular children, the likelihood of such a tremendous coincidence seemed so remote that he did not hesitate to take full credit for their cures. Terms like "psychosomatic" and "autosuggestion" were crowded from his vocabulary by the vanity and pride which grew in him like tumors.

During this period, which lasted approximately a month, Cathy lived in a fever of excitement. It was as though the prodigies attributed to Constantine amounted to a fulfillment of some wondrous prophecy in the realization of which she had proved indispensable.

"If I hadn't come to you, if I hadn't found you, you would have killed yourself," she said, fondling him, stroking his hair, looking at him worshipfully. "In a way I've given birth to you, a second birth. I've borne you and delivered you. I could never have a baby after this. It would be such an anticlimax. Even your baby. After this, even your baby would be nothing. I feel everything a mother feels. But more, more, more than any mother ever felt—more than the mother of Christ could have felt—because I'm your lover too. But it's strange: since you cured Toni Morini, I almost don't need sex anymore. Everything is sexual. I can get off just looking at you. It's like I'm living on the edge of a sexual knife blade day and night. It's like I've become part of your sexual nature, and when you go off like that I can feel the expenditure of your sexual nature vicariously—it is sexual for you, isn't it? Sex and religious ecstasy have always been inseparable; it's a documented fact. I have orgasm after orgasm, but somehow—I can't explain—I'm experiencing *your* orgasms."

The others expressed themselves in approximately the same terms. They were sexually exalted by Constantine's wonder-working. Before he arrived, their sexual relations with each other had been indiscriminate but too casual to be termed promiscuous. Sex was merely a necessary bodily function. But Constantine's ecstasies were a powerful erotic charge, stimulating them almost unbearably, producing in them erotic transports which spun themselves out to such extremes of emotion that they confused their feelings with the ecstasy they thought Constantine was achieving. Sex was beatific all at once, a revelation, they said. It made them feel godlike. The doctor had carried them along with him into a new spiritual dimension.

They could not imagine that they would very shortly become disillusioned and dissatisfied. When it happened, none of them, including Constantine, was prepared for the reaction.

CHAPTER 15

"WHAT'S WRONG, CATHY?"

"Nothing. Nothing's wrong. Why?"

"You look tired, tense," Marcia said. "You've been in a bad mood lately."

"I . . . I don't know. I'm sorry. I suppose it's all the excitement, the constant excitement. I feel all bloodshot." She smiled wryly at the figure of speech. Constantine had fallen into a trancelike sleep following another of his excursions, which he'd described at unusual length. The others were out; the girls were alone. "Yes, I'm just tired, I guess. I'm not sleeping very well."

"It's wonderful, isn't it?" said Marcia after a pause. "The doctor, I mean."

"Paul? Yes, wonderful," Cathy said absently. "You know, it occurred to me that by now my parents are probably looking for me. They've probably called the police."

"Do you miss them?"

Cathy thought about the question, frowning, and then shook her head. "No. This is my family now. No, I don't miss them really. But . . ." She left the idea uncompleted and sighed. "What an experience this has been. Amazing how I've changed."

"We've all changed."

"Totally! I've been away from the lab just a couple of weeks and yet it seems like . . . I don't think I could do a simple math problem anymore. And I used to be great in math. I feel like I couldn't add two and two."

"That's wonderful." Marcia smiled. They sat smoking a joint, not talking, Cathy reflecting on how many joints it required now for her to get off as opposed to the beginning, when only a few puffs were sufficient. Now she smoked almost constantly and never really got off. *Or maybe I'm permanently off,* she thought. It was hard to tell; everything was all mixed up. It was like making love to Paul. The first time he had merely to touch her and she came. Then it took longer, and she had to go away from him mentally for it to happen. Then she required external stimuli: watching the others make love, fantasizing that she was making love simultaneously with two, three, four of them at a time. Maybe, she thought hopefully, it paralleled the marijuana: maybe she was in a state of perpetual orgasm, which was why she didn't feel anything anymore when he was inside her. Which in turn might account for the comparative absence of emotion she felt listening to his accounts lately of his nebulous psychic adventures. Could that be? Could ecstasy, prolonged indefinitely, benumb you? What more could she ask for? He was a miracle worker. She had had visions, thrilling, remarkable states of mind and soul. And yet she could not help feeling that something was missing. She did want more; more of something.

Marcia, who had been watching her closely, stood up and began to undress. "I'm going to bed," she said, stripping off her sweater and her jeans. She'd lost weight, and though her figure was still very full, she was firm now, and looking at her Cathy was struck by how appealing her friend had become.

"You know, you really look great, Marcia. You must have lost about fifteen pounds."

Marcia curled up under the covers. "Damn cold in here," she said.

Cathy sat beside her on the floor, hugging her knees. "You ever think about your life before you came here?"

"I try not to. It was rotten."

"I think about it once in a while. College and all the stupid things I studied."

"Best to forget all that," Marcia said. "It just screws you all up."

"Yes, I know."

"Hey, you're shivering."

"It's freezing in here. I think I'll go to bed too."

"Leave the doctor alone, why don't you?" Marcia said. "He's all worn out. Come lie down with me; we can keep each other warm."

Cathy hesitated, then said, "All right. He is worn out."

Removing her clothes quickly, she slid under the covers next to her friend, wearing only her panties. Marcia moved up against her, slid one arm beneath Cathy's head and brought their faces together. "Nice and snuggly," she whispered. "Lots better."

"Do you want to smoke another joint?" Cathy asked nervously.

"Let's warm up first." Her hand was on Cathy's thigh and she began to massage the muscle lightly, and then touched her knee. Cathy drew her legs up and Marcia squeezed her foot experimentally, tickling her, and said into her ear, her breath warm and soft, her lips brushing her hair, "Your feet are like ice."

"Yes, I've always been cold. I think I have poor circulation or something." She would stay there a few minutes more, just to warm up, and then she would go and lie down with Paul. There was nothing wrong with lying in bed with a dear friend, even naked, there was nothing wrong with nakedness, their bodies all belonged to God and could not be considered in any way shameful. But she wished she knew what to do with her hands; wherever she placed them there was Marcia's leg or thigh or breast or stomach. "Hey, this is a one-way ticket," Marcia whispered, taking Cathy's hand and laying it on her own thigh, forcing Cathy to shift her position so that they were lying facing each other, and embracing. "I'm cold too," Marcia said. Cathy willed herself to move the flat of her hand up and down Marcia's heavy thigh; her flesh was incredibly soft and smooth. Marcia made a sound from deep in her throat, and twisted her hips. "That's really nice," she sighed.

Just a little more and then I'll go, Cathy was thinking, in spite of the pleasure of the warmth and contact, scarcely daring to admit the pleasure of Marcia's fingers, down inside the elastic of her panties, kneading and tickling her, as her lungs seemed to tighten and she felt wet and hot between her legs where Marcia's fingertips were so close and then brushing.

"You have such pretty firm little breasts," Marcia said. "I love to look at them." And before Cathy could prevent it, not really wanting to prevent it but apprehensive nevertheless, Marcia brought her lips to one of her breasts, working her head down under the covers, and ran her tongue over her nipple and then began sucking lightly at her breast, like a baby. Cathy stiffened, not wanting this at all, and yet excited and desiring not to offend Marcia, who was such a good friend, so loving and generous and full of self-sacrifice.

Girls sleeping with each other was no novelty. Marcia often had sex with Paula and Jennifer, although only Joyce Weintraub seemed to be exclusively homosexual. Cathy, however, had never done it with anyone but Constantine; she was faithful to him as a wife is faithful to a husband. She thought of them as married and could not imagine being unfaithful to him. What the others did, in whatever combinations, was not repellent to her —it wasn't ugly or offensive; if the girls wanted to have sex with each other, she was able to view it as a logical and defensible extension of the strong emotions which linked them. It was merely another form of the love that united them—the love of Christ, the love of each other, sexual and spiritual both being aspects of the comprehensive texture of their natures which collectively bore witness to the glory of God's creation. But she had never done it, and now she was frightened, in spite of everything, and the thought came to her as she was smothered in Marcia's sweet-smelling, sweet-tasting flesh: *But it's a sin!* However, Marcia was kissing her on the mouth then, her lips open, and Cathy opened her mouth, and when their tongues met it was like the first contact with Constantine, it was that thrilling, and she said to herself as she wrapped her arms around her friend, *There can't be sin where there's love,* and she thought some disjointed prayers, and tried to visualize the Virgin Mary, tried to concentrate on Mary and Jesus and the infant Christ, as Marcia slid her underpants deftly off her legs and licked the insides of her thighs, which were burning now, but the praying took hold and she grew more composed, and praying hard she began to respond to the girl's caresses and moved her hips, opening her thighs wide to accommodate her friend, and it was better after a while, easier then, and then it was much better, before it became unimaginable and could not ever be better or more loving.

Constantine was troubled by the alteration in the temper of the household. It was like fruit going bad, a perceptible transition from ripeness to decay. Cathy's behavior was a barometer of the change in attitude toward him which they were probably not fully conscious of but to which he was extraordinarily sensitive.

She stopped having sex with him. For a few days she was exclusively Marcia's lover, and then she slept with Jennifer, and then with Jennifer and Marcia together. When Marcia went to bed with Alan, Cathy was jealous, and the three of them quarreled. Soon everyone was quarreling. It was like a contagion.

Cathy began to look coarse and evil and debauched. Orgasm wasn't enough. She had to have better orgasms each time, ever more intense emotions, always ever higher plateaus of sensation, in which foredoomed quest she involved and corrupted all the others. And inasmuch as their original sexual transports had been stimulated by and confused with the psychic marvels he performed, as inevitably their excesses left them merely enervated, they turned on him irritably, as though it were all his fault.

He wondered what they expected of him, was distressed by their constantly escalating presumptions. Was it possible that so quickly he was losing his power to command their imaginations? Already it seemed that they were taking the sight of his stigmata for granted.

He was very apprehensive. He needed them. He felt that he derived much of the psychic strength on which his gifts replenished themselves from the group's devotion and admiration. But their devotion and admiration depended in turn equally on his performing ever more spectacular psychic feats. And where, he wondered, was the end of it? It was already insufficient for him to cure leukemia a second time. They would not be impressed by that. They were no longer impressed by his flights of bilocation. He would have to raise the dead to satisfy them. But then they would be bored again, and finally they would have to kill him to test whether he could raise himself from the dead.

Of course, he thought. *How could I not have seen that from the beginning, from the moment I came here?* Of course they would murder him. It was part of the logic of working miracles, of curing disease. You could not read the ultimate miracle in so limited a context as curing leukemia. He developed the formula. The end of all miracles was martyrdom. To be martyred was the highest plateau, the last plateau of psychic transfiguration, on which a man became the disease, all the disease, assumed the comprehensive burden of a society's afflictions, and then forced it to slaughter him so that his death would purge it and make it new. And you had to do it without flinching, you had to embrace that consummation gratefully, joyfully. You could not pray to be excused; you could not beg to have the cup pass away. You had to drain it eagerly. Only then could you approach divinity.

He knew he could not force the moment. There was a difference between suicide and martyrdom. But he was confident now that the time was coming. And when the time came, he would be ready. He began to prepare himself.

Advent came and then Christmas on the calendar, and passed unmarked by them in the boarded-up old house, in which they were scarcely conscious of whether it was night or day outside. It snowed the last week of December for several days consecutively, and the weather was warm. The first day of the New Year, the temperature dropped below zero.

Cathy got sick. It started with a simple head cold, but then a fever set in and she complained of a weight on her chest. In a few days she displayed all the symptoms of pneumonia. However, she resisted going to the hospital. Briefly her faith in Constantine's powers revived. "As long as you're here nothing will happen to me," she told him.

Her illness made him feel perverse. In her fever, her face burning, her eyes dull, all her features exaggerated, she seemed like someone else, as if she were performing a role. He was with her constantly. The others could not tell he was not trying to comfort or cure her; he secretly wanted to prolong her illness in hopes of contracting it himself.

But he did not, and when, after a week or so, she recovered, he felt a sense of loss.

She began to grow fat. Her breasts drooped. Her thighs went soft. Her waist thickened. She became careless about her appearance. She stopped bathing, her hair was dirty and oily, her breath rank. She rarely bothered to get dressed, usually wearing only a soiled slip, the straps dangling loose from her shoulders. She drank heavily and forsook marijuana for more powerful drugs.

And then Joyce Weintraub took them where they had to go, into the penultimate act. "Sadism, masochism—they're only labels the straights have attached. You can't have ecstasy without pain. Ecstasy *is* pain!"

Recalling the moment in his New London apartment when Cathy had exclaimed, "I want your pain . . . I want to *be* your pain," Constantine reflected mournfully that ironically Joyce was right. But there would be no ecstasy for them now, no apotheosis, as there would be for him. Only sordidness and squalor awaited them; they had long since surpassed the limits of their sensual natures.

They flogged each other. They attacked each other with crude sexual devices as they screamed out the name of Jesus in their pain. It was as if they were deliriously bent on stigmatizing themselves in hopes of thereby securing admission to the psychic realms until then reserved for Constantine. And failing, they were inflamed with jealousy and malice.

Constantine observed it all unmoved. He saw the pattern very clearly; he felt he had been endowed with preternatural insight. It had to happen this way. You began with quasi-religious rituals: smoking marijuana in rooms transformed into pseudo churches, burning incense, drinking wine, lighting candles. And you advanced to more powerful drugs, more elaborate rituals, like the peyote ceremony. But there was always a potential for carnal degeneracy in any form of religious ritual that contained sensual ingredients, and this potential was held in check only by the stabilizing influence of a formalized and intricate theology. Lacking that influence to organize and shape the volatile elements that stimulated the senses and emotions and channeled them into aspirations to spiritual ecstasy, the ritual, having no locus, became its own justification and declined precipitately into mere self-conscious theatricalism. And a debased theatricalism at that because, like religion without theology, it was performing without the desire or the ability to conceive a *telos,* the end of all desire.

Having rejected orthodoxy, the members of the group were left with no concept of a structured theology to which they might have affixed their combustible yearnings for ecstatic or mystical experience. Their rituals did not evolve out of a belief in God; they were attempting to evolve a beatific vision out of arbitrarily designed rituals. Sex and drugs were their sacraments; the sacramental act a desperate exhibitionism.

It was all supremely logical, Constantine thought. They had become religious addicts, religious junkies, hooked on their sensual self-flagellant rituals, requiring ever more potent doses of narcotics simply to maintain the level of stimulation which defined their addiction. The sadomasochism in which they indulged with such animalistic frenzy was the logical extension of the movement that began with the relatively innocent rituals of Bible reading, pot parties and peyote meetings. It was, metaphorically, a black mass—the doctrine of transubstantiation stripped of the stabilizing influence of a formal theology, in which sacrifice translated into physical abuse and transubstantiation was an incitement to cannibalism.

In the end, Constantine knew as he contemplated them with an almost astral detachment, they would devour him. He felt the time was very near. He insisted he would not flinch. His was a role unfolding according to higher laws. He was a drama, and the end of it would be apotheosis—an emerging into the sunlight, a breakthrough of the bottom of the infernal pit, going down and down through baseness and degradation and the positive renunciation of all human attributes until he broke through and emerged on the other side, soaring in sunlight.

The image of his destiny as an overflowing cup from which he was fated to drink was never absent from his thoughts. It was a culmination he felt was imminent as the January thaw set in. Tensely he waited for it, expecting it at any moment. But when day after day went by and nothing happened, when the cup did not appear, he gradually was made to realize that it did not after all exist at the bottom of the last circle, to be drained there and to transport him sacramentally to the other side, into the sunlight. He came to see that the descent itself was the draining of the cup; the spiraling down through concentric diminishing circles of the cone his Gethsemane. He was in the process of swallowing it all—the filth, the banality, the swinish self-defiling, the geometric reduction of the last vestiges of his humanity, which was the penultimate act preceding the sacrifice and the subsequent apotheosis. Before he could be reborn, it was necessary to atomize himself, to rearrange by means of a total moral dissolution the molecular structure of his nature, in order to be worthy of his destiny and to be purified.

Strange, frightened, forlorn children appeared. Runaways, dropouts, looking for a meal, a place to crash. The house was becoming notorious. "I heard about you from so-and-so," the vagabond children said.

There were reports of suspicious men in the neighborhood making inquiries about them. The drug consumption was heavy and constant. Everyone was quarrelsome. There were bloody fistfights. Constantine overheard talk of robbing a filling station. He knew that some of them were peddling narcotics at a nearby high school. There was a stabbing on the block.

Constantine passed no judgments. He was fatalistic. It all seemed requisite, inevitable, predestined; it was incumbent upon him only to be receptive, a sponge soaking up the vinegar until he was saturated and it would be time for them to squeeze him.

More miracles were described in the papers. Interviews with people who had been visited by the stigmatic. Statements from spokesmen for the archdiocese. But no one in the house was interested. Constantine's gifts were now merely incitements to buffoonery.

"Hey, look at that, old Jesus did it again!"

"Ekshay homo!"

"Shit! I'll take Barabbas anytime."

"Yeah, give us Barabbas."

"Crucify him!"

"Far out. Yeah, let's crucify him."

"Cathy is Mary Magdalene."

"Well, she's not the Virgin Mary, that's for sure."

"Ha ha ha!"

"If Cathy is Mary Magdalene, I'm Judas Iscariot."

"I'm the angel Gabriel."

"I'm King Herod."

"I'm John the Baptist."

"And I'm Salome," said Jennifer, "and I'll cut off your head."

"No, cut off his balls. Cut off his balls first, and then cut off his head!"

Constantine smiled to himself. *Mock me,* he thought. *Yes. Scourge me, spit on me, crown me with thorns.*

It would have been wrong and false had they continued to love him. They could not love you for curing them; they could not abide a perfection in their midst. They would reject it like antibodies rejecting a transplanted heart.

Their scorn substantiated his uniqueness. He was grateful for their taunts and jeers, for their coming at last to despise him wholeheartedly.

CHAPTER 16

One night in the middle of February a girl showed up at the house. She could not have been more than thirteen or fourteen years old. She was soaked and frozen and looking for a place to sleep.

"What's your name?" Fred, who had taken to calling himself Judas, asked her.

"Melissa," she replied, obviously lying. "Melissa Jones." She was thin and nervous and blond; she wore her hair long, down past her shoulders, parted in the middle. Large rimless glasses gave her face a look of naïve amazement, though the condition of the living room she had entered had as much to do with her expression, Constantine thought, regarding her attentively, trying to see them through her eyes, trying to imagine the impact of the sight on her, the garbage everywhere, rancid milk cartons, moldy food, the mattresses scattered on the bare floor, piles of newspapers heaped in corners, the overturned charcoal brazier lying amid piles of ash, and the weird, ugly people examining her, half-dressed, undressed, drunk, stoned, and the stink, the toilet smell of the place, the whole perceived only dimly, everything in long shadows, the candles stuck into wine bottles being the only light, the electricity having been cut off weeks before. It must have been stunning.

"How old are you, Melissa?" asked Judas Iscariot.

"Eighteen," the girl replied with a nervous smile. And then when she realized how absurd that was, she stammered an amendment. "Well, not actually eighteen. Seventeen. But I'll be eighteen soon. I've . . . always looked young for my age."

Twelve, thought Constantine. *No more than twelve.*

"Well, come on in, Melissa," the boy said. "Make yourself at home. My name is Judas Iscariot. And this is John the Baptist. Come in and meet the family. This is Mary Magdalene and this is Barabbas, and over there is Jesus Christ." He laughed. "And this is Salome and that's—oh, fuck. We haven't named the rest of them yet. They're waiting for their names. They're waiting to be baptized."

The child smiled bravely, baffled but pretending to understand, striving to seem amused. "A friend of mine was here a month ago," she explained, smiling, her teeth large and white, protruding slightly. "Debbie. Debbie Holloway?" Her glasses were fogged over and she took them off to wipe them and then returned them to her face and looked out through them and around her hopefully.

"Debbie. Sure," Barabbas said. "Take off your coat, make yourself at home, Melissa. Sure, we remember Debbie. Super chick. Far out." Of course there had been no Debbie. Holloway or anybody.

"She said if I ever needed a place to crash . . . that everybody here was . . . you know, nice."

"Couldn't be nicer."

"You've come to the right place."

"You're among friends here, Melissa."

"Yeah, right," said John the Baptist. "We're a real friendly bunch. They don't come any friendlier."

She was dressed in a tan corduroy car coat and jeans. When she removed her coat Constantine could see beneath her denim work shirt the slight swelling of breasts. She looked around for someplace to lay her coat where it wouldn't be soiled, but there was no place and she finally dropped it on the floor. Upper middle class, Constantine guessed, polite, well-raised. What was she doing here? He was very tense.

"Take off your shoes, you're soaked," Cathy said, coming up to her and putting her hand on the girl's head. Frightened, the child blushed, swallowed, but nodded, saying, "Thank you very much," and knelt obediently to untie her shoes.

"Take off your pants if you want to, baby," one of the nameless apostles grunted. "We don't stand on formality here." There was laughter. The child pretended not to hear, her hair in her face as she loosened the knots.

"It's okay, Melissa," Cathy said reassuringly. "We're friends. Lots of kids have stayed here. Are you hungry?"

"Starved," said the child gratefully. She was wearing white cotton socks stained from the wet leather.

"We got anything to eat?" Cathy asked the girl who had once been Jennifer but who now in Constantine's mind was irrevocably Salome.

"Just some cold beans. Maybe some bread."

"Beans would be wonderful," the child said. "I love beans. I'm really hungry. I'll eat anything."

"Where you from?" Cathy asked.

"Baltimore."

"You just out to see the world or what?"

"I had a fight with my parents. They grounded me for a month because I stayed out too late one night. So my friend and I took a bus to New York. She knew some people there, but we couldn't find them. So my friend went back to Baltimore, but somebody told me about this place, Debbie, and said it was cool here and so I came." She smiled self-consciously, looking amazed behind her large glasses.

She sat cross-legged on the floor in the midst of them, eating the cold baked beans out of the can, wiggling her toes in the stained socks, answering their questions, the candles flickering all around her. Her hair was wet and it glistened. Somebody gave her a bottle of warm beer, which she sipped at cautiously, properly. She wanted to please them and it was necessary to convince herself that they were—appearances to the contrary notwithstanding—actually as friendly and sympathetic as they kept insisting they were, not drunk and stoned and criminal in their intentions.

Constantine knew she was lying—not only about her age, but about her parents and the trip to New York and about Baltimore. She was very transparent, her efforts at lying complicated by the need she felt to seem older than she was, and to guess what it was that they wanted to hear which would make them like her. He watched her through a tension that made him feel cold in the center of his stomach, a cold which precluded emotions.

Cathy brought a towel. It was filthy, discolored. "Your hair's wet," she said, kneeling down in front of the child. "Let me dry your hair so you don't catch cold." The child submitted meekly as Cathy, wearing only her slip, gently buffed her hair with the towel, the girl stiff with concentrating on not taking offense, on behaving naturally. "You're such a pretty little thing," Cathy said, dropping the towel and fingering the girl's hair; she sat facing the girl, also cross-legged, with her breasts bagging loose from the torn slip and her nakedness exposed directly to the child, who kept smiling and smiling rigidly, looking Cathy straight in the eyes because there was nowhere else safe to look.

"You smoke, Melissa?" It was Alan, black hair covering his chest and his shoulders, pectorals that bulged obscenely, naked except for yellowing Jockey shorts. King Herod. Constantine was fascinated by his thick squarish feet, the toes covered with hair, the wormy veins, toenails like bent coins. In school their Bible history text was illustrated every other page with etchings of biblical men and women, saints and apostles usually in postures of extravagant martyrdom, being shot through with arrows or being devoured by lions or crucified upside down, or burned at the stake, and their legs were all muscle-bound with huge clots of muscle in the calves, all bunched and cramped, and with those huge granite feet which Constantine had been fascinated by and loathed intensely, for which this Herod could have been the model.

"Cigarettes? No," replied the child.

"Pot. Grass," said the man. "I mean, do you turn on?"

"Oh—sure. I turn on now and then. But only when I'm in the right mood."

"You want a hit?" Someone passed him a marijuana cigarette and he held it out to her.

She hesitated, but then, not wanting to offend them, she accepted. She pursed her mouth inexpertly and drew in some smoke, closing her eyes in a reflex action, coughed, made a face, blew out the smoke, and returned the cigarette with a weak, doubtful smile.

"It's very nice," she said.

"It's dynamite." He laughed, his genitals stirring in the pouch. "Dynamite shit."

"Thank you very much."

"Let's see what you look like without your glasses," Cathy said, and before the girl could move to defend herself, Cathy reached out both hands and plucked the glasses from her ears.

"I really can't see anything without them," the girl, Melissa, said, blinking in the firelight, blinking at Cathy, who was studying her features with approval.

"You're very, very lovely, Melissa. You should never wear glasses, you're so pretty without them."

"Thank you. You . . . you're very pretty too. But I'm really almost blind without them. Can I have them back, please?" Constantine could see the fear behind her steadfast smile.

"Just let me look at you for a while longer," Cathy said, holding the glasses behind her out of reach.

Constantine knew what was coming. He had seen Cathy like this before, knew her intentions and the mood of the group. He didn't move, tried not to think. He felt as though he were turning to stone inside, as though he were filled up with drying cement, solidifying from the inside out. He willed himself not to think; he just sat and stared, stonily.

"You ever turn on to smack, Melissa?" a man who called himself Ananias asked from where he was lighting a kerosene lantern in one shadowy corner of the room.

"Smack? I . . . I don't know. I . . . could I please have my glasses back now? I get very bad headaches if I don't wear them. I'm very near-sighted."

"Let's shoot her up with smack," sniggered a voice which Constantine, staring into the flame of the kerosene, could not identify.

I'll just look at the fire, he thought. He would lose himself in the flame. He would not look at her or listen to them or register anything that happened. It was a final testing for him. He would will himself to identify with the flame. He would become the flame and his core would melt and he would burn down and then he would be ash.

"I don't . . . I'm really not into a very heavy drug scene," the girl said, Melissa, the smile gone from her face now, feeling cornered, thinking how delicately and diplomatically she could extricate herself, how to do it courteously, without offending them, Constantine thought, his eyes back on her in spite of his resolutions.

No pity, he thought, trying not to think. *No mercy, no compassion, no feeling, no compromise. Nothing, nothing, nothing!* Because on the other side there would be sunlight, he would be climbing in the sunlight.

"There's a lot of ignorant talk about drugs," said Cathy soothingly, apparently entranced by the child, who looked naked without her glasses. She was kneeling again in front of her, sitting back on her raw heels, her slip taut against her rump, the towel twisted in her hands in her lap, two feet from the girl, who was starting to squirm. "You don't want to abuse them, of course, but they can be very helpful—they can help you see wonderful things, feel wonderful things, marvels, where the whole world is magical, magical and mystery. . . ." Constantine realized how drunk she was. Her hair lacquered with dirt, mouth rubbery, sloppy and wet, she swayed back on her heels, back and forth, rocking, talking nonsense that deepened the child's fear.

"I'm sure it's marvelous." She rose abruptly, scrambling her feet under her and pushing up quickly, springing erect. On her feet, with Cathy kneeling below her, she seemed for a moment even more vulnerable and perhaps even rude because she made a little dipping curtsy of apology, a springy quirking of her knees, like a schoolgirl on stage in the class play.

Constantine set his teeth so hard he felt them fusing. There were no teeth in his mouth. There was an iron bar between his jaws, a horseshoe curve of black iron.

"I suppose someday I'll try some probably." The girl swallowed, then took a breath as Cathy stood up too and faced her, grinning and loose-mouthed, her sloppy body coming out of her torn slip. Melissa peered down into the candlelit shadows of the floor, shuffling her feet, searching for her shoes. "Uh—I think I'll just run down to the corner—I saw a drugstore a couple of blocks down—to get some . . . some aspirin. I have a headache, I'm afraid. I'll be right back. Can I get anything for anybody? May I have my glasses back? I can't go anywhere without my glasses." She had jammed the toes of one foot into one of her shoes, and worked her foot into it, crushing down the heel, when Cathy, who was holding her glasses, said:

"If you give me a little kiss first. You're so pretty. Just a little kiss first—then I'll give you your glasses for a kiss."

"Of course," said the child, not understanding, blinking, feeling on the floor for her other shoe. She shyly extended her neck, meaning to kiss Cathy on the cheek, but Cathy put her arms suddenly around her shoulders and embraced her and kissed her on the mouth.

Constantine shut his eyes. It was very warm in the room. He tried to concentrate on the warmth, all the candles, the kerosene lantern, he did not know a kerosene lantern could generate so much heat, he did not want to know anything, ever; he would not look anymore no matter what, he did not want to see the slurring kiss, the sucking sounds of it, of Cathy slobbering on the child's face, nor interpret the whimper from the child, nor the amused and then interested and then excited growls and cackling of the others rising like the temperature that caused the sweat to leak down along his ribs. John the Baptist and Judas Iscariot and Herod and the angel Gabriel.

"No, don't, please!" the child exclaimed, gagging. She wrenched free of Cathy's arms, spinning off, and Cathy made a sudden move after her. The child, Melissa, gave a skip and then stumbled as her shoe fell off and, tripping over it, but young and quick, lithely recovering but blind without her glasses, danced over a candle in a wine bottle, and kicked another one, upending it, and came up dead against John the Baptist standing blocking the door who clutched at her laughing and as she jerked back from him there was a tearing sound and her blue denim shirt ripped open violently down the front, the buttons popping off and spilling on the floor. She tried to hold the shirt together in front with both hands, protecting herself. She turned, trapped, to face Cathy, who had come up still foolishly clutching the putrid wad of towel, and she smiled once again, putting everything into one last smile, still thinking to reverse it with a smile that said it's all right, I don't mind about the shirt, it was an accident, just a game that I really enjoyed and I didn't mean to insult you, and I'll just run down to the drugstore even with only one shoe and no coat and without my glasses for some aspirin and then come right back to all of you who are my true friends.

She was all rosy in the light, ethereal with her disheveled golden hair and her mouth glistening where Cathy had drooled on her, and the tension in Constantine watching, helpless not to watch, was such that he felt he was bowing, being bowed, his spine a bow being stretched to great pressure, tons of pressure, and still he did not snap though there was no elasticity left in him as the child, the smile gone, clutching her shirt to her breasts, searched the room with her dim shining eyes, starting to cry, and perhaps the tears correcting her vision for a moment or her only having remembered him where he was sitting, found him and cried out across the room, cowering down into her shirt, pressing herself down inside her clothes with both hands, *"Mister? Please?"*

At that moment Cathy and the angel Gabriel converged on her, but she ducked between them, head down, her hair flashing, charged between them and flung herself headlong across the room at Constantine, who raised a leaden arm to fend her off, which she ducked under also, and was in his arms then suddenly, crying hysterically and babbling. He felt her tears on his face, and her thin body quivering through his clothes. And then he snapped.

He exploded. It was like a stone bridge flying apart under intolerable stress.

He threw her body off him and without thinking, remotely conscious even as he did it that it was *instinctive,* he hurled his own frail matchstick body at the angel Gabriel and struck out wildly at him as Cathy, crazy, stumbled after the panic-stricken child scrabbling on hands and knees sideways, eluding her, screaming, and he was struck a massive clubbing blow on the shoulder that staggered him across the room, reeling, tripping on a mattress and sprawling face first into a pile of newspapers. He was stunned for a moment, then made a ball of himself and rolled out from under the assault of someone else, who hit him a blow that glanced off his spine, and he heard the child shrieking as he found himself grappling with a naked body, a man, straddling him and cursing, who had him now by the throat in both hands, a hideous streaming inhuman hairy face.

His fear was like liquid nitrogen, cold as stone, a liquid stone marbling him. And even as he felt himself losing consciousness, his windpipe crushed, he was aware that the nitrogen fear was in fact the long-awaited apotheosis, not sunlight after all, no climb into sunlight, just the epiphany of the entire opening of himself like a sunburst to the recognition, acute as a knife, of his inescapable, irredeemable animal human nature.

And terrified, with his last puny strength, wanting to live, he struggled; his hand groped for a weapon, found something, hot, a flash in the periphery of his fading consciousness, the kerosene lantern, and he flung it, skittering it along the floor, futile, but the kerosene spilled, and caught in an explosion, and in an instant the place was the inferno.

The force of the explosion seemed to blow his assailant off him. He was free and the hot air rushed searing into his lungs. He staggered to his feet, falling to one knee, getting up, colliding with someone fleeing for the door, and then he was crawling around, looking for the girl, as the walls went up and the mattresses, the smoke blowing thick and black and blinding, on his hands and knees beneath the smoke, calling the girl's name until he couldn't breathe anymore, believing she had escaped, finally yielding to save himself as the fire boomed all around him, crawled on his hands and knees, tumbling out the door and down some stairs headfirst into the cold, cold street where he fell down on his face in front of the first stranger running up to him, feeling himself being dragged a few feet by his arms, and then being lifted, hoisted, gaining his feet again stumblingly, his arm around a second stranger's shoulders, coughing and spitting, suspended between the two men, and hearing sirens in the distance, literally floating above the street borne along through the strange glare of the incendiary night, coughing out over and over again into the ears of his rescuers, who did not hear because they were shouting directions to each other, trying to coordinate themselves to accommodate his awkward unbalanced weight, "Help—help me—call the police!"

CHAPTER 17

"WELL, ARE YOU conducting an investigation? Is it safe to say that?"

"There is nothing to investigate," the Bishop said into the phone. "We are dealing with schoolchildren. If the same children testified that they had taken a trip on a flying saucer, you wouldn't give the matter one inch in your newspaper, even if you were desperate for copy."

"Yes, but this is different," the reporter argued. "We're not talking about flying saucers. We're talking about incurable disease."

"In that case you're talking about science, and I refer you to the chiefs of staff of the hospitals involved. Obviously the diseases were not incurable since the children recovered. I would say that makes it a problem of semantics, not theology."

"I must say, Your Excellency, you sound remarkably defensive about the subject."

"I am remarkably preoccupied with very pressing diocesan reforms," the Bishop replied. "I have more important things to do than waste my time discussing the hysterical . . ." He paused, a political instinct beaming a warning; he hastily reworded the sentence. ". . . than to waste my time discussing something as nebulous as this."

"One last question. What is your personal position on the question of the stigmata?"

"I have absolutely no comment to make on that."

"Off the record?"

"No comment!"

"Just one final question. What if these miraculous cures keep multiplying? What if the stigmatic surfaces?"

"He won't surface because he does not exist!"

"Is that on the record or off?"

The Bishop took a breath. "If you print it, I'll call you a liar."

He put down the phone, read quickly for the third time the story about the child in Stamford whose heart condition had vanished overnight. Then he flung the paper aside with an exclamation of disgust.

It was as though a collar of miracles were tightening around him, around his diocese, threatening to strangle him and all his works. They'd been relatively lucky so far; the press had been slow to pick up the story. But now it was edging closer and closer to the front page. Soon the Bishop would be unable to suppress the thing any longer. They would have a full-blown scandal on their hands, and he would be in the middle of it, and in that event there was no conceivable way he could emerge from it with his progressive image intact.

The pressures on him were enormous. The Cardinal in Boston was enraged, and the Bishop had just concluded a long and acrimonious conversation with the Archbishop in Hartford, who—senile as he was—considered the stigmatic a potentially formidable instrument for reviving the flabby morality of their congregations. More and more inquiries were trickling into his office every day from all over the diocese concerning the phenomenon of stigmatism. A Catholic bookstore in Norwich reported selling out all its copies of the life of Padre Pio. The Bishop felt besieged.

His anxiety was taking its toll. He had developed two bluish clams under his eyes; he had lost weight; he was taking pills for an acidic stomach; he slept poorly and his normally inexhaustible energy was sharply curtailed. His good humor had vanished too; he was testy all the time, short-tempered and sarcastic, even with his mother. He felt hounded, haunted, on the verge of ruin.

The door to his office opened and Michael came in.

"We have to *do* something!" the Bishop burst out at him. "About these goddamned reporters! We have to do something, we have to get a press spokesman, like the President has, to lie for us. I've spent more than seventy-five minutes this morning talking on the telephone. I'm reeling from the strain of all these evasions. I'm worn out, Michael. And then to top it all, that monosyllabic epitome of mental retardation in Hartford calls to say *he* thinks the stigmatic is new evidence of the proof of God's glory. You wouldn't believe—you would not believe the vulgarity, the banality—" He stammered to a halt.

"You mean the Archbishop?" Michael asked. "Oh, that's funny." He sat down, laughing.

The Bishop pounded his desk. "It is not funny! Why are you laughing? I forbid you to laugh! There is nothing funny about all this."

"Wait a minute, wait a minute," Michael interrupted. "They can hear you in the street. Calm down a minute and listen to—"

"I will *not* calm down! And I don't care if they hear me in Saskatchewan! I tell you—" The phone rang; he glared at it. "Answer the damned thing. I refuse to speak to anyone. I absolutely refuse!"

"Hello?" said Michael. The Bishop pushed his chair angrily away from the desk and stood up. The door opened again, and the cleaning woman started to enter with a vacuum cleaner in her hands.

"Get out!" the Bishop cried, rushing at her, waving his arms, pressing the door closed in her face. "Out! Go clean somewhere else!"

"No, I'm sorry," Michael was saying, shaking his head at the Bishop. "His Excellency is out right now. No, he won't be back till this afternoon." The Bishop tore his overcoat off the hanger in the closet and began to put it on. "No, for the moment I have nothing to tell you. We're looking into it."

"We're not looking into it!" the Bishop raged, jamming a button into the wrong hole without noticing. "You're contradicting me. I expressly told the other one there was no investigation!"

Michael gestured at him impatiently to be quiet, which infuriated the Bishop more. "These things are rather a common occurrence. The month rarely passes when we don't receive a report from somewhere in the diocese of a child having seen the Virgin Mary or Saint Peter or someone. No, it's not at all uncommon. So we're really not overly impressed. But we are looking into it."

"I'm going out to shovel snow!" the Bishop announced, his face flushed as he bent over to struggle with a pair of rubbers.

"You'll have a heart attack," Michael cautioned in a whisper, covering the mouthpiece.

"I don't care. I hope I do have a heart attack."

"Wait a minute. I have something to tell you."

"I don't want to hear!"

"Well, *that's* something else." Michael spoke into the phone, his eyes on the Bishop. "I'm not quite prepared to address that issue at this time."

"Where are my gloves? Where the hell are my gloves? Why can't I ever find anything around here?"

"We've got him," Michael said, covering the phone again.

"I don't care; I don't want to hear anything more about it—"

"I said we've got him. The stigmatic!" The Bishop halted. "That's right," Michael said to the caller.

"Oh," said the Bishop, standing in front of the closet, his buttons lopsided, a shiny black rubber dangling from his fingertips.

"You may say that we rejoice in the child's recovery and offer our prayers of congratulation and thanksgiving. And that's all I'm going to say for the moment." The Bishop came back across the carpet and sat down in the chair at the side of his desk. He looked blankly, almost meekly at his assistant behind the desk. "I'm sorry, no. No, I'm sorry, we have nothing else to say. No, nothing. No, not on or off the record. No, I'm very sorry. Good-bye."

He hung up. There was a brief silence. Then: "You said you've got him?" The Bishop's voice was subdued. An odd dependent appeal showed in his tired eyes. He twisted the rubber overshoe in his hands and then let it drop.

"He's in police custody. In Boston. He's been involved in some sex and drug scandal. A bunch of them, living together in a commune. I was just on the verge of breaking the case myself," he couldn't resist saying ruefully. "They burned down a house. The stigmatic is being held incommunicado."

"And the press?"

"Nothing." Michael shook his head. "So far the police are cooperating with the Cardinal's office. You know, the whole police force up there is Irish Catholic, thank God. They're keeping the lid on. But they say that eventually they have to let him go. Apparently all the evidence vanished in the fire."

"When did this happen?"

"Two nights ago. The only reason he's in custody now, aside from the Cardinal's intervention, is that he's evidently afraid of the people he's been living with. He wants protection. But when he doesn't want it anymore they'll have to release him."

The Bishop thought for a moment, scowling, then relaxed and brightened. "But it's out of our hands then, isn't it? He's not our problem any longer. It's in the Cardinal's lap now."

"Not quite. There are some other factors we have to consider and talk about."

"Like what?"

"I think we should have a drink first. You look like you could use a drink."

"Bless you, Michael, yes. Fix me a Scotch, please. No water."

Michael went out of the room and, sighing, the Bishop removed his overcoat, tugged the rubber from his shoe and resumed his seat behind the desk. He sat staring at the crucifix above the bookcases, his brain at a dead halt. Michael returned a few minutes later with two glasses, handed one to the Bishop, took the receiver off the hook and settled into the other chair.

"Cheers," he said, raising his glass.

"Cheers, Michael."

He drank off half the Scotch and then slumped down in his chair, clasping the glass to his belly, looking much older and physically reduced. "So tell me," he said. "What are these other factors? Why can't we just wash our hands of the whole horrible business?"

"Because for one thing it's too interesting. You would never forgive yourself for copping out on it."

"Copping out?" The Bishop lifted his eyebrows.

"An addition to my vocabulary—the result of the last several weeks scrounging through the Boston anticulture. God, you wouldn't believe it!" The Bishop smiled wanly. "But more important, he might still come back here. He's from this area. His name is Paul Constantine. He used to be a chemist, worked over in Groton, at Kaizer. The police can't hold him. So nothing's really settled yet. He could come back, and the whole nightmare might begin all over again."

"God, that's true. You're thinking very clearly, Michael. Much more clearly than I am. Go on. I trust you."

"Beyond *that*, the Cardinal is in a quandary. He would be very, very grateful to you if you could handle the thing for him. He would be heavily in your debt for a long time to come. A chance to patch up an old and obstructive antagonism there—obstructive to your career."

"Hmm," the Bishop said into his glass. "You're being extremely acute, Michael. Acute and profound. It does you credit. But what should we do? I tell you, murder is the only option that comes to mind. Seriously."

"We have to talk to him," Michael said. "We can't know what to do until we have a chance to assess his frame of mind. Who knows? He may be disposed to be reasonable. From what I can gather, he's frightened. Maybe we can reach some kind of agreement with him."

"Well . . ." said the Bishop slowly, toying with his glass. "Although I'm almost ashamed to confess it, you're right: I would never forgive myself for 'copping out,' to use your phrase. Damn it, I am curious. How can you not be curious? Pretty bizarre, all in all, isn't it? Yes, you're right. We have to go and take a look at him."

"There's something else. It turns out he has a psychiatrist. Or had one."

"Yes?"

"A doctor on Park Avenue in New York named Auerbach. They found his phone number on the man."

"A psychiatrist," the Bishop said, very interested. "That sounds hopeful. Better and better. A man who thinks he's Jesus Christ isn't likely to consult a psychiatrist, is he?"

"I think we should probably talk to Auerbach before we go to Boston. He may be able to give us some valuable guidance."

"Yes, a good idea. By all means. Call him up and make an appointment."

"I already have. We're going this afternoon."

The Bishop gave a surprised chuckle. "Michael, at times I can't keep up with you."

"That's because you're still awash in theological prejudices," Michael said with a thin smile.

"You've talked to him then, the psychiatrist—what's his name?"

"Auerbach."

"What's he like?"

"He sounds very civilized. There was some reluctance at first, on his part, to discuss the matter. Professional ethics and whatnot. But when I explained, he was very interested. I think he'll be helpful."

"I do too. I have great faith in psychiatry."

Michael looked at his watch. "We should be leaving soon if we're going to be there on time."

"Right. Fine. Let's go." The Bishop finished his drink. The color was back in his face; he looked lively and intelligent again. "You realize, of course," he said, "there really never was any question but what I'd have to see the man in the flesh. Constantine, you say? I feel as if somehow after all this time I practically know him. Don't you? When all is said and done—emotionalism quite aside, and the serious, even grave implications of the business notwithstanding—it's a damned exciting piece of adventure, wouldn't you say?"

"I could happily do without, thank you. The things I've gone through the past few weeks. I tell you. When this is all over, I want a long vacation. I want to go on an extended retreat."

"Ha ha ha!" The Bishop laughed. "I wish I could have seen you. Tell me all about it on the way. I want to hear about how you coped with all the immorality I understand is endemic in those circles. Weren't your morals subject to a certain amount of taxation in that libidinous environment?"

"After what I've gone through," Michael replied dourly, "trying to find this man, I don't feel the slightest obligation to regale your filthy imagination with prurient details."

"Oh, Michael!" The Bishop laughed as they went out together. "Poor Michael! Ha ha ha!"

"It's strange. I've always thought that if I hadn't gone into the priesthood I very well might have become a psychiatrist myself."

"As a matter of fact," replied Levy Auerbach, "I've always thought that if I'd been born a Catholic instead of a Jew I might have become a priest."

They both smiled; they had taken to each other from the moment they introduced themselves.

"I find you remarkably free of professional cant," the Bishop complimented him. "It's very refreshing."

"I wasn't quite prepared for your objectivity, either," confessed the psychiatrist. "Tell me, is it very representative? I mean, are there many more bishops with your intellectual proclivities?"

"What do you think, Michael?" The Bishop deferred to his assistant humorously. "Are there?"

"Fortunately, no," Michael joked.

"It is interesting, though, isn't it?" the Bishop remarked. "The similarity of our vocations. In the last analysis we're after pretty much the same thing, aren't we?"

"With minor variations."

"Yes, of course with variations. I'd enjoy it immensely if we could sit down together sometime and have a long philosophical chat."

"I'd enjoy that too."

"Do you like Spanish cooking? I know a place in the Village—below Washington Square, that street that looks like a continuation of Fifth Avenue, whatever it's called—it's on the corner of that street and Houston Street."

"In New York it's pronounced Howston for some strange reason," Auerbach said.

"Howston then. It's a slummy-looking place, but the food is marvelous. One dish especially, called Zarzuela; it's a kind of bouillabaisse—crabs, lobsters, scallops, everything—in a white wine sauce served on saffron rice.

Fabulous, really. Do you eat shellfish? Is that any problem?"

"No, I'm emancipated. I eat everything."

"Then we have to have dinner there sometime."

"With great pleasure."

"Make a note of that, Michael. At the first opportunity." Auerbach glanced surreptitiously at his watch, and the Bishop saw him and apologized. "We're taking up your valuable time, doctor. To get back to the stigmatic. What finally then *is* your diagnosis?"

Auerbach shrugged. "It's impossible really to make a diagnosis on the basis of one visit."

"But you actually saw the wounds?"

"I saw the wounds in his hands. I was quite willing to believe he had similar wounds in his feet and on his breast."

"He didn't strike you as being a religious fanatic in any way?"

"Almost exactly the opposite. He came across as fanatically antireligious."

"Well," observed the Bishop, "that's often pretty much the same thing. Fanaticism is fanaticism."

"True enough."

"Do you have any theories about how the wounds might have been formed?"

"Oh, there are dozens of possibilities. For one thing, he could have made them with a knife. That's not the most remote possibility either, by the way."

Michael uttered an exclamation.

"Oh, yes." Auerbach smiled. "It wouldn't surprise me in the least. But my guess is—and I emphasize that it's only a guess—my guess is that the lesions are probably psychosomatic."

"Something that horrible?"

"Let me show you something," replied Auerbach. He opened a drawer in his desk, removed a folder and laid it flat in front of him. "A patient of mine a few years ago." He opened the folder and shuffled through the papers. "I had a man a few years ago with a case of acute dermatitis. He went to half a dozen dermatologists before he came to me and none of them could help him. The whole problem started the year he got married. When he finally got to me he'd been married for twenty-five years. The first year of his marriage he noticed a scaling on his scalp. Afterward his groin turned scarlet, with eruptions. Further eruptions developed around his neck, in the creases of his elbows, behind his knees. All of which he scratched until he bled. The itching—and note this—he claimed the itching was similar to sexual pleasure, a voluptuous thing. When he came to me he was covered with scabs from head to foot. That's no exaggeration. He was a walking scab." Auerbach closed the folder and put it away. "He had this dermatitis for twenty-five years, remember. Within ten weeks after coming here there wasn't a mark on his body. No miracle. The scabs were simply correlatives for a very mixed-up life. Problems with his mother, a domineering wife, masturbatory fantasies, all kinds of complicated sexual guilts that carried over into his work and led him into alcoholism. Once we got all that into the open, the dermatitis disappeared. In a matter of weeks. And mind you, he looked as though he had the bubonic plague."

"Are you saying that with Constantine it could be the same thing?"

"I'm saying it could be anything. There are cases on record of hypertension, peptic ulcers, mucous colitis, severe dental problems, diseases of the gums, rheumatoid arthritis, asthma, urinary problems, a whole broad range of dermatological troubles, impotence, premature ejaculation, menstrual disorders—you name it, and they've all been treated more or less successfully at one time or another by psychotherapy. The subconscious ingenuity people employ to mutilate themselves is incredible." Auerbach looked at his watch a second time, more openly, and moved around in his chair.

"Do you think," the Bishop persisted, "that you could cure Constantine?"

"I think it's possible that whatever is bothering him might be straightened out in time—and if and when that happened you could be fairly sure that his stigmata would disappear."

"You say if and when."

"There are so many variables," Auerbach explained. "There's every likelihood that Constantine doesn't want to be cured. If he's placed himself at the center of a drug cult, it would suggest that he does not want to. He may have formed a deep dependency on the stigmata since I talked to him. Discovered a new, more compatible identity."

"How would you explain a shift like that in his orientation? I mean, you said that when he was here he seemed fanatically antireligious."

"As you observed, a fanatic is a fanatic. Besides, he's been living with the stigmata for six or seven months now. That alone could explain the shift in his thinking—if there has been such a shift."

"So you feel there's a chance he may turn out to be intractable in our dealings with him?"

"At this point I'm still not really certain I understand what your dealings with him are going to be."

"Well," said the Bishop, hesitating as he realized that he himself had not formulated a detailed plan of action, "obviously I want to help him."

Auerbach hitched his chair closer to the desk. "Please don't take this the wrong way, but exactly why do you feel any responsibility for this man's well-being?"

The Bishop looked into his lap, considered lying, realized at once that Auerbach would not be deceived, realized also that with a mind like his it wasn't necessary to lie, and, spreading his hands wide, said matter-of-factly, "Why, because he's rather an embarrassment to us."

"That's interesting," Auerbach said, swiveling his chair and tilting it so that his face was averted from his visitors. He was silent for a moment; the sounds of the traffic like winds in a tunnel came up muted from Park Avenue. "I would have expected that you'd want to exploit his problem. Sorry." He turned to them with a self-deprecating smile. "The word is ill-advised. I meant that I thought a miracle worker would be good for—uh—"

"Good for business?" the Bishop asked good-naturedly.

"Something like that."

"We're trying to get out of the miracle business," the Bishop informed him.

"I see. I didn't know that. That's very interesting."

"I'm not sure yet what our approach to him will be. In general, one way or another, I want to nip this thing in the bud if possible."

Auerbach nodded. "Well, then, let me give you a piece of advice."

"That's why we're here."

"I'd guess that whatever's been going on, Constantine isn't very happy about it. I think he probably wants help. I would guess that he'd prefer to be rid of the stigmata once and for all. On the other hand, at the moment the stigmata may be his only claim to any sort of self-esteem. It may be his only psychic support."

"Are you saying," Michael put in, "that it could damage him if we kicked the crutch out from under him?"

"It might kill him. I can see how he might be an embarrassment, as you put it, to you gentlemen. But remember—far from being evidence that he needs therapy, the stigmata may in fact *be* the therapy he requires. The stigmata may be the external evidence of the process of therapy he's undergoing. A sort of violent rebellion of all his physiological systems, rising up, in a manner of speaking, to repudiate and purge something in him that's essentially negative and unnatural. I think many people make themselves physically ill in order to provide themselves with a respite from the day-to-day pressures of their lives, in order to rehabilitate themselves physically or spiritually. That may be what's happening to Constantine. When he's had all he needs out of his stigmata, he may get well. Keep that in mind when you're dealing with him."

The Bishop could not follow all the connections in Auerbach's reasoning, which struck him as somewhat whimsical if not actually bizarre. "But a crazy man is a crazy man, isn't he?"

"Yes. The problem is in defining craziness. In my view, sometimes what we call craziness is obviously the disease. At other times—and in my experience this happens to be the case more often than not—craziness is the cure."

A button on the phone lit up and, excusing himself, Auerbach answered it. "Yes, all right," he said. "Five minutes." Michael signaled to the Bishop, who was looking thoughtful, and the Bishop nodded and they both stood up.

"You've been very helpful," the Bishop said, extending his hand.

"Thank you, a pleasure," Auerbach said, shaking hands and then shaking hands with Michael.

"Would you be interested in treating Constantine, if it should come to that?" the Bishop asked.

"I'm very expensive, and I doubt if he has any money," Auerbach replied, coming around the desk and walking them to the door. "But professionally of course I'm fascinated by the case. I'd certainly be interested to hear what happens, and if I can be of any help, if something can be arranged— Well, let's wait and see."

They shook hands again, and as Michael and the Bishop were going out, Auerbach thought to add, "Incidentally—you know, nothing we've been talking about will have any relevance or application, you understand, if in fact it proves that the stigmata are really a miraculous demonstration of the glory of God."

The Bishop responded with a loud, friendly laugh. "For the first time all afternoon," he said jovially, "I think I don't like you." And he turned and left without having understood that Auerbach had spoken seriously.

CHAPTER 18

IT WAS AN exceptionally brutal winter in Minnesota. One massive snowstorm followed another in an almost weekly rhythm dating from the middle of December well into February. The January thaw was absent and the snow piled up. Meteorologists had to go back to the previous century to find statistical precedents.

For Dr. Hermann Seltzer of the Department of Hematology of the Mayo Clinic the weather corresponded to an equally adamant and stifling winter of the spirit. He could not shovel out. A cold he contracted in November went into bronchitis. As he was recovering from bronchitis he was stricken with the Asian flu, which reached epidemic proportions in Rochester at Christmas. No sooner was he back on his feet than his wife, Marylou, came down with it, and he took more time off from work to care for her. Then, the third week in January, he slipped on a patch of ice in front of his house and fell heavily on his spine, incurring a hairline fracture of the coccyx which laid him up in bed for six more days. And Marylou hit a telephone pole with the station wagon in a blizzard.

It has to end sometime, he kept telling himself in the teeth of each fresh disaster. *Spring will come, the snow will melt.* After a while, however, he began to wonder. It began to seem entirely possible that it would not end. All those sputniks and satellites and moon probes had altered the delicate balance of the atmosphere. The polar caps were on the move. It was going to be winter forever.

Irrationally, he tended to ascribe most of the blame for everything bad that happened to him, including the weather, to the phantom scientist Dr. Constantine, who continued to obsess his thoughts. The phial of blood delivered to his lab the previous autumn now seemed in retrospect an evil talisman which had all but wrecked his life. A blood curse had been laid on him, disrupting the sane and well-ordered patterns of a professional lifetime. He considered himself fortunate that he had finally returned to his senses. It had been close. *Brother, was it close!* he would think.

In the space of eight weeks he had made four trips to Connecticut searching for the man. He was convinced that as much as anything else the physical and mental taxation of those desperate and ruinously expensive (not to say utterly futile) journeys to the east coast were responsible for the state of his health. They had broken him down, left him vulnerable to respiratory infections, robbed him of sleep, depleted his natural defenses.

And he had nothing to show for it, nothing whatever to compensate for the hours spent waiting in the chrome-and-plastic wastelands of airports; sitting in motel bars late at night smiling with stony politeness at the jovial scurrilities of traveling salesmen; lying at night alone and miserable in the Lighthouse Inn in New London, the Niantic Motor Lodge, the dreary Mohican Hotel, his stomach in rebellion against the plastic insults of the in-flight prepackaged hamburger steaks the airlines foisted off on him with an effrontery that did not preclude their calling it steak *au poivre;* driving in rented Plymouths up and down the coast between Boston and New Haven, interviewing everyone he could find who knew anything at all about Paul Constantine, who might provide the slightest clue to his whereabouts —Prescott, his boss; his technician, Cathy something or other; a man at

Harvard who had once collaborated with Constantine on a paper dealing with hematosis in monkeys; a former classmate who was now professor of neurology at the Yale Medical School; his physician, a drunkard named Morrison; his dentist; a tennis professional who had once given Constantine lessons; his wife, a bitter and enraged woman who had no doubt her ex-husband was living in South America with a fourteen-year-old girl.

Not that he failed to gather information. There was more information than he knew what to do with. "I could write a biography of the son of a bitch. I probably know more about him than his mother!" He had read every one of Constantine's dull and insignificant publications, looking for a lead. He had examined his notebooks. He had studied the personnel reports Constantine had written concerning recommendations for promotions and salary raises for his staff. And all the interviews. Yet despite this wealth of biographical facts he'd compiled, he had to admit he really knew nothing. He was no nearer to the truth of the man than he was that first morning after studying Clairborne's inexplicable data.

Part of the problem was the superficiality of his methods. You could not apply principles of academic research to finding a missing person. Obviously his investigation had not been very thorough. *But what else could I have done? I'm not a detective, I'm a scientist.* There was the family Fernandez, for instance, Constantine's neighbors. According to the landlord, Fernandez had mentioned one day while he was paying the rent that he thought "something funny" was going on next door. Something funny. But that was as far as it went. The Fernandez family had moved to California. *What am I supposed to do, fly to California?* Already the adventure had cost him more than a thousand dollars.

Seltzer's checkbook confirmed the dispiriting story: $167 plus, round trip, Rochester to Hartford. Times four. Avis, $38.82. Hertz, $42.19. And the credit card receipts: the Ship's Hold Restaurant, Mystic, $22.25, dinner with Constantine's girl, Margaret Bowen. Pretty but stupid. She got drunk and wept. A dreadful evening. "I thought we were getting along so well. I thought we were going to be married." She had talked to Constantine by phone, twice, after his "accident." He hadn't told her what was wrong, merely broke off the relationship abruptly, brutally. "If only I'd known he was sick," she sobbed. Margaret Bowen, engaged now to someone else.

$22.25. And Chuck's Steak House, $18.13. Dinner with the physician, Morrison. Waitresses in shorts and tennis shoes, all the salad you could eat. "Perfect health for a man his age," Morrison offered. He drank three double martinis, and Seltzer wondered, *What the hell do you do tonight if there's an emergency at the hospital?* "Blood normal?" "Blood? He never had any problems I knew anything about. Few pounds overweight, needed more exercise. We all do. I'll tell you this, Dr. Seltzer. If Paul's in a jam I can promise you it has nothing to do with his health. I'd be the first to know, believe me. Paul and I have been very close over the years. Like brothers!" Seltzer asked when he had last seen Constantine. "About a year and a half ago." $16.37, lunch at the Old Heidelberg in New Haven with Dr. Howard Ritchie, thirty-nine, double-knit sports coat and patterned tie, tinted aviator glasses, tinted (blue-gray) licks of stylish hair over his ears (and bald Seltzer in his wrinkled ten-year-old three-button dark-blue itchy wool suit and vest), eating shrimp cocktails and sauerbraten, recollecting with vast and mindless mirth a Halloween dance in college, Constantine the chairman of the decorations committee, a tale of stolen pumpkins and punch spiked with lab alcohol, the whole punctuated with bellows of laughter, absolutely the costly sum of what Ritchie could remember about his one-time classmate.

Finally there had been nowhere else to turn. He'd been forced to concede defeat. Constantine had vanished without leaving a trace. Seltzer didn't know what else he could do short of going to the police. He had considered that. But real life, he told himself, was not like life in the movies. Local police departments were not equipped to hunt down missing persons, even if they were disposed to try, which normally they were not. One of his friends in Rochester had appealed to the police there for help in locating his teen-age son, who had not come home for five nights. The police shrugged it off. "The highways are loaded with hitchhiking runaways," he was told. "And they all look alike. What can we do?" That left the FBI. But what could he tell the FBI? Had a crime been committed? Had a federal statute been violated? Constantine owed some money, true, but the FBI didn't go around collecting bad debts.

Maybe I should have placed an ad, he thought, *taken out a full-page ad:* DOCTOR CONSTANTINE YOUR BLOOD DOES NOT COAGULATE! There were plenty of things he should have done differently. In November he should have taken his vacation time, taken a month off, however long he needed to do the job properly. Instead of parceling it out a few days at a time across months, the trail getting colder and colder. But Marylou had her heart set on a vacation in the Bahamas. He'd promised her. He hadn't been able to bring himself to use up the vacation time. *I didn't really believe, I guess. I didn't believe in it hard enough.* Not that there would have been any guarantee he'd have found Constantine if he'd taken a month. Still, he would have felt better now as he prepared to abandon the project, would have felt that he'd at least given it all he had.

Well, but it was gone. Regrets were no good. You had regrets, sure, they were unavoidable, but they were terrible; if you let them they would devour you. You had to struggle. Work was the only antidote. Bury yourself in work, he advised himself. Constantine was gone, as good as dead.

But it was hard to interest himself in his platelet studies again. The platelets seemed insipid; he began to think he'd had it with platelets. "I feel like I'm in a change of life," he complained one night to Conrad Flesch. They were playing chess and Flesch was cutting him up; Seltzer made ridiculous mistakes.

"I've never seen you play so badly," said Flesch.

"I don't know what's wrong with me."

"You'll get going again. It's the aftereffects of the flu. You're not yourself."

"No, it's something else. I'm bored with my work. I can't concentrate. None of it seems worthwhile."

"Go away," Flesch suggested. "You haven't had a real vacation in how long? Take Marylou to the Bahamas. You keep talking about it. So do it. Treat yourself. Get your health back."

"It isn't that," Seltzer said with a shake of his head. "I've been thinking —it's all been so technical, my life. What the hell am I? Fifty-two years' worth of what? What have I contributed?"

"You've written some damned valuable stuff."

"Yes. On platelets! I ask you—what am I? A plumber, that's what. A highly educated plumber. Look, I'm intelligent, right?"

"You're very intelligent, Hermann."

"I've lived a lifetime. I've seen. I've experienced. I ought to be able to make a contribution. Not in the narrow sense. I want to do . . . something big."

Flesch looked at him, toyed with one of his captured pawns. "Like what?"

"I don't know. Yes. Maybe. I think I want to write a book. A philosophical book. A book about the philosophical implications of the chemical nature of blood."

Flesch smiled. "I think, Hermann," he said, unconsciously patronizing his old friend, "you'd be much better advised to take your wife to the Bahamas and soak up some healing sunshine."

Seltzer flushed. "Whose move?" he asked irritably, turning his attention to the board.

"The game's over," Flesch reminded him. "It's been over for some time. You lost."

Later, in bed that night with Marylou snoring beside him, Seltzer thought grimly, *The hell I have. The hell I've lost!*

The idea of a book had taken hold of his imagination. Marylou was reading a history of the Russian Revolution. She told him something he had not known—that if the czar had realized that Queen Victoria's granddaughter Alexandra was a carrier of hemophilia, he doubtless would have broken off their courtship, about which he had not been overly enthusiastic. "And," Marylou concluded, "if he hadn't married her, according to the author, there might not have been a revolution."

My God, Seltzer thought, *she's right! She's absolutely right.* He skimmed through the book. Alexandra's influence on Nicholas was all bad. She was a religious fanatic. The crown prince's hemophilia was the instrument of Rasputin's destructive power in the court owing to his mysterious gifts for treating the child's disease by psychic means. So that it really was possible to theorize that except for the fact that Alexandra was a carrier of hemophilia, Russia would be a constitutional democratic monarchy today instead of a communistic dictatorship. *And there wouldn't have been World War II. No atom bomb. Probably no sputniks. Maybe no Hitler, no slaughter of the Jews!* God, it was tremendous. The history of the entire twentieth century turned on the fact that the granddaughter of an English queen was a carrier of hemophilia. *It's staggering,* he thought.

"The Politics of Blood"! What a title for a book. What a thesis! Who had ever thought of such a thing? But, he cautioned himself, why restrict it to politics? Politics could serve as a point of departure for wider-ranging, more sweeping, comprehensive philosophical speculation. He could argue that everything—and that was *everything,* you name it—revealed itself in the chemistry of blood. Blood was infallible. Blood told no lies. It was a hieroglyph, true—but not indecipherable. It was the *tabula rasa* on which all the world's secrets were written. *The* primal element, as vital to an understanding of the nature of man as the sea was to an understanding of the nature of the planet earth.

He was excited. It would be historic. Politics, religion—yes, especially religion, religion too: Rasputin the monk, and the blood religions of Western man, the Catholics, their worship of bloody saints, their bleeding Christ, the connections between the disgusting blood worship and practices of the Catholics and the bloody age-old persecutions of the Jews. There was no end to it. He would include all of it.

He couldn't write, but that was immaterial; he would hire a ghost writer. What did you need in order to write? A knowledge of subjects and predicates. The ability to throw around a few subordinate things, conjunctions or whatever they were, adjectives and adverbs for decoration. A mechanical thing. Anyone could do it. The important thing was the ideas. *What he had to say.*

Monumental. He envisioned a monumental work, perhaps of several volumes. He would devote the rest of his life to the task. It would electrify the scientific world. He couldn't wait to begin.

The next morning, however, as he was sitting at the breakfast table dreaming about his great book, his wife called him to the phone. "It's that man in Connecticut, Dr. Prescott," she told him.

Seltzer jumped. "Prescott? What the hell does he want?" He hurried to the phone, his heart pounding. "Hello, Jim?"

"Hermann?"

"What's up?"

"Well, I've got some news." Seltzer braced himself; he didn't want to hear. "I don't know how you'll take it. Ready for this? Paul Constantine has been found."

"Found? What do you mean, found? He's been found? What do you mean? Found dead or alive?"

"Alive. And as far as I can tell, in good health. I just got a call from the Boston police department."

"Boston? The police?" His voice was shrill. "What's happened? How is this possible? I'd given up."

"I really don't know. They called me to verify that Paul used to work here. They wouldn't give me any information. Wouldn't tell me a thing. But I guess they've nabbed him for something. I thought, everything considered, you'd like to know."

"Jesus," Seltzer said after a moment.

"You there, Hermann?"

"Yeah, I'm here."

"What do you think?"

"Nothing, I'm stunned. I don't know what to think. I can't think."

"Are you coming out?"

"Coming out?" It was an outlandish, incredible question. "Come out there? Again? Christ—I don't know. I really don't know. What are *you* going to do?"

"I don't know either. If he's in trouble I sure as hell don't intend to get myself mixed up in it. Everything considered, I don't feel I owe him anything. He left me hanging high and dry. Besides, I'm a busy man."

"So am I. Especially now."

"I just don't want to get mixed up in anything," Prescott said. "I just don't like the sound of it. I have to think about the company, my job, my family. From my point of view I can't see anything but trouble coming out of this. I personally have too much to lose."

"Yeah, sure. Are you sure it's Constantine? You're sure they actually have him there?"

"If they don't, it certainly sounded to me like they knew where he was."

"I have to think about this," Seltzer said, frowning.

"I just thought you'd like to know."

"Yeah, thanks a lot, Jim."

"If you do decide to come out, you know you're always welcome to stay with us. Love to see you again."

"I'll let you know. Thanks very much. I'll give you a call."

He hung up and turned to Marylou, who had been listening at his elbow. "Constantine's in Boston," he said, feeling flat, sick. It was a bad joke. They were toying with him. A conspiracy to break him, just when he was inspired, just when he was onto something new and good.

"That's wonderful, Hermann," she said, hugging him. "I'm so glad for you!"

He pulled away. "It's not wonderful," he said.

"Of course it's wonderful. What are you saying? How is it not wonderful?"

"Damn it," he shouted. "If I say it's not wonderful, it's not wonderful!" He went back into the kitchen; she followed.

"So how can this man one minute be of historic importance and be not even wonderful the next?" she asked.

"I'm not interested in him anymore," Seltzer said, sitting at the table and leaning on his fist.

"How can you not be interested?"

"I'm exhausted! My interest in the subject was exhausted. I'm worn out! I don't care about his damned freakish blood anymore. What do you want me to do? Make another wild-goose chase out there? Throw more good money after bad? A man can only take so much. I'm up to here with Dr. Constantine." He indicated his throat. "In this life a man can be expected to take only so much!"

"But you can't back down now. Not after all you've invested."

"It's too late. A month ago it would have been different. Now I'm not interested."

"Don't tell me you're not interested."

"I'm telling you."

"Think of the challenge, Hermann!"

"I haven't noticed that life is running out of challenges," he said gloomily. "You don't have to go looking for challenges. They find you."

"You have to go. For your own sake . . ."

"No."

"I'll pack your bag, I'll call the airport."

"No! We can't afford it. I want to take you to the Bahamas. Conrad says we should go to the Bahamas."

"The Bahamas can wait. The Bahamas aren't going anywhere. This is your big chance! All winter you've been telling me, 'My big chance, Marylou, this is my big chance.' If you don't go now, next week you'll want to kill yourself."

"I'll take care of next week next week."

"Hermann, what's wrong with you?"

He blew out a sigh, puffing his thin cheeks. He looked out the kitchen windows; it was snowing again. It was going to snow forever. "I want to write a book—a great book," he said slowly.

"So why not? I always said if Conrad could write a book, you could write a book. What's Conrad got that you haven't? You could write a textbook. Who knows more about platelets than Hermann Seltzer?"

"Not a textbook. A *great* book," he said with feeling. "A great work of philosophy."

She drew back, startled. "Oh. You mean a *book.*"

"Yes."

She regarded him for a minute doubtfully. "But, Hermann, if you're talking about that kind of book, you have to be a writer. What do you know about writing?"

"I speak English, don't I?" he exclaimed with exasperation. "I'll just put it down the way I talk! In plain everyday English! Or I'll get a ghost writer. . . ."

"Then it won't be great," she said flatly.

He got up. "I don't want to talk about it anymore. I'm going to work."

She followed him into the bedroom, talking as he dressed. "Hermann, you're too old to start something entirely new like philosophy. You have to train for philosophy like anything else. It's a lifetime occupation. You know blood. You have to stick to blood, to what you know. Go see this Constantine. Maybe you can write a book about him."

"I don't want to."

"Are you afraid, Hermann?" She asked it gently, with affection, but he was stung anyway.

"What do you mean, afraid? What the hell's there to be afraid of?"

"You've had so many disappointments. Are you afraid, now that success is staring you in the face—are you afraid to reach out and take it?"

He turned red. He started to deny it, but the words wouldn't come. He stood with his trousers around his knees and hung his head, embarrassed and ashamed. There was a long silence.

"I don't care for myself," she said softly, persuasively. "If you write about platelets, or philosophy, or Constantine. I don't care if you're famous or if nobody knows your name. We've had a good life. I'm proud of you. And all I care is that you're content with yourself. That you go to sleep at night with a clear conscience. I care that you should be true to yourself, Hermann. That's all I want."

He sagged. There was a distant haunted look in his eyes. He didn't speak for several seconds, and he knew that she was finished talking and would say nothing again on the subject ever. She was a good woman, a faithful friend. She loved him. She would never refer to the subject again, but it would always be there, a specter like this goddamned Constantine himself. One way or the other Constantine would have to be exorcised. He wasn't going to drag Constantine along to the Bahamas. Was he really afraid? What a judgment. No, the great philosophical work would have to wait.

He raised his head, looked at her and forced a smile. "Okay." He nodded, pulling up his pants and buckling the belt. "Okay. So make me a reservation. I'll go. I'll try. One more time."

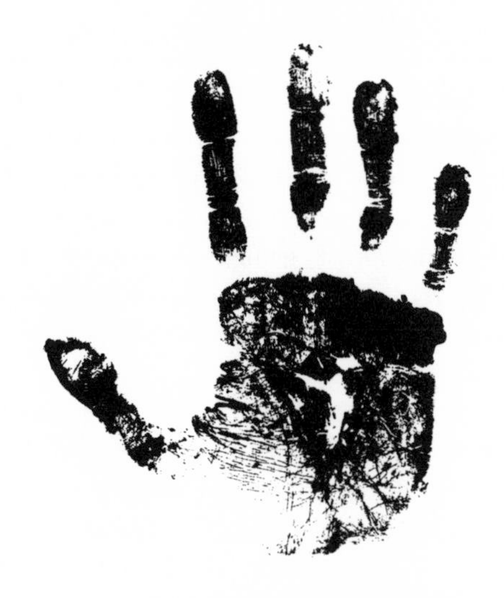

CHAPTER 19

THE LIEUTENANT was one of those dark-skinned Irishmen with black hair who could easily be mistaken for a Latin. He had an agreeable deferential manner toward the Bishop. His name was Mahoney.

"I've never seen anything like it, Father," he said. "I don't think he's eaten three or four ounces of anything. It's like he's on a hunger strike. He drinks some tea, a cup of chicken broth. But that's all. Just skin and bones."

"Has he been examined by a doctor?" the Bishop asked.

"We wanted to get a doctor for him but he wouldn't agree. We couldn't force him. Technically we couldn't have held him this long. The Cardinal asked us to charge him with something, anything just to detain him for a while. But we couldn't. We thought about arson but we couldn't prove anything. He says the fire was an accident. They were living there. It doesn't make sense for them to deliberately set fire to their own house in the middle of winter."

"Who were 'they'?" Michael asked.

"Bunch of hippies. We could have made a case against some of them. We had the place under observation for a couple of weeks. We're pretty certain there was a lot of drug activity going on in there, and some dealing in the neighborhood. But they all got away." He picked up a box of White Owls from his desk and removed a cigar. "Would either of you like one?" he offered.

"No, thank you," the Bishop said. "I don't smoke. But I enjoy the smell."

"Lucky for us, the man asked to stay for a couple of days. He was pretty scared. There's a woman on his mind—a woman he doesn't want to see. The Cardinal asked us to extend him every consideration. We've tried to oblige." He lit the cigar and dropped the cellophane into an ashtray.

"Have you been keeping him in a cell or what?" the Bishop asked.

"No, we made up a room for him in one of the offices."

"What does he do all day?"

"Nothing," the lieutenant replied. "He reads the Bible. Sleeps. Mostly just sits and looks at the floor." He paused and smoked, thinking about something. The two priests were silent. Then the officer cleared his throat and said, "The men have been saying some funny things about this guy. . . ." The priests exchanged a glance but did not otherwise respond. "Murphy, Sergeant Murphy, who was the first patrolman on the scene, he says—well, it was Murphy who called Father O'Shea because he said he saw the guy's hands—well—" He broke off, held the cigar in front of his eyes, turning it in his fingers. "Who is he anyway?"

"For the moment, Lieutenant Mahoney," said Michael carefully, "and believe me, I say this with the full authorization of His Eminence, the Church is very concerned that no one know who he is. It's a very strange, delicate, difficult matter we're investigating. It's vital—really vital—that we make every possible effort to discourage gossip or rumor or speculation."

"Then he's something big," the officer said. He was impressed. "Right. I'll tell Murphy to shut his mouth. He didn't see anything. Right." He got to his feet. "Well, is that it, then?"

"I think so," said the Bishop. "What if he refuses to talk to us?"

"I'll persuade him. He's pretty uncertain of his rights at the moment. He doesn't fully understand how clean he is. I'll be right back."

When he had gone out, the Bishop commented, "A fine race, the Irish. Devout, loyal, devoid of hysteria."

"It was a break for us," Michael agreed, "that it was a Murphy who got to him first and not somebody named D'Agostino."

"Evidence of the hand of God there."

"What exactly do you intend to say to him?"

"I don't have the foggiest idea. Just have to play it by ear, I suppose. I'll think of something."

"You usually do."

"Exactly." The Bishop walked around the room. A clock on the wall above a steel filing cabinet made a humming sound. He paused to look at a photograph on the lieutenant's desk. "Fine Catholic family. Have you ever been in a police station before?"

"No. And I'd be content never to be in one again."

"You have no social conscience," the Bishop said as the door opened and the stigmatic walked in.

The Bishop stopped and stared. He was supposed to be in his late thirties but he looked seventy; a frail, shrunken man in a long dirty black overcoat with an ash-colored beard that reached to the second button, and a weary, livid, haggard face, moving stiff in the knees, his heels dragging as though he were fettered with ankle chains, a stick figure, dry and wrinkled. Lieutenant Mahoney nodded from the hall and closed the door. His hands in his pockets, the man took a seat near the radiator and sat passively looking into his lap.

Michael glanced expectantly at the Bishop. But the Bishop felt as though his brain were paralyzed. He couldn't make it work. Here he was, in the presence of a man with the stigmata of Christ imprinted in his flesh. He never would have predicted his reaction. It was awesome. It was like being in the presence of death. You could not be ironic, you could not be supercilious or philosophical in the presence of death, in the odor of dying. Later, yes; afterward you could be ironic, rational, skeptical. But in the presence of death itself, like any child you merely gaped. Here was the Man at last. *Ecce Homo.* Here he was, long-haired, unwashed, sorrowful, one way or another, according to Levy Auerbach, having disfigured himself, branded with the wounds of Christ, and the Bishop who had come intending to negotiate, cajole, barter with possibly a lunatic found himself instead shaken by the raw testimony to the convolutions of human psychology, the capacity of men to visit terror upon themselves, which was in one definition the basis of all religion and the wellspring of man's belief in mystery and miracles. He felt Michael's eyes on him, Michael's expectation, Michael's impatience, his assistant wondering why he wasn't taking charge. But how did you take charge of the presence of something like this, of the odor of death, which for centuries was synonymous with the odor of sanctity? There was no way to begin. They would stand there like that mute for hours if it was up to the Bishop to find a way to begin.

Then the stigmatic raised his eyes and directed his gaze at the Bishop. There was no expression on his face. He seemed to stare straight through the Bishop as though the Bishop were transparent.

Finally Michael, sensing what was going on inside his friend, broke the silence. "Mr. Constantine—we apologize for disturbing you. We'd just like to ask you a few questions."

The stigmatic's eyes came slowly around to where Michael was standing. "Yes?" he said.

"But first let me say we're aware of your . . . affliction. We just got back from New York, where we talked to Dr. Levy Auerbach."

At the name, something kindled in the man's eyes. He smiled faintly. "Auerbach," he said. "How did you find out about Auerbach?"

"There were some phone numbers in your pocket. The police checked them out. We also know about the children, the so-called miracles. Naturally—"

"They were making life difficult for you?"

"We were naturally concerned about them."

The stigmatic considered the reply for a moment, then nodded. "Yes, of course. You would be." Then he asked with a sudden keen interest that caught Michael off guard, "What do you think of it all?"

"I . . . don't know," Michael said.

"Do you think I cured those children?"

"I don't know. I have no opinion. I—I think so far we've all suspended our judgment."

"Pending an investigation, is that it? Is that why you're here? To take me before an ecclesiastical court of inquiry?"

At last, overcoming the sense of awe and amazement which had rendered him dumb since the man had entered the room, the Bishop replied:

"Excuse me, Mr. Constantine. I think it's important for you to understand that we are interested primarily in your own well-being. We've come here as counselors, hopefully as friends. We're certainly not here as inquisitors. In order to be of any help to you, it's necessary for us to know a few things. To my mind, what we think about your relationship to those children is secondary to what you think about it."

"And if I don't choose to tell you?"

"That would be regrettable."

"And what would you do about that?"

"There isn't much we could do," said the Bishop with an effort to sound friendly.

"You see," Michael interposed, "we understand perfectly well that our interests—yours and ours—don't necessarily coincide. These so-called miracles have, to speak frankly, created certain problems for us. What we're trying to ascertain is whether you might be disposed to assist us in solving them. That in turn depends on our ascertaining how you feel about everything that's happened."

"In other words, you want to know if I consider myself a holy man."

"Something like that," Michael conceded. "Do you?"

There was silence again. The Bishop stared at the man who was such a threat to him, and he felt a strange fury stirring in him. There was a time when it wouldn't have been like this. When indeed they would have dragged the wretched man before the Inquisition instead of trying to bargain with him. *There was a time when I would have had jurisdiction over him, his body and soul!* And he realized with a kind of horror that he felt unfairly deprived, that he couldn't help responding to the temptation to exercise an autocratic, arbitrary tyranny over the man. It was horrifying to recognize the strength of the temptation because all his life he'd taken pride in what he believed to be his immunity to emotionalism. And yet now he could see that the side of him which prompted him to joke that he was a Borgia at heart was a far more developed aspect of his nature than he had ever suspected. Part of him was indeed a princely autocrat.

It was as though the generations of the Church were shaped and governed by laws of heredity as immutable as Mendel's laws. And which now tugged at him across four hundred years, ecclesiastical genes and chromosomes in a deadly combination, a sex-linked recessive type of inheritance that caused him to react to this apostate like any of the worst of the close-minded Spaniards and Italians prosecuting the Inquisition out of the Holy Office in the days when Jews and Arabs were flogged and burned and mystics and miracles were integral parts of the emotional fabric of everyday life. They were his spiritual ancestors, those Borgia princes and their lordly and bigoted retainers, and their hereditary strains were still potent in his spiritual blood. He realized with amazement how superficial his enlightened humanism actually was, how militant you had to be to avoid reverting all the way back. How easy, he thought, to let go of this fragile thing civilization, this fragile thing humanity, this fragile intellect, to burst like an animal out of these gossamer weavings which you deluded yourself into thinking were as tough as coils of baling wire, and to emerge naked, howling, your nostrils dilated, like something out of *Paradise Lost*, enraptured by the sweet black scent of warm blood.

At length the stigmatic said, "If I were a holy man, if I thought I were, what would your position be? What if it developed that I was another Padre Pio, if not another Saint Francis? What would you do, for example, if I should suddenly begin to levitate?"

The Bishop paled at the suggestion. Michael, however, managed a thin smile.

"I would probably faint," he said. "But to answer your question, I don't think we've dismissed any possibilities. I think we came here with open minds. And speaking for myself, I'm perfectly willing to entertain the possibility that your stigmata are in fact a direct and irrefutable miraculous gift from God. In that event, we would certainly be extremely desirous of helping to ensure your comfort and privacy, to provide you with whatever counsel and advice you might feel moved to request, and—"

"In other words, you'd lock me up in a monastery."

"This isn't the Dark Ages, Mr. Constantine. We couldn't lock you up anywhere, even if we wanted to. You mentioned Padre Pio. You're probably referring to the limitations placed on his freedom of movement. But that was different. Pio was in holy orders. So long as he did not renounce his vows, he was bound to obey his superiors. However, at any time Pio was free to renounce his vows and leave. Your situation is quite different. There's *nothing* we can do to you, Mr. Constantine, without your express consent. You're a free man—with all the rights and privileges of anyone else."

"And the police?"

"You're free to leave whenever you want."

The stigmatic closed his eyes for a few seconds, and then seemed to relax. "I'm sorry," he said. "I've been living under extreme tension. I don't mean to be uncivil. It's just that I'm out of practice. To answer your question—no, I don't think I'm a holy man; no, I don't believe my wounds are, as you phrased it, a direct and irrefutable miraculous gift from God. I don't believe in God. I'm an atheist. I regret I've caused you gentlemen trouble. I think you can feel confident that you've heard the last of me."

Michael was inclined to take him at his word, and he was puzzled to see that the Bishop demonstrated no corresponding satisfaction at the unexpectedly easy conclusion to the matter. He continued to look troubled, and then he said a bit awkwardly, as though reluctant to exact a further concession in view of what was, to put it mildly, a very reasonable and in its way remarkably accommodating posture on the part of the stigmatic:

"I'm afraid it's not quite that simple."

"I wasn't aware I was being simple."

"I didn't mean it that way," the Bishop said hastily. "Sorry. I mean—it's all well and good that you don't believe that you are in any way, shall we say, sanctified. And—and I want to be honest with you, Mr. Constantine. You've been cooperative and candid with us, and I think you've tried to understand our position, which must be very difficult for you, considering the ordeal you've evidently gone through, and I appreciate that more than I can tell you—and, as I was saying . . ." He was lost for a moment and couldn't remember what he was saying. Michael had never seen him so pompous and uncomposed. "Oh, yes. I never thought I would see the day when I was pleased to hear someone say he was an atheist. But on our side it clears the air. You understand. However, from the beginning the problem has been less, it seems to me, whether you considered yourself sanctified than the mass hysteria resulting from people's belief that you are sanctified. Do you follow me? What I'm driving at is that so long as people think they have another miracle-working Padre Pio in their midst, there will continue to be miracles attributed to you."

"Well, the only way out of that," Michael saw fit to interject reproachfully, "would be for Mr. Constantine to kill himself. And considering that he's an atheist, that would be an extraordinary sacrifice for the welfare and convenience of Mother Church, don't you think? It seems to me Mr. Constantine has gone as far as we can reasonably expect him to go. Perhaps even farther."

The Bishop gave Michael a fierce look. "I wasn't suggesting that the problem could be resolved only by the man's ceasing to exist," he said indignantly. "I was thinking that he might be interested in doing something to make the stigmata cease to exist. I was thinking about Dr. Auerbach. Originally, I take it, you had reason to believe that your condition was the result of a psychic disturbance of some sort. Since you disclaim any possibility that the stigmata are supernatural, I assume that is still your belief. It is also Dr. Auerbach's belief. He has expressed a desire to be helpful. I merely wish to apprise you of that desire. That's all I meant," he said, not quite truthfully, with another angry look at his assistant.

"No," said the stigmatic. "I can assure you I intend to go far away. I will effectively vanish. You don't have to worry about me being an incitement to religious hysteria. But as for Dr. Auerbach—no, I don't want to see him."

"You don't want to be cured?"

"I'm not hiding behind the stigmata, if that's what you're thinking, if that's what Auerbach suggested. Maybe at one point I was—that is, it occurred to me more than once that I was becoming dependent on them, that the stigmata represented an escape. But I don't believe that's the case anymore."

"Then why?"

"I don't want to be the man I was before," he said emphatically. "If a 'cure' entailed my reversion to the sort of man I used to be, then I'd want no part of it. As you can imagine, this experience has changed me. I now feel it's changed me for the better, fortunately. Suffering's a good teacher, I've discovered."

"I don't want to be indelicate," Michael said. "But what has the pain been like? Do you mind terribly talking about it? Of course, if it's too distressing . . ."

"No, I don't mind talking about it. Actually, it's a kind of relief to talk about it finally. To talk rationally about it. I've been trying to put it all together in my mind. To assess what it's all meant."

The Bishop walked to the window and looked out. It was raining. There was a courtyard of some sort below the window, the pavement covered with brown slush. A wing of the building jutting out at an angle faced him, three floors of barred windows. In one of the windows a black man was staring back at the Bishop.

"It's been a slow, persistent . . . there's been a sense of inexorable organic metamorphosis," the stigmatic was saying. The Bishop felt suddenly chastened by the man, by his ordeal, by Michael's surprising sympathy, Michael, whom he had always considered so cold and dispassionate and mechanically efficient. The black man across the way grinned and all at once stuck his middle finger into the air and wiggled it at the Bishop. The Bishop turned back into the room. ". . . a complete and categoric destruction of my personality. I'll tell you: I think the suffering has come more from my trying to hold on to what I was formerly than anything else, than from the wounds themselves—it's been the pain associated with becoming someone else. It must be the pain a fetus experiences when it turns into a baby. Funny, we always consider the mother's labor pains. Think of the labor pains of the fetus."

The Bishop thought instead of the abortion bill in Hartford, and the politics he'd been engaging in, and he felt slightly ashamed. It was an emotion he was not familiar with, and he shifted his weight with the partly physical effort of dispelling it.

"Still," he said, "there's the real world, your profession, your obligations."

"I haven't made myself clear," the stigmatic replied patiently. "What I'm trying to say is that the result of all this—this laboring has been to deliver me into the real world. That other one, my profession, all the rest of it, science—it's gone. Evaporated. That was someone else named Paul Constantine living that life. I could never go back to it. I could be condemned to go back to it, I suppose, through psychotherapy, through a process of obliterating this man, here, the man I am now." He pressed his hands against his stomach as though referring to something deep inside himself. "And though I could be changed by force into another man who could be made to acquiesce in that other life, could be induced to walk through those roles—Ph.D., taxpayer, so forth—it wouldn't be the same man who did those things before, it would be a different man in a similar envelope of flesh and blood. That reality is gone. And this reality has replaced it and I am beginning to think—no, I mean I'm beginning to hope—that possibly, in the long run, it may be a superior reality."

"Superior in what way?"

"I've thought about this a lot. There hasn't been very much else for me to do but think the past few days. Think about myself. So the stigmata in that regard have been a blessing in disguise." He looked at the Bishop with an expression of wry humor. "Sorry. A slip of the tongue. . . . You can't know anything about anybody else until you know yourself. Yet right from the beginning, from childhood, all the social pressures force you to think about everything except yourself. Sports, homework, high school, college, studies, exams, your job. By the time I was twenty-five there was scarcely a minute in any day I thought about myself. I began to drink precisely to make sure that I wouldn't think about myself. I thought about enzymes and prostaglandins and seducing girls and conniving for a raise. Most people are like that. Each year finding yourself more and more removed from even the possibility of contact with yourself.

"It's a little—it seems to me now that it's like accumulating fat, encumbering our muscles, straining our hearts, larding the bloodstream with cholesterol: deforming ourselves systematically, burying ourselves beneath all that lard and fat and flabbiness. That's what the life I led before now seems to me to have amounted to. Look at me. Look at this wrist." Extending his arm, he pulled up his sleeve to show a white skeletal wrist the circumference of a cornstalk. "You wince; you're making a face."

"I'm sorry, I didn't mean to," the Bishop stammered.

"It's painful to look at," the stigmatic acknowledged. "But only by comparison with very unnatural standards. What's enough? What's too much? I haven't the slightest doubt that in many ways I've never been healthier than I am right now. I don't know what I weigh now, but last summer I weighed a hundred ninety-five. I had pains in my chest, indigestion, I drank about a quart of Scotch every night just to get to sleep. I smoked two packs of cigarettes a day. I couldn't breathe without wheezing. Now I feel purged, purified. I require almost nothing to live. And these five wounds have been the agency. . . .

"I've been reading the Bible since I've been here. The story about the rich man, the camel, that it's easier for a camel to pass through the eye of a needle than for a rich man to go to heaven. That's what I'm talking about. The need to burn off all the fat from your bones, to reduce yourself to the essentials. It's ironically a prescription for godhead. We're made in the image and likeness of God. I think that's true. But only after we're reduced to essentials. The closer we get back to our essences, the closer we come to realizing whatever there is in us that for convenience we call divinity.

"I've had hallucinations, delusions. I've experienced long periods of hysteria, which in other times, other places, might have been called mystical ecstasies. Some very strange things have happened to me. To put it bluntly, at times I've been out of my mind. Literally. And at times I've come close to persuading myself that I was godlike. I've been tempted to think I could work miracles. For a while I did believe I was responsible for curing those children. I even fancied I could raise the dead. But what I failed to understand was that the condition I misinterpreted as an aspiration to divinity was simply the process of my coming to terms with my own manhood.

"I'm just a man, finally. But I'm a *man*. . . ."

The Bishop heard him now without actually listening to what he said. He was thinking about himself, his own weight, 192 that morning; the meal he'd eaten the previous evening—the peas in cream sauce, the filet mignon, the wine. He looked at his own hands; they were fat and soft, pulpy worthless hands, he thought. The diamond on his finger, his glossy black shoes, the expensive French after-shave his mother had given him for Christmas. His mother. He thought about her, and her fur coats, and her dyed hair, all her money, and he thought about his childhood when for a time he must have been lean and unspoiled, with instincts for something other than balancing fiscal accounts and political humbuggery. *When was the last time, was there ever a time in the last twenty years,* he wondered, *that I sat down to analyze myself?* He had always said he couldn't afford the luxury to stop and think. But was it a luxury? There were few other luxuries he could not afford. His Corvette. His tailored shirts. His books, his wine cellar. He had leisure for all of those. If stopping and thinking, critical self-examination, were truly a luxury, he would indulge in it too. Indulgence. A word that for him cut two ways. He was an indulgent person, but all his indulgences—did they secure him any remission of punishments still owing, still outstanding in his book of moral debits? He indulged himself in order to avoid self-scrutiny—yes, the man was right, that's how it worked—for fear that he would not like the glib, smooth-talking sensualist he'd become. To think, to see and then to measure the distance traveled, he could not abide the sacrifice required—to measure the overlay of, yes, fat, to measure the extent of the effort needed to punish all that moral corpulence off his bones and get back to his essences—if there were any essences left, if they weren't all stifled by now.

He looked at the stigmatic. He could not imagine what the man had undergone. But he knew he never could have endured a fraction of it. For the second time that morning he felt ashamed of himself, and this time he could not rid himself of the feeling. *After what he's gone through, I'm not fit to be in the same room with him,* he thought, failing to register the fact that he had expressed a humble sentiment, humility being so alien to him he couldn't name it when he experienced it. He only knew it made him uncomfortable.

"I won't bore you with the details of how it happened, but my eyes were opened to all of this fairly dramatically and very recently. I've spent my adult life looking at the world through a microscope, and I never saw anything. I never saw the relationships between things. Now, well . . . yesterday I was examining the floorboards, I was looking at the texture of the wood, the growth rings, and I realized I could—by extension—from looking at the floor understand what trees were all about and, understanding trees, what forests were all about, and step by step I could intuit eventually the plan of the whole natural world. The same with water drops on the window. And snowflakes. There isn't enough time in the rest of my life to exhaust the subject of snowflakes. Or a moldy piece of cheese. A piece of cheese by itself is a biological laboratory. Or a spider making a web. The real world? What should I go back to? I could spend the rest of my life in a jail cell without ever going out of doors more profitably than if you gave me the entire Yale Medical School to administer. This room is a laboratory. I'm a laboratory. It's enough, it's more than enough that I spend my time thinking about myself. It's a small enough thing to ask of the rest of the world—to leave me alone to indulge that ambition. Isn't it? Isn't it a small thing to ask?"

The Bishop regarded him pensively. "I don't know," he said. "I don't know, Mr. Constantine, if it's a small thing or a large thing to ask. But my guess is that no one's going to let you do it."

"But why?"

"Because in your present state of mind, you're a rebuke to everyone you'll come in contact with. They won't let you sit in your room and speculate on spider webs. They'll kill you first."

The stigmatic looked incredulous.

"Unfortunately," said Michael, "the Bishop is probably right. Ironically, the one place you would be secure is in the Church."

"Formerly," said the Bishop. "Not now. Not in *this* Church. *We* are the Church, Michael, remember." His expression was rueful. "And my instinct from the start, Mr. Constantine, was to have you murdered. That's true. At times I've come very close to praying for your death. That I stopped short of actually doing so says more about my attitudes concerning the efficacy of prayer than it does about any moral compunctions I may have felt. There's no place for someone like you," he insisted almost plaintively.

"I can't believe that," the stigmatic said quietly. "I'll make myself invisible." The reaction of the two priests brought a deprecating smile to his drawn face. "Just a figure of speech, I assure you. It's a big world. There's bound to be a corner in it somewhere for me—where I can do as I please."

"What exactly are your plans?" the Bishop asked.

"I'm not sure. I didn't realize I could leave whenever I wanted to. I think first I'll go to New York. New York's a wonderful place for being anonymous. I don't know why I didn't go there in the first place. I guess I didn't want to be anonymous. I guess I really wanted everything that has happened to happen; I guess I needed it."

"You'll need money," Michael observed. "Do you have any?"

"That is something of a problem," the stigmatic replied. "No—I don't have a penny. I didn't think about that." He made a vague helpless gesture. "Funny, I've gotten so out of the habit of thinking about money."

"Then I think we should help you out," Michael offered.

"You? Why should you help me?"

"Because I think we owe you something," Michael said, gazing thoughtfully not at the stigmatic but at his friend the Bishop. "We are in one sense," he went on, "as the Bishop pointed out, for better or worse, we are the Church. And if you have affected the Church on the one hand, the Church is responsible for the emotional climate that made all this possible. The Church educated you. The Church has to assume some responsibility for your welfare. We'd like to give you whatever financial assistance you'll require to get settled in New York, until—well, until you get on your feet, until, however you intend to manage it, you can support yourself again."

"No—but—I couldn't—" the stigmatic said in some confusion.

"I have learned, Mr. Constantine," the Bishop put in, "never to question the decisions of my assistant. He's never wrong. It makes him a heavy burden to live with, but it's true all the same."

"Wait. I just remembered. The company where I worked—they still owe me some money. Maybe I could borrow a few dollars from you and then . . ."

"Whatever you want," Michael said.

"I don't want them to know where I am. Someday I'll have to go back and clean up the mess I left behind, but I'm not ready for that. Maybe you could collect the money for me? When I get to New York I could let you know where I am, and then you could send the money on to me."

"You decide how you want to do it and let us know. We're at your service," Michael said. He drew a checkbook out of his breast pocket and wrote a check against the Diocesan Emergency Fund. He handed it to the stigmatic.

"But that's too much," he protested.

"Consider it an open-ended loan," Michael said. "Payable, without interest, at your convenience."

There was an awkward silence and then the Bishop, taking up his black hat from Lieutenant Mahoney's desk, said, "Well, then, Mr. Constantine, we'll be leaving you. Good luck. And remember, if you change your mind, Dr. Auerbach is available and he is interested, and as far as his fee is concerned—well, again, as Michael says, we feel more than a little responsibility in this matter. If you'll write me a note authorizing me to collect what money your former employer owes you, we'll send it along as soon as we hear from you. Good-bye."

"Good-bye, gentlemen."

"And, Constantine," the Bishop added, looking embarrassed, "I don't give blessings lightly, but—well, damn it, God bless you!"

"It was entirely too much!" the Bishop insisted.

"It was the least we could do, and you know it," Michael replied calmly. He cut into his lamb chop and forked the meat into his mouth.

"The least we could do," the Bishop complained sarcastically, watching enviously as his assistant chewed the meat. "He's probably got a suite of rooms at the Plaza! I don't see why you had to give him anything."

"You didn't object when I gave it to him," Michael said, buttering a slice of bread. "You blessed him, as a matter of fact."

"I was betrayed by—by the emotionalism of the moment. An emotionalism, incidentally, for which I hold you responsible!" He gave his plate an irritable little push with the back of his hand; on it were the remains of the paltry lettuce and cottage cheese salad. Michael was eating two thick lamb chops, rare and juicy, mashed potatoes, gravy, and bread and butter. He was also drinking a glass of wine; the Bishop moistened his tongue from time to time from a glass of soda water. "You of all people, succumbing to sentimentality. You're supposed to be so cold, so intellectual."

"I apologize! The next stigmatic we deal with I'll be different. I'll make him hitchhike to New York. He can sleep in the Bowery."

"You didn't have to sign away half the diocese!"

"Oh, you're just in a bad mood because of that absurd starvation diet you're on."

"My diet has nothing to do with it! And it's not absurd. It's marvelous. I'm not the least bit hungry. Your food looks perfectly loathsome to me, if you want to know the truth. I see those obscene glops of butter you're shoveling into your stomach turning into great lethal grease balls of cholesterol. You must have a repressed suicide complex to eat butter like that. As for me, I've never felt better. My mind is as clear as a bell. So don't try to obscure the issue by talking about my diet. We were talking about the stigmatic."

"Forget the stigmatic! We're finished with him. It's over and done with."

"I don't think so," the Bishop said. "It was a mistake to let him go. I don't like the idea of his roaming around New York on the loose like that. You mark my words—we haven't heard the last of him."

"I would be willing to bet," Michael said, dabbing at his mouth with a linen napkin, looking down the length of the long dining table at his friend, "that within a month he'll begin therapy with Auerbach."

"At our expense!" fumed the Bishop.

"Why are you on a diet anyway?" Michael asked seriously, laying down his napkin and resting back in his chair. The Bishop looked with disbelief at the amount of meat Michael was leaving on the bones. It was enough for an entire meal. "You're not fat, God knows."

"For purposes of self-discipline!" the Bishop exclaimed furiously, jumping up from the table, jolting the table as he did so. Michael darted out his hand to steady his wineglass. "Self-discipline!" the Bishop shouted. "A concept obviously far beyond *your* powers of comprehension." He turned and stamped out of the dining room just as the housekeeper entered with the dessert, which was a pineapple sponge cake covered with whipped cream.

"Just a small piece, Martha," he heard Michael saying pleasantly. "I'm stuffed."

Upstairs, in the bathroom, the Bishop removed his coat, then his shoes, and stepped onto the scale. One hundred ninety-one and three-quarters. He glared at the dial, trying to stare the pointer down to at least the five-eighths mark. But it wouldn't budge. He was *up* a quarter of a pound since yesterday. It was cruel. He had eaten nothing, *nothing,* except lettuce and cottage cheese. And one boiled egg. And he'd drunk nothing. With what results? He'd gained a half pound—and he was constipated.

He went into his room and in his shirt sleeves lay down on the floor and did some sit-ups. His bones creaked. His spine made snapping sounds. His face turned purple. He perspired.

Martha knocked on the door. "There's a man from the Mayo Clinic downstairs who would like to talk to you. A Dr. Seltzer?"

Sitting up, panting, the Bishop, his legs spread, his hands behind him supporting his weight, gasped, "The Mayo Clinic?"

"He says he's come special to see you."

The Bishop thought. Could it be some old college friend? Someone from Indiana, a med student from when he was at the university?

"Yes, Martha," he called. "I'll see him in the living room. I'll be right down." Washing his face in the bathroom, he tried to remember. Yes. There was a medical student—a large blond fellow, German, they'd played tennis, but his name—could it have been Seltzer?

On entering the living room a few minutes later, however, he realized at once that he had never before seen this short bald man in the rumpled suit.

"Yes. Good afternoon," the Bishop said, coming forward with an inquisitive smile. He held out his hand.

"My name is Hermann Seltzer," the man said, shaking his hand, also smiling, though somewhat warily.

"Dr. Seltzer, is it?" the Bishop said, gesturing for him to sit down. "My housekeeper says you're from the Mayo Clinic?"

"Yes, that's right."

"Well, you're a long way from home," the Bishop said, sitting on the other end of the couch, and waiting politely but expectantly for the man to explain his business.

"I was hoping you might give me some information," Dr. Seltzer began, raising his thigh to get at his handkerchief. "I'm looking for a man named Paul Constantine." He blew his nose, but did not take his eyes off the Bishop.

"Ah," the Bishop said. "Paul Constantine. That is interesting."

"Do you know where he is?" Seltzer asked eagerly, his handkerchief wadded tightly in his fist. "The police in Boston said you talked to him. They said you were the only one who'd talked to him while he was in the jail. Do you know where he is?"

"Yes, I do, Dr. Seltzer. Or, that is, I expect to know within the next few days."

"It's very important that I talk to him," Seltzer said tensely.

"Unfortunately," the Bishop replied, "I'm not sure I wouldn't be betraying a confidence by telling you." Seltzer started to say something but coughed instead. "Are you all right?"

"Yes, thanks. Sorry," Seltzer wheezed, wiping his eyes. "I've had bronchitis on and off all winter."

The Bishop stood. "A little whiskey's always soothing, I find," he offered.

"Yes. Thanks."

He went to the cabinet where he kept his liquor, opened it and asked, "Scotch? Bourbon?"

"Anything. I'm not a drinker. Don't waste anything good on me. I couldn't tell the difference."

The Bishop poured some bourbon into a glass, gazed longingly at the Scotch bottle, thought, *One hundred and fifty calories!* and regretfully turned his back on it.

"Thanks." Seltzer smiled stiffly.

"I'm on a diet. Drink up," the Bishop explained. Spying his housekeeper passing in the hall, he called, "Martha, close the door, please. And make sure there are no interruptions for anything, unless my mother calls." Seltzer took a large swallow and grimaced as it went down.

"Phew!" he said.

"Take the edge right off your throat, settle everything down inside."

"Constantine," Seltzer said, setting the glass down on the coffee table, leaning forward, his wrists on his knees.

"Yes. How did you find out he was in custody? That was supposed to be a deep dark secret."

"From his employer. The police called his former employer. I've been searching for him since October." He blew his nose again.

"Yes, I hadn't thought about the scientific side of it. Except for the psychoanalytical angle, of course. But then I don't really consider psychiatry a science, do you? Not in the same sense as chemistry or botany. Yes, I can see where from the point of view of the Mayo Clinic there would be an understandable desire to study the phenomenon at close range. It's not every day something like that comes along, is it? How did you hear about it?"

"Then it's true!" said Seltzer excitedly. "You know about the prothrombin times."

"Prothrombin times?"

"You said the phenomenon."

"Yes. The stigmata."

"The stigmata?"

"The stigmata of Mr. Constantine. That's what I'm talking about. Isn't that what you're talking about?"

"I'm afraid you've lost me," Seltzer said. "What is a stigmata?"

The Bishop extended his palms, touched first one, then the other with a finger. "Why, the five wounds of Christ, naturally." Then it struck him. "You mean you didn't know . . . ?"

"He has the five wounds of Christ?" Seltzer reached for the glass and drank again, this time without a grimace. "Oh, brother!"

"I suppose I've said too much," the Bishop murmured, taken aback. "But then—if you didn't know—then what . . . ?"

"This is something! Wow!"

"Now I'm lost," the Bishop said.

"God, yes. I'm beginning to see," Seltzer said. "Jesus, it's unbelievable."

"What's unbelievable?"

"Sorry," said Seltzer. "Let me explain." He took another gulp of the whiskey. "Last October a friend of mine, a very distinguished hematologist named Conrad Flesch—I don't know if you've heard of him . . ." And Seltzer told him the whole story, concluding with, "And we couldn't restore the prothrombin time of any of the clotting factors of the blood!"

"You mean he's a hemophiliac?"

"No. We couldn't restore the prothrombin time of *any* of the clotting factors; not just the hemophilia factor—none of them."

"I'm afraid I'm not familiar with the term 'clotting factor.' "

"It works like this . . ." and Seltzer explained.

"Then it was his own blood he sent you," said the Bishop.

"That's what I've suspected all along."

"Blood such as no one else has ever had?"

"That's right. And now on top of it, *this*—these stigmata. Do you realize how important this man could be to medical history?"

"It's amazing," said the Bishop. "I really don't know what to say. Damn my diet, I need a drink. You know this puts me in a hell of a moral quandary," he said over his shoulder as he poured the Scotch.

"Moral quandary? How?"

"Constantine is supposed to write to me. I have some money for him. He's supposed to send me his address. But I'm not sure I'm at liberty to tell anybody else."

"There's no overstating," said Seltzer as impressively as he knew how, "the potential benefits that may follow from unlocking the secrets of Constantine's blood. There may be a cure for cancer in the man. A cure for leukemia!"

"Yes, it sounds tremendous."

"I really don't know anything about stigmatics. The Church, I assume, views them as saints, or what?"

"That's a long story. But we needn't go into it," the Bishop said, deciding not to tell him about the miracles. "Suffice it to say that in this particular case there's no question that Constantine is not a saint. He happens to be an atheist. His stigmata are the manifestations of an illness. He recognizes them as such. The Church has nothing to do with him, nor he with the Church."

"Then—what's the problem? The man's obviously a scientific gold mine."

The Bishop pondered his answer. "The problem is he wants to be left alone. There was a tacit understanding between us that we would help him. He doesn't want to see a doctor. I can't in all conscience see my way clear to betraying his confidence in me."

"But he doesn't know!" Seltzer said with intensity. "He doesn't know that we couldn't restore the clotting factors! At the very least he ought to know that."

"Hmm. Yes. That does rather make a difference, doesn't it? If what you say is true, I wonder why he doesn't bleed to death. The wounds are open, you know. They bleed all the time."

"We have to find out," Seltzer said shrewdly, "for the man's own sake. You can't let him go walking around with blood in him like that without his knowing it. He's a scientist. When he learns about this it's bound to affect his thinking about submitting his condition to a thorough, comprehensive analysis. And," he thought to add as a clincher, "who can tell? His condition might be contagious."

"Yes," agreed the Bishop absently, thinking about something else, unrelated to what his visitor was saying. "For his own sake, of course." But he was thinking he had a chance to make amends for the deplorable slide into emotionalism two days before which had led him to offer that embarrassing, uncharacteristic "God bless you." A hundred times since that moment he had wished he could retract the words, the feeling expressed in the words. Now he had the opportunity—as well as the opportunity to rectify the dangerous tactical error of letting the stigmatic wander around loose and free in New York City with all that great potential for further mischief. Once Constantine was locked up inside the Mayo Clinic, that would truly be the last they'd hear of him. They'd cure him or kill him. If they cured him, Constantine would thank the Bishop. The Bishop would win every way. "Yes, of course," he said. "There's no two ways about it. The poor man can't be walking the streets in ignorance of his condition. You're right. What if he *is* contagious?" He thought a moment more, experienced a slight weak warning from his conscience, dismissed it and said, "He's in New York City. I expect to hear from him momentarily. As soon as I hear, I'll give you his address, Dr. Seltzer. After that you're on your own."

"I can't thank you enough," Seltzer said, unable to conceal his relief and elation. He pumped the Bishop's hand. "I must say, you've certainly revised my opinion of the Catholic clergy."

"In general, I'm sure your opinion of the Catholic clergy is very well founded. But some of us are trying to change, Dr. Seltzer. The Ecumenical Council was not for nothing after all."

When he had shown Seltzer out, the Bishop went into his study, feeling satisfied with himself and vindicated. There was no doubt in his mind he'd done the right thing. He rang the buzzer to summon Martha, and while he was waiting leafed through some financial reports requiring his signature. They looked good. Black ink everywhere. His fiscal surgeries were proving effective; if the patient was not exactly kicking, he was at least still alive.

Martha appeared. The Bishop wrote his signature with a flourish. "Martha—bring me some of that pineapple sponge cake," he said. "That is, if my gluttonous assistant hasn't eaten the whole bloody thing."

"Yes, Your Reverence," said Martha. "And oh, by the way, while you were talking to the gentleman you had a phone call from a woman, who was very excited. She said it's urgent that you call her back as soon as possible. Her name is Mrs. Bianca. I wrote it down."

"Thank you, Martha," the Bishop said. "After I eat my dessert."

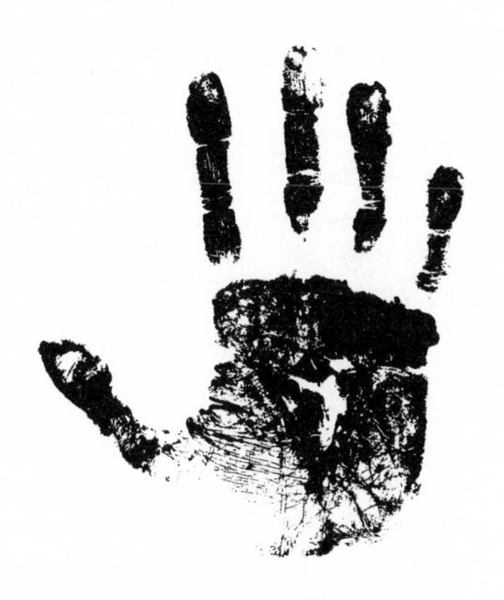

CHAPTER 20

Constantine was living in a three-room furnished apartment on the top floor at the rear of an old brownstone on Christopher Street in Greenwich Village. Compensating for the lack of windows on the street was a view from his kitchen down into a small garden at the rear. There were two rotting wooden benches in the garden, and a tree. The tree seemed a remarkable thing to be growing at the bottom of the funnel formed by the tall buildings. He could see a few green shoots starting to make their way through the naked branches. Soot fell daily like rain even in the sunshine on the tree; Constantine thought nothing could survive all that soot, but each day there were more green filaments. He never saw anyone sitting in the garden, which was littered with newspapers, soggy cardboard and broken bottles. From the front of the building nothing indicated that a tree was growing behind it. It was a secret place.

In his wanderings through the Village, he came across many concealed little terraces and patios similar to his own. Cobblestoned courtyards behind embellished wrought-iron fences, wooden tubs for holing ferns and flowers, the occasional piece of incidental furniture, at night as the fogs or the dew collected overhead lanterns making the flagstones gleam. The one he liked best (next to his own) was near the corner of Bedford and Barrow. But few of the others had a tree.

He loved the Village. No one seemed to have any more occupation than he did. Families strolled the sidewalks, mothers with their infants in slings over their shoulders, long-haired young men and women lounging in the cafés along Sixth Avenue looking out the opaque windows at Constantine looking in. It seemed pleasantly indolent to him, and graceful. Music came out of the clubs at night, and the bars and restaurants were jammed. It was not what he had read; he saw no crime and did not feel threatened.

On Sullivan Street he stood in the bright mist at ten o'clock at night peering through the window of a chess club up three or four stairs above the sidewalk, half a dozen tables, the players in ruminative attitudes, fists on their cheeks, frozen, a tableau, each night the same players, the same postures, as though they were sculptured reliefs on the base of a civic monument. It was still too early in the year for the chess players to be out at night in Washington Square. Constantine would shuffle across the square, his hands in his pockets, not feeling the chill, pause to inspect the garbage that had accumulated in the basin of the pool, move on to stand under the arch and gaze up Fifth Avenue, all the way up to midtown and the colored lights of the skyscrapers, which made him groan, they were so beautiful, especially when there was mist or fog and the colors were diffused and bled into each other and the buildings were crowned with gauzy nimbuses. Then back to his apartment, slowly, west on Eighth Street, through the crowds, jostled, bumped, approached by panhandlers just like everyone else, reviled by cab drivers just like everyone else, in a looping circle, peeking into hidden alleys and shadowy mews, through padlocked gates and over the tops of crumbling walls, and home, up the stairs, into his apartment, which was rent-controlled and had a pull-chain toilet and a braided rug on the living room floor and a table with chrome legs and a yellow Formica top, to stand over the sink and gaze down for long minutes at his tree in his garden.

It was a warm afternoon, the weather having gone over into a premature spring. Hermann Seltzer paced up and down the sidewalk across from the brownstone on Christopher Street. He had climbed the stairs to the door the Bishop had told him was Constantine's and knocked, but there was no answer. So he'd been waiting for half an hour. He was prepared to wait for several hours more.

He thought about the strange story the Bishop had outlined for him yesterday, on his second visit, after Constantine's note had arrived. The torture the man had evidently undergone for the past eight months. The Bishop had hinted at bizarre things but then backed off when Seltzer pressed him for details, pleading the privilege of a confessor. Seltzer did not insist. *Wait till I get him in Rochester,* he thought grimly. *I'll turn him inside out.*

He thought about Marylou, reflected how fortunate he was to have a woman like that for a wife. *Except for her I'd have blown this chance.* When it was all over he'd take her to the Bahamas for a month. Even if it meant mortgaging the house.

At length Constantine appeared, rounding the corner, coming down the street on the other side. Although the Bishop had described him extensively, Seltzer was amazed. *So small, so shrunken!* he said to himself. *He looks like he's eighty! My God, what he must have gone through!* He didn't take his eyes for a moment off the stooped, shuffling figure in the black outsize overcoat. With his long graying beard and his sunken eyes and his hollow cheeks, which made his nose prominent, he reminded Seltzer of an old Hasidic Jew. *All he needs is a skullcap.*

Constantine entered his building. Seltzer hung back, giving him time to reach his apartment. Then he crossed the street and, his heart pounding with excitement, followed him inside.

In front of Constantine's door, he leaned against the banister to catch his breath and collect himself. Then he knocked. The door was opened immediately.

"Dr. Constantine?"

"Yes, I'm Constantine."

"My name is Seltzer, Dr. Constantine. I've—uh—come from your friend the Bishop."

"Ah. You've brought my money? Come in. I thought he'd mail it. Please. Come in."

Seltzer took a deep breath and then entered. Constantine had not removed his coat. He was also wearing dark blue cotton gloves.

"Have you been waiting long for me? I noticed you outside. I was at the library. I've been going to the library lately."

"I'm sorry," Seltzer said, his eyes fastened on Constantine's gloves. "I don't have your money. My name is Hermann Seltzer. I'm an associate of Dr. Flesch, Conrad Flesch, at the Mayo Clinic."

The names seemed to mean nothing to Constantine for a moment; his face was blank. Then he remembered. "Oh, yes," he said, wary all at once, on the defensive. "Dr. Flesch. Yes. And your name . . . you said your name is . . ."

"Seltzer. Hermann Seltzer. I was in charge of doing the chemistries on the blood specimen you sent to Dr. Flesch last summer."

"Last summer?" Constantine stalled. "Blood? Oh, yes. Yes, I remember. Rather interesting, wasn't it?"

"I wrote to you about our findings, but by then you'd left your job."

"That's right. Yes. I . . . left my job. Went into another line of work." He frowned, lifted his shoulders, smoothed his beard, tapering it to a point as though he were holding a bouquet. "That blood . . . it came from . . . well, actually, it's a fascinating story; there's a fascinating story behind that blood. But I can't tell you the story. I'm not free to discuss it . . . without the donor's consent. Actually, to tell you the truth, the donor is dead. So. The case is closed. Too bad. But that's the way it is. Please, sit down, Dr. Seltzer. Would you like some tea? Afraid that's all I have. Let me put the water on." He went into the kitchen. "What are you doing in New York?" he asked, all of it false, artificial, perfunctory, as he seemed to realize himself, his performance being empty, Seltzer thought, of invention and enthusiasm. "Here for a convention or something?"

"Dr. Constantine," Seltzer said, "before we go any further, I should tell you that I know everything. I know about your stigmata. The Bishop told me."

At the sink, Constantine, his back turned, stopped, the teakettle in one hand, his other hand resting on the faucet. Seltzer watched him closely, watched him as though he were an experiment cooking in a beaker. Then Constantine said, half to himself, into his beard, "Funny. I trusted those priests. I liked them. I felt a genuine affection for the Bishop."

"He's a very fine man, and he's very concerned about you."

"Did he tell you . . . about the children?"

"The children? No, he didn't say anything about children."

"Well. That's something anyway."

"The Bishop wants to help, that's all. I made him see how important it was for me to talk to you."

Constantine came back into the room and sat down. "Why is it so important?"

"Dr. Constantine, there's something I think you don't know. That blood specimen. We could not restore the prothrombin time of any of the clotting factors."

Constantine's eyes narrowed, his brows came together as he tried to understand. "Prothrombin time . . . It's been so long . . . I seem to have forgotten everything I ever knew." He smiled confusedly. "Prothrombin time. Has to do with clotting, doesn't it? Oh, yes. Twelve factors. But"—he looked at Seltzer—"but if I remember correctly, that would be impossible, wouldn't it?"

"Yes. Exactly."

"But then it couldn't be."

"It was. I have the data. No mistake."

Constantine stared at the ceiling for some moments, fingering his beard reflectively. "It's interesting, isn't it?" he said abstractedly.

"That's one of the great pieces of understatement I've ever heard," Seltzer replied. He felt parched, his eyes burned; he was dried out from the decongestants he was taking for his cold. It was annoying that he was not at full strength.

"I'll tell you something even more interesting," Constantine unexpectedly volunteered with an ambiguous smile of what seemed almost to be childish vanity. "It's only the blood from here that doesn't clot." He extended one hand and touched the palm with his fingertips. Seltzer squirmed. He was dying to see the wounds with his own eyes. He had to keep lecturing himself to maintain control. "From my hands and feet and here in my side. If you took blood from a vein in my arm, it would coagulate. At various times I've doubted it really was blood."

"It's blood all right. Or we're redefining blood." He was stifled with excitement. "Are they—the wounds—are they open all the time?"

"Yes. All told, I would guess I lose about a cup of it every day."

"Is there any history," Seltzer asked, "of bleeding in your family?"

"Not that I know of."

"Have you dressed the wounds?"

"No. Never. I just wear these gloves."

"Have they ever become infected?"

"Never."

"It's fantastic!"

"I suppose it is, from your point of view. It seems somewhat less exciting from mine."

"Well, of course. You've lived with it. Still, intellectually, abstractly, you can't help but appreciate the potential implications of what we have here."

"What implications?" Constantine asked artlessly.

"Why—it's absolutely earth-shaking, what we have here. Earth-shaking!" He looked hard at Constantine, looking for some indication that he appreciated how earth-shaking it was. He saw nothing. Just a mild expression of almost blank innocence. *Jesus,* he thought, *he really doesn't understand!* It was possible that everything he'd gone through—the terrible tortured existence the Bishop had hinted at—had affected his brain. There were lapses in his concentration, vacancies in his eyes, symptomatic of people who had amnesia. *He's really not intellectually responsible for his actions,* Seltzer thought.

"How . . . earth-shaking?"

"Well—maybe that's an exaggeration," Seltzer thought it prudent to say. "I just meant that if we can figure out exactly what's taking place inside of you, it could very well be a landmark in the history of hematology."

"Oh. You're saying that you want to—to perform experiments."

"Naturally. Yes. I mean, you want this cleared up, don't you? Now that you know the truth."

There was a pause, and then Constantine said, "It's because I've come to know some truths, Dr. Seltzer, that it's really immaterial to me whether or not it's cleared up."

Seltzer felt his temper beginning to rise in spite of himself. *Stay cool,* he said to himself. *Don't blow up!* But he was getting hot.

"You're a scientist, Dr. Constantine. You were trained as a scientist."

"I'm not a scientist anymore." Constantine cocked his head, leaned his cheek in his hand. "I've forgotten almost all the science I've ever known. That's the truth. I was in the library today looking at a textbook, a college chemistry text. It might as well have been written in Hebrew."

"Yes. I can understand that. The Bishop gave me some idea of what you've undergone."

"Did he? Do you think he knows?"

"Well, but that's irrelevant, strictly speaking, isn't it? I understand you've gone through quite an ordeal. It's bound to have affected your emotional life, your—your psychology . . . perhaps even your memory. Or it could be that the unique chemistry of your blood is the cause. The cause of the stigmata, the reason your brain is . . . functioning, shall we say, peculiarly, as for instance in this case of having forgotten all your chemistry. You see, it's all just further evidence that something tremendous is going on in your bloodstream, and we have to find it. We have to make you well."

"But I'm perfectly well," Constantine objected. "I feel fine."

"By your own admission you can't read a college chemistry book!" Seltzer snapped, bringing his hand down flat on the arm of the couch, dry dust swarming from the upholstery like a flight of insects. *Watch it, Seltzer!* he told himself. *Watch it!* "I'm sorry," he said. "I'm not feeling well. I believe I may be developing a slight temperature. All right. It doesn't matter how well you feel. What matters—and please try to understand this, doctor—what is paramount is that whatever is causing your blood to behave the way it behaves may, if we can determine the cause, prove to be of inestimable benefit to all mankind. There's the possibility of your blood providing science with a truly historic breakthrough. As I told the Bishop, a cure for cancer might emerge from your blood. A cure for leukemia. For diabetes, for diseases that at the moment seem entirely unrelated to hematology. Schizophrenia. Autism. You name it. I believe you may be in fact a walking encyclopedia of medical knowledge." He paused. Constantine was listening to him with an expression on his face of almost simpleminded curiosity. Seltzer battled the rage which that expression provoked. "In view of which," he went on slowly, "I hope you'll agree to come back to Rochester with me and let us examine you at the Mayo Clinic." He paused again. Constantine's expression did not alter. Seltzer raised his voice. "Did you hear what I said?"

"Yes, I heard. And I understand. I'm not crazy; I'm not retarded. I've just forgotten my education, that's all. Which doesn't seem such a terrible thing to forget. More terrible in one way to forget your umbrella on a rainy day. But thank you, no."

"No? No, what?"

"I decline your invitation. I don't want to go to Rochester."

"But you must!" Seltzer blurted. "You have to! Can't you get it through your head that—"

"I'm sorry," Constantine interrupted. "I simply refuse to go."

"You wrote to us! Remember that. You asked us for help in the first place. Since then my private life has been turned upside down. I spent a fortune trying to find you. My work has suffered. You owe me some consideration at least."

"Everything you say is true. And I regret—really, profoundly—having inconvenienced you. But a great deal has changed since last summer. I'm coming out of a—an adventure, I suppose you could call it, that was very horrible and very wonderful. I survived. I'm beginning to understand some things, I'm beginning to put myself back together. I could not at this time endure being examined by anyone, for any reason. I couldn't take it. And I won't. I just want to be left alone."

On the point of cracking, of screaming and raging, Seltzer at last, with a stern effort, succeeded in mastering himself. *This isn't the way—you'll only scare him off. He'll vanish in the city like smoke. You'll never find him. Think! Take it easy! You have to get him some other way.* He stared at his shoes, chewed on his lip, pinched his nose. Constantine, composed, his hands folded in his lap, his legs crossed, watched him compassionately. He felt the man's frustration and was sorry for him.

At last Seltzer spoke. "Perhaps I've given you the wrong impression about . . . about the kind of life you'd be leading at Mayo. I'm prepared to guarantee your comfort and privacy. That goes without saying. We would naturally put your feelings ahead of every other consideration." He was thinking, *Conrad! Maybe Conrad can help me. Maybe I can get a warrant for his arrest.*

"Even so," said Constantine, "eventually you would want to publish your findings, wouldn't you? That goes without saying too, doesn't it?"

"Well, of course there wouldn't be much point to it if we didn't publish our findings. But I assure you—I promise that every effort would be made to guard you against any mental anguish or embarrassment you might feel." *A menace to the public health, he was thinking. Have the man declared a menace and lock him up. That might work.*

"I don't doubt your good intentions," Constantine replied. "And I would like to help you. I wish I could cooperate. But I can't take the risk. At the moment my psychology is a very fragile thing. I appreciate the extent of your concern, your desire to develop possible cures for cancer. If I were in your position I suppose I'd feel the same way. By the same token, I hope you can put yourself in my position, try to see things my way. I really feel that it's a matter of life and death, that my very existence depends on my doing things my own way."

Seltzer stared at the floor. "And there's not the slightest possibility that you'll change your mind?"

"It's exactly because my mind is changing every day that I won't go with you. I don't know from day to day what I'll think or how I'll feel the day after."

"Then it *is* possible that sometime in the future you might consider changing your mind."

Constantine smiled. "After what I've experienced, Dr. Seltzer, in the past nine months, I've become convinced that almost anything is possible."

"Well, then," said Seltzer, forcing a tight smile, "at least I can hope. Would you mind if I got in touch with you in a couple of weeks, just on the outside chance that you might have had second thoughts?"

"If I have second thoughts I'd prefer to contact you."

"Yes. Well. That's reasonable." *I could probably hit him over the head with something and kidnap the son of a bitch,* he thought. "You can call me any time, any time, at the Mayo Clinic. Seltzer. S-E-L-T-Z-E-R." *No, there must be legal avenues.*

"I won't forget," said Constantine.

"Well, then," said Seltzer again as he got to his feet, "I guess there's nothing for me to do but go back to Rochester and hope to hear from you. Remember, you can write your own ticket. I'll give you whatever guarantees you want, in writing."

"Good-bye," said Constantine. "And thank you for being so reasonable."

"Well, I can't pretend I'm not immensely disappointed. Dr. Flesch will be disappointed too. Science is my whole life. On the other hand, one has to guard against being carried away by scientific pursuits to the point where we become inhuman. In the last analysis, Dr. Constantine, humanity is what this is all about."

The next day the weather changed. Coming out of the subway at Forty-second Street and Times Square, Constantine was greeted by a sloppy wet snow that melted as it struck the pavement. He made his way east on Forty-second Street past the movie houses, the cut-rate char-broiled steak houses, the porno shops and the retail stores selling cheap lingerie, all the way to the library. When he emerged half an hour later, he was carrying an elementary Russian grammar. He walked back to the subway station, and before he descended he bought at a corner newsstand a copy of *The New York Times.* At home, snow was clinging wetly to the branches of his tree; there was, however, no snow on the ground; it was all mud around the roots of the tree. The green buds nosed up through the tatters of snow on the limbs. There were many more of them. Constantine sat down in his living room and opened the Russian grammar. He stared at the unfamiliar bramble of Cyrillic characters, which looked like pictographs. After ten minutes he laid the book aside and picked up the newspaper. The printing resembled Russian. He closed his eyes and, opening them, refocused on the page. The printing danced, then settled down. With dreamy, childish amusement he realized he had all but forgotten how to read English.

He turned to a back page and looked at the weather map and the meteorological symbols. He spelled out names and numbers, moving his lips. Barometric pressure, 29.84. Barcelona, 83. Rangoon, 90. It was cloudy in Moosonee. 45 in Calgary. It was clear over San Juan. " 'A cold front is a boundary between cold air and warmer air,' " he read slowly out loud. " 'An occluded front is a line along which warm air is lifted by opposing wedges of cold air, often causing precipitation. Isobars are lines of equal barometric pressure forming air-flow patterns.' " He looked out the kitchen window; his eyes felt fatigued. It was snowing. "An occluded front," he said. And he laughed.

"I can't explain now, Conrad," Seltzer said. His room in the Midtown Motor Hotel was costing twenty-four dollars per night. It was ugly and noisy and drafty. His cold was much worse; the decongestants had lost their potency. "I don't have time to explain. Just trust me, will you? Believe me! Have you ever known me to go off half cocked?"

Dr. Flesch had been waiting for a call from his son-in-law. His daughter had gone to the hospital the night before; she was in labor and having a hard time of it. He wanted Seltzer to hang up.

"But what are you doing in New York, Hermann?" he asked. "I don't understand."

"Look, I swear to you, I'm onto the most . . . stupendous discovery in the whole history of human blood! I can't tell you how important this guy is."

"Constantine?"

"He's got a rare disease of the blood. It's a long story. I don't have time to explain. But he refuses to cooperate. He's a little crazy. I'll explain everything. But I need help. Who do you know in New York? I need someone to open official doors for me. Didn't you used to be friends with somebody in the coroner's office once?"

"Yes, I have a friend who works in the coroner's office, Hermann, but—"

"Please! No buts!"

Flesch frowned. He scarcely recognized the hysterical voice.

"Call him for me. *Please,* Conrad. Now, right now, this minute. I need someone to open doors for me. And then call me back. Here's my number. You got a pencil?"

Flesch jotted the number on the cover of the phone book.

"Talk to Marylou. She can give you some of the details. The rest will have to wait until I bag this guy."

"Bag him? What are you doing, Hermann, are you stalking wild game?"

"That's close, Conrad; brother, that's close!"

"You sound terrible."

"I think I have pneumonia. But it doesn't matter. Don't tell Marylou. Tell her I'm fine. She worries. Stuart has some information too. Talk to him. But call this guy in the coroner's office first and fix it up for me to see him."

"It's very big, is it? Then that blood of Constantine's last fall . . ."

"I didn't fully realize at the time the scope of the thing. I made some mistakes. I'll explain later. Big? Conrad, in my life I've never seen anything bigger!"

Hanging up, he sat down at the desk to write his wife a letter.

> Please go to the bank and talk to Dexter. I need a thousand dollars. I may have to stay here for a while. Take out a home improvement loan and send me a bank draft at Chase Manhattan. And don't worry. It's even bigger than I thought. 1943 *pales in comparison!* Need I say more? As for this city, I can't begin to describe it. The air—you wouldn't believe the air. You can see it, you can actually see it, and it gets into your lungs like poison gas, and in your eyes. Your nose is dry, your eyes are inflamed, you cough, you're parched. You take a bath and ten minutes later your fingernails are black and your skin is covered with grease. The collars of my shirts look like someone's been walking on them. I don't smoke, but I might as well smoke two packs a day. How can anyone live in this hell? They shove you, they sneer at you, they poke umbrellas into your ribs and knock you off the sidewalks into the gutter. The cab drivers cheat you, in the restaurants they rob you blind. Nobody has a civil word. To ask directions from a cop you risk being arrested. To ask directions from anyone is to risk having your head broken. I carry my money in my shoe. I read that was the thing to do in New York. I don't go into the streets anymore without my umbrella. I have an umbrella with a sharp spike on the end for purposes of self-defense. So help me. It's a terrible

place. Be happy you're in Rochester. People in Rochester don't know how good they have it.

In ten more days it would be officially spring. Constantine sat in the main reading room of the library and looked at a diagram illustrating the relationship of the earth to the sun on the first day of spring. It seemed quite miraculous to him that in ten days' time the planet earth that he was sitting on would—tilted on its axis 23.5 degrees off the perpendicular—arrive at that moment of the year when magically Santiago, Chile, and New York City and Lima, Peru, and Shanghai, China, and Greenwich, England, and Vladivostok, Russia, would all enjoy exactly the same amount of daylight and darkness—one trembling balanced moment when that would be so—immediately after which the Northern Hemisphere would move into a period of longer days and moderating temperatures while the Southern Hemisphere moved inexorably into the shadows of fall and the storms of winter. This year that moment was calculated to occur on March 22 at 12:24 A.M. Eastern Standard Time in the United States. And then it would be spring in the United States and elsewhere, and it would be autumn in Tierra del Fuego and elsewhere. Constantine looked forward with special anticipation to that moment.

He went to the library every day. Sometimes he walked the entire distance; sometimes he took the subway from Sheridan Square. He would sit in the reading room and leaf through grammars. Russian. Arabic. Hebrew. Chinese. He made no attempt to study any of these languages; he simply passed the time in fanciful speculations, comparing their characters. He thought about the origins of language, decided that whatever other falsehoods the Bible might contain, the major falsehood reposed in the phrase that opened the Gospel according to John. In the Beginning, he felt, there were unquestionably many things. But he would bet the Word was not among them.

He also delved into books about astronomy and ancient religions that worshiped the sun. He pondered the history of the Rosetta Stone, studied diagrams depicting the circular Zodiac of Dandarah, puzzled over illustrations of the Tablet of Kings at Abydos. He perused esoteric charts showing the amplitudes at which stars of different declinations rose and set in different latitudes. He conceived a strong desire to visit Stonehenge.

Often he just sat and looked at the other readers. Sometimes he dozed, leaning on his fist. In college he only had to enter the main reading room of the library and open his textbooks, and he would be overcome by a delicious and irresistible drowsiness. One year, his sophomore year, he estimated that he slept on the average fourteen hours a day. In graduate school, however, it was just the opposite; he once went fifty-seven hours without sleep.

He thought a lot about his school days those afternoons in the New York Public Library, which he believed must have been the only place in the world where nobody seemed to find it curious for a man to be reading with his gloves on. He remembered roommates he hadn't thought about for years. Girls he'd dated. He wondered where they were, what they were doing. He felt sentimental about them. He wept frequently, something he had never done. He would come out onto the steps of the library late in the afternoon, with the setting sun slanting through the dissipating clouds of a thunderstorm fleeing raggedly to the north, and see the sunlight turning the skyscrapers golden and orange, the air fresh and washed with the rain, and he would look down from between the marble pillars, down the stairs at the buses, the traffic, the throngs of people, and a sweetness would invade him, and the tears would glide down his cheeks and into his beard. He would see a child take the hand of a smaller sister and guide her responsibly across an intersection, and he would cry. Lovers made him cry. The stars made him cry. A dandelion pushing up through the mud and debris in the garden made him cry. It was as though he were compensating for a lifetime of abnormal aridity. He gave himself up voluptuously to his tears.

He longed for spring.

"Let me get this straight, Dr. Seltzer. Are you trying to tell me that—"

"I don't know how I can make myself any clearer. Are we both speaking English?"

"But we can't just go around arresting people without—"

"You don't arrest people in this city on every goddamned imaginable flimsy pretext? The police don't bust prostitutes for stopping to straighten their stockings? I haven't seen that?"

"Yes, but you must realize—"

"You don't close down movie theaters and confiscate films? You're always so scrupulous about search warrants? I suppose habeas corpus is god in this city. Well, if habeas corpus is god in New York City, everyone does a hell of a job concealing the fact. You want evidence? I'm telling you—the goddamned man *is* the evidence. It's inside him. His blood is the evidence! At the airport they search inside a man's *asshole* to find contraband. I tell you this man is a menace to the public health. I can document it. I have the data in Rochester. I'm not some goddamned kook! I have a scholarly reputation, I'm an associate of Conrad Flesch, and when it comes to blood they don't make them any bigger in the world than Conrad Flesch. The man needs to be quarantined. You want a plague on your hands in New York City? You want a twentieth-century version of the bubonic plague? There are no antidotes to what this man has. Science doesn't know anything about it. Look, I'm not some ivory tower Ph.D. I'm a medical doctor. I've been in science for forty years. This guy has to be brought in, and brought in fast."

"I'll tell you what, doctor. Since this appears to be a health problem, why don't you go over to the city health department and—"

"I've been to six different departments in the last five days! I'm sick of being shunted from department to department. I want action. I want to see the mayor!"

"I'm sorry, but it's perfectly clear to me that this matter falls under the jurisdiction of the Department of Health. There's nothing I can do. I'll make an appointment for you. That's as far as I can go."

On March 20 the weather in New York City was perfect. It was sixty-two degrees at three o'clock in the afternoon in Central Park, winds were from the southwest at fifteen miles per hour, and visibility from the top of the Empire State Building was twenty-eight miles. *The New York Times* reported that a Russian nuclear submarine was on a voyage to the North Pole. Two tankers had collided off the coast of Santa Barbara, creating an immense oil slick. An executive jet had crashed in New Haven in a fog, killing seven passengers and a crew of three. Kaizer Pharmaceutical in Groton, Connecticut, announced a dramatic breakthrough on a new kind of fertility drug. The Midwest was languishing through a week of torrential rains. Local flooding was occurring in the outskirts of Moline, Illinois. In Lubbock, Texas, a tornado had flattened six houses and a barn.

Leaves were coming out on Constantine's tree. The chess players were active in Washington Square.

That evening, Constantine telephoned his daughter but there was no answer.

On March 21, Hermann Seltzer sat down at his desk in the Midtown Motor Hotel, where he had run up a bill in excess of three hundred dollars, and dashed off a note to his friend Conrad Flesch. "We've got him! We've got the bastard," he wrote. "I've finally got a warrant for Constantine's arrest!"

Constantine awoke around noon that day and prepared a cup of tea. He read the *Times* of the day before with interest. Then he went out and down the three flights of stairs to the street. The stairs corkscrewed down, winding around a stairwell illuminated dimly by a dirty skylight. It was a long, narrow building. Constantine occupied the top floor by himself. The foyer had a floor of black and white rubberized tiles laid down over cement; where some of the tiles were cracked the powdery cement was visible.

He let himself out. It was a sunny day. The temperature in New York City was 61. In Tegucigalpa it was 94. He entered a pharmacy a few doors down from his building and purchased a pair of scissors for $1.29. While he was waiting for his change, he overheard a woman talking to the pharmacist about a murder. Constantine didn't catch all of it, but evidently someone had been murdered the night before on the same block. Furthermore, it was the third slaying in the neighborhood in a month. "Nobody's safe anymore," the woman said. "I'm afraid to go down to the laundry room." Constantine was surprised; it seemed like such a tranquil neighborhood. "The goddamned mayor . . ." he heard the pharmacist say.

He went back to his building. As he climbed the stairs, glancing over the banister at the checkerboard pattern of tiles in the foyer, he thought about the murderer, thought how easy it would be for someone to enter the building and kill someone, and wondered why he was not afraid.

Back in his apartment, he snipped off the fingers of his gloves, reflecting that it was something he should have done long ago. He examined the wounds. There was almost no pain these days in either his hands or his feet, although the lesion in his side still caused him occasional discomfort. He went into the bathroom, carrying the scissors, and looked at himself. It occurred to him to cut off his beard. Then he thought better of it and merely trimmed it a few inches. He went into the kitchen, where, standing at the sink peeling an orange, pleased at the increased efficiency provided by the fingerless gloves, he gazed with proprietary satisfaction at the tree at the bottom of the deep shaft which was the back yard. It was speckled with bright green curled-up buds. It was shortly after one o'clock when he left the apartment for the second time that day.

He walked east toward Fifth Avenue, very warm in his long black woolen coat. He considered that he would soon have to buy a less cumbersome garment as summer approached. At Sheridan Square he looked through a sidewalk bin of used books. He came across a volume entitled *Principles of Astronomy*. It was very dirty, and the spine was broken. He bought it for fifteen cents and put it in his pocket.

Continuing east, he purchased a bagel from a pushcart and a little farther on drank a glass of orange soda at a counter of a hot dog stand. The sidewalks were crowded; it was a beautiful day. Girls in jeans and flowery halters, their arms and shoulders white from the winter, gossiped on street corners, eating ice cream cones and taking in the sun. On the steps of the pool in Washington Square, boys played guitars and sang. A cop on horseback patrolled the perimeter of the park. There was water in the pool now, cellophane bags floating in the water, glistening like silver. Pigeons scattered up and down the walks pecked at spilled popcorn. The trees were green.

Dr. Constantine proceeded across Fifth Avenue and into the East Village, where soon the atmosphere changed. The streets became dirtier, the people on the steps of the brownstones hostile and sad. He saw a cannibalized car, a shell, its wheels stripped, windows smashed, upholstery charred.

A drunk up ahead was accosting pedestrians; Constantine crossed the street to avoid him.

At Saint Mark's Place, he turned north and began to wander uptown for a few blocks. Then he turned east again and moved toward the river. It was three-thirty by the time he crossed the pedestrian bridge over the FDR Drive and found a bench by the water. He sat there resting for half an hour, alternately watching the barges churn upriver and leafing through the book he'd bought on Sheridan Square.

By four-fifteen he was outside the UN Building, walking north. Inside the UN a delegate from Libya was denouncing Israel, and the Israeli delegation was threatening to boycott the debate. Half a dozen pickets were in the street with signs reviling Red China. A few blocks north, some students were sitting at a card table collecting signatures on a petition that had to do with grape-pickers. Constantine declined to sign the petition. A few blocks farther on, a black man tried to shove a circular into his hand; he declined to accept it.

At five thirty-two he went into Grand Central Station and sat down in the waiting room to rest again. Commuters flooded up and down the ramp from Forty-second Street. The church pews were packed. Constantine read his book for a while, realized that several pages were missing, dropped the book into a trash bin and went outside. He stood in front of the station looking at the traffic, undecided whether to go north on Lexington or west on Forty-second to Times Square. After a moment or two, he bought a Yiddish newspaper, folded it, tucked it into his coat pocket and set out toward Times Square.

It was almost dark when he got there. He turned north on Seventh Avenue, walked past the international magazine shop, crossed over to the west side of the street, looking into the souvenir shops, the cut-rate camera and record stores, the pornographic movie theaters, the dance halls and massage parlors. The traffic roared and bellowed. Constantine stood in the middle of the sidewalk and raised his face to the sky. The news of the world raced in a belt of winking lights around the middle of the Allied Chemical Tower: IN SANTIAGO CHILE FOUR BRAZILIAN HIJACKERS . . . PRIME MINISTER INDIRA GANDHI SAID TODAY THAT . . . THE PENTAGON ANNOUNCED THE DEPLOYMENT OF . . .

He watched the ribbon of light until the words blurred and ran together into a stream of continuous tracer fire.

He was not conscious of making a decision to do it; he was not aware that he had done it until several seconds after he removed his gloves.

Then he realized with a start that he was standing in the middle of the sidewalk, the mobs dividing to pour around him, with his stigmata exposed, his hands outstretched, the palms up and fingers spread wide, for everyone to see. He waited, his heart beating rapidly, frozen in that posture for thirty seconds, a minute. The noise of the traffic did not abate. The news of the world did not falter. People scarcely glanced at him. Nothing happened.

He looked around. He saw a multiple amputee like an oversized amphibian scooting down the sidewalk on a skateboard. He saw a blind beggar with a white cane jingling a tin cup. He saw a hunchback zigzagging across the street, dodging cars and trucks. He saw an old gray-haired Negro lean over the curb and vomit. In the window of a bookshop he saw seated at an elevated desk a gross triangular mountain of flesh, a structure shingled in fat, a man who must have weighed four hundred pounds. He saw two midgets, a man and a woman, with pink faces all bunched and wrinkled as though they'd been pressed out of cookie cutters, hand in hand, skipping in and out among the legs of the human traffic towering over them. He saw a man with lipstick painted on his mouth, a mouth like a scarlet blossom, his eyelids painted blue, a beauty mark on his powdered cheek, mincing down the street wearing bright blue satin trousers very tight across his buttocks, and high-heeled shoes. Behind the counter of a pizza place he saw a man twirling dough; he had a large bulbous bald white head like a mongoloid. He saw a man with a goiter eating pizza, the goiter purplish and distended, dangling beneath his chin like an enormous swollen testicle the texture of uncooked poultry, wobbling as he chewed. He saw an old woman with no teeth playing an accordion. Her legs were hairy, doglike, and covered with scabs. She was wearing a pair of ruined corduroy slippers on her feet. She had one eye. He saw an old man with trousers ripped at the knee, the cloth sagging open like a flap of skin, a crazed expression on his stubbly face, do a slow pirouette and collapse on his back on the sidewalk, people hurrying by, stepping over and around him, unconcerned.

Constantine began to laugh.

He stood there, his head back, his face turned up to the enormous billboards high above the street, waterfalls of amber whiskey flooding over icebergs in a glass, a twenty-foot-tall giantess in a bikini that would have housed a family of four, with breasts that would have nourished a Brownie troop, with enough ivory in her smile to make a grand piano, and Dr. Constantine, his hands stretched out at his sides, laughed and laughed, as the great neons flowed on and off and the curtains rose in the theaters and the old man who had fallen struggled feebly to rise, he laughed, and the horns blared at him, and he continued to laugh as the woman with the accordion crooned a gibberish song and the Negro spat up and hacked out his vomit and the man with the goiter dabbed at his lips daintily with a napkin while the circle of dough danced on the fingers of the mongoloid like a huge airy Frisbee, Constantine laughed until he thought he would rupture himself.

And then a policeman was growling in his ear, "Okay, Mac, move it along before I run you in!"

He was famished when he arrived back in the Village. His hunger did not seem unusual to him. He knew where he wanted to eat. There was a restaurant near the corner of Bedford and Barrow, adjacent to one of the concealed patios he was fond of. The restaurant had no sign outside. The door was indistinguishable from any of the other doors on the residential street. If a person didn't know it was there, he could not find it.

Constantine entered, went up a short flight of stairs and then down into a dark smoky room with bare wooden floors and scarred wooden tables. The walls were streaked with soot. Framed photographs dark with age hung from the walls. A jukebox was playing. A small coal fire burned in the fireplace. The room was half filled.

A young man in a denim shirt and Levi's took his order. At first Constantine did not know what to ask for. Then he decided on a bowl of bean soup, and when he finished that he was still hungry and ate a steak with fried potatoes. For dessert he had a cup of tea and a dish of vanilla ice cream. He ate with his gloves on.

It was eleven-twenty EST when he emerged. The temperature was forty-nine and the wind was from the west. It was chilly and Constantine walked rapidly. Not many people were on the streets. Traffic was light. He stopped in a café on Christopher Street and drank another cup of tea. He did not want to go home, and he stayed in the café until after midnight, coming out again on the morning of March 22, which was a Friday.

The sky was partially clouded over as he arrived at his building. He looked at the clouds, which would give way to reveal the moon and a few pale stars and then re-form again, covering the stars. He was tired. He had walked for miles. He wondered how long it had been since he'd walked so far.

He opened the street door and went in. He stood for a moment at the bottom of the stairs looking up to his landing. There was only a single weak light bulb hanging from a cord in the ceiling, dangling free in the middle of the stairwell at the second floor. The hall was dark and shadowy.

He began to climb, slowly, his shoes rasping on the stairs. It was very quiet. He ascended step by step, his shoes striking the stairs in time to his heartbeat. He gripped the banister with one hand; his other hand was in his coat pocket, clutching the Yiddish newspaper. As he ascended he was thinking about two things principally—Stonehenge and his daughter. He would telephone her again in the morning. He didn't know what he would say to her, but he promised himself that he would call. And he wanted to see Stonehenge.

He reached the first-floor landing, looked up past the light bulb, but could not see anything beyond it. He heard a muffled cough. He continued on up, his pace lagging a beat behind his heart now. He would sleep very well tonight, he thought. No trouble falling asleep after a day like this. He began to try to calculate how many miles he'd walked, adding up the blocks approximately over to St. Mark's Place, dividing by eight, eight city blocks to a mile, they said—but which blocks, the long ones or the short ones? —and then thirty-four blocks roughly to midtown and another mile to Times Square. . . . He couldn't keep the figures straight in his head. Miles and miles, though. Maybe ten, maybe more. He was very tired.

At the second-floor landing he reached out over the banister and gave the light bulb a tap. It swung back and forth like a pendulum on the long wire, sending strikes of shadows up and down the walls. Constantine glanced down, thirty feet to the checkered floor in the foyer, the shadows washing back and forth on the tiles. Then he rounded the corner and began to climb the last flight of stairs to the landing in front of his door.

He would need money soon. He thought about the Bishop, the money owing to him from Kaizer. The Bishop had never sent it. The Bishop, he thought. Oh, my, that Bishop. Well, he would need money anyway. Eventually. He couldn't work. How would he get money? There was a clinic near Times Square where you could sell blood. He wondered what they paid. He smiled at the notion. He remembered one of his roommates in college who was always broke; he had sold blood once to pay for an important date. What was his name? A Polish name. Baranowski or something. He was always selling things to pay for his romances. One semester he sold all his textbooks. Then he pilfered books to sell. Then he pawned his watch. Then he dropped three courses to get a refund. Then he sold his blood. *I wonder what the going rate is for blood these days?* Constantine thought as he arrived at the top of the stairs.

It all happened very quickly then. It took only ten or fifteen seconds. He was feeling in his pocket for his key when he became aware of them in the shadows. He looked up and saw them, three of them, and his heart gave a great bound of terror. There was a murmur, a scuffling of feet. Constantine instinctively leaped backward. Seltzer, whom he did not recognize, lunged for him. Constantine saw uniforms. But his backward leap had brought him against the banister, and he almost lost his balance, his feet coming up off the floor a few inches. Seltzer tried to grab him, to pull him back, but one of the uniformed men, who also sprang forward to save Constantine from tumbling backward over the banister, collided with Seltzer, and Seltzer was knocked off his balance for a split second and lurched against Constantine, whose legs kicked straight out into the air as he waved his arms in a windmill motion clutching at space, and Seltzer, recovering, grabbed at the front of his coat, but lost him, and grabbed at the legs of his trousers, but lost him, and Constantine's feet came up and went over the banister, and Seltzer grabbed again at his ankles, and then got his hand on one of Constantine's shoes and almost went over the banister himself and would have if the third man had not clamped his arms around his shoulders from behind and pulled him back to safety as Constantine somersaulted free and dived down through the stairwell, all of this without a word being uttered by anyone, in less than fifteen seconds from start to finish.

It was twelve twenty-four in New York City as Constantine dropped through the air, feet downward at first, catching at the light cord, tearing it loose from the ceiling. In Fairbanks the sun was setting; in Athens it was dawn. As Dr. Constantine fell, over on his back now, tangled in the cord, his legs spraddled, a Russian submarine was nosing under the icecap at the North Pole and Constantine's daughter was brushing her teeth before going to bed. As he plummeted, headfirst now, coins spilling from his pockets and floating in the air alongside him, Seltzer's white face above transfixed at the railing staring down at the cartwheel his body described as it dropped in accordance with the laws of gravity at thirty-two feet per second per second, a freezing rain was falling in Tierra del Fuego, a warm front was invading Asunción, and Melissa Jones came awake in her bed in her father's house in New Rochelle with a little scream which failed to arouse her pet kitten, who was sleeping beside her.

As Dr. Constantine's skull struck the floor, and his neck snapped, and his spine was crushed, at that instant in one of the labs in the Medical Research Building at Kaizer Pharmaceutical Company in Groton, Connecticut, a guinea pig which had been injected with a new and powerful fertility drug gave birth to a tiny horror with no legs and two heads which the mother promptly tore to shreds with her sharp teeth.

Five of his ribs were shattered in the fall. One of the broken ribs punctured his lungs. His liver burst. His lower intestine exploded. His pelvis was jammed upward against his rib cage, rupturing his stomach. His kidneys were perforated by shrapnel from his vertebrae. His femoral artery was severed. Most of the bleeding was internal. His heart continued to beat for several minutes after he was dead.

Seltzer came clattering down the stairs ahead of the two officers, sobbing, babbling. Constantine lay motionless on his side, curled up in the fetal position. One of his shoes had come off in the impact. There were coins scattered all over the floor. The light cord was wrapped around his broken neck.

"Call for an ambulance!" Seltzer screamed, rolling Constantine on his back, clawing at the buttons of his overcoat. "He's still alive, he has a pulse, call for the ambulance!" He knelt beside Constantine and tore open his shirt and listened at his chest. There were no marks on his torso, no blood at all on his breast. "We have to save him, my God, quick, get help, get help! I tell you he's still alive, I can feel his heart!" Seltzer's face shone a sickly yellow in the light from the officer's electric torch; he was covered with sweat. "He's scientifically invaluable!" He ran his fingers over Constantine's chest, stopped, caught his breath. Then, his eyes glazing with disbelief, he took first one of Constantine's hands and then the other and stripped the fingerless gloves from the hands and snatched the flashlight from the officer's grasp and directed the beam onto the dead man's hands, and gave a groan of deep anguish. The flesh was pink and clean and soft. He touched the palms with his fingers, turned them over, stroked the backs of Dr. Constantine's hands, which were covered with thin black hair. They were the hands of a child. The fingers were rather short and fleshy, the palms plump and dry. And there was not a mark on them. There was nothing.

CHAPTER 21

THE GIRL WATCHED without emotion as her parents drove off. Her mother had wept; her father had chewed on an unlighted cigar.

She followed the mother superior down the gravel path, beneath the trees, to the retreat house. It was very quiet. She saw no one else.

"Here we are," said the mother superior. She was an old wrinkled woman with whiskers on her chin. She smelled of camphor. "Dinner is at six. If you need anything, ask."

"Thank you," the girl said tonelessly. "It looks very nice."

The mother superior went away and the girl closed the door and locked it. The room contained a single bed with a crucifix attached to the wall at the foot of it, where she would see it the last thing at night before she went to sleep and the first thing in the morning. The window afforded a view of a small pond covered with water lilies. The floor was bare and the walls, which were cream colored, were also bare except for a cheap framed print of a winter landscape hanging above the wooden dresser. A cane-bottomed rocking chair stood in one corner opposite the door. There was a coat hook on the door, and the girl hung her bathrobe on it and put the rest of her clothes in the dresser, arranging everything neatly and carefully as her mother had always insisted when she was a child. Then she unbuttoned her dress and tossed it carelessly on the rocking chair, and in her white cotton bra and panties, sat down on the edge of the bed, next to her empty suitcase, and stared at her bathrobe for almost half an hour.

A bell rang somewhere. Goose bumps formed on her flesh. She absently ran her hand up and down her arm. The setting sun turned the room rosy. Another bell rang, and she stood up and walked somnolently to the window and watched the lily pads rising and falling gently in the water and saw the sunset edging the clouds with mauve and crimson.

Someone knocked at the door. The girl did not answer. She leaned on the window sill with both arms and pressed her face against the glass and looked at the gorgeous colors in the sky. The knock was repeated. "Yes?" she said, her breath smudging the windowpane.

"Are you all right, dear?"

"Yes, I'm fine, thank you. I was just taking a nap."

"Dinner in fifteen minutes."

"Thank you."

She did not go to dinner. She expected someone to return, but they left her alone. She knew she would have to conform or they would send her away and she would be forced to live with her mother and father again. She didn't want that. She had to be careful, smile when it was expected, eat when they called her, be courteous, be modest. Or else there would be more sessions with the doctor.

You're fine, he told her, patting her head as if she were a child. They all talked to her that way, as though she were five years old. Well, let them think whatever they pleased. She was alone now, finally, for the first time in months, free to think, unmolested, free to try to remember.

It was so hard to remember. But she would remember, now that there was no one to interfere with her. She would recapture every sensation. She would reconstruct every moment of it. He would help her. She could see

Him clearly, even though it was very dark now in the room and she could see nothing else. But she could see Him, with His arms outstretched, and the blood on His hands. He was luminous, and His face was kind and loving. He glowed, He lighted up the whole room, He was refulgent.

Yes, she thought, smiling, it would all come back to her. It was coming now, already. Her heart was beating very rapidly. He was smiling at her, He loved her still, and with a rapturous little cry she knelt down on the floor in front of Him and began to pray.

75 76 77 78 79 10 9 8 7 6 5 4 3 2 1